WHO PAYS THE PIPER

MACKENZIE SMITH

arrow books

Published by Arrow 2012

2 4 6 8 10 9 7 5 3 1

First published in Great Britain in 2012 by
Arrow
Random House, 20 Vauxhall Bridge Road,
London SW1V 2SA

www.randomhouse.co.uk

Addresses for companies within The Random House Group Limited can
be found at: www.randomhouse.co.uk

The Random House Group Limited Reg. No. 954009

A CIP catalogue record for this book
is available from the British Library

ISBN 9780099576761

The Random House Group Limited supports The Forest Stewardship
Council (FSC®), the leading international forest certification
organisation. Our books carrying the FSC label are printed on FSC®
certified paper. FSC is the only forest certification scheme endorsed by
the leading environmental organisations, including Greenpeace. Our
paper procurement policy can be found at
www.randomhouse.co.uk/environment

Typeset in Palatino by Palimpsest Book Production Limited,
Falkirk, Stirlingshire
Printed and bound by CPI Group (UK) Ltd, Croydon CR0 4YY

To Arabella

Acknowledgements

With thanks to Tony, Gryller, Major VS, Helen, Blofeld, Tim, NRC, Ben and the others within.

Prologue

Loud music was playing in the house above. Between tracks, he could hear familiar clicking noises that sounded like snooker balls.

He wondered what the rest of the Squadron were doing by now. They would have been flown out to the Destroyer lying off the coast and debriefed. Technically speaking, the operation would be deemed a success. As far as Christian knew, three men had been killed in return for twelve saved lives. Also, the WSBs had been neutered as a fighting force and a message sent to other groups not to grab British soldiers, or face a full kicking from the SAS.

Unofficially, it had been a mess. They had underestimated the WSBs, who had regrouped much more effectively than anticipated and had used mortars, which had not been foreseen. The river extraction was a fall-back plan and, for all he knew, could have been

1

a disaster. Not much better than that time when the Americans left Vietnam from the roof of their embassy in Saigon.

His next thought was of his family getting the news of his death. He imagined his elderly parents receiving a telephone call and a visit from the Colonel the following morning. He could see them taking the news bravely and hearing an exaggerated account of his heroic death. He saw Sam offering sincere condolences at the funeral at the regimental church near Hereford. He could see friends turning up, his ex-girlfriend Kate shedding tears.

The others would have concocted a watertight story and there would be no reason to dispute them. The fury and frustration were unbearable and took over from the pain in his shoulder. He kicked out at the wire and felt tears rolling down his face. This was as bad as it could get. He thought of the pills. If he took the lot, he would be unconscious in twenty minutes and dead from liver failure in an hour. But then that bastard would have got away with it.

Sitting cross-legged in the darkness, Christian breathed deeply and vowed revenge. Somehow, he would get out, get home and get even. He would find a way to make him pay.

1

An hour after dark, on 29 August 1999, an RAF C-130 Hercules transport aircraft started a steep descent into Lungi airport just to the west of Freetown, the capital of Sierra Leone. The landing lights had long since been stolen, forcing the pilots to work on instruments and improvised beacons placed at intervals on the crumbling tarmac. The usual ironic comments over the intercom from the co-pilot about putting seats in the upright position and fastening seat belts did not amuse the members of D Squadron 22 SAS, who were sitting or lying among crates and pallets of equipment.

Once the aircraft had landed safely and come to rest, the whine of the winch motor signalled the rear door was opening. Warm tropical air filled the belly of the aircraft as the first soldiers emerged, casually dressed, each shouldering a bergen and a kit bag. As the engines closed down, conversation broke out. The Squadron were assembling their kit on the tarmac when a familiar face appeared out of the darkness. Major Mark Day, a wiry Welshman, stopped in front of the men and waved his torch in the air.

'Quiet please,' he shouted. Then, lowering his voice a little, he continued, 'The Irish Rangers, those that have not been temporarily detained' – a snigger broke out among some of the men – 'have set up some accommodation for us over there behind that hangar. There's washing facilities, so to speak, in the white, low-level building round there too. There will be scoff in the hangar at twenty-one hundred, and a short briefing afterwards.'

Last out of the Hercules was Captain Christian McKie. He was in his late twenties, tall, with a crisp and effective look about him. Knowing one of the RAF pilots, he had secured a seat in the cockpit, a useful move on the nine-hour flight from Brize Norton. A friendly jeer went up from the assembled soldiers, to a retort of, 'It's not what you know, folks!' Christian picked up his kit and continued to elaborate on the benefits of the flight deck to his mates as they made their way across the runway.

The tents were ancient army issue and smelt, but had been rigged up with electric lights. Each one could accommodate eight men but fortunately this time the allocation was for three.

Christian dumped his stuff next to a camp bed and

was pleased to be sharing with his two close friends, Corporal Jamie Baxter and Trooper Tim Symonds. It would have been unusual for three different ranks to be so close in a regular army unit but in the small, unorthodox world of Special Forces, no one was too fussed about job titles.

'I bet you, after all this, it gets called off,' Jamie muttered under his breath, tipping the contents of his bergen onto the camp bed.

'Well, it usually does,' replied Tim.

They left the tent, making sure the mosquito netting was securely shut, and made their way over to the hangar that served as the operation's headquarters. Christian slid back a metal door and entered to find one end was set out with tables and catering facilities. The other end contained a number of Portakabins, housing hastily improvised offices. Most of the forty members of the Squadron were already either seated and eating or queuing for food at the canteen.

While some of the guys finished the last of their dinner, Colonel Nigel Deverall stood up at the front of the tables and asked for quiet. He was a tall, dark-haired man, aged forty; three years earlier, he'd been one of the youngest men in the British Army to be promoted to Lieutenant Colonel.

'Right, everybody, listen up please. As you know, it's now four days since the Rangers were taken. There is also a Sierra Leonean corporal with them, making the group twelve in total. The Int. Boys have had a meeting of sorts with representatives of the West Side Boys and the Major. During the meeting, Major Moore managed to pass over a map showing the layout of the remote jungle camp where they are being held.

'We are still hoping for a peaceful conclusion, but our job is to prepare for a hostage extraction. There are about two hundred and fifty people living in the village, most of whom are fully signed-up West Side Boys; the rest are various women and other hangers-on. I don't need to remind you that these guys are truly savage. Their idea of fun is taking bets on the sex of an unborn child and then cutting open the mother to see what's what. There are a hundred thousand people in this country missing arms and legs. Need I say more?'

Deverall glanced around, before carrying on.

'Over the next twenty-four hours, we will be evaluating the best modus operandi for what has been code named Operation Barras. You will be kept informed and involved in the planning. You will collect weapons from the armoury after this briefing. Before you go, we have some photos of key people. You will get copies, so you can familiarise yourselves with their faces.'

The Colonel flicked a switch on a slide projector and an image of a soldier appeared on the screen behind him.

'This is Major Moore. He's a respected Royal Irish Ranger with an excellent record in Belfast. This next guy is the local corporal who was guiding them. We don't know for sure, but think he is being held separately in very poor conditions. He's likely to be in a bad way and may not look quite like this if and when we end up going in.'

The hangar was silent. Deverall continued. 'This next guy is Udor Foday, the West Side Boys' chief. Be aware, it's an old shot.' A picture of a skinny Rastafarian in a grubby white vest appeared on the screen. He had a number of gold teeth, hair in a green, red and gold Rasta hat and carried a grenade launcher.

'He might look like more hat than cattle, but this guy can rustle up two thousand psychos whenever he wants. He controls most of the diamonds coming out of this part of Africa and has held onto his position for seven years – a record for round here. As I said, take these guys seriously.

'That's it for now, folks. Get your heads down and we'll see where we are in the morning.'

The men of D Squadron started to stand, and conversation broke out. They made their way to the sliding metal door and around the corner to another hangar containing dozens of pallets, laden with jungle-warfare equipment.

Sergeant Frank Norman, a small, stocky man with red cheeks and wild eyes, known as 'Armalite', the Squadron armourer, was waiting for them. A long-serving member of the Squadron, he had earned his nickname the hard way, in County Armagh, having lost half his hand dismantling a roadside bomb. Fortunately, only the detonator had gone off.

Each man picked up his own M16 A2 assault rifle and headed back to the tents, through the warm night air.

2

It was light in the tent when Christian woke at 07.00. There was a chill in the air and a thin mist hung in the trees as he walked barefoot over to the building that contained the washing facilities. A row of grimy washbasins along the far wall gave him the feeling he was back at school. He pushed open the white wooden door into a shower cubicle and hoped for hot water. After a moment of disappointment, a nearby clanking sound heralded the ignition of a boiler, followed a few moments later by a single jet of hot water; the shower head had long gone no doubt.

He stood under the water and reflected on the past three days' preparation and travelling, during which he had hardly slept. He often wondered how soldiers felt on the eve of battle. Could this finally be the occasion when he would face the enemy for real, as opposed to endless counter-terrorism deployments when the enemy did his best to avoid you?

How would he cope under enemy fire? Almost half the Squadron could honestly say that they had been in a fire-fight of some description. Some had seen incoming rounds in Bosnia, two guys had even served in the Iraq War, and a good number had seen a few rough patches in Northern Ireland. Apart from that, D Squadron had had a fairly quiet time, working largely with the CIA in South America.

Christian knew full well that the toughest-looking guys, those who could carry the heaviest weight the longest distances, were not always the guys who could handle the pressure of real-time fear. Everyone knew members of athletics clubs never passed Selection because they always got injured, and the more normal guys who came last, but never gave up, usually got in. But no one could tell how people would behave when the bullets started flying.

Back in the tent, Tim and Jamie were both stirring.

'Wake up, you guys,' Christian called as he sat down on his camp bed and looked across at them. 'I had no idea a tent could smell so bad.'

'Fuck off, you tart!' retorted Jamie, still under his blanket. 'It was you that lost the bog roll in Kenya and didn't wipe your arse for two weeks.'

Before the conversation got any further, the flap of the tent opened and Major Paul Cornwallis poked his head inside. He had served eighteen years in the

British Army and, with his thick black moustache, very much looked the part.

Before he had had a chance to open his mouth, Tim interjected, 'Sir, would you say it smells in here?'

The Major looked at him in a matter-of-fact way. 'Well, if this airport needs an enema, I know where they'll stick the pipe.' Anyway, Christi, I want you dressed and in the hangar in ten minutes.'

Inside the hangar, Christian walked to the first Portakabin and knocked on the door he had seen Colonel Deverall emerge from the night before. Cornwallis opened the door and asked him in. There was a large table covered in maps and papers with chairs around it. There was also a camp bed covered in equipment, including a leather shotgun case. Colonel Deverall saw Christian's eyes were drawn to it.

'You know, this country does have some good points. There is excellent wild fowling to be had where the Rokel Creek flattens out into mangrove swamps and joins the sea. There are some amazing blue snipe, although no one has ever managed to shoot there because you can't get in on foot.

'Christi, let me introduce Dan Miller and Steve Rayner. These guys are with Int. and have been on this job from the minute it started. I've asked you in here so Dan and Steve can tell you the latest, and bring you into our current thinking and how it may involve you.'

Colonel Deverall looked tired and scruffier than he had the night before. Christian had the impression that he may have had an all-nighter with the Int. guys. His breath stank of coffee as he leant forward and oriented the map towards Christian and Cornwallis.

Deverall continued: 'We are talking to these guys. We know, one, where the hostages are, and, two, that they are more or less OK except for the poor old corporal. He's been knocked about a bit and is being kept separately in a hole in the ground. It's touch and go whether we'll be in time for him. My fear is that if the talks go badly, they may separate our boys. If this happens, we don't stand a chance unless we know who's gone where and when, which brings me on to you, Christian. We need to get some eyes on the village and see what is really going on there.'

He pointed to a site on the map next to the river.

'This is Gheri Bana. To call it a shanty town would be flattering. It does, however, have a few concrete buildings, one of which contains our guys. As I mentioned last night, the Major managed to slip one of the negotiators a basic map showing what's what. This is an enlarged version.'

The Colonel pushed an A4 sheet towards Christian. 'It shows the house where they are held in relation to where the West Side Boys sleep and spend most of the day. It also shows where the Russian anti-aircraft piece is, and where they think the .50-cal from the Ranger's Land Rover is set up. This area is their football pitch, and this is the hole where the corporal spends most of his time. The other large building is Udor Foday's HQ. It's only single storey, but is properly built and well guarded.'

He glanced across at Dan, a skinny man in his late forties who looked knackered too. His heavily receded forehead glistened with sweat.

Dan cleared his throat. 'I was brought into this five days ago now and become less optimistic by the hour. These guys will not be able to resist butchering eleven British soldiers once they have had a few bargaining counters out of us, wouldn't you agree, Steve?'

Steve was smarter in appearance than Dan, more diplomat than spook. He nodded in a resigned way and added, 'Yup, I reckon so.'

Dan continued: 'It's essential to get a team in there to keep an eye on things. We need to insert a patrol and set up an observation post somewhere where we can see this building.' He tapped his finger on the hostage house.

'We have two problems. The first is going to be getting a team in there unseen and the second, finding somewhere to dig in that's close enough to see what's going on. The jungle is seriously thick, which means any OP has to be within 30 yards of the village to have any chance of being worthwhile.'

The discussion continued for the best part of an hour before they agreed to break for a few minutes. Christian began to register the heat and went back over to the canteen to get breakfast and a cup of water.

He loaded up a plastic plate with toast, bacon, eggs and baked beans. Clocking Jamie and Tim, he made his way to their table.

'So, are we on or not, mate?' Tim asked.

Christian knew he had to evade the question and replied, 'They don't know yet,' carefully using the word 'they' as opposed to 'we'. 'They have another meeting with the West Side Boys later and that should dictate the course of action.'

Christian ate his breakfast as quickly as possible, keeping an eye out for the others returning to Deverall's Portakabin. Fifteen minutes later, they reconvened and Major Cornwallis initiated the talk.

'I think we all agree getting an OP set up is an important step and we have been looking at the best way to insert. Walking in will take too long and the helicopter option is too noisy. It leaves us the river. We could get you within about twelve K of the village by boat if we were to drop you off here.'

He pointed to a bend in the river on the map. 'The area between this point and the village is largely jungle, with one or two patches of open scrub. It should not be too difficult to get over to the village in five hours, give or take. The idea would be to drop you around twenty-three hundred hours tonight, which would give you ample time to get in and set up by first light tomorrow. How's this all sounding, Christi?'

'Well, it's doable, if we get it right,' said Christian. 'Who else do you have in mind?'

Deverall interjected. 'It's your job to pick the team and I am not going to put forward anyone, but Sergeant Sam Carter has spent half his life in OPs and knows a lot about this part of the world.

'Now, I know you get along with Baxter and Symonds, which will be important and they are as good as any for this sort of thing. I reckon that would work, but it's your call.'

Christian was trying to imagine the four-man patrol in the hot and cramped environment of an OP, which would be nothing more than a scrape in the ground, covered with a camouflage net. They would be within spitting distance of 250 heavily armed psychos and not able to sneeze without attracting attention. Getting the right guys was essential and, although he knew he could veto any of the Colonel's suggestions, it was clear he would need very good reason. Also, he thought, going with the Colonel's suggestions would lead to fewer issues if things went wrong.

Christian nodded. 'I'm happy to go with that, sir, and we can't have any more than four.'

'Good decision,' said Deverall.

3

It was agreed that they would take rations for only seven days; otherwise they would be too laden. Their calorie burn, sitting in an OP, would be low, which meant they could hold out for the best part of three weeks if they had to.

They all signed out silenced side arms as well as several grenades. Christian was happy to take the M16 he had already collected. Jamie exchanged his for a belt-fed Minimi machine gun capable of putting down 1,000 rounds a minute. Tim kept his M16 but also signed out a long-range sniper's rifle with a collapsing stock, which would fit in his bergen. Sam, a big muscular guy with ultra-short black hair and Para Reg tattoos down both arms, chose an M16 that had a 203 grenade launcher attached below the barrel. This would be useful in the event of enemy fire from a fortified position. The most significant weight would be water. They would each need three litres a day in such a hot environment. They agreed to take two five-gallon jerry cans, which would last several days, and find further supplies of water once they were in theatre.

It was 06.00 hours when Cornwallis pushed open the door of the Portakabin.

'Right, folks, I need you ready in twenty minutes. The talks were a complete waste of time. It looks like we are on, so I want to run through your kit and get a radio check sorted before eighteen thirty. Then load up the van and get back in the Colonel's office for a chat. Is everyone sure they've memorised the rendez-vous points?'

The patrol signalled their agreement, continuing to stuff their bergens with kit. There was the usual problem of weight, but the walk in was not too long. However, they still needed a hand to stand up, once strapped into their bergens.

'Right everyone,' said Sam, 'let's dump this lot in the van and get some grub into us.'

'Good plan,' agreed Jamie, as they lifted their gear across the floor of the hangar towards an ancient-looking van. The canteen staff had laid on steak and chips. They sat together at one of the tables, without saying much. The next step was to consume as much fresh fruit as possible, in the knowledge that this would be the last non-vacuum-packed or freeze-dried food for a while.

Christian was wondering if he could face one more banana when Colonel Deverall approached. He looked frustrated. 'Guys, as Cornwallis has told you, the talks have come to nothing. We are going to arrange for ten minutes' airtime for them on the BBC World Service. This is being scheduled for the day after tomorrow, which probably means they won't try anything too clever between now and then. They also want some guns and vehicles that we have said we will consider.

'The bottom line is we have bought some time to get you in and work out the details of the extraction. Once you've finished your chimpanzees' tea party, I will come down to the port with you and the SBS boys will fill you in on the drop-off. They are just going to dump you on the bank of the Rokel Creek but they want to explain it all in SBS talk.'

The hangar was filling up with members of the Squadron, all of whom knew exactly what was going on and had turned up early for dinner with the express purpose of mobbing up the members of the patrol and wishing them good luck.

'Have fun; but if you fuckers start without us, there'll be trouble. You do know that, don't you?' bellowed Trooper Grant MacDonald, nicknamed 'The Beast' for being the biggest and ugliest man in the regiment.

Christian started to feel the butterflies in his stomach as the moment of departure drew closer.

Cornwallis and Deverall sat in the front of the van, MP5 machine guns across their laps. Sam was last into the back. 'Cheers, boys, see you later.'

The engine started and immediately the back of the van filled with diesel fumes. They passed through the main gate and turned left towards the port.

'What the fuck is the twenty-four-hour RV again?' said Sam, quietly making sure only the members of the patrol could hear him.

'It's nineteen twelve forty-one,' whispered Jamie.

'No, it's fucking not,' chipped in Tim, as Jamie started to chuckle.

'It's eighteen twelve forty, or is that the twelve-hour RV?' whispered Christian, giving the first three digits of the twelve-hour RV and the third three of the seven-day RV.

'I don't give a shit anyway,' said Sam. 'If we have to evacuate the OP, I'm not waiting around at any of the RVs for you lot to turn up, or not. We should just leg it back here. I reckon it would only take about twenty-four hours at a push, forty-eight if you did it according to the book.'

'You're right, Sam,' said Christian, feeling it would do no harm to exert his authority at this point, 'but we would be better off doing it together, so we'll all stick to the RVs – OK, everyone?'

'Of course, of course, if you insist,' said Sam, rolling his eyes as the others nodded agreement.

The van bumped on down quiet suburban streets

in what looked like any African city. There were kids playing and some market stalls still open. Life was going on as usual despite the threat of the West Side Boys. After a few minutes, the van took a sharp turn and stopped. They were parked behind a warehouse in a disused part of Freetown port. Two SBS troopers sat on the roof of a low concrete building, keeping watch. A slipway led down to the dirty brown water of the port. Moored at the bottom was a 22-foot rigid inflatable boat – a RIB – painted in light green and black, with two large outboard engines. There were another two SBS soldiers on board looking relaxed and ready to go.

Christian could smell the sea salt in the air, and for a fleeting second it reminded him of being on holiday. He could see a large tanker a few miles out to sea and knew that somewhere beyond that was a British Destroyer lying in support. He began dragging the equipment out of the back of the van. They were already sweating, despite wearing lightweight jungle kit.

The two soldiers from the boat walked up and introduced themselves as Simon and Don. They helped drag the remaining kit down the slipway and strapped down what they could towards the front of the RIB.

4

As the RIB made its way up the first section of the Rokel Creek, Freetown lay to their right. There were no streetlamps, but lights twinkled from the windows of some houses. A few small fishing boats still trawled their nets as the RIB passed them by. Christian was relieved they were finally on their way, and that there was now a specific sense of purpose. They cleared Freetown and saw cultivated farm land. It was not possible to distinguish the crops but it was clear that this part of Sierra Leone had not been abandoned, as the land to the north had been.

By 22.30 the evening had long given way to darkness. The river had narrowed and was overhung by dark-looking trees and dense vegetation. The moonlight, reflected on the water, allowed them to navigate down the centre of the river. They had reduced their speed from almost flat out on the first

21

section of river to around 10 knots to reduce noise and disturbance.

'ETA ten minutes.'

Christian raised his hands, fingers outstretched, in the direction of the others and mouthed the word 'ten'. They vacated the comfort of the jockey seats and lay among the equipment at the front to disguise the number of men. Each one now had his weapon in his hands and Sam surveyed the river bank through his night-vision scope. The temperature had dropped and dew formed on the metallic handrail along the edge of the boat.

Simon tilted forward and his face reflected the pale yellow light of the GPS screen. He switched it off quickly and raised his outspread hand to indicate five minutes to arrival. He moved the RIB out from the middle of the river, cut the speed to walking pace and continued forward, the boat now hugging the right bank.

It was just about possible to hear noises from the jungle and the sound of the water gently washing down the side of the RIB. Christian felt increasingly alert as the right-hand bend in the river loomed towards them through the darkness. This was the drop-off point. He made eye contact with Simon who was carefully guiding the RIB forward to a sand bar in the slow-moving water on the inside of the bend. Don stood on the front of the RIB, a bow line in his hand. He had his M16 looped over his shoulder and his ops vest on, in case he became separated from them.

He dropped carefully into the water in front of the bow as the RIB came to rest on the bar. The water was just below his waist as he pulled forward on the line to secure the RIB against the current. Sam held his bergen on his arm and followed behind Don, doing his best to keep his kit dry. Simon kept the engines running slightly to keep the bow as close to the bar as possible while the other members of the patrol followed Sam, lugging their bergens, rifles and the jerry cans.

Don looked at Christian and whispered, 'OK?', to which Christian gave a thumbs-up and patted him on the back. He then signalled to Simon, who nodded and slipped the engines into neutral as Don swung himself back aboard.

The current took hold of the RIB, swinging it round and moving it gently back in the direction it had come. The patrol watched it glide silently away as they grew accustomed to the quiet chatter of jungle noises. The priority was to get into a secure position on the bank as quickly as possible, to lie low for a few minutes and make sure they had not been spotted. The bank was some thirty feet away across a shallow stream.

Christian signalled to Tim to go first. He waded into three feet of muddy water and made it across with no problem. He climbed the bank and took up a position looking into the jungle while the others crossed, doing their best to minimise any tracks in the mud. They squatted down at the base of a tall tree and listened.

They waited for ten minutes and let their senses acclimatise to the jungle, each covering an arc of fire. The mosquitoes wasted no time, so the men rolled down their sleeves and buttoned up their combat smocks to reduce exposure. Christian broke the silence by tapping Jamie on the back and telling him to lead on the first bearing. This was a 4 km line slightly uphill, which would lead to an intersection with a disused track.

After an hour pushing through rough jungle vegetation, they reached the track. Christian told Sam to lead and they swapped around the two jerry cans that were a serious weight in addition to their bergens and weapons.

Christian was happy with their progress but eager to reach the village soon to give themselves time to dig in and set up a proper OP. He regularly glanced at his watch and counted the paces to keep an idea of distance covered. They completed the second leg without any hitch and stopped for a break where the jungle gave way to an area of open ground. They squatted down, covering their arcs, and slipped out of their bergens. They listened for a minute before feeling safe to talk quietly.

'Fucking mozzies,' started Tim. 'It's always the same on these things. I'd love it if it weren't for the bloody mozzies!'

'If someone could invent a mozzie spray that

actually worked, they should be knighted in my book,' whispered Jamie.

'If someone could invent a jerry can that wasn't so heavy, they should be made king,' said Sam.

'So what do we do for the guy that tarmacs this whole jungle?' added Christian.

'Well, send him to Staff College, surely,' replied Jamie, taking a swig out of his water bottle. 'So, when are we going to be there, Dad?' he continued.

'It shouldn't be too bad from here,' Christian replied. 'We cross this bit of higher ground, follow the line of the river and then shimmy on in from there. It's two thirty now and I reckon we should all be tucked up in OP hell by fourish. That's assuming we don't bump into Udor Foday and his band of merry men on their way back from a hard, all-night lock-in at the AK and Machete.'

'And what if we do?' whispered Jamie, starting to chuckle. 'Do we tell them we are local chaps on our way back from an SAS fancy dress party and do they know where we can get a cab?'

'Well, either that or we slot the lot of them and then ask them,' contributed Sam.

'No, no, I expect we'll get right in there, dig in the OP and then get a call from Dev to say there's been a big misunderstanding and the Rangers were released yesterday,' whispered Tim.

'And have been holed up in the AK and Machete ever since celebrating their release,' added Christian.

The moon appeared, illuminating the area of open ground in front of them. The sudden increase in light came as a reminder that dawn was only a few hours away and there were still 7 km to go. They helped each other up, under the weight of their bergens, and Sam continued to lead. The going was easier than in the jungle as the ground was firmer underfoot and they were not pushed off their bearing by clumps of trees and thickets. The downside was that they were more conspicuous and could be seen from some distance. With the greater feeling of vulnerability, the pace quickened. Within forty minutes, they had crossed the higher ground and were descending a gentle gradient, back into thicker vegetation. The river was now a couple of hundred metres to their left and would act almost as a handrail, guiding them to their destination.

Christian stopped the patrol. They each dropped to one knee and covered an arc of fire. He pushed his global-positioning device as close to the ground as possible, to avoid the light giving them away, and checked their position. He was sure he knew where they were but needed certainty. He indicated to the others that they were 3 km from the village.

The atmosphere was now noticeably more serious. Christian swung the jerry can he had been carrying back to Sam and moved forward to lead the patrol. He knew that this leg of the approach was the most dangerous, as they could walk onto an enemy position at any moment and his night-vision goggles were no good in such thick vegetation. They progressed slowly, looking and listening, weapons at the ready. They were entering the lair of the most barbarous group of killers in the world and, if it came to a fight, would be outnumbered to the tune of fifty or sixty to one.

Christian expected to reach the top of a small ridge that ran along the south side of the village. They would make their final approach from this point. They continued to move silently but would all stop simultaneously at the slightest sound. To Christian's relief, the ground started to rise. He would feel better once he could see the village, because there were only a couple of hours of darkness left. Within a few minutes the ground levelled out and they reached a clearing on the crest of the ridge. Below them, some 500 yards away, it was possible to make out the outlines of houses and a large open area that had to be the football pitch. Christian felt a rush of excitement knowing that the West Side Boys would be carrying on as usual, unaware they would soon be observed through the rifle sights of the cream of the British Army.

5

It was approaching 04.00 hours. They had an hour, perhaps an hour and a half, to find a suitable site for the OP, get it dug in and camouflaged.

They came across a track in the jungle down which they could see the outline of a single-storey building that marked the edge of Gheri Bana. Crossing one by one, they soon dropped back into the cover of the vegetation. Christian signalled to the others to stop. He eased off his bergen, slung his rifle over his back and drew out his silenced pistol. He pulled his night-vision goggles out of his combat smock and moved gently forward through the vegetation in the direction of the village.

His adrenalin rising with every step, he was soon trembling with nerves and needed to pause to get a grip of himself. The final approach was ultra risky, but he had to check he was in the right place. He moved forward on all fours. Finally he came to a point where the jungle thinned out and he could see buildings 30 yards away, close enough to make out the outline of the corrugated iron roofs. He could see clothing hung out to dry on a line and the silhouette of a pick-up truck with a machine gun mounted in the rear. He smelt wood smoke. He raised his night-vision goggles and surveyed the village. Nothing stirred.

There was a track leading down the centre of the village with simple mud and concrete houses built along it. He imagined snoring WSB soldiers inside, sleeping off last night. Some, no doubt, were awake, with their weapons lying close. Christian's heart pounded as he peered around a wall and looked down the row of houses. He pushed past the line of washing and saw the large building, with a terrace in front of it, which fitted the description of where the Rangers were held. He could also see the outline of the Russian anti-aircraft piece sitting prominently in front of the building. He had seen enough to know he was in the right place and was desperate to get back into the jungle before anything went wrong. He crept back the way he had come and felt relief as he ducked back into the trees. He found the others where he had left them and signalled to follow him. They moved a couple of hundred yards around the southern side to a point where they could see the village, but were still 20 yards into the jungle.

The priority was to get the OP built. Christian gestured to Tim to move forward of their position and keep watch and indicated to Sam and Jamie to start digging in. They slipped out of their bergens and started work. Christian wanted to get a better understanding of the village and moved quietly into the jungle to see if there might be an observation point nearby that would command a better view. He came across a tall tree about a hundred yards from where Sam and Tim were digging the OP. It had a couple of low branches and without much difficulty he was able to pull himself up to a point from which he had access to the higher branches. He climbed 20 feet up and, with the benefit of the sloping ground, was able to see over the top of the thickest vegetation.

He could now see the whole village and the shimmering Rokel Creek on the far side. He looked at his watch: 04.45. He had been on the go for twenty-two hours and suddenly felt a wave of fatigue wash over him. He was pleased that he had led the patrol successfully into the heart of WSB territory. His main concern was that Sam's somewhat abrasive personality might become an issue in the confined space of an OP. With Jamie and Tim, his only worry was that they were both eternal optimists who had not necessarily considered the worst-case scenario of the mission they had embarked upon – the very real possibility that they all might be captured or killed by this rogue gang of unpredictables. Under normal circumstances an OP would be hundreds of yards or even miles from the location under observation, but the jungle prevented this. It was easy to imagine something like a dog smelling them in the OP and raising the alarm. If a fire-fight broke out, they were vastly outnumbered and would eventually run out of ammunition. It did not bear thinking about, but the chances were all too real given their proximity to the village.

He swung his leg over the branch, slithered down the tree and made his way back to the OP. Sam and Tim were still digging a hole in the soft jungle soil. It was a bare minimum, three feet across and five along. Christian immediately started scooping earth and scattering it about. The hole was close to three feet deep, creating enough room for the patrol and their kit. They covered the remaining debris with leaves. Sam draped the hole with a small camouflage net. They kept an observation hole pointing in each direction and placed branches and other foliage on top to break up the outline.

Christian moved forward to fetch Jamie, and within a couple of minutes they were all crammed into the newly dug OP. Sam opened his bergen and extracted four Claymore mines. He glanced at Christian for permission to lay them around the perimeter. With a nod from Christian, he crawled out and placed the mines at strategic intervals around the OP. He wired them to a small hand-held detonation device that could be triggered in the event of attack.

Whilst the mines were small, they would still cause major destruction in all directions whilst the patrol could flatten themselves on the bottom of the OP to avoid the blast. Sam made a couple of adjustments to the outside of the OP and slid back in. The time was 05.30 hours. They were filthy, wet and exhausted. Christian whispered to the others to get some sleep. He would do the first stag duty.

In less than an hour, the morning sun flickered through the trees and the temperature in the OP started to rise. The damp jungle soil had been easy to dig but was full of insect life. Christian had a load of mosquito bites on his face and was concerned to see the array of weird and wonderful bugs that had been disturbed by the digging. Things that looked like flying ants buzzed in the air, dropping through the camouflage netting and settling on him. Several marched across Sam's hood, which he had drawn tightly around his face in an effort to protect himself. Christian quietly rummaged for some biscuits from a side pouch of his bergen and settled down to watch the village through his binoculars. He could see most of the football pitch, the anti-aircraft weapon, the rear walls of a number of buildings and the track leading into the village.

By 11.30, the others were stirring and fidgeting. Christian was pleased they were waking up as he was keen to get some sleep himself.

'Anything going on, mate?' Tim whispered.

'Fuck all, really, except these bugs,' replied Christian.

'What are we using as a piss pot?' asked Sam.

'Empty that jerry can into whatever you can find and we'll use that,' whispered Christian, still looking down into the village.

They filled their water bottles and two plastic water-carrying sacks from the jerry can. Sam then adopted a kneeling position and relieved himself into the opening.

Christian told Sam to take command. Then he settled down and did his best to shut his eyes and get some sleep. He always found it difficult to sleep on exercises. He had slept in some very uncomfortable, wet and cold places in his time and this was certainly ranking with the very worst, but after an hour of lying there, with his eyes shut, he decided not to bother.

'This is hopeless,' he muttered as he sat up. 'What's going on?'

Jamie put down his binoculars. 'There's a bit of milling around and a couple of lads knocking a footie about but no sign of our guys yet.'

'OK, Tim, it's time to check-in. Turn the radio on and let Dev know we are in, but yet to have visual on the Rangers.'

6

It was mid-afternoon when Christian picked up his rifle, pulled his hood up over his head and whispered to the others that he would be back in an hour. He slithered out of the rear hole and moved slowly in the direction of his lookout tree. It was good to stand after so many hours in the OP. The air felt fresh against his face and he noticed how his wet clothes clung to him. It took under a minute to get to the base of the tree and no more than thirty seconds to get back up to the branch where he had sat earlier. He had a feeling of comfort being back there, away from the claustro-phobia of the OP, and he liked the fact that he was able to see around him. He spent a few minutes sitting still on the branch making sure he had not been seen, and then raised his binoculars to study the area. Now that he had the advantage of full daylight, he was able to appreciate the view the tree afforded him. He could see a tall, skinny youth leaving one of the houses. He saw the relaxed expression on the boy's face and the picture of a rap star on his faded T-shirt. He could make out horizontal scarring down his right arm, as if he had had some nasty encounter with a machete, or perhaps it was the scarring from an unpleasant coming-of-age ritual. Across his shoulder was slung a self-loading rifle and from his belt hung a Western-style holster that had to contain some sort of pistol.

The youth wandered out of the house and turned along the track that ran down the middle of the village. Christian lowered his binoculars and lifted his rifle. He popped off the covers that protected each end of the telescopic sight and, despite the much narrower field of view, had little difficulty finding his man gently strolling along. He was no more than 75 yards away, only ten per cent of the accurate killing range of his weapon. The boy looked different with a cross-hair dissecting his face into quarters.

Christian lowered his rifle and picked up his binoculars in time to see a battered pick-up pulling up. Several gun toting men jumped out. The last one out wore a proper shirt with sleeves, as opposed to the ripped vests and T-shirts worn by the others. He did not have a gun in his hand, which also suggested that he might be in command. The pick-up had stopped in front of the biggest house, which had a veranda built along one side. The men pushed the door open and went on in like they owned the place. Christian could not see the face of the man in the shirt but thought it likely he was the infamous Udor Foday.

The next hour was uneventful. All he saw were various West Side Boys wandering about aimlessly. There were a couple of women hanging out washing on lines and some cooked on small stoves raised on bricks just outside their houses. A few kids were kicking a ball around on the football pitch and shouting at each other.

Christian had just decided to stay on the tree for another five minutes when the door of the main house opened and the man in the shirt emerged. He was followed by a couple of his cronies with their guns raised. Behind them trooped a group of men in green army fatigues, the Irish Rangers.

Christian recognised the Major. He appeared to be talking to the man in the shirt as they walked towards the vehicle. Both men seemed agitated and Christian wished he had some idea of what they were saying. He counted the group and was relieved to clock eleven, although three of the men needed support to walk.

The Rangers sat down on the veranda and along the grass just in front of it. Three WSBs sat on white plastic chairs around them with their AKs across their knees. Christian was surprised to see one of them pass what looked like a joint to one of the Rangers who took it, had a couple of puffs and passed it on.

He whispered into his personal role radio, 'Come in,' and almost immediately heard Tim's voice.

'All right, Tarzan?'

'Fine thanks, Jane, I've forgotten what he called the monkey . . .' replied Christian. 'I'm on my way back now, so please don't shoot me and, if possible, no funny ones with the mine field. Seen the Rangers, by the way, all eleven of them.'

A minute later Christian slipped back into the OP.

'Fuck me, it hums in here,' he said. 'They'll be able to smell us before they see us at this rate.'

'Are all eleven of them OK?' said Jamie in a concerned voice.

'Fine-ish,' replied Christian. 'All I could see is that they are all there, sitting on the grass outside Foday's place, smoking his ganja, by the looks of things.'

'What?'

'That's right, on the grass outside, smoking his gear,' continued Christian.

'Fucking hell,' hissed Tim, 'we really do get the bum deals round here. I'm giving myself up right now.' The others smiled and Christian continued to give them a more detailed summary of what he had seen.

A few more hours passed with little activity in the village. The patrol settled down to consume their second meal of dried and vacuum-packed rations. The conversation soon drifted round to a discussion about who was going to take the first crap, which had to be done using a plastic bag. This conversation always took place on the first day in an OP and invariably seemed ridiculous later when all inhibitions and self-consciousness had been well and truly forfeited. Tim did the honours, pulling strained and satisfied expressions to amuse the others. Towards the end of his theatrics there was the sudden sound of an engine and shouts. The patrol immediately took up positions, each one scanning the jungle. The old pick-up was leaving the village with at least eight WSBs standing in the back. They were in a hurry and seemed to have shaken off their laid-back appearance of earlier. The patrol could see them through the undergrowth going down the track within 30 yards of the OP.

'Just one grenade is all it would take,' said Sam under his breath.

'I wonder what they're doing,' said Christian, noting down the departure. 'Let's hope they haven't realised that things are not necessarily going their way.'

'They'll work that out once and for all when a couple of Chinooks drop in here and pay their respects,' Sam muttered.

The patrol maintained their vigilance for the next few hours, as the light began to fade and the temperature fell slightly. The insects had been less of a nuisance during the afternoon but now large brown moths appeared, flapping in an ungainly manner around the OP.

'I'd rather these fuckers than those ant things,'

observed Sam, as he watched one walking across the back of his hand. Tim, who was keeping watch on the village, turned and whispered, 'I'm sorry to interrupt, David Bellamy, but you guys really need to see this.'

The others hauled themselves into kneeling positions, squeezed together next to Tim at the front of the OP and raised their binoculars. A game of football was in full swing on the pitch. The ground was about half the size of a normal pitch but relatively flat, although the grass was long and uneven. There were about fifteen aside and, much to the amusement of the patrol, most of the players still carried their weapons. The age range was from about six to forty and some of the women had joined in too, wearing long multicoloured dresses and some were in hats.

'Is it a carnival, a riot or a game of footie?' asked Christian.

'Or a blood-bath if someone fouls in the penalty area,' whispered Tim, suppressing a laugh.

'The tall guy with the ball and the AK is actually quite good,' said Jamie. 'He's got round a couple of the others very nicely.'

'Yes, but they're not armed, are they?' replied Tim. 'Most of them seem to slip on invisible banana skins every time he gets the ball. Imagine what would happen if Foday turned up. It would be thirty–nil in five minutes!'

The game continued for an hour until the light had

nearly gone. The pitch gradually emptied and the players drifted back to their houses. Christian whispered to the others that he wanted to see if he could catch a final glimpse of the Rangers. He spent a minute adding camouflage cream to his already filthy face, picked up his rifle and slipped out of the hole.

Back in the tree, he looked over the top of the vegetation down into the village. There were a number of gentle orange glows coming from the stoves outside the houses and he caught the smell of wood smoke and cooking food. He wondered what would be for dinner in such a place and thought even the twenty-four-hour ration packs supplied would be haute cuisine by comparison. He would have loved to have let the Rangers know help was at hand. They would be feeling scared and isolated, not knowing that the best of the British Army would soon be descending like an avalanche on the village.

He flicked the switch on his binoculars to turn on the night vision. He saw the odd person wandering between the houses and heard the occasional shout. There was no sign of the Rangers but he was sure they would be back in Foday's house, for another night in captivity. Suddenly, a boom of music came from the direction of Foday's place. The front door opened and light spilled out onto the veranda. A couple of men sat down on the plastic chairs, bottles in hand. They seemed to nod and tap to the beat of the aggressive-sounding rap. Judging by the intensity of the light, Christian guessed there must be a generator running to create power.

Christian's eyes had wandered from the house and were fixed on the shimmering reflections of the river on the far side of the village when he saw the man who he had assumed was Foday appear from another house. He suddenly felt alert and realised that he had been more or less dreaming for a few minutes. He shrugged off his tiredness and focused on Foday, who walked slowly towards his own house. As he passed, he waved casually to the men on the veranda and made some strange break-dancing movements in time to the rap music. He carried on in the direction of the river. After 100 yards, he stopped, turned around and lit a cigarette. He moved on again and Christian assumed he was walking down to the water, when he turned off the path and walked straight into the jungle. Christian pushed the switch on his binoculars around again from light intensity mode to infrared. This setting showed the heat of Foday's body as a red glow moving about in the dense vegetation.

The red blob moved uphill into the jungle and stopped by a clump of tall trees that grew up above the rest of the jungle. The blob remained stationary for five minutes and then moved behind a tree for a brief moment before re-emerging. Christian saw him light another cigarette and make his way back to the village. He walked towards his house and sat down on the veranda with the other men.

Christian decided nothing further could be gained from sitting in the tree. His eyes stung from tiredness and from squinting through his binoculars. He had been up for a day and half and needed to sleep. The mosquitoes buzzed round him and he felt an increase in humidity which made him think it was going to rain. He slithered down from the tree and announced his return over his personal role radio. Back in the OP, Tim and Sam were asleep and Jamie was still keeping lookout. He turned on the radio and made a brief report to base.

As he took off the headset, he felt the first drop of rain on his cheek. This was followed by several more, and a mournful whisper of 'here we go' from Jamie. Then there was a short but unmistakable build-up as the drops turned into a torrential downpour. There was not even the time to pull out the ponchos from their bergens before the rain was pouring down their faces.

7

'I'm glad you're back,' Tim said to Christian. 'Do you want to enter the moth competition?'

'What, a "Who has sat on the most" competition?' whispered Christian, sounding confused.

'No, there're two classes,' replied Tim. 'A wingspan class and a hairiest body class. Sam's probably ahead on wingspan, but I have the hairiest one here.' He opened a pouch on his bergen and produced what looked like some brown mush.

'Looks like you won the "Who's got the most drowned moth award", mate,' said Christian.

'It's got to be alive to win,' Sam joined in, leaning forward to inspect.

'That's right,' chipped in Jamie. 'All entrants must be alive, have two operational wings and a minimum of four legs attached. Otherwise, they don't count.'

'I can't believe you spastics are running a butterfly

beauty contest when we're about to drown! What about a sweepstake on when the first piranha pops up in this OP!' said Christian, no longer needing to lower his voice due to the intensity of the rain.

After a few minutes, one side of the OP slipped in, causing the camouflage net to fall in on their heads. The rain was several inches deep in the bottom of the hole and they were forced to squat to keep themselves out of the water. Sam did his best to scoop the saturated and crumbling soil out of the side of the OP where it had fallen in, but his efforts had little effect other than to cover him almost entirely in soaking mud and leaves. The others were trying to steady the netting above them, which was now flapping noisily in the wind that accompanied the rain.

After an hour, the rain eased off, turning from torrential into a steady pour. The wind became stronger, which Sam assured the others was a sign of the storm passing. The atmosphere in the waterlogged OP was far from upbeat and Sam's meteorological predictions were shot down aggressively by the others. However, in keeping with Sam's forecast, the rain let up by around 04.00 and the wind died down.

Fortunately, the radio was safe in its own waterproof carrying pack. By 05.30 hours, the light started to appear through the trees, revealing the true extent of the filth they were living in. They were caked in blackish mud from head to toe. The mud had found its way into all their clothing, boots, pockets, hair and ears. Each of them was barely recognisable. Christian was asleep, slumped in one corner, his face sunken into the soft earth, his hood pulled tight round his head, oblivious to the filth and water in which he was submerged. Tim was kneeling, keeping lookout with his binoculars raised, while Sam and Jamie sat doing their best to clean their weapons. With the light came a welcome increase in temperature that was followed almost immediately by mosquitoes and various new insects that the patrol assumed had hatched as a result of all the rain. A thin mist hung in the air and the birdsong and other jungle chatter seemed louder than the previous day. Christian slept on. Sam and Jamie shut their eyes and dozed while Tim scanned the village.

A couple of hours passed with no sign of activity when suddenly two approaching pick-up trucks broke the silence. Tim had not seen these particular vehicles before and shook Jamie awake.

'Check these out, mate . . . What d'you think?' he whispered.

'Not sure, but we need to note it down,' Jamie replied, reaching for the notebook.

Christian and Sam were awakened by the movements in the OP and sat up to see what was going on. The arrival of the pick-ups in the village caused shouts and yells and people to appear. The noise soon settled down and the village went quiet once again.

Sam opened the jerry can designated as the piss pot, and relieved himself.

'Can you get trench cock?' he muttered, as he buttoned himself up.

The atmosphere lightened and Christian suggested it was time for their next meal. They opened their ration packs and sifted through the contents. Tinned fruit in sugary syrup, slices of dried bread, on which they spread margarine and jam, were the order of the day.

Christian felt more exhausted than ever, having finally had a few hours' sleep. He told Tim to take over from Jamie and lay back on his bergen in an attempt to get more. To distract himself from the discomfort, he tried his usual technique of thinking of comforting thoughts of home. He worked out what time it would be in England and thought of what his parents might be doing. They would have finished breakfast and his father, a retired engineer, would have probably just got back from walking his two Irish terriers. His mother would no doubt be busying herself around the house.

His mind skipped on to Kate, the girl he had been seeing. He knew thinking of her would be depressing and that she was not right for him in any case, but she still popped up. Christian could see her face and hear her talking. She was in the kitchen in his flat in London. They had not been together for long but had had great times before they had been bothered by the practicalities of real life. He had been dumped. She was now going out with a guy with a good City job, a fast car and a huge flat in Notting Hill. He had been dumped for a cliché, albeit a successful one.

It was obvious she was going to need a man around who was able to pick up restaurant bills, as opposed to someone on the end of a satellite phone in a rush because another guy needed to call home before the battery went flat. Exciting stories of foreign parts were all very well, but mostly they were highly confidential or involved tales of waiting around in a hole and crapping in a bag. He was reassuring himself that she was too much of a material girl when Sam shook him. He was not aware that he was asleep, but sat up with a start and realised he must have been. Sam signalled to him to be quiet, with his finger across his mouth. Jamie and Tim were looking intensely through the sights of their rifles.

'The Rangers are on the football pitch and it's not looking too clever,' whispered Tim. Jamie made room for Christian in the opening through the netting and passed him his rifle. Christian looked down the sight and saw the Rangers all kneeling in a row, several WSBs standing around them, their AKs at the ready. One waved a long machete. Christian scanned the area and saw more WSBs appearing. Then, to his horror, he saw a man being dragged along the ground. His hands were tied to his ankles, bending him backwards. He was naked and offered no resistance. Christian guessed this must be the Sierra Leonean Corporal who had been captured with the Rangers. Christian turned his head and snapped instructions to the others.

'Sam, Jamie . . . I want you two thirty yards out to the left and wait for my command. We may have to go in on our own. Tim, get Deverall on the radio and tell him what's happening. We need authority to act. We need air support, everything they've got. Tell him we will be on the ridge just above here, about half a K to the south. That's somewhere we could hold for an hour max. Radios on, now!'

Sam and Jamie zipped up their ops vests, which contained their ammunition, grenades, a basic ration pack and water bottles. They wriggled out of the OP and moved off out of sight. Tim had the radio headset on and was calling base: 'This is Blue Snipe, this is Blue Snipe, over?'

'Hello, Blue Snipe; hello, Blue Snipe,' replied the voice of the radio operator.

'We have a potential execution in progress,' replied Tim, trying to sound calm.

'Will fetch Sunray, standby,' said the operator. 'Send sitrep?'

'They may be about to kill the Rangers and the Corporal on the football pitch. Do we have authority to intervene?' Tim responded.

'That's for your Sunray or our Sunray; he's coming,' said the voice.

Christian saw the man in the white shirt standing among the crowd. He could not clearly see the Rangers and the Corporal was out of sight completely. A jolt ran through his body as he heard a couple of shots fired.

'Sam, what can you see?' he asked.

'Not a lot, but the Rangers are all OK. Can't see the Corporal. Hold on, they are moving back; looks like it was one of Foday's guys trying to shut them all up,' replied Sam.

'OK, OK, hold your horses. Jamie, prepare to open on the far left; Sam, inside left. I do the inside right and Tim the right flank. Waiting for Deverall,' said Christian.

The crowd had moved back a little and Foday became visible, standing in front of the kneeling Rangers. The Corporal lay near him. Foday shouted to his crowd. Some punched their fists in the air in applause and others waved their guns and machetes.

Christian told Tim to switch the frequency of the radio to the same one they were using for their personal role radios, which meant the whole patrol was effectively in touch with base.

'Do not fire without my express authority. I will call it. Half a mag on auto, then choose targets. We have enough ammo for every one of them if we don't go crazy. Sam and Jamie, you fire while Tim and I get out and get them. We withdraw up the hill and hold the top of the ridge until the helis get here. OK?'

Foday continued to rant and wave his arms around. After a further thirty seconds, the patrol heard Deverall's voice: 'I hear things may be warming up your end. You are in command. It could be mock, you call it. You call it. Don't let him shoot anyone, just to make sure. I'd rather eleven Rangers and a court case. The same applies to the Corporal – he's one of us. Good luck.'

Foday still lectured the crowd when he turned around and kicked the Corporal several times as he lay bound on the ground. His body twitched and convulsed. Next he raised his gun and aimed it at the Rangers. He paused, lowered it and continued with his address. He turned around to point it at the Corporal and then again to the crowd.

Deverall's voice sounded over the radio again: 'Blue Snipe, are you sure it's the Corporal they have there? Can you see for sure, over?'

'Not for sure, but it must be him, over,' replied Christian.

Christian heard a vehicle approaching. He glanced around and saw one of the pick-up trucks bumping along the track with WSBs sitting in the back and hanging onto the sides. The vehicle drove into the village and straight out onto the football pitch. It stopped next to Foday and eight men jumped out. They dragged another man out, hogtied the same way as the Corporal. They let his body drop to the ground. There was more frenzied shouting and Foday waved his arms around, inciting the onlookers still further.

'Who's that? Can anyone see?' said Christian.

'Judging by his red shorts, he doesn't look military; but I can't see for sure,' replied Jamie.

Foday raised his arms and one of his men fired again in the air. He spoke in a quieter voice, pointing at the new arrival on the ground. He bent down and cut the man's bonds with a knife. The man was hauled to his knees. A group of the youngest WSBs formed at the front of the crowd, each holding a machete. Foday raised his hand and the kneeling man, now shaking violently, stood up and was allowed to run.

Foday let him get 20 yards before waving to the mob of children to give chase. They moved like a pack of wild dogs and had little difficulty gaining on the man. He made it to the edge of the jungle but no further. There was a sickening scream followed by more. The next sounds were triumphant shouts coming from the bushes. A minute later, a child emerged waving a severed arm.

No member of the patrol spoke. Christian broke the silence.

'You all know our remit. We are here to observe and only get involved if and when the main extraction force turns up. If anyone does not wish to go in, then none of us do, OK? There are two hundred and fifty of them and four of us. No one will think the less of you. It's fucking madness, obviously, but we stand a chance. I need to hear from each of you.'

The other members of the patrol all spoke at once. Christian spoke over them. 'Sam first.'

Sam replied. 'We can't sit here with a thousand rounds of ammo and watch these psychos butcher our boys.'

'Too fucking right,' added Jamie.

'We do it if we have to,' replied Tim.

'OK, this is Blue Snipe, this is Blue Snipe. We will be going in. Will require evacuation on the ridge asap. What is your timing, over?'

'Getting ready to go now, over,' replied Deverall. 'Will have air support in situ within forty minutes, Chinooks will take fifty max. This is beyond remit, your call, your call.'

Foday allowed the crowd time to indulge in the killing before shouting for silence. He continued to speak, pointing at the Rangers, all of whom stared at the ground. The Corporal lay motionless by Foday's feet.

Another minute passed. Christian poured with sweat from the tension. He had Foday in his sights but found it hard to keep aim. He was no more than 100 metres away. In theory an easy shot, but this was different, knowing that the moment he squeezed the trigger a full-blown battle would break out. He kept his breathing under control and blinked away the muddy sweat from his eyes.

Foday raised one arm in the air, as if arriving at his final point. He took an AK from one of the men standing closest to him. He walked slowly down the line of Rangers, giving the impression he was carrying out an inspection. He stopped in front of one man and moved to the next. He grabbed the Ranger by the shoulder and dragged him out of the line. He was young, with fair hair. He was made to kneel in front of the others. Foday stood to his side and held the muzzle of the gun to his head. The Ranger was visibly shaking and staring around as if expecting his fellow Rangers to do something. They remained motionless. Christian spoke calmly into the radio. 'Get ready, wait for my command. I've got Foday. Tim, take the one manning the gun on the truck, then the driver.'

Christian guessed the WSBs would not bother with the safety catch and assumed the rifle would be ready to fire. He watched Foday's hand and decided he would fire when his finger touched the trigger.

Foday kept the muzzle of the rifle pressed against the Ranger's head and walked around behind him. He raised his foot, planted it between the Ranger's shoulder blades and kicked him forwards onto the ground. Then he began to laugh. The onlookers all roared with delight and some clapped their hands. The Ranger remained motionless where he lay and was finally pushed back into line. Foday paraded up and down for a few seconds and then, very suddenly, walked off in the direction of his house. The Rangers were pulled to their feet and marched away. The remaining onlookers wandered back to the village, while others started a game of football.

Christian spoke into the radio. 'This is Blue Snipe, air support no longer required; repeat, air support no longer required.'

'Affirmative, affirmative, Blue Snipe,' came the voice of the operator.

8

Once relative calm had been restored, Christian moved back to the tree where he remained until dark. Just as he was swinging his leg off the branch, he felt the first few drops of rain on his face. His spirits sank at the prospect of another few hours of misery. He announced his return over his personal role radio and approached the OP. He slid in and squatted down next to the others. They nodded quietly to him but Jamie seemed to avoid eye contact. They began to whisper to one another about the proposed assault in the morning. Christian detected a strained atmosphere but Sam changed the subject from the attack onto the somewhat lighter issue of what he was going to have for breakfast back at the base. Christian dismissed his feelings, reminding himself they were all very short of sleep and had been sitting in a muddy hole for far too long.

He tucked his head back against the camouflage netting and cleared his mind. He was conscious of insects and the occasional sound of vehicles, but managed to sleep for nearly three hours before he sat up, feeling raindrops once again splashing on his face. The floor of the OP was full of water again. He could make out Sam and Tim keeping watch out of the gap in the netting. Jamie was beside him. He looked at his watch and saw it was 23.30. He lay back down and shut his eyes again. The next thing he knew, he was being gently shaken. He sat up and looked into Jamie's face.

'It's three fifteen,' Jamie whispered. 'The other two have been kipping for a bit. Thought you might need to wake up.'

'Yeah, yeah; quite right, mate,' whispered Christian.

'It's still raining, not sure if that's a good thing or not,' Jamie went on.

'Don't know, but it doesn't make fast roping any easier. Mind you, if you drop off the rope, at least you are on for a soft landing,' replied Christian.

Inside the hangar at Freetown airport, Deverall addressed D Squadron, the helicopter pilots and gun crews. It was an informal affair, with some men seated and others standing behind. The hangar was dimly lit and the windows draped in black plastic sheeting to reduce signs of nocturnal activity. The Colonel held a mug of coffee in one hand and the remote control for the slide projector in the other.

'Right, everybody, we can't hang around indefinitely. We are going in after all. You have all been through the operation and know your roles. There isn't a great deal to say other than to remind you that this will not be a pushover. They may be running around like lunatics initially, but once they work out what's going on and regroup, there will be stiff resistance. They are not to be underestimated because they are not part of NATO. The likelihood is they will fall away into the jungle and then bounce back. By that stage, we'll have the perimeter secured and will have established clear lines of fire. The first hostage rescue team, HRT 1, should have the Rangers out and at the holding point here.'

He switched on the projector and gestured to a red circle on a map of the village.

'The next issue will be the Corporal. Our Intel tells us he is in a pit, we can't see exactly where from the satellite imagery but we reckon it's close to the hostage house. HRT 2 will have him out, but may take longer if he is secured or needs to be carried. The OP team will provide a full sitrep in the next hour but the current thinking is that the enemy have no idea we are on the way. Once HRT 1 and 2 are at the holding point, the first Chinook will land on the football pitch and extract. Once they are out, fall back to the inner perimeter and wait for the second one. Beware – there is nothing they would like more than one of our Chinooks as a trophy for the mantelpiece. They will attract fire, fire that must be suppressed at all costs. This operation is vulnerable in that respect, it's our Achilles heel. Body armour is an individual choice. Go, stand by your kit and be ready to board in thirty minutes. Good luck, all of you.'

Christian looked at his watch. It was nearly 04.00. The rain had eased to a fine misty drizzle. He whispered to Tim to wake the others and that he was going to take a final look around. He zipped up his ops vest and decided that he would take his M16 as well as his silenced pistol. He would not normally have wanted the inconvenience of taking a hefty assault rifle on such a close-quarter recce, but he instinctively felt he might need it this time. He wriggled out of the OP and moved quietly over to his favourite tree. He knew the village best from this angle. He stood still for a couple of minutes listening. The village was quiet.

He approached the edge of the track and looked along it into the middle of the village. The mist had been hardly noticeable when close up, but now he was looking at a distance of nearly 200 yards, it appeared much thicker. He could barely make out the houses at the far end. This was ideal for the purpose of a close-quarter recce, but hopeless for a coordinated airborne assault.

The operation would be postponed if the visibility did not improve. The prospect of another twenty-four hours in the OP did not appeal and he wondered if the Rangers could handle any longer in captivity, not to mention the Corporal. He took one more careful look down the track. He felt convinced there were no undercover preparations taking place. He turned around and crept slowly back towards the OP, wishing he could somehow let the Rangers know what was hopefully about to happen. He announced his approach and slipped back through the gap.

The others were all awake and eating rations. Christian was not in the mood for food and was keen to make the sitrep. He put on the radio headset and contacted the base.

'Go ahead, over,' said the voice of the radio operator.

'Situation normal. Nothing to report other than ground mist, over . . .'

'Understood. Sunray is here, over,' replied the operator.

'What's this mist like, over?' said Colonel Deverall.

'Difficult to say as it's still half dark, but it's quite thick. It could be early-morning mist or it might be coming off the river,' replied Christian.

'Roger that, require sitrep in thirty minutes. Out,' said Deverall, his tone agitated.

Christian turned to the others and whispered, 'This mist is not looking good. You can't see much from here but it gets worse in the village. If it doesn't clear, the whole thing could be aborted.'

'Fucking bloody marvellous,' said Sam under his breath.

'We'll see what happens,' said Christian, 'but we can't let them drop in and fuck up, otherwise we'll end up rescuing the whole bloody Squadron, too.'

'Imagine the humiliation when A Squadron gets sent in to dig us all out,' Sam said with a grin.

'I'd rather A Squadron than the Paras,' replied Tim.

'If we aren't careful it will be Delta Force. Then we really will be in trouble. This OP would look like Dresden before they even landed,' said Christian, grinning. 'Anyway, let's get a weapon check in. Sam, can you get out there and make sure the mines are OK? I reckon we need three facing forwards and one pointing back over us. Obviously, on individual settings.'

Once Sam was back in the OP and they had all been over their weapons, Christian checked his watch and made another sitrep.

'It will be about one minute from when we first hear the helis to when they get over the drop zones. I don't think there will be much activity until they get overhead,' whispered Christian. 'Sam, I want you on the mines, one at a time. We need to stay in here and hold this point against anyone coming out of the village. They won't be expecting us dug in on the ground so we should have the edge.

'What I don't want is us to get stuck in, reveal ourselves and then for some reason the helis abort and we find ourselves taking on the whole village. That is not the plan, challenging and invigorating as it may be. Once our guys are on the ground, we move forward. We are linking in with the team holding the western perimeter that starts to the right of the hostage house and stretches back down this side. Cornwallis said there would be us plus two others, who better have Minimis. We'll leave the rations, water and rubbish in the OP and get it later if we can. We'll take the bergens with us, as they should be light enough, and drop them somewhere where we can get back later. Then, we just slot in with the others and get stuck in. Any questions?'

'Is the mist getting any better, do you think?' asked Sam.

'I reckon it is. Once we get a bit more light, we should be able to see,' replied Jamie.

'Well, it's four fifty-five now, which means it's got fifty minutes to go,' said Tim.

Back at Freetown airport, the door of the hangar opened and forty heavily armed soldiers filed out. They made their way in two lines towards the helicopters stationed on the runway. The crews were already aboard and the pilots making various pre-take-off checks, while waiting for the signal to start the engines. At the far side of the runway, the ninety men of 1 Para were already crammed into the back of two Chinooks, ready to be dropped the other side of the river to remove any threat from the second WSB settlement.

Deverall sat at a table covered in maps next to the radio operators with Cornwallis and the Int. guys. He was tired, stressed and sweating. Cornwallis dragged on a cigarette and looked equally done in.

'This is going to be close, guys,' said the Colonel. 'We need that mist to clear otherwise we are going to mess up. We can't risk hovering about over that village looking for the drop zones. We will be sitting ducks. It has to clear. Get me the OP.'

9

Christian pushed his head out of the netting one more time. Dawn was breaking and he saw the mist had cleared considerably. He could see the makeshift goalposts on the football pitch that had been invisible twenty minutes earlier. This was the measure he'd had in his mind. There would be a few more minutes for the light to improve still further. He pulled back into the OP and grabbed the headset.

'This is Blue Snipe. Situation normal, over.'

Immediately, Deverall's voice replied, 'Roger that. Confirm, again, over.'

Christian replied, 'Confirm, situation normal. Proceed as planned, over.'

'Roger that. Good luck. Out,' replied Deverall.

Christian took off the headset and began to slip the radio into the plastic carrying case. He looked at the others. The light was improving and he could see just what a mess they looked, caked in mud and grime, their weapons the only clean things in the OP. They were already sweating with nerves and the rise in temperature that accompanied even the first glimmer of sun. They were squatting in six inches of liquid mud and the insects were out in force to see them off.

The seconds crept past. They knew the holding point was ten miles away and would only take a few minutes to fly.

They looked at one another again. They could hear the sound of incoming helicopters. No one spoke. They all nodded to each other before turning to look skywards. Sure enough, there was no waiting. The tranquillity of dawn in Gheri Bana was shattered by an explosion of noise.

The Chinooks came thundering over the treetops releasing canisters of firework-like chaff to confuse heat-seeking missiles. Inside, D Squadron sat in a column down each side of the loading bays. Each man wore a Kevlar helmet and some had body armour beneath their ops vests, which bulged with equipment and ammunition. They were armed with a mixture of Diemaco and M16 assault rifles. Some carried Minimi machine guns. Each man also had a Sig Sauer 9 mm pistol in a holster strapped to his leg.

The hostage rescue teams were armed with smaller 9 mm MP5 machine guns, which would be easier to manoeuvre in the close quarters of a building. They also carried day sacks containing plastic explosives, fragmentation, stun and smoke grenades, and water bottles, and two had large metal cutting shears strapped to their fronts. Their faces were blackened with camouflage paint.

Inside the leading Chinook, Major Mark Day shouted encouragement to his men. They could see his face but not make out many of the words. 'We are going in. We are fucking going in. Go, D Squadron, you are the best in the world.'

The men stood up and held onto the rails to look out of the windows. They could see Rokel Creek out to the left and the tops of the trees only a few feet below. They were over the landing zone. The gunners had slid back the doors and were firing belt-driven M134 mini-machine guns into the village 50 yards away. The rear door opened and the first men grabbed hold of the fast ropes and began sliding down. They crashed to the ground under the weight of their equipment, flicking off the heat-proof gloves and running for cover.

The Lynx gunships worked in two pairs to reduce the likelihood of collision, roaring over the village with guns blazing. Earth flew in all directions. Trees and vegetation were torn up by the gunfire. Some corrugated-iron roofs had been blown clean off houses to reveal terrified people still lying on their beds. Naked and partially clothed men ran around madly, bent double, cowering from the aerial assault. Some fired their AKs wildly in the air. Some had already been shredded by machine-gun fire and lay in mangled heaps. The soldiers were now grouped by the edge of the clearing waiting for the command to enter the village. The Chinooks lifted off and veered away sharply from the village to avoid incoming gunfire.

In the OP, the patrol kept their heads down. The helicopter gun crews knew exactly where they were but there was still the fear of accidental fire coming their way or a ricocheting bullet. A stream of empty bullet cases clattered down through the trees above, several of which landed in the OP. Christian pulled the camouflage netting downwards and pushed it into a corner. Jamie raised the Minimi and rested it on the ground just in front of them. Christian leant forward and covered the arc to the right, Sam to the left and Tim to the rear.

They heard desperate shouts and screams. To their surprise, the first escapees were two mangy dogs charging into the jungle. Christian had time to exchange a glance with Jamie who had only just prevented himself from instinctively opening up on them. A moment later, a shout drew their attention to the left. Three men were running into the jungle. They wore shorts and nothing else. Each held a rifle and one waved a machete. They ran headlong in the direction of the OP. Jamie did not move until the last second. Just as the lead man came within 10 yards, he adjusted the aim of the Minimi and opened fire.

The first man was hit in the chest and upper legs by the hail of bullets and was hurled backwards. Another burst from the Minimi, combined with several accurate shots from Sam, killed the other two in an instant. They fell and lay motionless on the jungle floor.

On the other side of the village, Major Mark Day gave the order to advance. A barrage of covering fire erupted from the edge of the clearing and twenty soldiers ran towards the village and reached the outermost houses. They fired short bursts as they rounded the corners of buildings and took up defensive positions. It was pandemonium as more WSBs appeared from houses and returned fire. Most were too panic stricken to take aim, firing their weapons randomly in the general direction of the attack. The Lynx helicopters swooped over the village once again, directing their fire on the unattended anti-aircraft piece.

The sound of automatic gunfire was deafening. Christian could smell and taste cordite from spent ammunition as he fired again and again at anyone he saw holding a gun. He heard Jamie's voice shout 'loading' and turned to see what was happening in their direction. There was still activity in the bushes and the odd rattle of fire. As Jamie released the empty metal ammunition box from the bottom of the Minim box, four more WSBs appeared and started to fire at the OP. Sam fired at one who dropped and Christian opened up on another who fell instantly to the ground.

More WSBs appeared and ran towards them.

Christian grabbed the detonator for the mines and shouted to the others to get down. He snapped the safety catch to one side, piled himself into the corner of the OP and pressed two buttons. The first detonated one of the mines to the front of the OP and the other set off the mine directed over to the rear. There were two cracks. The mines showered thousands of ball-bearings in 140-degree arcs, lacerating anything in their paths.

Christian waited a couple of seconds and set off the third mine. He raised his head and looked about. The vegetation between the OP and village looked like a giant lawnmower had just swept past. To the rear, he saw similar devastation. In among the tangled mess lay a horrific sight. He could see the remains of a number of mutilated bodies and limbs that had taken the full brunt of the blasts. One man crawled away in the direction of the village. Christian knew there was no time to be lost. He shouted to the others who were still keeping down, waiting for the fourth mine, 'Last one now and then we go, OK.'

Crack went the last mine. The blast shook the ground and more debris flew. The crawling man lay flat on the ground, unidentifiable as a human being.

Jamie fired a long burst into the jungle and stood up. Christian led the way into the now open area of ground in front of the OP. It was a terrible sight. He could see the scorch marks where the mines had been placed and some bits of metal casing. He stepped over harrowing remains of the WSBs who had been hit by close-range machine-gun fire and then riddled with the ball-bearings from the mines. He saw a house in front of him and wanted to use it as cover. He heard the other members of D Squadron on the radio.

'This is Blue Snipe, approaching village from OP,' he said as calmly as he could.

'Roger that, Christi,' replied Major Day.

He ran forward. He had to cover the 30 yards of open ground between the edge of the jungle and the first house. Jamie and Tim crashed against the wall beside him while Sam covered them from the edge of the jungle. Christian raised his rifle and waited. A second later, two men appeared around the corner and almost ran into him. They had staring eyes and mouths wide with fear. Without hesitation Christian opened fire from point-blank range. The bullets tore through the first man and into the second. Their bodies collapsed. Tim took no chances and fired a single round into each of their heads.

Christian took a deep breath and wiped the sweat from his eyes with his sleeve. He glanced quickly around the corner of the building and saw a mêlée of WSBs, running in all directions firing their weapons. He was desperate to get the patrol into an identifiable area of cover that they could hold while the rest of the Squadron took the village. He could then let the others know where they were and prevent any 'blue on blue'.

The next-door building was no more than 10 yards away and had a metal door facing them. He turned around and signalled to Sam, who was now running across the open ground. Sam reached the wall and fired a grenade straight at the metal door. There was a massive bang as the door broke clean in half and was left swinging on its hinges. Christian threw a fragmentation grenade through the opening and ducked back round behind the wall. There was a dull thump as the grenade exploded in the confined space. Grey smoke billowed out the door. Tim pulled the pin on another grenade and lobbed it around the corner of the building. A second after it went off, Jamie stepped forward firing through the smoke whilst the other three dashed over and piled through the broken door.

Christian looked about. The dust and smoke were clearing to reveal shattered furniture and the frame of a bed. On the floor lay the shredded remains of two people. Even in the few seconds since the grenades had gone off, a ghoulish white dust had settled on the bodies. Christian did not dwell on the sight. He flicked the remaining shutter out of the way with his rifle and started to fire out of the window. Tim joined him while Sam and Jamie fired intermittent shots from the door. Christian now had a view of the centre of the village.

He could not see any of the Squadron yet but knew they would be appearing to the right any second and that he should concentrate his fire to the left. A door opened on the other side of the track. Christian raised his rifle and was on the point of firing when he noticed several women, one holding a baby. A sickening pang of guilt passed through him. He barely had time to think before he saw two men carrying a general-purpose machine gun into a two-storey building. He fired but missed.

Moments later, they appeared on the roof, scrabbling about trying to set up the gun. They were partially hidden by a parapet running around the roof. He shouted into his radio as he raised his rifle. Tim saw the threat and took aim. They both fired and saw one man jerk backwards and disappear. The other man had seen where the shot came from and popped his head up, took aim with the machine gun and opened fire. Christian and Tim ducked down as the gun opened up. The first burst hit the wall of the house, cracking into the concrete building blocks. Large sections of concrete fell off the inside walls, creating choking dust. Christian could hardly see but was aware that the walls were no match for a heavy machine gun. A second burst, lasting nearly fifteen seconds, must have come through the open window as the rear wall of the house disappeared from view in a cloud of dust.

'Where the fuck is that coming from?' Jamie shouted.

'Tim, get some fire on him,' yelled Christian. 'I'll take him from outside.'

Tim leapt up from his position on the floor by the window and fired a long automatic burst at the building on the other side of the track. Christian stepped out of the door and used part of the hanging door frame to rest his rifle. He knew roughly where the WSB would pop up and that he would have a split second to shoot before he would be able to adjust his aim and fire. A couple of seconds after Tim's burst of fire, a head popped up to see what was going on. Christian fired one shot. The head kicked back and disappeared.

10

Christian darted back inside. Tim was covered in dust and had a dark patch of blood fast appearing on his right thigh. Sam had been hit in the face by something and had blood pouring from his chin. He had also broken a blood vessel in his right eye and it was now a demonic-looking red. Jamie was unscathed.

'Tim, you OK?' gasped Christian, his mouth dry from dust.

'Fucking agony, but fine. Must be a splinter or ricochet.'

'Sam, you all right?' Christian said, turning to Sam.

'Never better,' bellowed Sam.

At that moment, Christian heard Major Day on the personal role radio.

'Where the fuck are you guys?' said a calm-sounding voice.

'In the remains of a house just in front of the OP,'

Christian replied, standing up and starting to drag the filthy-looking remains of the mattress off the bed. 'It's the one with the mattress sticking out of the window. Can you see us?'

'Not yet, but we'll be with you. Clearing more houses our end first,' replied Day.

Outside the house, there was still the odd WSB appearing and running for cover. Most of the village seemed to have fled. The patrol covered the windows and door. They had decided to wait for the Squadron to move to them, as opposed to risking an approach. Some of the gunfire in the immediate vicinity had died down yet there was still the ongoing clatter of automatic weapons coming from the far end of the village.

'Christian, I reckon I can see you now. Is the mattress grey?' said Major Day's voice.

'Yes, that's it,' replied Christian.

'OK, I need you. There are a couple of guys, two buildings down from you on your side, with a machine gun and an RPG launcher. Get round the back and take them out. The one with the rusty red roof,' replied Major Day.

'Will-co,' answered Christian, nodding to Jamie.

They left the house and crawled down through the long grass on the edge of the village. Christian saw the building with the rusty red roof 20 yards in front of him and could hear the muffled roar of automatic fire coming from inside. It was on the end of the row and commanded a sweeping view of the centre of the village. He still couldn't see the rest of the Squadron but knew they would be just behind the houses at the far end. He was worried he would be visible from the jungle behind and that anyone lurking there would have an easy shot. He turned to Jamie and gestured to him to stay put and cover the rear. He crawled forwards and made it to the back of the house. As he got to it, he felt the vibrations of the machine gun through the wall. It was firing almost constantly and had to be of serious calibre.

He unzipped a pouch on his ops vest and took out an explosive charge about the size of his fist. He tore off the plastic coating and stuck the sticky underside to the wall. He turned to catch Jamie's eye as he twisted the timer through ninety degrees, giving him fifteen seconds. He jumped up and darted around the corner of the wall. There was a huge boom. Christian reappeared, a grenade in hand and threw it through the five-foot-wide hole in the wall. There was a second boom and a cloud of smoke billowed through the hole.

Christian ducked through the opening, his weapon raised, and fired a burst into the room. Through the dust, he could see it was a store of some kind but with no trace of bodies. There was a wooden door to his right leading to a second room. He heard shouts and realised the WSB with the machine gun had been protected by the dividing wall. He took a gamble and fired a burst straight through the wooden door into the room beyond. The top half of the door disintegrated, splinters flying in all directions. Christian could hear screams of panic and pain. He moved around carefully to see further into the next-door room. He saw the body of a man collapsed against the wall with a coil of machine-gun ammunition in his hand. As he moved further round he could see a second body fallen forwards and hanging half out of the window. He fired a second shot into both bodies. The first body hardly moved but the second body slipped forward and fell through the window.

Christian took a deep breath and wiped his face on his sleeve. He looked down and was concerned to see an unpleasant mixture of sweat, blood and dust. He stammered into his radio between deep breaths, 'Machine-gun threat neutralised, over.'

Jamie appeared through the door behind him and took up a defensive position at the window.

'Stay put; we'll come to you,' said Day.

'Roger that. Two of us are in the machine-gun position and the others are in the house with the mattress. Any news of the Paras?' replied Christian.

'Well, good news and bad,' answered Day. 'They got dropped off in four feet of swamp, but then came under intense mortar fire. Sounds like they could be bogged down a bit but they've done their job and soaked up any potential reinforcements. Hold on, we're coming over.'

A few seconds later, a barrage of fire broke out from the far end of the village. Grenades whistled down the track along the centre of the buildings, hitting houses and areas of cover, bushes and clumps of trees – any one of which could be hiding snipers. Automatic machine guns rattled as figures appeared running from house to house clearing any opposition. Within two minutes, Day's sweaty face appeared at the window.

'Are you going to open the fucking door or do I have to blow it off?' he shouted.

'Why change the habit of a lifetime?' Jamie retorted, lifting a metal bar that was holding the door shut.

Day burst in followed by a couple of other members of the Squadron. 'Good effort, boys,' he gasped, short of breath. 'It's gone down fine on our side, but the Paras have had some shit. Right, Christi, get your guys and join Andy and his team on the west perimeter. Get them to divi up if you're low on ammo.'

Just as Christian made for the door, the Beast charged into the room, his bright red hair poking out under his helmet and his ops vest visibly straining to fit his massive chest. He held his M16 in one hand, making it look like a toy gun in proportion to the rest of him.

'Christi! Good to see you, lad,' he croaked, in a thick, guttural Glasgow accent.

'All right, Beastie. Good to have you onside,' Christian replied with a grin.

On the other side of the track, the HRT 1 approached the hostage house. Two soldiers covered the front of the building while three more ran across the veranda to the front door. A couple of seconds and two small explosive charges later, the door blew off its hinges and fell forwards. As the soldiers raised their weapons, two WSBs lurched out of the doorway with their hands in the air. There were two short cracks of fire and both fell on the veranda. The soldiers moved into the building. 'British Special Forces . . . Identify yourselves!'

There were shouts from the Rangers in the room immediately on the right.

'Stand back, we're going to blow the door,' yelled one of the soldiers. With that he fired a couple of shots into the lock, sending splinters of wood and concrete into the air. Kicking the door open, he burst inside.

The Rangers stood in a huddle on the far side of the room.

'Which one of you is Major Moore?' shouted the soldier, his weapon pointing at the stunned-looking Rangers. Major Moore raised his hand. The soldier turned to him: 'Are these all your men?'

'Yes, but the Corporal is in a pit round the corner,' replied the Major.

The first soldier did not reply as he was counting for himself. 'Is everyone able to walk?'

The Major replied again. 'Yes, but the Corporal needs help. He's in a bad way.'

The soldier took a pistol from a pocket on his ops vest and handed it to the Major.

'Right, follow this man here.' He pointed to the second soldier, standing by the door. 'You will follow him to the landing zone and wait there until a helicopter arrives to get you out of here. Is that clear?'

The Rangers nodded. The second soldier led the way across a track towards a building next to the football pitch. He instructed the Rangers to sit against the wall and keep their heads down. The second hostage rescue team found the pit where the Corporal was held. There was a metal grate measuring six foot by six foot on the ground just behind the house. The first two soldiers scouted around it, looking for booby traps. They lifted and pulled it back to reveal a water-filled pit. Lying in one corner, with his head barely above the waterline was the Corporal. His hands were still tied to his ankles; his eyes shut. Flies and insects crawled across his swollen face, encrusted in dried blood and filth. The black stagnant water smelt putrid. The soldiers laid him on the ground gently and cut the rope securing his hands and ankles. His body jerked forward and he cried out in pain. The second two soldiers unfolded a stretcher and slid the Corporal onto it. Another helped him drink from a water bottle.

They all picked up the stretcher and carried him over to where the Rangers were sitting.

'Major, here he is. Try to get some fluids into him. There will be medics on the heli who'll sort him out,' said the soldier who was carrying the front of the stretcher.

Christian and Jamie followed Day out of the building and ran back to the house where Sam and Tim were waiting. There were still shots from the far end of the village and the odd burst of machine-gun fire coming from the jungle. Christian popped his head through the window with the mattress hanging out of it. Sam and Tim were inside standing by the door, their rifles raised. They were talking to one another and glanced back at Christian.

'Guys, we've got to get on our perimeter. Come on,' he shouted.

11

Christian tucked himself into the dry drainage ditch that ran along the edge of the village. He was able to lie down, allowing him to rest his rifle steadily on the ground in front of him. To his right, he could see Lance Corporal Andy Curtis and, further along, Tim was visible in the rubble of a house that had been totally destroyed. Beyond him, he knew Sam and Jamie would have taken up positions. On his left was Trooper Paul Bignall, holed up under an abandoned pick-up truck. To his rear, the Beast lurked in a building, covering the track down the centre of the village. They talked quietly over the personal role radios and agreed arcs of fire.

Christian released the used magazine from the slot underneath his rifle and replaced it with a full one. He counted his magazines and realised that he had used four full ones and most of the last one. This was about half his ammunition. He tried to remember switching magazines and found that he couldn't actually recall reloading other than the first time when still in the OP. He had been operating on autopilot.

He was still breathing heavily and was soaked in sweat. He gingerly touched his face to see where the blood was coming from. He had a nosebleed, a split lip and his right ear was also bleeding. He noticed the knuckles on his right hand were grazed and that he had a nasty burn on the underside of his left forearm. The taste in his mouth was awful. He tried to spit but his mouth was dry. He reached for his water bottle and took several long gulps and felt immediately better. He replaced the cap and slipped the bottle back into its pouch.

He looked around and could see the remains of several WSBs lying 20 yards out to his left. Judging by the mutilated state of their bodies, they must have been hit by the heavy belt-driven machine guns from the helicopters. The bodies lay in a twisted tangle. He was pleased their faces were looking away from him. Off to his left was the site of the OP. He could see his favourite tree. Everything had changed in less than half an hour.

Christian heard a suppressed cry from behind him. He spun round with his rifle at the ready. He was amazed to see a child of no more than six years old, standing in the remains of a building, in front of the Beast whose face was twisted in pain.

Christian was unable to work out what was going on until he saw the Beast's face contort even further as he pulled a long bone-handled hunting knife out of his thigh. The child simply stood and stared. Christian realised the child must have ambushed the Beast from somewhere in the rubble of the building and stabbed him in the leg.

The scene was surreal. He had no time to react before he saw the Beast reach forward and grab the boy who was still rooted to the spot. Christian braced himself for something violent. The Beast stooped, picked up the boy, bent him across his knee and gave him several hard slaps across the bottom. He stood up, still holding the knife, and raised his hand as if to hit the boy, who turned and fled screaming into the jungle.

Christian was still staring in bewilderment when he heard the Beast mutter, 'Bloody kids', as if the child had squirted him with a water pistol.

The momentary distraction came to an end as a mortar round landed in the jungle just the other side of the village. Immediately there was swearing and cursing over the personal role radios. A couple of seconds later, a second mortar thundered into another area of jungle to Christian's left.

The area of open ground between Christian and the jungle was suddenly ripped up by fire. Mud and debris kicked into the air in a long line. A second burst tore into the buildings behind him. Christian scanned the jungle, desperately looking for targets. The mist was still lingering in the trees and masked any tell-tale smoke from the WSBs' weapons.

Christian's eye was caught by a movement directly in front of him, 50 yards into the jungle. He squinted into his sights and could make out two men squatting down with an RPG launcher. He fired immediately and saw both men drop to the ground. He was wiping the sweat away from his eyes when a third man appeared, picked up the RPG launcher and disappeared from view.

Seconds later, a trail of white smoke emerged from the jungle. Christian had time to shout 'RPG' before ducking down. The RPG slammed into the side of a house 20 yards behind him. There was a massive boom and pieces of concrete rained down all over the place. Christian turned and glanced over his shoulder. He could see a gaping hole in the wall of the house with pieces of broken and twisted metal inside. He made a mental note that this would be a useful place to fall back to, if need be.

The incoming fire continued. Christian took the odd shot at possible targets in the jungle. Day's voice came over the radio telling everyone to preserve ammunition and that the Lynx helicopters would be back soon having been re-loaded at the base. He added that there was no way the Chinooks could land until the enemy fire had been controlled. He was still talking when a mortar round made a direct hit on the pick-up truck to Christian's left. There was a boom and flash of light. Shrapnel and pieces of the pick-up truck were blown into the air. A couple of seconds later, the smoke cleared to reveal there was nothing left of the vehicle other than a large black lump that had been the engine block.

Christian knew that Trooper Bignall would have stood no chance. He resisted his urge to run over and check, just in case by some miracle he had survived. There were bits of pick-up truck lying about, some bits still smoking in the grass. The remains of a wheel lay within six feet of him and gave off an acrid smell of burning rubber. He wiped the sweat from his face again and this time felt pain from his bleeding nose.

The first Christian knew of the Lynx helicopters returning was the swirling dust. He was surprised that he had not heard them coming in and put this down to the ringing in his ears from the mortar that had gone off so close to him. He saw two pass above him firing into the rising slope of jungle above the OP.

They circled around again and fired missiles into the jungle. Christian knew they would be after the mortar positions. He turned around and spotted the Rangers crouching by the building next to the football pitch. They would be wondering why things were taking so long. Another boom erupted from the other side of the village, indicating the mortars were still operating. This was followed by a dramatic increase in fire from the other side of the village. He could hear other members of the Squadron talking calmly to each other and selecting targets.

12

As the first Chinook landed on the football pitch, the jungle erupted with gunfire. The WSBs had been waiting for their opportunity and were doing their best to prevent any airborne evacuation. Bullets rained down in a random pattern all around.

The Rangers had disappeared and Christian assumed they had boarded the Chinook, along with the wounded. Despite the incoming fire, half a dozen members of the Squadron were piling WSB bodies into the back of the Chinook to lower the head count for the world's media, who would, by now, be aware of the operation. They would be dropped far out to sea.

Christian could not make out any specific targets. He saw the odd movement and guessed the fire was coming from some distance away. As the Chinook took off, a second appeared overhead, its guns roaring.

He took a quick look at his watch and was amazed to see it was only 07.45. He felt the battle had been raging for hours. It was worrying that they were still on the ground and he wondered how they had lost momentum. The rescue plan was based on the element of surprise and the longer they occupied the village, the longer the WSBs would have to mount a counter-attack. They obviously had weapons stashed in the jungle and were regrouping.

The second Chinook screamed overhead, before rearing up in position to land on the football pitch. The Lynx helicopters appeared again and poured down covering fire into the jungle. The Chinook lurched in the air and began its final descent from 100 feet. It came down agonisingly slowly.

Without warning, an RPG slammed into its side. It jerked and instantly lost 20 feet of height. The light armour had deflected the majority of the blast, but Christian was sure there would be casualties on board. He had no idea from where the RPG had been fired and desperately scanned the jungle. The Chinook's engines roared louder than ever. It started to rise as another RPG exploded in exactly the same spot. It jolted backwards and a cargo net fell from the open rear ramp, which was billowing black smoke. Christian glanced and saw the Chinook lower its nose, move up and away from the landing zone and out of sight, over the canopy of the jungle. He could still hear the engines and assumed it was capable of flight.

Immediately, the Lynxes appeared overhead in formation and fired rockets into a wide area of jungle. There was a series of explosions, which sent powerful echoes around the village. Smoke appeared among the trees.

Christian knew he had to keep focused and continued to search the jungle through his sights. Suddenly, out to his left, he saw the white smoke trail of an inbound RPG. He had only just seen it when he saw several more. There were a number of explosions followed by a massive amount of gunfire.

A jolt of fear ran through him as he saw a group of some forty or more WSBs running out of the jungle towards the village. Several fell immediately. They had the look of a crazed lynch mob. He fired several carefully aimed bursts at the group. More fell, but many had reached the buildings at the far end of the village. He could hear screams and what sounded like battle cries amongst the gunfire.

A second, smaller, group appeared from the jungle immediately in front of him. He fired two shots and snapped on a new magazine. The group ran headlong out of the jungle in a wild charge. Christian saw several more drop to the ground to his right and knew this would be Andy's shooting. He fired nearly half a magazine in one burst and saw three more collapse. He continued to fire as accurately as he could, making sure he was taking specific targets. His mind was a swirling blur of noise, confusion and fear.

Several WSBs had made it within a few feet of him as he changed magazine again. He managed to raise his rifle and fire. Their bodies fell among the rubble of the collapsed wall. He saw their contorted faces and wide eyes.

Christian heard Andy scream, 'Reloading!' He glanced Andy's way and saw that a group of WSBs had made it to his position. A second later, Andy's body fell forward into view from the building where he was positioned. He tried to stand but only got to his knees when his body jerked forward to the ground. Oblivious of danger, two WSBs set about him with their machetes. Christian felt fury, and fired. They fell on top of Andy's body and that outraged Christian still more.

He could not understand how a relatively small group could have rushed Andy. He had been defending his own stretch of line, but Jamie, Tim and Sam should have covered him while he reloaded. Christian saw more WSBs appear out to his right and fired. They darted back into the cover of the jungle. He realised that with Andy down, he had a larger section to cover and should move along to where he could see the others. He fired a couple of shots in the direction the WSBs had been and clambered back through the house and out the other side. He ran around the back of some houses, across the veranda of the hostage house and entered it.

He stepped over the remains of the shattered door.

He could see the room where the hostages had been held on his right. With his rifle raised, he moved quietly down to the next door, which was shut. Over the din of the firing outside, he could make out some kind of argument.

He heard Sam shouting and someone screaming. He heard Sam's voice again, 'This is your last fucking chance. I know you understand me. Where are the diamonds?'

He heard a shot, followed by a sickening scream. There was more shooting, this time from an automatic rifle. His mind swam in confusion.

He yelled: 'It's McKie; I'm coming in.'

He pushed open the door with his rifle raised, then stopped in his tracks. Udor Foday knelt in the middle of the room, his hands secured behind his back. Sam stood in front of him, a pistol in his hand. Tim was holding Foday in position with a piece of wire wrapped around his neck. Jamie was by the window taking shots. Part of the roof had fallen in and the room was littered with rubble and broken furniture. Foday's face was swollen and bleeding. He was trying to balance on one knee to take the weight off the other, which was pouring blood.

'Get out of here, Christi,' yelled Sam.

Foday looked at Christian, and a glimmer of hope passed across his face.

Jamie shouted, 'Christi, we found him in here, hiding in the rubble. We'll cut you in. I promise.'

Christian had started to speak, but Sam lurched forward, grabbed his personal role radio mouthpiece and snapped it off.

Christian jerked backwards and shouted. 'You've killed Andy. You're fucked on this, you fucking idiots, what are you doing?'

Foday began to shout at Christian to save him, but Tim yanked the man back with the wire around his throat. Jamie still took shots out of the window. Sam pushed Christian hard against the wall and pinned him there with his shoulder. Christian decided not to resist. Sam turned around and snapped to Tim and Jamie to get out. Tim pushed Foday to the floor and as he moved towards the window, Sam raised his pistol and shot him twice through the head. Foday's body jolted and a pool of blood encircled his head where it lay on the dirty concrete. Jamie and Tim took a quick look out of the window and then climbed out and immediately started firing their rifles.

Sam turned his face to Christian, still holding him against the wall. Christian's mind was spinning. Sam's face was purple with anger and his blood-filled eye gave him a demonic look. Spit had built up in the corners of his mouth and he gleamed with sweat.

'One word, Christi, and I will . . . I will kill you. Nicking off this lot is not a crime,' he roared in Christian's face. 'They are fucking vermin, you know it.'

'You will be court-martialled for this,' Christian

shouted back. 'Not for the diamonds, you idiot – for Andy. You abandoned him and he's dead, hacked to shit by machetes while you were in here, fucking looting, not holding the line.'

Sam's face took on a new dimension of anger. Christian saw fear, too. He could see Sam's personal role radio was switched off so no one could hear what had been said.

Sam raised his pistol and pushed it into Christian's cheek, growling, 'Just one word, and I will kill you and your whole family; you know I can. Now don't move.'

Sam released his grip and stepped back a couple of paces, pointing his pistol straight at Christian's face. He knew Sam would not shoot and stood stock-still. Sam lowered the pistol slightly and fired a shot into Christian's right shoulder.

Christian would have fallen over backwards but the wall stopped him. He sank down in shock and pain. Now he realised that Sam was going to kill him, but without using a signature SAS double-head shot. Christian was slumped against the wall, unable to move his right arm to use his own rifle. He tasted the blood in his mouth and felt he was going to be sick. He heard the shouts and yells of WSBs in the corridor outside. He looked up at Sam, who was still pointing his pistol at him. He knew he was dead one way or the other. He stared at Sam defiantly. An intense look came over Sam that Christian could not read.

Then several things happened at once. The door burst open, Sam swung his pistol firing three shots into the doorway and an RPG exploded against the outer wall of the building. The wall collapsed inwards covering Christian in rubble and corrugated-iron sheets from the roof. Struggling to keep on his feet, Sam fired again at the doorway whilst throwing himself backwards out of the window.

13

Christian was unable to move beneath the concrete blocks and roofing materials. He could not see anything and felt suffocated beneath the weight. He tried to move but felt searing pain from his wounded shoulder. He heard shouting around him and voices crackling through the earpiece of his personal role radio. His thoughts were unclear but his sixth sense told him to keep still and quiet.

Christian was not sure what was happening in the room as there was so much firing taking place. He had to keep still until things quietened and then call for help. A minute or so passed. He felt he could not take another second under the rubble with the agonising pain from his shoulder. His tried to speak but his mouth and throat were clogged with dust. He coughed and then croaked into the personal role radio.

'This is McKie, I am trapped in the hostage house;

repeat, I am trapped in the hostage house, require urgent assistance.'

He could hear voices over his earpiece including Day telling the Squadron to re-form the perimeter. Then Christian felt the worst feeling he had ever felt in his life. He remembered Sam had ripped off his mouth piece to prevent the rest of the Squadron hearing what was going on. Panic ran through his body. He was wounded and trapped in a part of the village that sounded like it had been overrun.

He tried to move and found that there was some give in the rubble and corrugated iron on top of him. He could have pushed some of the debris off him but his right arm was out of action. He wriggled and writhed to get himself free but the pain in his shoulder was unbearable. He heard more shouts from the WSBs and guessed they must be somewhere close. He tried to listen.

He heard Day talking once again. 'I don't need to remind you to preserve ammunition. Find your targets, watch your arcs. We can't get a heli in here and are going to fall back to the river. The Chinooks are dropping four ribs a mile downstream in fifteen minutes, which means they should be here in twenty-five. I want the Northern perimeter held—' His voice was drowned out by the roar of a helicopter overhead.

Christian heard Day again giving orders for the fall-back to the river. Then he heard him ask for a casualty report. Someone reported Andy as dead. Day then asked for Christian to confirm this, knowing they had been next to each other.

There was a pause, and then he heard Sam's voice. 'We were in the hostage house but he didn't get out. We were overrun. Christi was holding the door and was shot.'

'Can anyone confirm that?' replied Day.

There was pause. Then Tim spoke. 'Yes, Christi's dead; I was there.'

Lying in the rubble, Christian became aware of figures moving in the room. He was not sure if he had lost consciousness but had little sense of passing time. He listened for voices but could only hear a continuous hum in his ears.

For the second time, he felt a desperate feeling of abandonment and betrayal. The pain in his shoulder surged as he tried once again to move. He tried to concentrate. He knew his situation was dire and that death would most likely be a better option than becoming the target of the WSBs' revenge. His thoughts were interrupted by a sudden clamour. He closed one eye and tried to focus. Two men were shouting to each other and lifting the corrugated-iron sheets off him. He tried to speak but was only able to croak and splutter.

He shut his eyes, hoping for one final moment of relative peace before the horror began. He felt a series of slaps across his face and opened his eyes to see an older man staring at him. The man had grey hair, wispy stubble and trembled with rage. More debris was pulled away, including the beam that lay across Christian's chest. He tried to sit up but was pushed back down by the muzzle of an AK-47. He wondered if he stood any chance of making a grab for a weapon. This option was very quickly removed as a second man, younger looking, but equally irate, seized Christian's M16 from the rubble and was busy ripping open the pouches on his ops vest. Both men were shouting instructions at Christian but he was more or less oblivious due to the ringing in his ears.

Once all the equipment had been grabbed, the second man scuttled over to the window and fired a couple of shots. He then leant out and yelled. Within half a minute, the room had filled with a wild-looking mob. Christian was shaking uncontrollably with fear but was doing his best to focus on the older man, who still had his AK pressed hard down on his chest. He hoped he might be in charge and have some kind of grip.

A furious argument ensued with two obvious factions. Some brandished knives and pointed at Christian while others yelled and screamed at each other. The older man shouted back at some of them and then became the recipient of all the aggression in the room. Christian hoped there might be a sudden blood bath that would provide him with an opportunity to escape.

The row was quickly escalating into a frenzy of rage, with guns being pointed in all directions, when the remains of the door were suddenly kicked open. The shouting ceased instantly. From where he lay, Christian could not see the man's face but whoever stood in the doorway had brought instant control. He heard a deep voice snap out a couple of words which were met by nods by those in the room. The new arrival stepped into view and turned to look down at Christian. Like Foday had been, he wore a clean white shirt and full-length trousers. He had slick-looking sunglasses pushed up on his head and the feel of authority; behind him stood four guards clearly not fresh from battle, like the others in the room.

'Looks like you put up a fight, soldier,' he said, in good English.

Christian was not sure what to say. The man continued, 'I expect you are going to tell me you are a medic with the British Army Air Corps, aren't you, soldier?' He dropped down to one knee with an amused expression on his face.

'So, they leave you behind. That's not so nice for you, is it? You people are quick to leave when they no longer have a use for a man or a place.'

He picked up a brick-sized piece of concrete and thumped it down on Christian's wounded shoulder. Christian screamed in pain. The man looked pleased, as did the others in the room.

'Now you are going to tell me who you are and

exactly what the so-called Special Air Service is going to do next.'

Christian could hardly speak due to the pain pulsating through his shoulder and upper body. He turned to speak but was only able to gag and then be sick all down his chest. The group of WSBs looked delighted with this and chatter broke out amongst them. The man in the white shirt raised his hand for quiet, unclipped his pistol from its holster and placed the muzzle against the entry wound in Christian's shoulder.

'Who said lightning doesn't strike twice, soldier?' he said, smiling.

Christian had wondered so many times how he would stand up to torture. It was every Special Forces soldier's worst nightmare and it had become his reality. There was no training for this apart from being told, roughly, what one could expect in each different country. He knew the reasons for not talking were to give your comrades time to escape and not to jeopardise the remainder of an operation. In this case, neither applied as the Squadron were long gone and the operation was over. There was nothing to be gained by keeping quiet.

'My name is Major McKie, 22nd SAS.' He hoped the elevated rank might have some sway and make him a little more useful. 'I am part of a hostage extraction force sent here to liberate British servicemen captured during a peace-keeping mission.'

'That's all obvious. Are they coming back here or are they finished with us?'

Christian replied, 'Our remit was to extract the hostages and withdraw. The chances are the whole Squadron will be back in Hereford by tomorrow.'

'Not all the Squadron – you are here with us for the time being.'

Christian was concerned by his choice of words but chose to consider them in a glimmer of hope.

'May I ask who you are?' he mumbled.

'They call me Colonel Cambodia,' the man replied.

Christian was surprised that a man with this much authority opted for what sounded like a silly fictitious name, but he replied, 'Yes, Colonel.'

'Anyway, it's your lucky day – you are coming with me,' Cambodia said, turning to his guards and gesturing to them to carry Christian. Two moved forwards while the other two stood with their weapons at the ready. Christian had no idea what they were expecting as his only weapons were a half-full water bottle and a medical kit that had not been stolen because it was in a pouch on the back of his ops vest. As he was lifted up roughly from the rubble, his shoulder made him wince with pain. Cambodia spotted the medical pack and ripped it from Christian, looked inside and then pushed it into Christian's hand with a grunt.

The pain of being suspended by his arms made Christian cry out.

'I can walk,' he said, looking towards Colonel Cambodia who, to his surprise, nodded at the guards who promptly lowered him to the ground. He stood up slowly and could finally see the appalling carnage strewn about the floor and walls. He could tell the atmosphere was changing and the dozen or so WSBs were looking less in awe of Colonel Cambodia and more like a lynch mob again.

Cambodia detected the change too and snapped instructions to the guards who pushed Christian out of the door into the corridor and towards the front door. Cambodia backed out of the room and pushed past Christian and the guards. Christian crossed the veranda and surveyed the shattered remains of Gheri Bana. Bodies littered the ground and houses lay in rubble or were riddled with bullet holes. It was obvious why these people wanted his blood. One of the guards nudged him with the butt of his rifle towards the back of a black pick-up that was parked just outside. He clambered into the back and sat down among a pile of empty bullet cases. He pushed his back against the cab and his feet against the base of a .50-cal. machine gun mounted on a stand.

Three guards climbed in the back with him while Cambodia got in the front with the fourth. As the engine started, Christian sat low and stared at the floor to avoid eye contact with the large group of WSBs milling around the vehicle. As they started to move, he glanced sideways and saw the situation was very tense. There were wild-looking men that had been in the thick of the fighting, still holding weapons, some with bleeding wounds, some shouting and running along with the pick-up. Christian was amazed they were letting him go and hadn't lynched him there and then. Then it dawned on him that perhaps they had interpreted the battle as some kind of bloody victory in which they had seen off the British superpower.

The guards looked nervous and squatted in the middle of the back of the pick-up to avoid the grabbing hands of the crowd. The vehicle gained pace and soon passed the last house of the village, making for the track that Christian had seen so clearly from the OP. He glanced up and saw his tree flash out of sight.

As the pick-up bounced along, Christian tore off the remains of his right shirtsleeve and administered basic first aid to his wounded shoulder. He tore open a sachet of purple antiseptic powder and tipped the contents into a field dressing which he managed to stick over his shoulder so that it covered both the entry and exit wounds.

Next, he swallowed four painkillers and three antibiotic pills. He then pushed the plastic container into his cycling shorts in case the medical pack was taken from him.

He looked about him and at the three guards. He was surprised how relaxed they now seemed. He had been part of numerous escape and evasion exercises and could hear Major Day's voice in his head asking the question: *So how many mistakes have these guys made since they captured Christian? I count ten. Who can give me the first six?*

He should have been hogtied, blindfolded and face down on the floor. The fact that he was not tied and could see what he was doing was a great advantage, but his right arm was out of action and causing him unbelievable pain. He could not jump and run for it and he stood no chance of overpowering three guards with only one good arm. His only option was to keep a low profile, watch out for landmarks and keep an idea of the distance and direction that they travelled.

14

The journey continued for hours and Christian gave up any idea of making a heroic escape. He was conscious of the passing jungle and that the sun was no longer overhead. He guessed it was late afternoon. Without warning, there was a jolt as the pick-up bounced up a steep slope and down onto a tarmac road. The engine revved loudly as they increased speed. Whilst the smooth ride and cooling breeze came as a relief, Christian knew that he was now travelling much faster into hostile territory. As they passed a run-down village, the guards shouted at the passers-by and waved their weapons triumphantly.

The pick-up veered off the tarmac and started down a narrow track with roughly cultivated fields on either side. They turned through a gateway into a walled compound containing a large, well-built house. The rusting metal railings had an ornate look that made him think the house must have been built when the French occupied Sierra Leone. Several scruffy men appeared from the front door and ran down the steps towards them. They exchanged excited greetings with the guards. Colonel Cambodia got out and issued various instructions before walking up the steps into the house.

Christian was in such pain that he did not really care what was happening. As the guards jumped out of the back of the pick-up, he slipped a couple of empty bullet casings into the top of his boot on the off chance they might be of use. Then he was dragged out of the back of the pick-up by his legs and landed on his back on the dusty concrete yard. He lost grip of his surroundings and thought he heard familiar voices calling for him. For a split second, he imagined he was being rescued. He opened his eyes and saw the faces of the WSBs looking down at him. Fear surged through him as he was dragged to his feet and frog-marched around the side of the house. He did not resist as the medical pack was snatched from him.

He looked about for any potential escape routes. He could see a rough area of wasteland behind the house and some encouragingly thick-looking vegetation beyond. He was still looking around when he was pushed down some steps towards a metal door under the house. A guard opened the door with a wrenching sound. Christian was worried by the amused expression on the guard's face. There was virtually no light inside but Christian saw a movement in the darkness at the back of what must have been an old wine cellar.

Down the left wall were a series of cubbyholes, some of which still contained wine racking. Along the right was a row of wire cages. Christian shuddered as he felt hands pushing him forwards. There was a terrible stench, so strong he could taste it. He was pushed along to the third cage and had to duck down to fit in. He moved into the cage and sat down against the brick wall at the back. The door was shut and padlocked. As Christian's eyes became accustomed to the darkness, he spotted the cause of the smell. His heart missed a beat as he saw most of the cubbyholes contained severed human heads in various states of decay. He couldn't see the heads clearly but realised this was some kind of trophy room, designed to terrify anyone held in the cages opposite.

Moments before he blacked out, Christian could just about see the outline of a man rocking to and fro in the next cage.

15

The next morning, at Lungi airport, the pilots of the Hercules C-130 made their final checks before take-off. There was a strange atmosphere on board amongst the men of D Squadron. In military terms the operation had been a success. The objectives had been achieved, yet there was none of the jubilation that some of the men had anticipated on their way home. They had done the job they had trained to do, but any feeling of triumph had been washed away by the loss of their comrades. Deverall had debriefed them on the Destroyer and congratulated them, but everyone knew the final extraction had been a mess.

Sam sat apart from Jamie and Tim. He had been talking about the fire-fight and filling in the rest of the Squadron over and over again about what had happened to Christian. He was eulogising about what a great officer Christian had been and what a professional job he had done. Jamie and Tim were quiet, grateful when the roar of the engines became so loud as to make meaningful conversation all but impossible.

The return flight felt even longer than the outward leg. Two medics moved among the men offering their services and checking out minor injuries that had not been attended to by the Navy medical crews.

Back on the ground at Brize Norton, D Squadron hauled their personal kit bags out of the back of the Hercules, across the tarmac into two waiting Chinooks. It was a warm summer's evening with calm-looking ground staff directing the proceedings. At Stirling Lines, on the outskirts of Hereford, a welcoming party were hanging around the buildings next to the helipads, eager to congratulate the returning soldiers.

Deverall was quick to bypass any backslapping and handshaking. He moved around the back of the Chinook and set off towards the office block, planning how he was going to break the news to the bereaved families. He felt particularly uneasy about Christian's parents as he was short on facts. He had met the McKies on several occasions and knew that they lived in the New Forest. He had arranged for a driver to take him there the following morning.

The melancholic mood that had prevailed on the return flight soon lifted as the men of D Squadron filed into the Sergeants' Mess and tucked into the pints of lager already waiting six rows deep on the bar. Souvenirs such as a rusty AK and a machete were placed in the glass cupboard on the wall, alongside all kinds of other peculiar trophies picked up in various theatres of war.

Sam descended on the lager. To the outside world, he appeared very much the returning hero, yet his insides were knotted with fear and anxiety, which he sincerely hoped the lager would settle.

An hour into the celebration, Deverall entered the mess, to a rowdy round of applause. He smiled and raised his hand for quiet. 'Now listen up a moment please, folks. I have a short note to read you from the Prime Minister. Don't worry, I have persuaded him there is no need to come down here in person – that is, until we have had time to hide all the new kit and get the crappy old Land Rovers out the front. Anyway, he says he is very impressed and by all accounts you are the best of the best. If only he could see us in two hours' time.'

Deverall continued to read aloud the note from Tony Blair, with his own commentary thrown in at various points, to raucous applause from all present.

The evening descended into a drunken party. Sam, stripped to the waist, was attempting to consume his second yard-glass of ale to screams of delight from the crowd around the bar. Others sat around at tables endlessly analysing the assault and working out ways it could have been done better. By 2 a.m. most had cleared out of the Mess and had made their way back over to their living quarters.

At 09.30 the next day, a grey Vauxhall Senator pulled up outside a pretty, well-maintained Georgian rectory on the outskirts of Lymington in Hampshire. A smartly dressed elderly man with an ashen face was waiting by the dark green front door. He took a deep breath and stretched out a hand towards Deverall as he approached across the gravel drive.

'Please come in, Colonel.'

'Thank you, sir,' Deverall replied, stepping into the hall where Mrs McKie gestured him into the drawing room. Deverall was guided to a wing-backed chair next to a walnut table displaying a bank of photographs of Christian, from a grinning boy in a tiny sailing boat to a grown man standing proudly in military uniform.

Deverall sat down and began the most painful half-hour of his military career.

16

On the morning of his fifth day in the cellar beneath Cambodia's house, Christian was dragged outside. He lay on the ground blinking in the sunlight through half-closed eyes. He had only been outside once before to receive basic medical treatment on his shoulder. Apart from that, he had sat in the dark, surviving on a diet of green bananas, stale bread and foul-tasting water.

Cambodia appeared and looked down on him where he lay.

'Get up now, lazy boy!' he shouted, almost in a friendly tone. 'We are all going up country.'

Christian got to his feet, wondering if this was good news or bad. He was flexi-cuffed and hurried around the house towards the pick-up. He sat himself in the same place as before, with his back against the cab. He did not know the exact time, but guessed it was still pretty early as the back of the pick-up was wet with dew. The impact of the first major pothole slammed Christian's shoulder hard against the side of the pick-up. He gulped with pain and braced himself as the vehicle gathered pace. The guards adopted a more professional attitude this time and looked stern as they bounced their way along the track leading out of the village. Cambodia was driving, the radio on full blast.

Christian knew they were travelling northwards as the sun was rising out to his left. He guessed they were doing at least 30 mph and that, with each hour, he was one more day's walk from Freetown. By late morning, he concluded that a 'walk-out strategy' was close to impossible.

He noticed that he had not seen any form of cultivation for some time. The condition of the road was worse and vegetation had become taller and hopelessly overgrown. Just as Christian was thinking that it might be a good moment to jump, due to the abundance of cover, they burst out of the vegetation into a clearing. A few minutes later, the pick-up slowed and the music coming from the cab stopped. Cambodia's head appeared from the window. He grunted a few words to the guards who immediately cocked their AKs. Christian saw a new-looking twin-engine aircraft in a makeshift hangar of bamboo poles and camouflage netting. Next to it, in two deckchairs, was a very worrying sight. There were two Arabs dressed in dark T-shirts, combat trousers and sunglasses.

Cambodia stepped out of the pick-up and confidently approached the men. Christian heard Cambodia talking, but could not make any sense of what he was saying. A moment later, he found himself being pushed out of the back of the pick-up and forced into a kneeling position.

A guard held an AK against his head as Cambodia and the Arabs approached. The atmosphere was tense and Cambodia seemed worried. The first of the Arabs looked closely at Christian. He was clean-shaven and purposeful, his hair held back by a black bandana. He had a hard look to him as he assessed Christian's clothing and boots. Cambodia produced the medical pack and thrust it at the second Arab, who was standing back, holding a Heckler & Koch G36 assault rifle.

The first Arab spoke in perfect English, but with an identifiable American accent.

'Tell me, how long you have been in the SAS?'

Christian did not answer, wondering what approach to take. Before he had time to think what to say, the Arab kicked him with all his strength in the stomach. Christian was bowled over backwards by the force of the kick and totally winded. He lay gasping for breath in the dusty grass.

The Arab spoke again. 'If you aren't British SAS, then you are of no value to me other than bush meat. I will ask you the question again.'

Christian was barely able to speak, so simply nodded his head.

'So it was an SAS operation. Get in and out as quick as possible. Shoot the place up and go – your usual sort of thing, then. I wonder how the hundreds of wounded African freedom fighters are getting on lying in the jungle being eaten by maggots? Have you given them any thought?' The Arab spat, his coolness fading fast.

'This reminds me of your American friends killing and wounding two thousand civilians in Mogadishu not so long ago.'

Although Christian had now recovered his breath, he knew to keep as quiet as possible and to avoid eye contact at all costs. He lay on the ground waiting for the next wave of pain.

Cambodia and the Arab walked slowly back towards the makeshift hangar, talking quietly. A couple of minutes passed before Cambodia returned with an expression on his face that Christian found hard to read. He looked more relaxed, but awkward too. The two Arabs approached and pulled Christian roughly away towards the aircraft and pushed him to the ground by the hangar. Christian had his last view of the WSBs as dust kicked up from the rear tyres of the pick-up.

The Arab in charge squatted down in front of Christian and spoke. 'Now, we can do this one of two ways. Either we treat you like the sack of shit you are or we can be a little more civilised. You need to tell me your name, your unit and the name of your commanding officer.'

Christian knew there was nothing to be gained from lying as it was so obvious he was from a British Special Forces unit: 'My name is Captain McKie and I serve with 22nd SAS. My commanding officer is Colonel Deverall.'

'Very good,' replied the Arab, standing up and pulling off Christian's flexi-cuffs. He then walked to the aircraft and returned a few seconds later dropping a bottle of mineral water and a packet of biscuits in Christian's lap. The other Arab chucked a packet of cigarettes onto the ground in front of him too. Christian nodded his thanks.

For several hours, Christian sat quietly in the shade of the hangar, watched closely by the Arab guarding him. The senior Arab wandered around making endless calls from his satellite phone.

All of sudden, the Arab ended his call and directed his attentions to the aeroplane, making pre-flight checks. Christian cleared his throat.

'Excuse me, sir. May I ask what you are planning on doing with me?' he said as calmly and politely as possible.

'Yes,' said the Arab, pausing. 'Yes, you can. It's very simple. I have just arranged to sell you back to your people for three million dollars. Not bad for me and lucky for you. Al Qaeda only bid one million dollars and wanted to behead you live on TV. So, let's go, but it's flexi-cuffs on.'

It was difficult for Christian to get into the back of the aeroplane with his hands cuffed behind his back but he was soon inside. He had now identified from the conversation between the Arabs that the senior one was called Mo, and his number two, Farq.

Mo turned the key and started the engines. The sudden rush of air flowing into the cabin through the open windows was pleasantly refreshing. Christian watched Mo go through his basic checks and pull the throttle out towards him. The aeroplane moved forward and gathered speed along the grassy runway.

The aeroplane bumped for the last time and took to the air. Mo pushed the nose down to gain speed and skimmed along just over the tops of trees below. Christian wondered why he had not been blindfolded. From the new aircraft and the modern weapons, these two guys looked professional and would surely put a bag over his head to stop him looking around. His conclusion was worryingly negative and fear surged through him once again.

If he were being handed back to the British Army, surely the Arabs would have hidden their faces for fear of being tracked down in the future? Christian's next thought was worse still. The Nazis had never told the Jews they were being taken off to be gassed. They were told they were being relocated and there-fore the majority went along quietly. The fact that he would be able to provide an accurate description of Mo and Farq implied he was on a one-way flight.

He was still analysing the intentions of his captors when his next unpleasant shock came. Farq pulled down the sun visor at the top of the fly-splattered windscreen revealing a small mirror. Christian caught a glimpse of a face he did not recognise. This ragged-looking man had matted hair encrusted with blood and dust. He had sunken eyes with entrenched black bags. His skin appeared tight, stretched and grey, covered in filthy stubble, bruises and cuts. This was a desperate-looking wreck of a creature, clearly on his last legs.

He slumped back in his seat and watched the aircraft gauges They were flying north at 120 knots. He had no idea where they would be heading but after three hours they landed to refuel. They set off again on the same northerly heading.

The organ played in St Martin's Church in Hereford as the first of the mourners arrived for the 3 p.m. funeral service. Deverall had insisted that the bodies of the dead should be laid to rest as quickly as possible. This was for two clear reasons. Firstly, he knew from experience that this helped family, friends and indeed the whole regiment from protracted depression and moping around. Almost every year the SAS lost people, and a long interval before a funeral always made things worse.

His second reason was that there was a noticeable

atmosphere around Stirling Lines. There was a bad feeling amongst the soldiers and he knew what they were thinking. The feeling was that three of them had died to rescue eleven and that this ratio was not necessarily worthwhile. Sure, the WSBs had been knocked back into the Stone Age, but so what? There was also the issue of Andy. He had been chopped up by the WSBs, which was quite extraordinary – he should have been covered by his mates. Everyone understood that trawling through the actions of men in combat was unhelpful from the calm of a briefing room, but still there were questions being asked.

Another factor contributing to the atmosphere was that of Christian. What was he doing in the house and why wasn't he outside on the perimeter? Everyone knew he was the last guy on earth to run for cover. What had happened to him?

The feeling was that the 'spirit' of the regiment had somehow been tarnished. They had not fought as a cohesive unit, more like a group of individuals. It was mooted that the SAS had not fought in such large numbers before, and were now only used to operating in tiny units of just four men. There were too many chiefs, not enough Indians. Everyone had been rushing around making decisions and not getting on with following orders. Some people were even saying the Paras or the Marines would have done a better job, and that the SAS was really only any good at counter-terrorism.

The church filled up and many mourners had to stand outside where some speakers had been erected. Mr and Mrs McKie were already seated in the front row, surrounded by their family and friends. Extra chairs lined the side aisles and a dozen soldiers perched uncomfortably on a wooden bench beneath the lectern.

Deverall made his way towards the front of the crowded church looking for a seat. He had expected to find one reserved for him and was starting to feel awkward when the Beast stood up with some difficulty and offered his. Deverall tried in vain to decline his offer, as the Beast muttered something deep from the back of his throat which sounded like, 'Noot ba wee scratch, seer.'

Deverall's position had moved from awkward to downright uncomfortable as he sat down next to the sobbing mother of Paul Bignall. He did not need to look but he knew Andy's family were right behind him too.

He glanced to his right and received a dignified nod of recognition from Christian's father. This stoic man understood the sacrifice his son had made. Several rows back, behind the McKies, a large dark blue hat caught his eye. As discreetly as possible, Deverall glanced over his shoulder to see Margaret Thatcher sandwiched between her husband and the Chief of the Defence Staff. He had not seen her on the list of dignitaries, but knew she always liked to keep the MOD guessing. She had always admired the regiment from the Iranian Embassy days and referred to them as 'my boys'.

The Regimental Chaplain, Tom Evans, known affectionately as 'Evans Above', appeared from the vestry. Silence fell as he walked slowly to the lectern and offered a subdued but warm welcome to the congregation. The organ struck up again and the rear door of the church opened. The congregation stood, turning sideways to watch the slow procession of coffins move towards the altar, each supported by six soldiers in uniform. As they drew parallel with him, Deverall could see the discomfort on Jamie's face as he supported the empty coffin that represented Christian. Due to his height, he was bent forward awkwardly, to keep the coffin flat. Sam supported the rear corner. His face was bright red, a large vein stood out on his neck. Deverall noticed that he had sweated right through the uniform around his armpit.

17

Ten thousand feet over a mountain range in Guinea, Christian slept through his own funeral. He awoke to find he could hardly move as the numbness from his arm and shoulder had spread over his whole body. He was disorientated and confused. He pulled himself upright and saw it was getting dark.

Farq turned around and produced a plastic bottle of water. Christian leant forward as Farq more or less poured it down his throat. Christian gulped as much as he could before having a square-shaped piece of pita bread shoved in his mouth. Farq seemed to find the process of feeding him amusing. Christian capitalised on this by making a fool of himself to encourage Farq, who was now rummaging around trying to find anything he could to stuff in Christian's face.

When Christian felt he was close to being sick, he pushed himself back into his seat and grunted some words of thanks. He shut his eyes again and slouched back.

His next sensation was his head banging hard against the window as the aeroplane landed again. He saw Farq's amused expression looming at him in the darkness. He sat up and saw a series of small fires marking out a basic landing strip.

Christian looked at the clock on the dashboard. It was 19.00 hours, which meant they had flown several hundred miles. He did not even know the name of the country to the north of Guinea. He knew from endless escape and evasion lectures that knowing one's whereabouts was essential to getting out and important for morale. Now he was not sure even what country he was in.

As he pondered his whereabouts, the aircraft came to a standstill next to a clapped-out hangar. A small group of men stood around an oil drum containing a fire. Several were African and others appeared of Arab origin. Mo and Farq looked relaxed and confident.

Christian had difficulty getting out of the back of the aeroplane without the use of his arms. From the light of the fire, he saw unimpressed expressions as the men looked over their shambolic wreck of a prisoner. One man even slipped his pistol back into the belt of his trousers. Christian was clearly no threat.

A hand pushed him forward. He was marched around the side of the hangar towards a surprising sight. A British army 4-ton lorry was parked in the darkness. He was escorted by Farq around to the rear and then manhandled into the back. He felt strangely reassured by the familiar smell of diesel that was always present in the back of these trucks in which he had spent so much time bumping around in the Welsh hills.

Christian stumbled along the back of the lorry and sat down with his back against the cab. Farq was close behind with several other men. He settled down to the most uncomfortable journey of his life as the lorry bounced, crashed, tipped and revved its way through the night.

By the evening of the second day, Christian had given up keeping track of how far they had travelled. The scenery had become more arid, which suggested they were heading into a hotter area which he assumed had to be the Sahara.

As a way of passing the time, he tried to guess when the truck would next stop. So far, he had been way out each time but for some reason he now had a stronger feeling that his journey would soon end. And this time, he was right. The metal-on-metal screech of brakes sounded and they came to a halt. Chatter broke out and Christian felt something was different. He could hear approaching shouts and yells.

A crowd of militiamen surrounded the back of the lorry. Christian could see their aggression as they jostled one another to see into the lorry. Christian was pulled forward by his good arm by Farq and shoved along the back of the lorry. He lowered himself feebly to the ground. Mo shouted a few words, triggering a jeer from the assembled onlookers who were already drifting off.

Christian's sixth sense had already told him his journey was coming to an end and he knew he needed to wake up and start paying attention. As he was pushed forward by Mo, he looked about, noting as much as could about his new environment. He was in the middle of what appeared to be a traditional North African farming village. The ground beneath his feet was dusty earth and the vegetation a scant covering of wispy grass. There were a number of ancient-looking single-storey stone buildings with high mud walls built around, linking them together. Over to his left, Christian saw a thirty-foot-tall communications mast built next to a modern concrete building. A Toyota Land Cruiser was parked outside.

He rounded the corner of an eight-foot mud wall and was pushed through a gateway into a small empty compound. Opposite was a new-looking house built in concrete blocks with a dirty whitewash. Mo marched forward and yanked open a heavy metal door that groaned on unoiled hinges. Christian lowered his head slightly to enter and was immediately met by the foul stench of stale urine. It was darker inside and his eyes needed a moment to acclimatise. The room was about four metres deep and three wide, with the back half separated from the front by steel bars from the floor to ceiling. It looked like the kind of jail he had seen in Western movies. There were two small glass-less windows in the front section and one with bars in the back. Mo pulled open a door section in the bars and pushed Christian inside. He then secured the door with an old motorcycle lock.

'I will see you in a day or two.'

Christian simply nodded and watched Mo pull the outer door half shut and disappear from view. He looked around and assessed his situation. The building was newish and made of proper concrete blocks with hard-looking cement. The bars also were new and it was obvious that this cell had been purpose built. He was sure he would not be burrowing out with the help of a bullet casing. He quickly identified the source of the smell. An old oil drum had been cut in half and served as a loo. Flies buzzed around and Christian saw it was six inches deep in piss and shit. The only other object was a filthy-looking blanket lying in the corner.

The walls had once been whitewashed like the outside, but were now stained and filthy. Christian tried not to think what had made the dark marks on the back wall. As he surveyed his new surroundings, he felt a strange feeling of relief, despite his enormous fatigue, that he was no longer travelling; relief that for the first time in days his body was still. He felt sure this was the final destination, as opposed to another stop-over. He squatted down on the floor and pulled the laces on his boots undone for the first time in nine days.

He was not expecting a pretty sight. The revolting smell in the room was no match for the stench from his boots. He slowly pulled off his socks. They were rigid with sweat, dust and caked mud, which he guessed came from wading through the Rokel Creek. His feet were luminous white. Bits of skin hung between his toes with oozing red sores beneath. To his disgust, the flies buzzing around the oil drum now seemed more interested in him than the raw shit, and homed in on his rotting toes.

Christian's next area of exploration was his shoulder. Gingerly, he pulled up the remains of the sleeve of his shirt and examined the bandage. Just as he decided it was best to leave it alone, he heard voices approaching.

Instinctively, he reached for his boots and was just getting his first one back on, when the outer door opened.

18

A group of six men appeared with a look about them that meant trouble. Christian looked up nervously, feeling the fear running through him once more. Without a word said, the door to his cell had been unlocked and swung open. Christian tried to smile and look as relaxed as possible, but was hauled to his feet by a grinning Arab with a black beard and broken teeth. He offered no resistance as they pushed his hands through the bars of the cell and tied them tightly together through the other side. They were talking and joking amongst themselves, clearly enjoying the look of panic on Christian's face.

One of the men moved forwards and waved a dirty pillowcase in front of Christian's eyes. Its contents were moving. Christian felt another jolt of fear crash through him and his whole body shook. His breathing became faster and adrenalin pumped around his overloaded system as it tried to reassure him that he would not have been transported halfway across Africa just to be tortured by a bunch of tooled-up goatherds. The man opened the sack and shoved it towards him.

Christian saw at least four large rats writhing inside it. The men roared with delight as he turned his face away. The man swung the pillowcase around and crashed it hard against the wall several times. As Christian looked on in total bewilderment, the man pulled down his trousers and shat into the mixture of crushed rat. There were further roars of delight from the group and two more pulled off their trousers and crapped into the pillowcase.

Christian knew for sure what would happen next. Two men held him by the shoulders as the pillowcase was pulled over his head. More laughs and screams of enthusiasm broke out. Christian tried to control himself and remember his training. He knew you had to try to make the torturers think they were winning and yet remain a boring, grey subject who inspired as little interest as possible.

The smell was truly unbearable and Christian retched uncontrollably. The more he did, the worse it became as he felt more of the foul mixture in his mouth, nose and eyes. He could feel strong hands holding the pillowcase in place and knew there was no way he could flick it off. A minute passed as he received what sounded like a lecture from one of the men. He could not understand the language but it was punctuated with pauses and grunts of approval from the others.

His next sensation was vomit racing up from inside his stomach and the feeling of drowning. The strength in his legs vanished and he fell forwards to the ground, his hands still tied through the bars. His shoulder burnt with pain as it took the weight. He struggled back onto his feet as he felt tiny claws scratching frantically against his face. At least one of the rats had survived the pounding against the wall.

Christian had to gasp for each breath and it was at that point where he could no longer taste or smell the gore in the pillowcase. His mind had blurred from the lack of oxygen. His next sensation was his trousers being pulled down and his cycling shorts yanked down too.

There were more screams and yells of delight, along with taunting comments. He felt hard slaps across his arse and then the butt of the rifle hit him hard between the legs. Christian fell forward, his full weight once again on his arms. He was pulled back onto his feet and held, his torso bent forward. He was sure the worst was still to come. He knew being buggered was a likely outcome of capture in certain countries and was used as a method of breaking down prisoners. He felt his legs being pulled apart and could feel someone standing close in behind him. The pain in his balls was unbelievable and shot up into his stomach and spine. There was no point in resisting and he tried to think of something to transport his mind to a different place.

He felt something brush across his arse and braced himself. The noise in the cell reached a peak. Christian was sure whoever it was behind him was revelling in some kind of sadistic showmanship and procrastinating to amuse the others. For what felt like an age, the man hovered behind him, slapping his backside with his erect penis.

Sam's face flashed through his mind. He saw the vein bulging in his neck as he had yelled moments before he pulled the trigger. All this was Sam's fault, a direct result of his disgusting greed. Andy hacked to pieces by the WSBs, Christian shot, left for dead and now about to be gang-raped by a sadistic rabble.

Strangely, it was the anger that took Christian to a higher plane. He no longer heard the noise and the chaos in the filthy jail cell. The searing pain from his wounded shoulder and ache from his groin were gone. Even the dying rat scratching at his face was left behind now. Whatever was happening was happening to his body because his mind was somewhere else. He was in a place called Survival.

Christian's thoughts rejoined his body as the pillowcase was pulled off his head. The room was quieter but he could not see properly due to the muck and crap in his eyes. He heard Mo's voice but could not hear what he was saying. Mo stood on the other side of the bars looking at him. Christian was aware that he was still being held but that the man behind him had stepped back.

Mo looked hard at Christian, then he spoke: 'That's just the start of option one. You stay in here and take this and much more until your people pay up.'

He paused for effect and then continued, 'But I can arrange for you a second option if you want it?'

Christian nodded his head slowly, still unable to see Mo's face clearly. He imagined for a second what he must look like. Naked, except for a filthy shirt, battered, wounded and covered in shit and rat entrails.

Mo continued: 'I run a training academy here for soldiers from all over the world. They come to learn the ways of modern warfare. My academy is the finest and my clients will only send me their best men. They pay a great deal for the privilege and it would benefit me to offer training from a genuine member of the British SAS. In return for your cooperation, you will receive favourable treatment from me. Understand, I will only make this offer once.'

No, fuck off, you goat-fucking piece of shit, was the answer that sprang to Christian's mind. But doubt filled him and he knew he could not take much more knocking around without getting in a serious state.

He cleared his throat and did his best to speak as calmly as possible. 'OK,' was all he could say.

Following a clipped one word from Mo, the men holding Christian let go. Another man cut the rope that secured his hands. Christian straightened himself, took a couple of steps backwards and sat down against the rear wall of the cell. He could feel tears welling up in his swollen eyes. The relief that he had avoided gang rape was hard to cope with. He understood how the enemy could play mind games on prisoners to break them down without doing much real harm, but this had gone to the next stage. Teaching these guys a few basic tricks would be a small price to pay.

The men trooped out of the cell, disappointment written all over their faces. Christian sat alone, watching pathetic twitches coming from inside the rancid pillowcase lying on the floor. He leant forward and pulled it towards him. Gingerly, he lifted the opening. The surviving rat that had scratched his face struggled out, looking bewildered and stunned. It was caked in shit and the blood from its less fortunate companions. Christian gazed at the rat. It looked back at him and then turned and limped off slowly on three legs.

Christian sat alone on the concrete floor of his cell. He tried to wipe as much of the filth from his face as he could but was feeling so low that he did not really care. He hardly dared swallow due to the foul taste that lingered in his mouth. He remained motionless, his mind as empty as possible, his knees pulled up under his chin.

The light was fading when the metal door swung open. Farq appeared with an African woman wearing a brightly coloured skirt and a clean white shirt. She looked at him and then said in reasonable English: 'So it's you causing all this smell, is it?'

Christian was not sure if she meant it in a pleasant way or not. He simply nodded.

'Well, get out of here and we sort you out.'

Farq unlocked the chain around the door to the cell and gestured to Christian to get up. As Christian approached the door, Farq instinctively drew the pistol from the front of his trousers. Christian was amazed this man could perceive him as threatening in any way.

He stepped out into the small walled courtyard where he saw a metallic water trough had been placed. The woman gestured to him to kneel down. He stripped off the torn remains of his shirt and pushed his head into the water. It was refreshingly cold but, more importantly, the immediate stinging sensation all over his head meant it contained disinfectant. Every nick and scratch on his head now screamed out but he found the pain reassuring, knowing it was doing him good.

Next, he took off his combat trousers and minging cycling shorts. He sat in the water trough and washed himself with a small bar of soap and an old tea towel. Farq and the woman looked on as he splashed around, trying to get clean without getting the bandages on his shoulder wet. Finally, feeling a little more human, Christian stood up and stepped out of the trough. He was way beyond any feeling of self-consciousness, standing naked in front of this unlikely couple. His concern was more for the condition of his body. He had arrived in Africa in super-fit shape and reckoned he must have lost two stone since his travels up the Rokel Creek. His ribs stood out and his knees were now knobbly, like those of an old man.

Still naked, Christian was told to sit down. He plonked himself cross-legged on the dusty ground. The woman squatted down next to him and carefully began undoing the bandages of his shoulder dressing. Instinctively, he flinched.

The woman spoke calmly. 'I have treated more gunshot wounds than any doctor in your country, and many of them on young children. So, be still.'

Christian watched as the front section of bandage came away from his chest with a tearing noise. He had no idea quite what to expect but prepared himself for the worst. He was pleased to see only a small black hole, about the width of a pencil, surrounded by an angry-looking purple bruise, the size of a saucer. Around the bruise, the skin was a nasty pale white and there were still traces of the antiseptic powder he had originally applied shortly after the battle.

As Christian contemplated the entrance wound, the woman pulled the bandage up and over his shoulder towards the exit wound. This was altogether different. A shocking pain ripped through him as she peeled off the gauze that protected the wound on the back of his shoulder. Christian had been expecting pain but was not prepared for this. He sprang to his feet and marched about the courtyard swearing uncontrollably.

Farq appeared taken aback and nervous while the woman looked cross and unimpressed. She pointed at the ground and told Christian to sit back down. Once he was seated on the ground again she busied herself re-dressing and bandaging the wound. Christian sat still and quiet and paid little attention to the various comings and goings in and out of the cell block. Twenty minutes later, the woman finished her work. She gathered up Christian's filthy clothes, including his boots, and said she would be back to see him tomorrow.

Christian made his way back into the cell block. Despite the absence of any lighting and it being almost dark outside, he noticed some remarkable improvements. The most noticeable difference was that the stink of raw shit had been replaced by that of strong disinfectant, reminding him of a recently cleaned school changing-room. The rancid half-barrel had gone and in its place was a small plastic bowl with its own cover. Christian guessed this was the loo. A mat, just long enough to lie on, lay on the floor along the back wall. There was also an old wooden chair in the middle of the cell with a bottle of water and two small loaves of bread. Most surprisingly of all was a long blue robe, draped over the back of the chair and a pair of flip-flops placed neatly between the legs. Christian stared at his unlikely collection of new-found luxuries. He turned to Farq, whose expression implied all these wonders were his doing. He had the look of an obsequious hotelier gauging the reaction of an important client to his best suite.

Christian nodded to Farq who was already winding the chain around the door. Christian managed to get himself into the robe and sat down on the chair, all too well aware that this might be the next phase of a nasty tricks campaign. He held the bottle of water between his legs and twisted the top off. He drained it and set about the bread.

19

In his office at Stirling Lines, Colonel Deverall laid three pieces of paper side by side on his desk. It was dark outside and he had been at his desk most of the day. His coffee machine had been on overdrive, as had he. He poured himself another mug, knowing he did not really want it. Wishing he was still a smoker, he swirled the coffee around, watching it as it reached the top of the cup. The atmosphere in the barracks was still very tense.

He had spent the day combing through the reports written by each man who had taken part in the assault on the village. Everyone had been tasked to write down each action he had taken and everything he had seen. This was a standard procedure and, as usual, the perceptions and recollections of men fighting for their lives differed widely. Deverall knew that two soldiers fighting 5 metres apart could

137

see things completely differently and their reports might therefore appear to be from entirely separate engagements. This was normal and to be expected.

He reached into the bin and pulled out a piece of scrap paper. He smoothed it out and drew two vertical lines down it. He noted each key fact from the three reports in front of him into a separate column. Next, with a yellow highlighter pen, he circled each fact that appeared in all three columns. He replaced the cap of the highlighter and swivelled around on his chair to look out of the window. He contemplated the dim orange glow from the street lights coming from Credenhill village behind the barracks. Clearly Sam, Jamie and Tim had played huge roles in the fire-fight and their reports reflected as such, but it was what they did not say that worried him. There were none of the contradictions that he would have expected, which, ironically, usually gave these reports a collaborative air.

He swivelled around on his chair, again holding the piece of scrap paper covered in yellow rings. He remembered in Northern Ireland that on several occasions he had actually told soldiers to discuss events among themselves before putting pen to paper to make sure they did not contradict each other. He remembered that these three soldiers had been debriefed on the Destroyer, all together, and would therefore have relayed their accounts as one. This was the likely reason they now wrote similar-sounding reports. Feeling better, he reached for the TV remote control, swung his feet onto the desk and flicked on the Ten O'Clock News hoping to catch the closing headlines.

A little distance away, across the car park, Sam ordered another pint in the Sergeants' Mess. This was his sixth so far and likely not to be his last. Since returning from Africa, he had enjoyed the attention of having played such a major part in the assault but found it hard to be his usual relaxed self. The less relaxed he felt, the more he worried that people might notice his tension and get suspicious. He had been over and over things in his mind and was absolutely convinced he had nothing to worry about but still a nagging fear constantly bugged him.

It was not guilt, as it was certainly no crime to try to take a few diamonds from a bunch of murdering psychos. He had never intended to hurt Christian. It was simply a by-product of a difficult situation and would not have happened if Christian had not been such a self-righteous fool. Sam also knew that Jamie and Tim were as deeply implicated as him and would therefore be mad to say a word. He was safe, but he still felt better with alcohol inside him.

A hundred miles to the south, John McKie squatted down by a large blue bean-bag in the corner of his kitchen. He fondled his Labrador's ears affectionately and rubbed the dog's tummy. He stood up and spoke his wife's name in a soft voice. He paused for a moment and, on getting no reply, moved out of the kitchen towards the elegant Georgian staircase in the hall. He reached for a bottle of eighteen-year-old Macallan from the tray that sat on an antique chest which neatly filled the space beneath the stairs. He took two large swigs before carefully repositioning the bottle. He popped back to the kitchen and stuffed half a banana in his mouth before slowing making his way upstairs. As he opened the bedroom door, he saw his wife was already in bed watching television. Before he had a chance to utter a word, she raised her hand in a silencing motion. On the screen were the eleven grinning faces of the rescued Irish Rangers standing outside their barracks in Belfast.

Each and every time Christian had woken during the night, he had been accompanied by a suffocating feeling of gloom deep inside his chest as the relative peace of his dreams was swapped for the dismal reality of his situation. This time, however, he did not feel quite the same sense of misery engulf him as his eyes opened. He knew it was still very early in the morning but he must have slept without interruption for at least four hours. He lay quietly on his back, thinking.

Farq was asleep on a bedding roll pushed up against the door of the cell block. He was well out of reach but still the two grenades and the satellite phone clipped to the front of his ops vest looked very appealing. Christian stood up and quietly placed the old wooden chair against the wall beneath the window. He stepped up and looked out. The first thing he noticed was that the wall was over two feet thick and that the three bars blocking the space were each considerably thicker than his finger. He looked across a wide open dirt track with a low row of single-storey mud buildings down the other side. Beyond these, he could see a sandy ridge covered in sparse wispy grasses. He could not see much to the left and right due to the thickness of the walls. As he absorbed his new surroundings, he heard the patter of small cloven feet. He pushed his head against the bars and was just able to catch a glimpse of a small herd of goats trotting out of the village. A moment later a dog barked, setting off a chorus of barking from all around.

Sitting back on his mat, Christian felt reassured by the farmyard noises and wondered if this was a terrorist training camp or a genuine desert settlement. His thoughts were interrupted as Farq stirred. Immediately Farq reached for the reassurance of his pistol, which was wedged between his leg and the wall of the cell block. This instinctively jumpy reaction answered Christian's question. He knew there was nothing pleasant about a place where a man reaches for the cold metal of his gun before even opening his eyes in the morning.

Farq eyed Christian suspiciously before grunting and getting to his feet. He zipped up the front of his ops vest and rolled up his bed-roll. He pulled open the metal door and stepped out, closing it behind him with a clang. He returned an hour later, a bowl in one hand and a large piece of pita bread in the other. He gestured to Christian to move back against the rear wall of the cell and then placed these on the floor within easy reach. Once he had stepped back, Christian moved forward to collect his breakfast of lamb stew and under-cooked pita bread. He sat on his chair and munched away. It was the first proper food he had had and the heat of the stew stung the endless ulcers that had developed in his mouth.

He was on his last mouthful of pita bread when the woman who had washed him appeared. Over one arm she had draped his combat trousers and shirt. In her hand she held his boots, which appeared to have been scrubbed. She dumped his kit within reach on the floor with a look that said she was a nurse, not a washer-woman. Christian thanked her and pulled his clothing through the bars. He was pleased to have his own clothes but knew this was no act of kindness. This was to make sure the newly recruited training officer looked the part in front of the paying guests.

Back in his own kit, Christian felt more in control. Whilst he appreciated the clean blue robe, he did not feel he was equipped to make a break for freedom in a flapping nightie and flip-flops. This was the reason experienced troops always deprived prisoners of their boots. The ragged remains of the right arm of his shirt had been cut off neatly to make it short-sleeved and the left arm had been made to match. The problem was that he could not get his boots on with one hand. They seemed to have shrunk and his feet had definitely swollen after so long in boots. He pulled as best he could but the pain of cramming his rotten feet into a confined space was too much. 'Fuck it,' he thought. He knew he was unlikely to get a chance to run for it that day, so he slipped his feet back into the flip-flops.

The village was waking up. Christian could hear people passing by the window, chatting in a relaxed, everyday manner. He could hear the odd engine start up and the occasional shout. The sun was rising and shone strongly through his barred window. He sat quietly on the chair, wondering what was going to happen. So far during his captivity all he had wanted was to be left alone, but now he felt he needed some form of interaction. He needed something to take his mind off the pain of his predicament. He wondered if he was really going to have any involvement in the training of Mo's punters, or whether he would be paraded around, as a mere trophy?

The temperature in the cell was getting to the point where Christian could feel himself sweating. He heard a vehicle approaching, followed by the sound of squeaking brakes. The engine turned off and he heard footsteps coming from the yard outside. The metal door swung open and Mo stepped inside. 'Good morning,' he said, his tone up-beat and businesslike.

Christian rose to his feet and nodded in reply.

'Here, you will need this.' Mo passed through the bars a sheet of material, knotted at one corner to make a sling for Christian's arm.

'This morning, you will be required on the ranges. We have four groups of ten soldiers at hourly intervals. Today, we are working on single-round firing, but before we start I want a ten- minute briefing from you on the weapon and firing technique. I assume you are familiar with the AK-47?'

'Yes, I am,' replied Christian, trying to remember when he had last done the foreign weapons course.

'Good, but before we go, I will remind you that I will not tolerate any tricks or lack of respect.'

'Understood,' replied Christian.

'Let's go, then,' said Mo, as Farq stepped forward and removed the lock.

Christian passed through the iron door and into the yard. Two more men stood there with surly looks on their faces. Both wore desert combat trousers with long baggy shirts hanging down nearly to their knees. They were unshaven and wore wraparound sunglasses. Christian observed their ops vests bulging with all kinds of pistols, grenades and spare ammo.

'Good morning, gentlemen,' Christian said, stretching out a hand towards the nearest one. 'So where's the embassy, then?' he asked sarcastically, a big smile on his face. The nearest man straightened up, with an awkward look, clearly taken aback by Christian's apparently friendly approach.

Christian felt heartened by his subtle piss-take of these ultra-macho-looking guys who clearly thought they were as hard as nails. They walked out of the yard into the main street that he had seen the night before. He looked around and saw the communications building with the mast down to the left and several pick-ups parked around the place. There were people wandering about. It was pretty obvious that most were Mo's trainees and that the rest of the inhabitants were there to make a living providing for them.

Christian was directed towards a dusty-looking pick-up and told to get in the back. The two hard men got in too and sat there looking moody and bored. Christian looked around as much as he could as the vehicle moved off. It bumped down the simple street that formed the backbone of the desert village. Christian guessed there could be no more than seventy individual houses, which seemed to be arranged mainly along two wide dusty tracks. After a hundred yards or so, there was a wider area where the houses were set back around something of a square. In the centre was an open area with two sets of goalposts.

They bounced on out of the village and onto a soft sandy track. There was no sign of any real farming, just a few withered-looking plants and long-dead grass growing out of rough undulating scrub.

Within a couple of minutes, the pick-up stopped. Christian saw a small group of men standing around a table outside a wooden hut. They had the same hard, unimpressed looks as the two tough guys. Each held an AK-47 and most were smoking.

Mo got out and walked up to them, talking and waving his hands around. He gestured towards Christian and was greeted by several shrugs of the shoulders and one man even turned his back. Mo turned and glanced back at Christian who detected a pleading look in his eye. Christian saw he had an opportunity here. Mo was on the back foot and needed him now, his credibility at stake. Christian decided he would take advantage and do what he could.

He stepped forward confidently and stood next to Mo, who was now addressing the group. Mo turned to him.

'Right, you will now introduce these men to the AK-47 and then we will conduct a live firing exercise on the range.' Mo gestured at an earthy bank, a couple of hundred yards away with a series of yellow oil drums at intervals, along the far end.

'Very good! We'll do this Sandhurst style,' replied Christian, turning to face the assembled mob standing the other side of the table. He paused before he spoke. He looked at them carefully.

'Please take two paces backwards and form a semi-circle,' said Christian with an unmistakable tone of authority. Ten blank-looking faces turned to Mo, who instantly waved his hands in a semicircular shape and snapped some words. The men exchanged sideways glances and stepped backwards into an orderly semicircle.

'You,' said Christian, pointing at the biggest, most aggressive-looking man, 'dress forward and place your weapon on the table. Then get back in line.'

Before the man had a chance to utter a word, Mo snapped another instruction and he took a step forward and dropped his weapon from about four inches onto the table.

'My name is Major McKie. You may address me as Major, Major McKie or sir.' Christian turned to Mo, waiting for the translation. Christian enjoyed the moment of hesitation as Mo translated.

'This is a Kalashnikov assault rifle known as the AK-47. It was designed by Mikhail Kalashnikov in nineteen forty-six and went into mass production in the Soviet Union from nineteen forty-nine.'

He paused for Mo to translate.

'The weapon fires a 7.62 mm cartridge from a magazine of thirty, with an effective killing range of up to 800 metres. The weight of the weapon is approximately four kilos and it comes with a standard wooden stock, or a folding version.'

A more relaxed Mo continued to translate.

'To fire the weapon on semi-automatic mode, you attach the magazine and move the selector lever to the lowest position. You then pull back on the charging handle to draw the first round into the chamber. Pulling the trigger will now fire one round. With the selector in the middle position, the rifle will continue to fire on automatic mode.'

Christian drew his breath and paused to allow Mo to catch up.

'To disassemble the rifle, you first remove the magazine. You should then pull the charging handle to the rear position to make sure the chamber is empty. Then press the button on the back of the receiver cover while pushing it up. You can now push the spring assembly forward and lift it up and out. The moving parts will now slide out.'

'Is there anyone here who would like to demonstrate this procedure?' said Christian. Without allowing enough time for anyone to volunteer, he pointed at a scrawny young man, wearing a red and white baseball cap the wrong way around.

'Dress forward, and remove the working parts from the rifle,' said Christian. Bewilderment spread across the young man's face as Mo translated. He stepped forward, yanked off the magazine and then struggled with the button on the back of the rifle. Christian stood there quietly as the soldier eventually slid the moving parts out and onto the table.

Christian made the tough guy in the middle strip and re-assemble his own weapon before indicating to Mo that they should proceed to the live firing. He knew he would have to teach them something slightly useful without giving away any real trade secrets.

The group wandered over to the range in a cloud of cigarette smoke. Farq skulked around behind them with his hand twitching around his pistol in the top of his trousers. Christian knew that even the slightest sharp movement would result in a bullet in the back.

Christian gestured to the group to form another semicircle around him. He pointed to the young man in the baseball cap again and asked him to step forward and adopt a standing firing position. Once Christian had told him to widen his stance, he ordered him to fire one round at the far right yellow barrel at the end of the range, some 200 metres away. The bullet kicked up dust in the bank at least a metre over the top of the barrel.

Christian spoke to Mo. 'I need you to take the weapon from him, appear to check it and remove the bullet from the chamber. Cock the weapon and pass it back to him.'

Mo did what Christian said and passed the AK-47 back to the young man. Christian told him to take a second shot. After a moment of almost theatrical aiming and expressions of concentration, there was a loud click from the firing pin striking into an empty chamber. Simultaneously, the young man jerked the rifle upwards in anticipation of the recoil.

'That's why the first shot missed the target by in excess of one metre,' said Christian. There was a moment's silence as it dawned on everyone that Christian had just demonstrated something they had not seen before. Mo translated, but there was really no need as the point had been made.

For the next half-hour Christian had the group working in pairs. One would load the rifle and pass it to his mate without him seeing if it was loaded or not. The improvement in accuracy was immediate, as they learnt to keep the rifles still and steady when firing. Christian walked from pair to pair offering bits of advice. Mo moved with him, looking pleased.

By now, the Tsetse flies were buzzing about, landing everywhere. Christian could see a noticeable deterioration in concentration and called the group back into a semicircle. With the exception of a couple of surly-looking faces, it was apparent that Christian's tuition had been pretty well received.

Mo flicked his hand forward in an indication that it was time to go.

Once the men had lit cigarettes and shuffled off, Christian turned to Mo.

'How much longer will I be here?'

Mo shifted his weight from one foot to the other before he replied.

'I can assure you, my friend, that having you here is not doing my blood pressure any good at all. You have no idea the kinds of problems you are causing. I have every intention of getting you away from here as soon as I can.'

'Well, if I am causing that much of a problem, I am happy to walk out of here right now. You will never see me again,' said Christian, with an incredulous expression.

'Not so simple. The negotiations with your people are not so easy. These things will take time. And in the meantime, you will earn your keep working for me.'

Christian got the impression he may have said a little more than he intended. It sounded like the conversation was coming to an end.

'OK. You're the boss,' Christian replied quietly.

The next group arrived just in time to break the tension. Christian rolled out the same introduction to the AK-47, but seemed able to remember more random facts about it than in his first talk. Mo translated and things went well.

By the fourth group, Christian was starting to feel tired. The flies were bugging him and his shoulder ached. He was thirsty and his ears were ringing from the constant rattle of gunfire. Under normal circumstances, soldiers with this little ability would still be in a classroom and nowhere near the ranges. He was making a big effort to keep upbeat but what these men really needed was a morning's square-bashing followed by a twenty-mile run around the Brecon Beacons in driving rain.

Eventually, Mo called an end to the fourth group. Christian hauled himself awkwardly into the back of the pick-up and sat down on the uncomfortably hot metal floor. He was dusty, dirty and knackered. The two tough guys in sunglasses clambered in too, still not speaking. They bounced back towards the village where Farq shooed Christian into his cell.

He plonked himself down on his wooden chair. He had not been wearing a hat and felt he had been too long in the sun. He looked down to see the tops of his feet were a bright pink from only wearing flip-flops. The fact he was so tired from four hours standing around demonstrated what poor condition he was in. This was not a promising sign in terms of making a run for it. On a normal escape and evasion exercise he could cover forty miles plus in a day, but that was on the premise of starting off in reasonable shape.

Whilst it was good to be out of the sun and away from the tsetse flies, they had been replaced by mosquitoes, which now hovered around his head, repeatedly landing on his face. Christian also noticed that the smell of stale urine seemed to have returned. Farq appeared a while later and passed a bottle of water through the bars along with a small basket containing a piece of pita bread, two oranges, a packet of cigarettes and a book of matches.

Christian thanked Farq and tucked into the bread and water. Once he had devoured the oranges, peel and all, he picked up the packet of cigarettes. As an ex-smoker, Christian could never imagine himself ever feeling excited by the prospect of a cigarette, but right now he was. The packet felt a bit light. He looked at the front cover and was surprised to see they were Craven A, a brand he thought had died out decades ago. He flipped back the top and saw why the packet was so light. He pulled out the last remaining cigarette, put it in his mouth and opened the book of matches to reveal one last match.

The hit of nicotine gave him an instant head rush. The smoke also dispersed the mosquitoes and masked the smell of piss. As he puffed away happily, he decided he would let himself smoke but only until he was back on British soil.

20

Sam stepped out of the newsagent's with a packet of cigarettes in his hand. He had been a smoker from a young age but had quit with some difficulty during pre-selection training. He had always had the odd one when really drunk, but not too often. Since returning from Africa, he felt much better with a cigarette in his hand and thought they made him look and sound more relaxed. Lighting up could be a useful pause in conversation, as could taking a big, long drag. As he reached for his lighter, his mobile phone rang.

The duty officer from the guard room introduced himself and told Sam he was needed in Deverall's office as soon as possible. A terrible jolt of adrenalin pumped through his body to the point where he actually felt light-headed. He had not dared ask if there was a particular reason, as he had to appear unconcerned. But this sort of thing never normally happened.

He had finished his cigarette by the time he got to his car. Nodding politely to the two MOD plods at the gates of the barracks, he drove slowly around to the car park. He took the stairs, in his usual two-at-a-time fashion, on his way up to the first floor where Deverall had his office. He walked down the corridor and past Deverall's door, knowing he needed a moment to compose himself. Just as he was turning around, he heard a door open and saw Jamie emerge. He cast a glance his way but said nothing. Sam had never seen such a tall guy look so small.

Sam was paralysed with nerves. In a trance-like state, he knocked on the door. There was a pause before he heard Deverall's voice loudly calling, 'Enter.' As he pushed open the door, he heard his own voice speaking: 'Good morning, sir. How can I help?'

Deverall sat behind his desk, rocking on his swivel chair. Sam had only been in this room once before, and that was when he had been promoted to full sergeant, two years before. He glanced about, noticing how nothing had changed. The coffee machine still bubbled away, and the clock on the wall still ticked rhythmically. Deverall gestured to the chair in front of his desk.

On the desk, next to a photo of a young-looking Deverall posing by an Apache helicopter, was a map. Sam could see an outline of a large, oblong country with lots of huge open spaces. It looked like somewhere in Africa.

Deverall smoothed the map out with his hands and looked at Sam. Then he spoke. 'Thanks for popping in. Now, this morning I was in rather a good mood until I got a telephone from our friends in Cheltenham.'

'GCHQ, you mean?' replied Sam.

'Yes, well, kind of, anyway,' continued Deverall. 'We have picked up a great deal more chatter coming out of the various countries in and around Sierra Leone than we would usually expect, even after an operation like Barras. Strangely enough, the focus seems to be in the southern end of Mauritania.' Deverall jabbed at the map with his finger. 'This would not cause undue concern if it did not coincide with two particularly unpleasant people applying for visas to Mali, which is bang next door.' Deverall tapped a different section of the map.

Sam felt his face reddening as he did his best to pull his features into a slightly surprised expression. Deverall continued: 'One intercept tells us there is a high-profile Western hostage being held somewhere in the region. But our problem is that no one is missing. Satellite imagery shows at least six terrorist training camps in the desert area near Bukonda. The Int. guys reckon there is what they call a "convergence" going on. In other words, more people heading there than usual and more electronic chatter than there should be.'

Sam nodded helpfully to show he understood.

'So, Sam, my question to you is a simple one. Do

you think there is any possibility, even the most remote, that someone's got Christian? I know the situation in there was bad but could Christian have survived? Is there any, tiny chance?'

Sam cleared his throat and adjusted his position in his chair. 'Well, sir,' he said in a gruff, stifled way, 'I . . . we were under a lot of pressure on our perimeter and fell back, as you know. To be honest, I can't see any way he would have made it. He was hit and went down. The area was then overrun and he could not have survived. That's why I said he was dead; otherwise we would have gone back for him. No, I can't see any chance he made it . . . It's quite impossible, sir.'

Deverall did not respond, giving Sam the chance to keep talking. After it became obvious that Sam was not going to allow himself to ramble on, Deverall spoke. 'Well, that's what we thought. I can't see it myself. How could he have made it? But you appreciate I needed to ask the question, don't you?' He said it with a wistful note to his voice.

'Uh, yes, sir; quite right to ask the question, sir,' said Sam. 'He was an excellent soldier and a good friend to us, you know. He did an excellent job in the OP and very much had the respect of the men, sir,' Sam went on.

Deverall nodded. 'Well, if you think of anything, you will let me know.'

'Of course, sir,' Sam replied, standing up and

making his way towards the door. He was desperate to get out of the room. As he pulled the door closed behind him, he felt short of oxygen. He made his way along the corridor and down the stairs. As he walked towards his car he turned and looked back over his shoulder. Deverall stood at the window.

For the next ten minutes, Deverall fidgeted in his chair, not doing anything, just thinking. He had now spoken to Jamie, Tim and Sam. He had not learnt anything new, but still their tales were conspiratorially accurate. Jamie and Tim had not seen Christian go down and were working on the assumption that he had done, firstly because Sam had said so and, secondly, he was no longer with them. The first point relied on Sam and the second was an assumption.

He lifted up the map and pulled out his large desktop diary. He flipped through to the page towards the back, to the Time Zones section. He decided he should probably wait another hour before calling the US, especially as he was about to ask a favour.

Jamie had reached the top of the stairs and was already fumbling for his mobile phone. He scrolled through to find Tim's number. He made his way quickly to a quiet part of the car park and pressed the call button. Tim answered immediately.

Before Jamie had even said a word he was

interrupted by a casual-sounding voice. 'Hi, mate, glad
you called. Are you on for a pint?'

Jamie realised that if Deverall was suspicious of
something, he could easily have put a tap on their
phones and this explained Tim getting his word in
before he had had a chance to say anything unwise.

'Well, to be honest, I would rather a walk,' replied
Jamie.

'OK, how about we RV at the Pen y Fan car park
around two p.m. and head off from there?'

21

An hour later, Jamie's Saab turned off the main road into a large gravel car park in the Welsh hills. Apart from one minibus, the place was empty. Jamie turned off the engine and pointed his rear-view mirror at the entrance. He was desperate to see Tim. He had to know if Deverall had revealed anything else that might give a clearer impression of whether the high-profile hostage could be Christian.

Since the funeral, he had been racked with guilt and infuriated by the dispassionate sense of smugness he picked up from Sam. During one brief conversation, Sam had gone as far as to say that Christian was only any good as a peacetime soldier and had brought this death upon himself by being too squeaky clean and self-righteous.

Jamie had only known Christian since Selection, but they had become very good friends and been through a lot together, both inside and outside the army. He had no idea that Sam had tried to kill Christian but he knew that his own personal greed had resulted, albeit indirectly, in his death. With hindsight, he thought that they should have included Christian in the wheeze to get hold of Foday's diamonds. It was perfectly possible that he would have been on for it. Jamie had told Sam in the OP that having Christian onside would make things much easier. Tim had agreed, but Sam was convinced Christian would talk the others out of it. In the end, Sam had been so persuasive that they had both agreed to exclude Christian.

Since they had returned, Sam had pointed out that things could have turned out exactly the same way, even if the diamonds had not been part of the equation. Things had gone to rat shit and they were right to have taken refuge in the hostage house during the fire-fight. The fact they were bashing Foday around only changed things very slightly.

Jamie's thoughts were interrupted by the sight of a familiar motorbike drawing up at the far end of the car park. Without a word, he and the motorcyclist nodded greetings and pulled their small civilian daypacks onto their shoulders.

Both men were similarly dressed in jeans, walking boots and fleeces. They crossed the road and started up the all too familiar muddy path towards the peak of Pen y Fan, the highest peak in the Brecon Beacons.

It was only once they passed through a stile, after a few hundred yards, that they began to speak.

'So do you reckon it is Christi down there?' Jamie said, tilting his head towards Tim who was a metre or so behind him.

'It has to be, doesn't it, for fuck's sake. You can't believe a word Sam says. Let's face it, no one saw Christi go down. He's the type of fucker that would survive, isn't he? If anyone got left behind and could make it out of there, it's bloody Christian, isn't it?' Tim hissed, as if every clump of bracken was crawling with MPs.

'Well,' replied Jamie, talking in a much more normal voice, 'we have to work on the assumption that it is him. Deverall says it's a high-profile Western hostage but no one has anyone missing. How much of a coincidence is that? It's bloody well him and we have three choices.'

'Yup, yup, no, no, I agree with you. We don't have any option other than go on the worst-case scenario. It's Christi and he's in some godforsaken cage halfway to hell and it's our fault. This is a fucking disaster.' Tim was speaking more normally now.

It was a minute before Jamie spoke again. The path started to steepen and the autumn afternoon showed signs of rain. A party of rosy-cheeked walkers passed them by, coming downhill with good-humoured nods and mutters of, 'Afternoon . . .' They had the cheery look of people on the home straight.

'We don't have any choice,' said Jamie. 'Well, we do, but as I see it, we can do one of three things.'

'Which are?' replied Tim.

'Well, option one is come clean to Deverall. If he takes it the wrong way, which he will, we end up getting court-martialled and done for manslaughter at the bare minimum. Not that great. Also, that doesn't help Christian, as he's still in the shit and we don't know what Deverall can or can't do to help him.'

'OK, OK,' replied Tim. 'That's a non-starter, so what's option two? It had better be a bit fucking better than option one.'

'It is and it isn't,' replied Jamie.

'Oh, bloody marvellous, then,' boomed Tim, clearly giving up any concerns of imaginary eavesdroppers lurking in the undergrowth.

'Hold on; easy, mate,' continued Jamie, calmly. 'Option two does have some merit. We simply do nothing. We don't end up in prison and we just wait and see what we find out. This way, we only act on the basis of the right information, which we don't have right now, do we?'

'We do have quite a bit of information, if you ask me,' Tim snapped. 'Like, for example, we know that we don't know for sure if Christian was killed. Also, we know no one high-profile is missing and there is a high-profile hostage somewhere very near, by African standards, to Sierra Leone. Deverall also said something about a couple of, and I quote, "particularly nasty pieces of work" heading down there. What's that meant to mean? At best, it's someone who's not going to be very nice to the mystery hostage, isn't it?'

'We don't know for sure, do we?' grunted Jamie, now walking so fast, the Chinese Long March would have been over in minutes.

'Well, do you want to sit around for the rest of your life not knowing?' Tim was interrupted by Jamie.

'Which brings me to option three.'

'Thank fuck for that,' gasped Tim.

'Option three is we get down there and have a look. Deverall has more or less told us where he is – if it is him, of course. We could go down there, check out if it's him or not and if it is, we could get him out.'

Tim paused for thought before answering. He wiped the first specks of rain from his face.

'Mate, that is the only option as I see it. We can't sit around here in the UK like a pair of twats waiting for Deverall to impart the odd piece of information. We need to get our arses down there, and at least get to the point where we know if it's him or not.'

'Which brings us on to the million-dollar question of how we get down there to the middle of nowhere with the right kit in the next couple of days,' replied Jamie.

For the next twenty minutes, Jamie and Tim stomped through the thick red Welsh mud towards the top of Pen y Fan. Despite their fitness, they both huffed and puffed due to the speed that they were walking. The

ground flattened out as they reached the summit.
They crossed the flat grassy area on top of the hill
and briefly took in the panoramic views to the south.
The rain eased to a fine wet mist. They turned around
to the right and headed down a steep path known as
Jacob's Ladder, and off along the top of a ridge. They
talked as they stormed on, with the odd silence, both
feeling calmer and benefiting from the unspoken
significance these hills held for them. By the time they
emerged back in the car park, they had covered 18
km, the last hour in darkness.

22

Two days later, at 09.00, a long wheel-based army Land Rover pulled up at the checkpoint outside Brize Norton airbase. The driver wound down the window and passed his ID card to the civilian security guard. With a momentary flash of his torch into the back of the vehicle, the yellow waistcoated guard gestured to the driver to enter the base.

Lying still, under a pile of kit, Jamie and Tim were relieved not to have fallen at the first hurdle. They were taking the most almighty risk. They had concluded, during their tab round the hills, that neither of them could possibly do anything other than get down to Africa and do what they could for Christian. They had agreed how they would get there and what they would need to take with them. They had decided to postpone any decision about busting Christian out of wherever he was being held until they were there. They thought the overwhelming likelihood was that they would not find the right camp and, even if they did, it would not be Christian held there anyway. On this basis, it seemed pointless spending time working out a purely hypothetical extraction strategy.

They had divided the task of preparation. Jamie agreed to do the planning while Tim sorted out the kit and transport. The first issue was getting leave. They had spoken to their commanding officer and got two weeks' leave to go on a fictitious climbing holiday in Chamonix. It was just the sort of holiday commanding officers liked and had not been a problem as half the Squadron had disappeared on leave since Sierra Leone. Sam was also away in Scotland leading a survival course, so he wouldn't even be aware that they had gone; for a while at least.

Jamie had studied maps from the part of Mauritania that Deverall had shown him in his office. He needed to work out exactly what they were going to do and what they could expect in terms of terrain, river crossings, local tribes, temperatures and, above all, how to procure food and water. He planned a drop-off site and how they would walk from one possible camp to the next, using the southern border of the country as a handrail. From Deverall's description, there were six possible camps all just inside the border with Mali.

He had worked out what kit they would need and given Tim a list. There were no issues in terms of clothing, boots, bergens and so forth, as they had their own, but the tricky bit was weapons. They had three options. Firstly, there was going in, unarmed, purely to observe. No way. Secondly, they considered buying weapons down there. The problem was where to buy and how to buy without causing suspicion. Also, it could take a week and they would end up with rusty, unreliable junk. The third option was best.

Tim had always had good rapport with 'Armalite', who ran the regimental armoury, and had popped in to see him, knowing he was as warlike as he was unorthodox. Armalite had seen more action than most of the regiment put together, and would be the last person on earth not to help. Tim got him alone in his office and put his cards on the table. He did not mention the diamonds or Sam, but said he feared they had left Christian behind. After twenty minutes' very tough questioning and a rant about the moral fabric of the British Army, Armalite went quiet. Tim knew he knew there was more to it. After a pause and some huffing, Armalite nodded slowly and said he would help.

The next issue was getting to Africa. After his success with Armalite, Tim tried it again with Christian's friend, the RAF Hercules pilot in the corps attached to the SAS. Unfortunately, Flight Commander Oliver Daily lacked Armalite's mad dog nature. When he mentioned the implications for his RAF career and pension, Tim thought he was on a losing streak. It was only Tim's reference to Christian possibly being decapitated that swung the balance. There were still regular RAF flights to Sierra Leone passing right over Mauritania, and it would just be a case of juggling the rota.

They now had basic regional intelligence, kit, weapons and a ride, it was time to go.

Armalite fumbled the Land Rover into first gear with the stump of his left hand and they moved off into Brize Norton airbase. He was now finally silent, which was a welcome change, after spending the hour-and-a-half drive from Hereford lecturing Jamie and Tim. The first half had been about how you never ever left anyone behind, the second a pre-op-style briefing on exactly how and what to do once they got there. Because he was doing them such a massive favour, Jamie and Tim made all the right noises. Finally, Armalite gave them a detailed introduction to the weapons he had laid on for them.

The first was a ten-year-old, but almost unused, AK-47, decorated with solid gold panels. Armalite had brought it back from the Iraq War, having grabbed it from an Iraqi colonel. This was a highly treasured and valuable piece that he definitely wanted back. The next weapon he had conjured up was his own personal .375 stalking rifle. He had shot three buffalo with this large-calibre, and highly accurate, sporting rifle and it came with an expensive Zeiss telescopic sight. Again, he wanted it back.

Antiques fucking Road Show, Jamie mouthed to Tim, before Armalite finally moved on. There were two Sig Sauer automatic machine pistols that had broken during testing. Armalite had fixed them, but as far as any inventory was concerned, they no longer existed. These were state-of-the-art, large-calibre machine pistols with magazines of thirty rounds. Armalite had also thrown in six grenades of various types and ages.

He drove slowly past the office buildings by the entrance, turning on the hazard lights before heading onto the concrete hard-standing, by the runways. They drove past a series of massive dark green hangars, making their way towards the looming shape of a Hercules C-130 at the far end of the airbase.

Armalite swung the Land Rover around the rear end of the aircraft and parked it on the far side of the open rear ramp. 'Don't move until I get back,' he said.

He opened the door and had hardly got a foot on the ground when Oliver Daily appeared. Compared to Armalite's relaxed composure, the pilot was panic stricken.

After a stutter lasting several seconds, he spat out the words, 'He . . . he . . . hello there, hold on a second.'

Armalite sensed his fear and spoke calmly. 'Don't worry, lad, all the time in the world.'

Oliver ducked behind the ramp of the Hercules and

strolled around, looking anything but casual. A few seconds later, he waved to Armalite and said, 'OK. Let's get the equipment on board.'

Armalite opened the back door of the Land Rover and pulled a 90 lb desert bergen onto his shoulder. Jamie and Tim clambered out of the vehicle laden with equipment. Oliver looked surprised to see them, with three days' stubble growth and obvious fake suntan on their faces, necks and hands. They followed Oliver up the ramp and into the belly of the aircraft, pushing past large wooden containers secured for transit with elastic straps and ropes. They came to a gap between two crates.

'Right, guys, get through there and you will find a gap behind. Sit there, and I will get you when it's time to jump. I'll slip you a piece of paper with our position, air speed, etc., when it's time. There won't be anyone in the cargo deck, but there will be a few passengers up front. You will be going out of that door,' hissed Oliver, pointing back towards a side door at the rear of the aircraft.

Jamie and Tim nodded their agreement and squeezed between the wooden boxes. They dropped off the first load of equipment and came back to relieve Oliver and Armalite of two jerry cans of water and a sports bag containing the weapons.

'Keep yer heads down, boys,' said Armalite, with a nod and a raised thumb, turning and making his way back down the ramp.

171

Jamie and Tim heard the engine of the Land Rover start up as they began sorting out their kit in the cramped and dark gap between the wooden containers and aluminium fuselage of the Hercules. Within less than a minute the lights were turned off. They decided it would be too risky to use a torch, and any accidental bangs or noises might be detected, so they simply sat still and quiet in the dark. Oliver had said the flight had to leave before 23.00 hours due to the local noise pollution guidelines. That meant a maximum wait of two hours. Jamie checked the luminous face of his watch.

They both had parachutes and large bergens containing food for eight days, or fourteen at a push. They were dressed in a strange mixture of kit. They wore long, baggy, Arab-style shirts tucked into faded desert combat trousers. They had on what Jamie had put on the list as 'Arab fancy dress' under their desert combat smocks. They each had a grab-sack that contained a twenty-four-hour ration pack, a one-litre water bottle, $1,000 in cash, a compass, torch and ammunition.

The plan was to parachute in, find a place to stash spare kit and water, and then get themselves into a suitable lying-up position where they could sleep for a few hours before starting the search.

At 22.30, the sound of voices broke the tedium. The crew were approaching the aircraft and the rear tail-gate ramp was being raised. They sat on their kit and did not move a muscle. Soon after, the first two engines started with a roar that sent a judder through the whole aircraft. A couple of seconds later, the second pair thundered to life.

Two minutes later, the aircraft was gaining speed down Runway 240. As the wheels left British soil, Jamie leant forward and patted Tim hard across the back. Oliver Daily sat on the flight deck in charge of the aircraft. Next to him sat his co-pilot, a younger man, still learning the intricacies of flying C-130s. Behind them, and to the right, sat the navigator. As they reached 300 feet, Oliver pulled the controls towards him with his left hand while holding the throttle in place with his right. The nose lifted and the engines groaned under the increasing strain of the climb. They made a large left-handed arc until they hit the correct bearing where Oliver set the course.

After the distraction of the take-off and setting the course, Oliver found himself becoming increasingly tense. He busied himself by looking something up in the aircraft manual that lived in a pocket by his knee. They reached the standard cruising height of 28,000 feet and had the advantage of a 30 mph tailwind.

Jamie and Tim lay back on their equipment and tried to doze. Despite it being 02.00 hours, they were both unable to get any real sleep. Oliver had told them it would be seven or eight hours to the drop zone.

When he appeared they would have just a matter of seconds to grab their kit and dive out of the rear door. They had agreed that Oliver would slow the aircraft down to an acceptable jump speed.

As 04.00 approached, they were now well into the drop-off time. The seconds crept past. Both men had a parachute harness strapped across their bodies and lightweight plastic goggles already over their eyes. On their fronts, they had their grab-sacks and their bergens slung below.

In the cockpit, Oliver felt a thick bead of sweat run down the side of his chest inside his shirt. He had allowed his imagination to torture him for the duration of the flight. He had entertained the wildest and most ludicrous thoughts as to the repercussions of what he was doing. He had thought in terms of civil, military and aviation law. The best-case scenario, if he were caught, would be a court-martial, being thrown out of the RAF and banned from flying ever again by the CAA. The worst-case scenario included a lengthy prison sentence.

With these thoughts in mind, he turned his head to the co-pilot and said, 'OK, now, we are a little ahead of schedule, so I'd like you to bring the aircraft back to 150 knots and put her on a bearing of 160. Take her down to 22,000, nice and gentle. I am off for a piss and when I get back I want you to run me through a HELP – a Hostile Environment Landing Procedure.'

The co-pilot nodded, and Oliver scrutinised his face

for signs of suspicion. He was now deviating from the usual route and knew that their course would be monitored by the black box on board, as would every word they said to one another over the internal intercom. He also knew that every minute he took off the course would equate to about five miles less walking for Jamie and Tim. It could make all the difference.

Oliver jotted down a few details on his notepad and pulled off his gloves. He dropped them casually over a carefully chosen area of the dashboard, covering the small blue light that would come on when the rear door was opened. He stood up slowly and stretched. This was the moment he had been rehearsing for two days.

'Can I get anyone a coffee?' he said, with a yawn.

'Nah, I'm good thanks, skipper,' came the reply from the co-pilot.

'White with one, please, boss,' said the navigator, turning around in his seat with a grateful smile.

Oliver opened the door from the cockpit and moved into the seating area immediately behind. Having taken off his headset, he was relieved by how noisy things seemed in the back. Hopefully none of the dozing passengers would hear a thing.

Jamie and Tim looked at their watches every few seconds. It was eight hours from take-off when suddenly the light flicked on. A moment later, Oliver's face appeared around the side of the containers.

Without a word, Jamie and Tim hauled their kit off the floor and pushed through the narrow gap towards him.

'We are doing about one hundred and eighty knots and there is a twenty mile an hour westerly wind, which should help you,' hissed Oliver, pushing a piece of paper into Jamie's outstretched hand.

'We're about forty kilometres north-west of the drop zone. I did what I could, now go, go, go and good luck. Keep your heads down, and all that.'

'Cheers, mate. Nice one,' replied Jamie, straining under the weight of his kit. Tim simply patted Oliver on the shoulder with his free arm and mouthed something that no one heard as the small rear door swung open, creating a riotous blast of wind.

Jamie was straight out with Tim less than a second behind him. The door slid shut on its runners and the wind ceased in the rear section of the C-130. Oliver took a deep breath and, for the first time since he had agreed to help out, felt he was somehow enjoying his role in this madness.

He flicked off the light in the rear section of the aircraft and re-emerged in the seating area. None of the passengers had moved a muscle. He made the coffee in the narrow canteen area and pushed open the door into the flight deck.

'Oh, cheers,' grunted the navigator, taking the plastic cup from Oliver's hand. Oliver slipped back into his seat, buzzing with adrenalin. He picked up his gloves and glanced at the controls. His co-pilot was still making the descent to 22,000 feet.

As his feet left the aircraft, Jamie pulled a star position. He balanced himself in the air and pulled the D-shaped alloy parachute deployment device on his chest. His next sensation was a sharp cracking sound, a hard jerk on his chest as his chute opened, followed by quiet. He swung in his harness and looked up to check his canopy. Above and to the right, he caught a glimpse of a shadow that had to be Tim.

The purpose of any high-altitude, high-opening – or HAHO – jump is to get the parachute open as high as possible and to travel as far as possible on the wind. Jamie and Tim now soared, side by side, moving as far laterally as they could while maintaining height. They were travelling in a helpful easterly direction and desperate to avoid carrying their heavy kit any further than necessary. Despite the goggles, their eyes streamed with tears from the wind and the icy, high-altitude night-time cold.

23

The next few days followed a routine. Christian helped out on the ranges and with teaching house-clearing techniques. He was fed well and his wound was treated every evening. The cigarettes came frequently and he noticed he had begun to look forward to them. Having had several good nights' sleep, things did not seem quite as traumatic and he felt less paranoid.

He had not stopped looking for a way out, but had decided he could not risk making a mess of it. Each day, he grew stronger and became more familiar with his captors, their ways and routines. He would keep his head down, eat all the food he could and look for the right opportunity.

On the evening of his fifth day in the village, he was watching the familiar beam of sunlight from his window move slowly up the wall as the sun set, when he heard a distant but all too familiar noise.

He shoved the chair up against the wall beneath the window, pushed his head against the bars and listened. It was an approaching helicopter. A bolt of excitement ran though him. No one in this part of Africa used helicopters – the odd light aircraft, but certainly not helicopters. It had to be someone official, probably army, maybe an SAS team to get him out or to sort out a ransom demand. He knew the British government paid off kidnappers when it really mattered. He had seen it with his own eyes.

Straining at the window, Christian heard the *chop, chop, chop* getting closer. A rush of activity in the village confirmed that the helicopter was in-bound. Twenty seconds later, he felt the downdraught as it passed above. Dust swirled up around the cell, forcing him to shut his eyes. Any moment, someone would come for him. He was in the last moments of his ordeal. A minute later the engine sounded a different note as it began to shut down.

This was surprising. You would never shut down the engine in circumstances like these. You would keep the rotors turning, in case of a quick get-away. Perhaps some final stage of negotiations was still needed. Christian shook with anticipation and held onto the bars of the cell to keep his hands still. A few more minutes passed . . . Still nothing.

Christian's feeling of excitement was turning to anger. He knew the first thing a negotiator would ask for was sight of the hostage. This would be the prerequisite to any talks. Otherwise you could be negotiating for no hostage, the wrong hostage or a dead one. Christian's world started to wobble. He paced across his cell and once again stuffed his head against the bars of the window in a desperate effort to get a glimpse of something that might explain what was happening.

After half an hour of pure misery, he heard footsteps approaching and voices speaking in English. His mind was in a frenzy of anticipation. This was the moment. He had survived. The metal door clanged open and Mo stepped into view with a smile on his face.

Right behind him was a European man with short fair hair. He was in his late forties and wore a plain green T-shirt and beige canvas trousers, with pockets on the sides. He had an effective, military look about him. A second man followed, smaller with dark hair and sunglasses, but also European in appearance.

'Hi, I'm Conrad Lennep and this is Martin Roote,' said the big fair-haired man, in a South African accent, gesturing over his shoulder.

Before Christian had time to do anything other than nod, he continued, 'We work for a security agency based out of Jo'burg. We've been tasked by your government to negotiate your release and get you home as soon as possible. I can see from the photographs that you are who you are meant to be, so that's good. Are you OK?'

Christian nodded, then said, 'Well, not really that great, actually. Pretty shitty, in fact.' He took several deep breaths in an effort to hold back a wave of emotion.

'Don't worry,' said the dark-haired man, also with a strong South African accent, 'your people are very keen to get you home and they have paid a lot of money. We just need to confirm it's you, collect the payment and we should have you out and home in a couple of days.'

Christian had tears in his eyes. He had been so resilient for such a long time and felt overwhelmed that finally he was talking to someone on his side. He just nodded and took deep breaths. Mo stood there grinning, in an 'I told you I had everything under control' sort of way.

The dark-haired man continued. 'We have got you some stuff that might make things easier.' He slipped a small backpack off his shoulder and opened it. 'It's just basic bits and pieces; chocolate, vitamins, mozzie spray, stuff like that. Do you smoke?'

'I do now,' grunted Christian, with a semblance of a smile.

'Well, here're some fags and a light, too.' The man squeezed the backpack through the bars. 'We just need to photograph you to keep your people happy and then we need to get going.'

He produced a small digital camera and took a couple of photos of Christian. Mo was guiding them

181

out of the door when Christian called out, 'Hold on just a second, does my family know I am alive?'

The fair-haired man turned around and paused. 'Well, I can't say for sure, that's one for your people, isn't it?'

Christian just nodded his head, knowing he had asked a silly question.

A feeling of confused elation washed through his mind as he heard the footsteps walking back through the courtyard. He was surprised someone like Deverall would have opted to get the cheque-book out when the first choice would have been a smash-and-grab. It had to be because of a lack of intelligence and Mo, or the people behind or above him, would have insisted in dealing via a third party, hence the guys from Jo'burg. Christian sat and rummaged through the backpack. He went straight for a bar of chocolate, ripped off the foil and squeezed the soft melted mush into his mouth. He chewed slowly, savouring the sweet taste of sugar, something wholly excluded from his diet since his capture. Next, he demolished a packet of digestive biscuits. He washed them down with water and then paused to enjoy the sensation of not feeling hungry.

Having got over the immediate delights of the food, he decided he needed a smoke. He had difficulty peeling off the cellophane from the packet of cigar-ettes, due to his heavily bitten fingernails. A long flame instantly burst from the brand-new lighter, and he happily drew on a Marlboro Red.

The question that filled his mind was: who knew he was alive? Obviously Deverall did, but what about his family, Sam, Jamie and Tim? He guessed that Deverall would have gone absolutely mad when he found out that his own troops had left one of the team behind. He would not have been told the real circumstances but, however it had been presented, he would be outraged. Perhaps he was planning on getting him back and finding out the full details before tackling the culprits?

He finished his cigarette and lit another. Not having to wait to be given one cigarette and one match at a time felt great. He thought of the looks on everyone's faces if he made it home. He assumed correctly that he would have had some kind of funeral and that, by now, he would even have a gravestone. He knew that once he revealed the truth, Sam would end up behind bars for attempted murder. The only problem was that there were no witnesses to the actual shot.

Sam would argue that Christian was making things up to get back at him for making a mistake and accidentally leaving him behind. Christian had imagined that, if he made it home, the record would be put one hundred per cent straight and justice would be done. Now, for the first time, he could see that there was a way Sam could get out of the most serious part of what he had done: he could simply deny shooting him. No jury would do him for murder without any witnesses. The wound was healing and could not be linked to Sam's pistol. No clever forensic detectives in white suits could visit the crime scene and analyse the blood on the floor or find the bullet embedded in the wall.

Sam would argue that if he had wanted to kill Christian at point-blank range, he would have gone for a head shot, just as he was trained to do. This would sound very plausible in court. Why would a highly trained member of the SAS bungle a simple shot at a range of 2 metres? Christian was becoming more and more wound-up. He dropped his fag end on the floor and stamped on it. It was becoming clear that his homecoming was not going to be as marvellous and joyful as he had thought. Worse still, maybe Sam and the others had concocted some story about him giving himself up to the WSBs or something equally outrageous.

Christian was interrupted from his thoughts by Farq's arrival with his dinner. He wore the same pissed-off expression on his face as Mo had had. He slid a plastic bowl of lamb stew and beans into Christian's cell and then hovered like a hotel porter waiting for a tip. It took Christian a moment to catch on. With a sigh, Christian lobbed him a pack of Marlboros.

As Farq clanged the metal door shut, a pang of fear struck Christian. Why had he not heard the helicopter take off? He was surprised enough to hear the engine shut down under these circumstances, but it was very strange that the two South African negotiators had not left. He fumbled for a cigarette in the darkness. The flame shot from the lighter and lit up the dingy cell, casting long, exaggerated shadows of the bars against the wall. He decided there was no need to panic because there could be any number of reasons why the South Africans had either stayed or, more likely, left by other means. Christian reckoned the most likely reason was that the two men were staying in the village to make sure he was not moved before the handover. Also, Mo would not want them leaving and coming back with an army. It started to make sense.

He ate a couple more of the biscuits, swallowed three multi-vitamins and applied himself with mozzie spray, before lying down on his mat to sleep. He got off to sleep quicker than expected, his thoughts spinning from dealing with Sam to seeing his parents, sleeping in his own bed and drinking endless pints of very cold lager in his favourite pub on the water-front in Lymington.

24

Straining in their harnesses to keep their bearing as easterly as possible, Tim and Jamie tried in vain to catch any kind of thermals to keep them high. They could see nothing in the darkness below, but out to the east there were tiny glimmers of light heralding dawn. They shouted to one another – at three miles up they could make as much noise as they pleased.

Twenty minutes later, they were down on the hard sand of the desert floor.

'Fuck me, that was cold,' Jamie muttered, pulling off his gloves and frantically rubbing his hands together.

'We must have covered twenty ks,' replied Tim, as he knelt on the ground checking the weapons.

'Let's bury the chutes and crap and get going. We're still sixty clicks from the nearest camp,' Jamie grumbled.

'There's no point digging too big a hole,' Tim suggested. 'It's hardly like anyone is looking for us. Let's just hide them.'

'Suits me.'

A couple of minutes later, they had rolled up the parachutes and covered them with sand and rocks. They took off their overalls, gloves and goggles, covering them, too. They wound their Arab-style shemaghs around their heads and untucked their long shirts.

Once they were properly dressed, Tim fiddled with his GPS unit and established their position. According to their coordinates, Jamie was right to within one km. They were 61 km from the nearest possible camp. They had agreed that they would split up and get round each of the planned sites as fast as possible. If one of them found Christian, they would call the other on the sat phone and they would meet. It was a pretty basic plan, but practical.

First, they were going to walk in and hide their excess rations and water at a central point, as they knew Arabs never wandered around the desert with huge military packs on their backs. Within less than ten minutes of hitting the ground, they were on the move. It was 05.00 and getting lighter by the minute. Usually they would have walked at least 20 yards apart in open ground, but there was no real threat, so they walked side by side. Tim had the AK-47 suspended on a shoulder sling, so it hung across his lower chest under his shirt. Jamie carried the .375 slung down his back, still in its sleeve; their pistols swung from their belts under the cover of their shirt-tails.

The increasing light revealed a wide, arid and empty landscape. The ground was a dry and crumbly mixture of dust, soil and sand, which cracked beneath their boots, leaving an unhelpful trail. They passed occasional rocks and clumps of bushes with the odd gully and dry river bed. With little conversation, they walked and walked, aiming to keep up an average pace of 4 km per hour.

By 08.00, the sun had risen sufficiently to increase the temperature to the point where both men were sweating heavily.

'You do know that most of your fake tan has run off into your shirt, don't you, mate?' Jamie said, pointing to Tim's front.

'We'll have real tans by lunchtime at this rate,' replied Tim. 'Anyway, you look a fucking sight yourself. Let's take a breather and get some fluids on.'

They slipped out of their bergens and sat in the shade of a small pile of rocks. Jamie checked his GPS and confirmed they had travelled almost 12 km.

After two minutes sitting in the shelter of the rock, the tsetse flies appeared. Tim swatted the first one on his arm, muttering, 'My bite marks haven't even cleared up from Barras, and here we go again.'

'These things just ruin Africa, just like midges ruin

Scotland,' Jamie replied. 'Someone said about being in the army that you spend eighty per cent of the time bored to death, nineteen frozen to death and one per cent, scared to death. What about being annoyed to death?'

'I think that bit needs to be put in the eighty per cent category as a subsection along with being underpaid to death,' replied Tim, with a laugh.

Jamie chuckled. 'Well, I suppose they do keep you on the move. So we need to include walked to death, too.'

'OK, we need to find somewhere with a breeze next time we stop. Let's give it five minutes and fuck off,' replied Tim.

They hauled their bergens onto their backs, straightened out the shoulder straps and set off. Jamie tucked in behind Tim and they continued on their easterly bearing. They knew the sun would be in their faces for the next few hours and slipped on their sunglasses. In every direction, the terrain was the same slightly undulating, dusty scrub without any particular landmarks. They knew they would eventually intersect a desert road that ran north–south across their route.

It got hotter as the morning wore on. Both men were pouring in sweat and taking regular gulps from their water bottles. Maintaining 4 km an hour was hard going with the soft ground and the weight of their kit. By midday, they were both tired and in need of a real break. With the sun directly above them it was difficult to find any natural shade, so they used a plastic groundsheet as a basic tent with the .375 acting as the central pole. They crawled in and lay down. After establishing that they had covered a satisfying 27 km, they tucked into their first meal for twenty-four hours.

Jamie slept for an hour and a half, while Tim lay quietly next to him listening. Every twenty minutes he would slip out from under the groundsheet and scan the horizon with his binoculars. By the time they had swapped over, the heat of the day was beginning to ease off. They rolled up the groundsheet and set off, hoping to hit the desert road within a couple of hours.

With the exception of boxing around one very small village, which had not appeared on their map, the afternoon was uneventful. They talked through the various scenarios as to what they would do if they found Christian, but agreed the subject was pretty much academic as they had no idea where he was being held, or by how many people, and under what circumstances. They had agreed that this was an observation exercise, but the more they talked, the more gung-ho their ideas became.

'We should be getting close to the road in a k or two,' Jamie said, squinting at the screen of his GPS unit.

'Yeah, but these desert roads do move from time to time, with the sandstorms and stuff,' replied Tim.

'Sure, but it won't be far away, even if it has taken a new course,' retorted Jamie.

'Well, let's find it, wherever it is, and then stash the excess baggage,' said Tim.

'I can assure you, mate, I'm as keen as you are to dump the clobber and get moving for real,' huffed Jamie.

After a few more minutes, and with no warning at all, they hit the desert highway.

'It's just two long parallel ruts in the sand,' said Tim.

'Ah, the M4,' replied Jamie.

'Don't forget to look left and right before you cross,' continued Tim, with a laugh.

'And you said we should hide the excess kit near an easy-to-find landmark, so we could find it on the run and without the GPS. You could fart and cover this road with enough sand that you would never see it again,' answered Jamie.

'No need to be quite so negative. This excellent piece of infrastructure provides us with a textbook feature that we can handrail off if necessary, right back to this precise spot. So, shut up and let's get digging,' Tim replied, still laughing.

They crossed the road, paced out 100 yards and started digging with entrenching tools in the soft ground, just in front of a small dead tree, which was the only visible landmark. They dug a small trench, a couple of feet deep, then emptied half their ration boxes and one of their plastic containers of water into the hole, all wrapped in black bin liners. They filled in the trench and kicked away the excess sand and earth.

'OK, mate,' said Tim, clicking on his GPS to set the position as a way point.

'See you back here in forty-eight hours, and do call if you're going to be late. I can think of better places to hang out.'

'Ditto,' replied Jamie. 'You recce your two camps and I will do my two. That's doable from here in the time and then we can do the further-away camps together. And don't forget to turn your sat phone on for fifteen minutes at twelve and six, will you?'

With a casual nod, the two men set off to reconnoitre four out of the six possible camps where Christian could be held, according to Deverall's intelligence. Both men knew the likelihood of finding him was slim, but the exercise had to be done. They would walk through the night and get to the first camps in the early hours, sneak in around 04.00 and have a look. Then fall back to a lying-up point and observe the morning activity. Then, they would move on to their second camp and repeat the process. It would be tough going to get back to the central point in forty-eight hours, but without the weight on their backs, they would be substantially faster.

25

Back in Hereford, Deverall was using the end of an ornamental commando knife to clean out the nozzle of his coffee machine. It had fallen off the little wooden shield it had been mounted on, commemorating some long-forgotten tour in Northern Ireland. Having finally served a useful purpose, he lobbed it in the bin and sat down at his desk to enjoy his coffee.

The atmosphere around the place had improved, although he had not been there much due to commitments in London. He had kept his ear to the ground and had tabs on Sam. According to his daily reports, the intelligence chatter from the countries around Sierra Leone was getting even more intense. It was frustrating that there was still no one missing.

Having agreed with himself that he would give up smoking the moment he got back home, Christian felt no guilt in lighting his first cigarette so early in the morning. He had never liked smoking and usually was appalled to see people lighting up first thing after any exercise.

He puffed his way through several cigarettes, listening to the sounds of another day starting around the village. On cue, Farq pushed open the door and dumped a bowl of rice and stew on the floor. He slid it under the bars with his foot, not looking at Christian. As he turned to walk out, Christian's words of thanks fell on deaf ears.

Christian wondered if he would be summoned for his usual morning on the ranges when he heard a noise he had not heard before. It was the high-pitched whir of what sounded like an electric saw or an angle grinder. It stopped and started and was interrupted by the bang, bang, bang of a hammer bashing a nail. He listened carefully and thought the noises were coming from somewhere in front of the cell block and a bit to the right.

By midday, the cell buzzed with mosquitoes that seemed undeterred by his spray. He reckoned that the smell might even be attracting them. He paced around, increasingly frustrated by the lack of information regarding his release. He knew things would be based on African timescales, which were never going to be quick, but he thought it would be reasonable for him to be kept informed. The noise of drilling, sawing and hammering outside was also starting to annoy him.

To add to his worries, he had now smoked a full packet of twenty cigarettes in less than twenty-four hours. With only two packs left, he was going to have to slow down and ration himself with this important new part of his life. The afternoon wore on slowly with Sam never out of his mind for more than a minute or two.

The one break in the tedium came as Farq clanged open the metal door to deliver what was either a late lunch or a very early dinner. Christian tried to catch a glimpse through the door but could only see into the outer courtyard, which looked unchanged.

'Do you know when I am going to be released, please?' he said, trying to sound as pleasant as possible.

'Soon,' Farq snapped back, as if he had been asked rather a personal question.

'What does soon mean – a day or a week?' Christian replied, a distinct ring of desperation in his voice.

'I don't know. Soon,' Farq hissed, sliding a plastic bowl of dates and bread under the bars.

Christian tried a different tack. 'So the men who came for me, are they still here?'

In an instant, Farq's expression changed from agitated to furious. Christian was surprised at the reaction as he did not think he was pushing him too hard.

'Stop asking me,' growled Farq, flashing his eyes at Christian.

'I am sorry, very sorry,' replied Christian, quietly raising his hands.

Farq looked calmer, glanced over his shoulder and made as if to say something, but as he opened his mouth, he must have changed his mind. He closed his mouth, nodded to Christian and left, pulling the metal door shut behind him with a clang.

Christian plonked himself on his chair and thought. He lit a cigarette and watched the beam of light move slowly up the wall as the sun set. He could hardly claim to know Farq, but his manner was out of kilter with how he had been. He looked stressed, on edge and shifty. The building noises were still coming from outside and Christian could hear many more vehicles revving in and out of the village than on previous evenings.

26

Jamie strode off as fast as he could. Tabbing long distances on your own was the bedrock of Special Forces and was no issue for him. In many respects it was easier than being in a patrol, where you had to fit in with the pace of others. He could now walk as fast or as slow as he wanted, and stop when he wanted.

It was 30 km to the first camp. Although he could feel the strain of the day's walk in his legs, he was determined to cover the remaining distance before 03.00. This would give him time to get in and out during the darkest part of the night. Also, if things went wrong, he would have several valuable hours of darkness to play with.

Tim was equally happy setting off on his own. He knew how fast Jamie covered the ground with his long legs and that he would have to move fast to get round his two camps in forty-eight hours. Once Jamie was out of sight, he broke into a slow run that he maintained for an hour.

This was the first time Jamie and Tim had had any real time on their own since the operation. Tim cleared his thoughts and concluded that they had made a mistake in the jungle and that they were putting it right now. He was not a worrier like Jamie, who was now striding along in the African twilight analysing why he had let greed get the better of him and trying to reconcile whether this rescue mission neutralised being such a terrible friend to Christian. The other worry in Jamie's mind was that they were now operating behind enemy lines without the usual back-up. Jamie knew Tim could be very cavalier and would be sure to opt for amateur heroics, as opposed to identifying Christian's whereabouts and calling in proper support. He thundered along, easily exceeding 4 km an hour, until the sun had set way behind him. By 22.00, he reluctantly acknowledged he was exhausted. He looked around for somewhere to sit down and, on seeing nowhere obvious, dropped himself on the ground right where he stood.

Despite the drop in temperature, he was still sweating and reckoned he had not stopped all day. His hands, face and neck were stuck with a combination of fake tan, dust and sweat. He could feel itchy lumps popping up on his arms and legs where the tsetse flies had bitten through his shirt and trousers.

'Time for a nip of the Macallan,' he thought to himself, pulling out a small silver hip flask from his grab-sack. He unscrewed the lid, sniffed the contents and took a small satisfying gulp. Now came the serious business of eating. He ripped open a hamburger and beans ration pack and squeezed the contents into his mouth. A bag of tomato soup and a sickly squirt of treacle pudding followed in quick succession, washed down with half a litre of water and a final swig from the hip flask.

He had only been sitting down for twenty minutes, but could feel his legs stiffening as he started to get cold. He had intended to take a proper break of an hour but felt the urge to get moving. He hauled himself to his feet and flicked on his GPS to check he was heading off on the right bearing. As the yellow glow of the screen faded, he became aware of the darkness around him. The moon was obscured by passing clouds. One minute he could see for miles around, the next the darkness was near complete.

He could not decide if he felt safer during the dark or in the moments of clear moon. The noises of the night had started and the empty desert now buzzed with nocturnal activity. He heard the hoots of an owl and sniffling noises, which felt like something was behind him. Several times, he stopped and looked back but could see nothing. He thought of throwing in a snap ambush but dismissed the idea as paranoid.

All day, he had been on a roll of excitement, parachuting unofficially into the desert to rescue a mate from a bunch of terrorists. He had been with Tim and things had felt good, but now his mood had changed. He questioned what he was doing and tried to convince himself he was not making the mother of all mistakes. He argued both sides of the case and increasingly thought he was a naive fool acting out an idiotic Boy's Own fantasy. He felt alone, very alone. Normally, he would have the full weight of the British Army behind him, not to mention the Americans and the UN, too. This time he was solo, with the back-up of a borrowed hunting rifle and a nicked machine pistol that had already broken once. Sure, Tim was there, somewhere about 30 km away with no transport and a museum-piece AK. Marvellous, if the shit hit the fan.

He knew that he had hardly slept in the last thirty-six hours and that things always felt worse when he was knackered. He could normally control any low feeling because he knew he just had to get on and finish the exercise, but this was worse. He could cope with the physical tiredness, but he would have swapped the nagging doubts for the steepest of hills or the heaviest of rain.

On he trudged. He could still hear the snuffling noise behind him. He slipped the .375 out of its sleeve, checked there was a round in the chamber and carried it in his arms.

200

By 02.00, he was cruising on autopilot. He had stopped thinking, which was a relief, and had found a path going in roughly the right direction, which made the walking easier. He checked his GPS and was irritated to see that he had got 'track happy' and followed the path, even though it had veered ten degrees off his course.

Back on the right bearing, Jamie's mind slipped into gear as he began to think how he would recce the first camp. The satellite imagery showed activity, but it could be the normal day-to-day goings-on in a regular African village. The six sites had been identified as possible training camps for a number of reasons. Firstly, on the basis they supported a disproportionately large amount of inhabitants compared with a standard farming community, and had, therefore, more vehicular comings and goings than would be expected. Another telltale factor was that most traditional farming activities were no longer viable in this arid and sandstorm-prone part of the sub-Sahara. These factors were combined with GCHQ picking up an unlikely amount of satellite phone traffic from the area and the fact that the sites were in a lawless part of Mauritania, where terrorists could train without interruption from any government.

When the GPS showed he was 3 km from the camp, Jamie squatted down on the ground and pulled open his grab-sack. He fumbled for some biscuits and took a long gulp from his water bottle. Next, he pulled out his night-vision goggles and positioned them on his head. He flicked them on and adjusted the sensitivity. He put the .375 back in the sleeve and checked over the machine pistol. Standing up again, he made sure that all his pockets and bags were zipped shut. He glanced down at the GPS unit and set off at a fast walk. He wanted to get in and out as quickly as possible. He knew there was only a tiny chance of this being the right camp, but still he felt a twinge of nerves.

He was ahead of schedule as it was not even 03.00. There was no sign of dawn and the moon was still sliding in and out of sight behind the clouds. He walked across open, untended land with no sign of organised farming. The night-time noises were now very much at the back of his mind as he got closer to what could be a massive concentration of heavily armed thugs. He had no idea if they would have sentries placed at night but he could take no chances. He peered into the goggles and looked around the eerily yellow image of the landscape. Subconsciously, he repeatedly pushed the safely catch on the machine pistol forward into firing mode. With his left hand, he felt the reassuring outline of an Armalite grenade in his trouser pocket. He slowed his movements and paused every few yards to listen.

The GPS showed '275 m to destination'. Jamie took deep breaths and peered hard into the goggles, trying to interpret the yellowy shadows ahead. When the distance to destination dropped to 175 m, he made out angular objects that had to be houses.

He paused and was conscious of his heart pumping faster. He listened but could hear nothing other than the slight breeze. He smelt wood smoke. He felt his hands shaking as he moved forward, casting his head around in exaggerated movements due to the goggles' narrow field of vision. It dawned on him that he had really expected to find a series of deserted settlements, which meant he could have then headed home with a clear conscious before anyone had even missed the two of them. This was now real.

He could see the outlines of houses in more detail. They had flat roofs and small dark windows. His next sensation was the smell of goats. He found this reassuring as he guessed terrorists would not also be farmers. He moved on, aware of the sound of his feet crunching on dead vegetation. He planned what he would do if he disturbed anyone. If it was a genuine farming village, he would just turn and run. If he had walked into the heart of a terrorist training camp, he would lose off half a magazine of the machine pistol, lob one grenade, turn and run 500 yards before stopping and putting down the other half of the magazine as suppressing fire. It was pretty basic, but he was short on choices.

He approached the house on the right end of the village. He brushed his hand along the flaking white paint of the crumbling back wall. Slowly, he turned around the corner of the house, peering at the ground to avoid treading on anything that would make a noise. He kept going, his finger still involuntarily checking the safety catch was in the forward position. He rounded the front of the house and saw an open doorway. Inside, on the floor, he could see sleeping bodies. He was close enough to hear breathing and see the rise and fall of the chest of the person closest to the entrance.

He moved on, peering into the yellowy gloom. He crept up to the next house and noticed that the entrance was blocked with a wooden gate. He decided not to look inside due to the strong smell of goat. He walked on with more confidence, feeling that he was most likely in a farming settlement. There were no cars or pick-ups so far, nothing out of the ordinary. He carried on and looked in more houses. They were either empty or contained sleeping people or animals. With a feeling of relief, he retraced his steps and quietly made his way out of the village the way he had come in.

Once he was fifteen minutes' walk away, he sat down and got out his GPS. He scrolled down the menu and clicked on the next destination. 'Calculating route' appeared briefly on the screen, and then '22.82 km to destination'. Jamie stood up and set off, determined to get this down to 15 km before he found somewhere to lie up for a sleep.

He locked on the next bearing, put his head down

and walked. Despite his rigorous pace, he felt cold and dizzy. He glanced down at the GPS every few minutes, watching the 'distance to destination' figure drop at an agonisingly slow rate. It was 04.05 and the dark thoughts were back with a vengeance. He could see an incredulous expression on Deverall's face and hear him saying, *Why on earth didn't you just tell me what you knew? We could have done this properly.*

The mission seemed absurd and he felt both immature and selfish. This was more about his conscience than rescuing a mate. Christian's best chance would be a full-scale operation to get him out, not two gung-ho pricks with fake tans, padding round the desert in fancy dress.

By 05.30, Jamie was 14.5 km to his next destination. The sun was visible on the horizon and provided enough light to see his surroundings. Nothing had changed. It was still an open, undulating wasteland of dust and the odd wispy tree or bush. He knew it was time to stop and get holed up before he either collapsed or bumped into someone. He spotted a small pile of rocks and headed towards them. He laid down his kit and sat himself down against the largest, most upright stone. He felt low and reminded himself that it was because he was so tired, and not for any other reason. He took a swig of the Macallan and then squeezed a full meal set of ration packs down his throat. By the time he had finished and got his groundsheet out, it was nearly 06.00 – time to turn on the sat phone. He knew Tim would only call if he had news. 6 a.m. came and went. By 06.10 it was obvious that neither of them had any need to call. He waited until 06.16 and switched off to preserve the batteries. He tucked the machine pistol closely by his side and slipped inside the folded groundsheet. Within two minutes, he was fast asleep.

He awoke with a start. He sat up and looked around, thinking he had heard something. He instinctively reached for his weapon and flicked the safety off. By now, he was fully awake and getting a grip. He looked and listened. Other than the frantic buzzing of tsetse flies, everything seemed calm. He laid the machine pistol down and wiped the sweat from his face. He kicked off the groundsheet and found himself drenched in sweat from the heat of the sun, which was now high in the sky. He glanced at his watch. It was 11.40. Having kipped for over five hours was a great feeling. It was quite an achievement on his own, in the middle of the desert; he'd been expecting to get an hour or two at best. He drained his second water bottle and squeezed more rations into his mouth.

He checked through his kit and had a look around through his binoculars. There was nothing much to see other than endless, dusty desert. He checked his watch and flipped up the aerial on the sat phone. It was very nearly 12.00 and time to switch on in case Tim had anything to say. He pressed the 'On' button and, before he had even found somewhere shady to put the handset, it rang. Jamie jumped and snatched up the phone.

'Hello,' he said.

'Jamie, Jamie, it's me. I've fucking found him, I have found him, I am sure of it. Listen— '

'What? Oh shit,' injected Jamie.

'I am sure, it has to be. There is some shit going down, too. Where the fuck are you?' gasped Tim.

'Hey, hey, man, just tell me what's going on,' Jamie replied calmly.

'Right, I got to the first place, which was pretty much abandoned but I did manage to nick a motor-bike,' continued Tim, breathlessly.

'You thieving gypsy twat.'

'Yes, yes, thank you, mate, but it meant I got to my second camp about an hour ago. And there must be forty vehicles parked up, two hundred rag heads knocking about, a communication tower, the fucking lot. I didn't get too close because it's light, but if he's anywhere in Africa, that's where he is.'

'OK, OK,' Jamie replied, trying to sound in control. 'Where are you now? Give me your coordinates and I'm inbound.'

'No, no, you sit tight and I'll pick you up on the bike. Give me your coordinates. That will be much quicker,' replied Tim, sounding ultra stressed.

An hour and a half later, Jamie heard the distant revving of a motorcycle. Through his binoculars, he saw Tim approaching. He was doing about 20 km an hour, his baggy shirt flapping wildly behind him. Jamie revealed himself from behind the rocks and saw Tim adjust his course towards him.

'Nice wheels, man,' Jamie said as Tim pulled up beside him, cutting the engine by pulling apart two red wires that had formed an improvised ignition.

'Yeah, how African can you get? It actually goes really well, you know,' Tim said, standing back to look at the dusty wreck of a 1970s Honda, with a rusting brown fuel tank.

'Better than that souped-up piece of Jap crap you tart around on back home,' laughed Jamie.

'Well, I think we will have to agree to differ on that, mate,' replied Tim, also laughing.

'Anyway, you seem a bit calmer now. You OK?' said Jamie.

'Knackered, mate, knackered . . . been there before. But the camp looks rammed with guys and they're all well tooled-up. Anyway, how was your camp?' replied Tim.

'Bunch of snoring farmers and a load of goats,' said Jamie, with a slight shrug that implied that he always got the boring jobs.

'We need a plan.' Tim plonked himself down on the ground next to the ticking and cooling motorbike and lit a cigarette.

'Well, nothing has really changed, has it?' replied Jamie. 'The only difference is that we reckon we know the camp has some life in it before we get there. We still don't know if Christi's in there and, let's face it, he probably isn't. It's most likely some local militia piss-up and nothing to do with any real terrorists at all.'

'They don't drink down here, so it's not going to be a piss-up, is it?' retorted Tim.

'OK, a fucking regional Scrabble tournament then,' groaned Jamie, rolling his eyes. 'Whatever, but we still need to get in close and check it out. We get our shit together here, you get some sleep and we go in tonight. After all, it's only fourteen ks, which won't take long if we use your hooky super bike, which I still think you need to return to its rightful owner.'

'I bet you it was nicked in the first place,' Tim replied, rubbing some of the encrusted dust off the exhaust pipe with the toe of his boot.

'Stop being so utterly pedantic and get some kip. I slept all morning, so you sleep for a bit and I'll do stag,' said Jamie.

'Suits me.' Tim pulled his groundsheet out of his bergen.

27

Christian had a bad night. He felt too anxious and stressed to sleep. He spent most of the night sitting on his chair assessing the Sam situation. For the last couple of nights, Farq had slept elsewhere, which, in an extraordinary way, made things worse as Christian felt even more isolated on his own in the cell block.

Eventually, there were signs of dawn. The village was waking up to another day but there were more sounds than usual. He heard more voices and more vehicles. Christian smiled to himself and wondered if terrorist training camps had 'changeover days' like holiday resorts.

Farq arrived with breakfast and clanged open the metal even more noisily than usual. Breakfast was slid under the bars at lightning speed. Farq turned and left before Christian even had time to think of asking him any questions. As Christian sat down to eat his lamb stew and half-raw pita bread, the screech of power tools started up.

With all the extra activity in the village, Christian had a feeling he would not be called to the ranges. He sat on his chair with his foot tapping on the floor. He blamed Sam for everything. He promised himself that under no circumstances would he ever let the matter drop. He looked around at the tiny bare cell and down at his filthy body. He would get Sam, one way or another, whatever it took.

The morning continued and took on the tedium of the night. Christian knew exactly why Farq had dashed in and out so fast. Christian was desperate for information. He wished he was at least out on the ranges doing something. Being holed up in his cell for a second day was bad enough but it was the not knowing that was eating him up. He paced around, swiping at mosquitoes and rubbing their bloody remains into the walls. The only distraction was the activity in the village.

By late afternoon, he was down to eight cigarettes. He reckoned he would probably be freed either the next day or the day after. This meant he could smoke two more today and then have three on each of the next days. He regretted giving Farq a full pack. He felt that if things took any longer, the negotiators would be likely to revisit him to check he was still there and hopefully stock him up with fags and biscuits.

Holding cigarette number seven between his thumb and forefinger, Christian watched the beam of light from the setting sun begin its evening crawl up the wall. He knew that prisoners with nothing to do developed a strange reliance on minute details in their routines. He could see it in himself as he pondered the mundanity of taking an interest in watching the microscopic movement of a ray of light. Still, it passed the time and helped him get away from thinking about Sam.

Jamie spent the afternoon going through the kit. Tim lay on his side in a foetal position, his mouth open, in a state of near coma. Jamie resisted the temptation for practical jokes and spread out all the kit on his groundsheet. He needed to check the weapons were working properly and had not been damaged in the parachute drop or had got clogged up with dust on the walk in. He dismantled them one at a time and gave the working parts a rub with a toothbrush soaked in gun oil. He tested the radio headsets and made sure the battery contacts were in the right positions. Next, he unscrewed the tops of the grenades and checked they were primed properly. By 18.00 everything had been checked and he knew that he was really just killing time. Nerves were building in his stomach and he wanted to get on with the job, but it was only fair to let Tim kip for the same five hours he had had, so sat quietly eating biscuits until 19.00. Tim had not moved a muscle since he'd shut his eyes.

'Time to wake up, mate,' Jamie said, quietly shaking Tim.

Tim's eyes flashed open. 'For fuck's sake, what time is it?'

'I make it nearly dinnertime and you've been asleep all afternoon. Hopefully, you might have woken up in a slightly better mood,' replied Jamie.

'Well, I have definitely woken up with worse BO,' Tim grumbled, pulling his soaking shirt away from his chest.

' I'm sure you'll fit in just fine with the after-dinner entertainment, then,' Jamie said, laughing.

'So what's the plan?' Tim sat up and looked around.

'Let's just wait for dark and get in as close as we can. The problem is going to be knowing if he's there, so we may need to get right inside or lie up somewhere close and see if we can see him in there in the daylight,' said Jamie.

'I don't like the idea of an OP much. There's no cover if we get rumbled in the daylight. We haven't even got the right stuff for a fighting retreat.' Tim sounded worried.

'I think the secret's going to be not being seen,' said Jamie in an equally serious tone.

'Yup, I think that's going to be the gist of things. Shall we make this the twenty-four RV then, and where we left the food, the seven-day one?' said Tim.

'Makes sense, I guess.' Jamie nodded.

After a meal of lukewarm meatballs in pasta

followed by a soft squeeze of gloop calling itself 'Traditional Spotted Dick', it was time to pack up and get going.

'Right,' said Tim. 'Let's get this little baby on the road.'

He twisted the throttle with one hand, touching the ends of the two red wires together with the other. Instantly there was a small blue spark and the engine revved into life.

'Don't you ever be rude about my bike again,' shouted Tim, twisting the throttle to keep the engine running.

'Impressive, I have to confess,' said Jamie, lifting his leg over and sitting himself on the back seat. 'I'd better take the bags if you're going to drive,' he continued.

'It's about forty ks; should take us a couple of hours,' replied Tim. 'Don't know if we've got enough juice to get us the whole way.'

Gingerly, Tim turned the Honda round and set off, following the tracks he had made earlier. Despite the relatively soft surface they found they could make quite reasonable progress if they kept a steady pace of about 15 km an hour. Every so often, they would have to lift the bike over a river bed or get off and push when the gradient got too steep.

After an hour the light had faded to the point where progress had to be slower. Tim could hardly see the ground in front of him and was having problems avoiding obstacles such as rocks and holes. They reduced their speed to a slow running pace but agreed it was still a lot better than having to walk.

Suddenly, the engine gave a shudder. Tim twisted the throttle frantically but to no avail. A second shudder and the engine cut out.

'That's it on the petrol,' said Tim. 'I checked it earlier and it was only a third full. To be fair, I'm surprised we got so far.'

Jamie pressed the button on his GPS. 'Not bad, mate, we did twenty-five ks and that would have taken us six hours plus.'

'Sadly, it looks like this may be it,' said Tim, getting off the Honda and laying it on the ground.

'The end of the road for you . . . '

'That bike has survived at least twenty years in just about the harshest environment on earth without a whiff of a service or a drop of oil. You find it, or nick it I should say, and it's knackered in less than twenty-four hours,' said Jamie in a satisfied way.

'Out of petrol is not the same as knackered, mate, is it?' Tim replied with a laugh.

'Come on, it's nearly twenty-three hundred hours and we need to keep going. It's still fifteen ks to go.'

Both men wrapped shemaghs round their heads, covering their radio headsets, and set off on foot. Jamie had the .375 out of the sleeve hanging down his back and Tim had his AK across his chest in a sling.

Despite their best efforts to keep things light-hearted,

nerves had taken over since they had dumped the bike. This was not a normal patrol. They weren't properly equipped and did not have the usual back-up. Also, they were almost certain to be going in against an unconventional enemy who were anything but followers of the Geneva Convention. If they were caught, it would most likely be a nasty drawn-out death and no one would ever know how, why or where. Armalite would probably come clean with Deverall after a few months but it would not make much difference.

The night before, Jamie had felt a sense of excitement and purpose as the GPS counted down his distance to destination. This time the 15 km was frighteningly close and, each time the km dropped down a digit, he felt the tension increase inside him.

'OK, what's the similarity between a fat girl and a clapped-out, rusty nineteen-seventies Honda?' said Tim, after over an hour of silence.

Jamie instantly chuckled.

'They are both fun to ride till your mates find out!' carried on Tim, with a schoolboy laugh.

'You'd fucking know, mate,' replied Jamie. 'Mind you, we'd be pushed to shag anything looking like this,' he continued, turning around to grin at Tim.

'What's the Mauritanian word for sandpaper?' said Tim.

'Oh, heavens, come on then,' replied Jamie, still grinning.

'A map!' laughed Tim, kicking some sand towards Jamie.

'Dismal, truly dismal,' replied Jamie. 'Has my life really come to this? Using up hard-earned leave to walk round a desert with a loony, to spy on some other loonies because of what another loony did, and probably losing my job in the process. Not to mention, having an almost one hundred per cent chance of not being able to return this prized rifle to its owner, who is then likely to kill me.'

After more silly jokes, the conversation took a more serious turn.

'Right, my GPS says it's five ks to destination,' said Tim.

'Well, that was the fastest ten ks I've ever tabbed,' replied Jamie.

'The quicker we get in, the quicker we get out. That's the way I see it,' said Tim.

'Well, we need to find the place and get into a decent vantage point. We are going to need a super discreet OP if we're going to watch the place tomorrow. Personally, I want to get in tonight and see if he's there,' said Jamie.

'Me too,' replied Tim. 'At least in the jungle we had some cover and some bloody shade. Out here it's going to be tricky.'

Jamie watched the GPS as the last full km changed to a zero and showed 990 metres to destination. They squatted on the ground and took out their night-vision goggles. It was nearly 02.00. An unhelpfully bright moon had at least enabled them to spot the desert road running into the village before they had walked right across it.

With Tim leading, they edged their way up a slight rise in the ground.

'We should be able to see it from here,' whispered Tim.

Jamie nodded.

They reached the crest of the rise on their hands and knees. They could see the light-coloured shapes of the houses and the dark silhouette of the communications tower. There were a number of lit-up buildings and a glow coming from the centre of the village.

'Smells like a fire to me,' whispered Tim.

'I can hear them talking, too. Can't be more than three hundred metres. Sounds like we might be missing out, mate.' Jamie turned to look at Tim with a grin.

'Perhaps it is Ali Baba's birthday bash after all,' replied Tim, lowering his night-vision goggles over his eyes and adjusting the settings.

'You can't see them from here but there were a load of vehicles parked the other side of the houses yesterday,' Tim went on, still whispering. 'Basically, like I said, you have about sixty houses built along two tracks with a bit of an open area down the far end. That's where the fire must be. It's like a village green without the grass, if that makes sense.'

'Yup, and the road comes in from this side, which is the south,' said Jamie, also looking through his goggles.

'The question is where would they hold Christian if they've got him? All the buildings look roughly the same from here. If this is a training camp they're sure to have some kind of central building or guard house where they keep stuff. My guess is it's near the comms mast,' said Tim.

'Would make sense,' replied Jamie.

'The real shag is these boys aren't in bed yet. Sounds like they're hanging out round the fire and having a piss-up,' said Tim.

'They don't drink down here, do they, you twat,' hissed Jamie.

'Well, we can't risk going in any closer till they settle down for the night, whatever they're doing down there. We can go round the other side and get a better idea of the place and see if the vehicles are still there. I can't see any sentries but, if they had any sense, they'd have a couple of guys way out here somewhere, patrolling.'

'Yes, but they aren't us and they aren't expecting any trouble, are they? Even if they're a bunch of extremists,' replied Jamie.

They crawled back down the rise to the point where they felt they were low enough to be well out of sight of anyone in the village. Five metres apart, they walked slowly in a large right-handed arc around the village. Both men surveyed the desert for signs of life, expecting at any moment to see a sentry.

As they rounded to the north, the ground rose into a long, low ridge, giving a slight degree of elevation above the village. A river bed dissected the ridge at one point, along which flowed a trickle of foul-smelling water.

'Guess this must supply the village with water in the rainy season,' said Tim.

'And double up as a sewer the rest of time,' Jamie replied. 'But this could be the place if we need to lie up. Also it's our exit route if the shit hits the fan. They wouldn't be able to get vehicles through here very easily, which would make things a bit fairer.'

'Yup, and with the height, we'll be able to get a reasonable look into the place. The only issue is we can't see down the middle of the houses,' Tim said.

They continued around the bottom of the ridge until they could see a bonfire burning in the open part of the village, with a large group of men milling around it – some stood and others sat in small groups.

'Well, there we are,' whispered Tim.

'I reckon I can see forty and they're all stacked with guns,' replied Jamie.

'And there'll be a whole load more we can't see, in the houses,' said Tim.

'What the fuck is that?' continued Jamie. 'To the right, it looks like a raised platform and there's a beam built over the top of it.'

'It wasn't there yesterday. Hang on a second,' answered Tim. 'Look, look. I can see the tail of a bloody helicopter sticking out of what looks like a tent.'

Jamie adjusted his goggles and stared in the direction of Tim's pointed finger.

'Yes, yes, it's a helicopter with the rotors folded back, just like when they're being stored,' said Jamie, baffled.

'The tent is a disguise. They are obviously hiding it from satellites,' said Tim.

'Mate, I'm liking this less and less. There's nothing normal going on round here at all,' whispered Jamie. 'We need to get the fuck out of here, call Dev and start being a bit more—'

'We still don't know if he's here or not,' interrupted Tim.

'Let's get back to the river bed, recce the area properly and sort out our exit strategy,' said Jamie.

The two men turned and crawled away on their hands and knees in the direction of the river bed. Once they reached the bank, they slipped down and began making their way along the wide-open bed, stepping from one large stone to the next.

For the next forty minutes or so, they wandered about quietly in the darkness exploring the area and looking for firing points and places to climb out onto the desert floor.

Once they had a good idea of the river area, they

made their way around the perimeter of the village. Jamie suddenly gestured to Tim.

'Look, this is a firing range. You can see where they've scooped up the earth over there and there are thousands of empties everywhere,' he said, squatting down and running his fingers carefully through a pile of empty bullet casings on the ground.

'Yup, I think we can safely say this isn't your regular farming community scratching a living from the land,' replied Tim.

'It's getting on for three thirty and we need to find somewhere to lie up where we can see what's what,' said Jamie.

'OK, let's find a scrape on top of the ridge where we can lie. Something that'll allow us to get back down and into the river,' replied Tim.

A few minutes later Jamie and Tim were back on the top of the ridge a couple of hundred metres from a gap that dropped down into the river bed. They could see directly along the line of the houses and had the advantage of 5 metres of elevation. The top of the ridge was covered in thin grass with the odd large stone lying about.

After a minute of debate, both men laid their kit on the ground and dug a long, narrow trench with their entrenching tools; it was just deep and wide enough for one man to lie in. The plan was that one of them would lie in the trench and the other would lay a groundsheet over the top and disguise it with sand and debris. He would then wait behind the ridge, keeping a lookout to the rear. If compromised, they would put down some rounds and get down to the river bed and then run for it with the odd burst of suppressing fire. They reckoned it would work at night but such action would be pretty foolhardy by day.

Once the scrape was finished, they slipped back down to the river bed to get themselves organised. They checked their weapons, squeezed some rations down their throats and had a large drink. As the first glimmer of light broke the darkness, Tim offered to take the first shift in the trench.

'OK, mate, you go first, but you know it's going to be very hard for me to swap with you,' said Jamie. 'Are you sure I shouldn't just bluff it and take a walk round the village? It looks like they've all fucked off to bed.'

Tim shook his head. 'You'd probably be fine but you're six-foot-six. How many Arabs have you seen round here of your height? This is Mauritania, not Ethiopia; you'd stand out like a sore thumb snooping round in there.'

'I guess so, but it would mean we don't have to hang around here in broad daylight. We could make it out in the dark with the whole lot of them in tow but if we get seen in daylight, there's no fucking cover,' Jamie whispered anxiously.

Tim sighed. 'So you reckon the risk of one of us

walking in there now is better than the risk of lying up for the day?'

'Well, I reckon there's a twenty per cent chance we would get compromised going in there now and then have a ninety per cent chance of getting out OK. We have a ten per cent chance of being compromised lying up for the day but then have a ninety per cent chance of getting wasted on the way out,' muttered Jamie.

'The way you're talking, we need a fucking calculator,' replied Tim, with a nervous grin.

'We need to make a decision,' Jamie said, looking hard at Tim in the breaking darkness.

'OK, you get in the trench with the .375. I'll walk on in and take a look around. You'll be spotted a mile off,' Tim hissed, taking his AK off its sling.

'Sure,' replied Jamie. 'Let's do it.'

28

A minute later, Jamie lay in the trench straining to see through the sight of the .375 in the half-light. He had the machine pistol and a grenade next to him. Tim walked casually across the open ground, straight towards the village. He held his AK in his left hand and in his right, a razor-sharp commando knife, the blade hidden by his wrist. He had his grab-sack over his left shoulder and secured around his waist.

Jamie felt his heart pounding against the hard sand. Adrenalin pumped around him as he surveyed the village for signs of life. No one was visible, although the fire was still glowing and giving off smoke. In some ways, this was the perfect time to recce. There was just enough light to see things without night vision and it did not look quite so suspicious to be walking around at first light as opposed to the pitch dark.

Tim was within 20 yards of the closest house. He shook with nerves and felt the sweat forming on his face and dripping down his cheeks. His grip on the knife felt weak and slippery. He approached the fire and looked around. Keeping his head low he walked around the burning embers and approached the stage-like construction in the middle of the open area between the houses. He stopped and looked. A large wooden platform had been built and obviously very recently, judging by the new nails and freshly sawn timber. Over the top was a strong wooden beam supported at each end, reinforced with scaffolding poles.

Without warning, there was a scraping noise as the door to a house about 50 yards away opened. Two figures stepped out and walked slowly towards Tim.

Jamie was sure he saw Tim jump as he clocked the two men. Jamie squinted desperately into the sight of the .375 and took aim on the larger of the two men. Tim, however, immediately changed course and walked diagonally across the dusty area between the two rows of houses. As he approached the other side, Jamie felt Tim had probably got away with it as the two men disappeared into the gloom.

Jamie spoke quietly over the radio, knowing that Tim would be able to hear but would be unlikely to reply. 'You're OK. No problems. They've disappeared.'

Tim raised his hand to where his microphone stick was wrapped up in his shemagh and tapped the end twice with his finger to confirm he had heard. He took a quick glance over his shoulder before turning into a narrow alley. With his finger hovering on the trigger guard, he made his way between the high mud walls. Halfway along, he froze. He could hear conversation coming from a small window on his left. Ducking down, he stepped under the window and carried on.

Sweating heavily and with his jaw trembling with nerves, he reached the end of the alley and could see about a dozen four-wheel-drive vehicles and open-back pick-ups parked under some trees.

He had just taken his first step towards the vehicles when Jamie spoke again: 'Inbound vehicles, coming up the road from the south. Pull out, pull out if you can. Turn left and come along the back of the houses.'

Jamie heard a tap, tap of acknowledgement.

Tim swung around sharply and made his way at an increasingly sharp pace along the back of houses in the direction of the ridge. As he scurried along, he glanced up and noticed that one window was barred whereas the rest had wooden shutters. He paused, glanced around and, seeing no one, laid down his AK and knife, grabbed hold of the bars and hauled himself up to look inside. Despite the increasing light, it was still pitch black inside. The only sign of life was the strong smell of stale cigarette smoke.

Tim lowered himself down and carried on. Now, able to hear the noise of at least one approaching vehicle, he moved on quickly past the next house, glancing anxiously down the dividing alley. A dog barked and he heard more voices.

A thought suddenly flashed through his mind. He stopped in his tracks, turned around and ran back the 30 yards to the barred window. He rested his AK against the wall, reached up with his commando knife and tapped it very gently on one of the bars. He paused, listened and then tapped again. He ducked down low and looked up at the window, feeling sure a bearded face or the barrel of a gun would appear. He heard a scraping inside. He held his breath and felt his whole body shaking with nerves as he gripped his knife in one hand and the AK in the other. Sweat dripped into his eyes as he looked around, trying to work out where he could run.

A thin beam of headlights appeared between the houses and lit up a strip of desert. Tim was on the point of moving when he saw a hand grip one of the bars.

'Is anyone there?' whispered Christian.

Tim stood and reached for Christian's hand.

'Yes, yes. It's me, Tim. Christi, is that you?'

'Shhh, shh, yes, yes,' replied Christian almost inaudibly.

'We're here to get you out,' hissed Tim. 'But it's unofficial. It's just me and Jamie.'

'What? But— '

Tim did not hear the rest of Christian's words as Jamie's voice crackled through his earpiece demanding to know what was happening. Simultaneously a large pick-up appeared around the side of a house, on its way to where the other vehicles were parked under the trees.

Tim crouched in the shadows below the window as Christian pressed his face into the concrete wall in a desperate effort to see what was going on. As the pick-up stopped, a second vehicle appeared, its head-lights shining brightly.

In one smooth movement, Tim stood up, placed his commando knife on the window ledge, turned and walked off with his back to the pick-ups. He reached up, pulled down his microphone stick from in his shemagh to his mouth and spoke.

'He's here. He's bloody well here. Just seen him. He's here . . . '

Jamie gasped and felt momentarily deprived of oxygen. He paused before spluttering, 'Roger that. Fuck, Roger that.'

Tim was aware of activity all around him. The arrival of the two pick-ups had set off every dog in the village and doors and shutters opened everywhere. His mind was a whirl of lights, barking dogs, voices and men with guns. He saw the wooden platform and the glowing embers of the fire. People passed right by him. He walked forwards with his head down. Slowly, in a nightmare of fear, he concentrated on taking each step, every second expecting a hand on his shoulder or a bullet in the back.

He heard Jamie's voice in the background but was not listening to the words. He just kept walking. It was still almost dark but, in Tim's world, the lights were on full.

Jamie's voice suddenly became clear, mid-sentence: '. . . covered, got you covered, it looks OK from here, mate. Just keep on going, just like you are. There is no problem behind you.'

Tim had passed the last house in the row. He allowed himself a tiny glance behind and was surprised to see that no one was following him or taking any interest in him at all. He could see several men by the fire and a couple more milling around. There was the glare of headlights in the background but no vehicles coming his way. He cleared the immediate area of the houses and decided he would not make directly for Jamie but for the river bed. A few seconds later, he was stepping down the bank into cover. He smelt the strangely comforting smell of sewage and knew he was nearly out of sight.

As he felt the soft wet sand under his feet, he took a deep breath.

'Reckon I'm clear,' he gasped into the microphone.

'Come on down the river bed and I'll see you,' replied Jamie.

Christian's heart thumped as his hand gripped the handle of the commando knife. His mind churned, grappling with the enormity of the last few seconds.

He had been sleeping one moment and the next he had been speaking to Tim outside the window. He had gone from fast asleep to high trauma in a matter of seconds. If it weren't for the knife on the window ledge he would have thought he was dreaming.

He replayed Tim's words in his mind. He was there with Jamie, unofficially. How could that be? What about the South African negotiators? Were there two forces operating separately and independently of each other?

With trembling hands, he lit one of his few remaining cigarettes, put it to his mouth and took a long drag. It felt good. He sat down on the floor with his back to the wall and tried to guess what time it was. Judging by the light beginning to fill his cell, it had to be very early morning. He was surprised at all the activity so early. This was not the usual routine.

The word that troubled him was 'unofficial'. He did not like the connotations. They implied amateur, cavalier and without back-up. Very soon, it started to make sense. Of course it was unofficial. So was abandoning the perimeter during the fire-fight, beating the shit out of Udor Foday to find a load of conflict diamonds and, most unofficial of all, Sam shooting him. That was as unofficial as you could get. It therefore made sense that his so-called mates would be messing about unofficially trying to rescue him, when a proper official rescue was taking place.

Christian reached for cigarette number five. Things

still did not stack up. The South Africans had troubled him as much as the shock of suddenly seeing Tim's face at his window. The one good point was that people on the outside knew he was not dead. Even if the wrong people knew, it was still a good thing. He thought of Deverall. If a pair of Muppets like Tim and Jamie could find him 'unofficially', surely the likes of Deverall could too.

The more he thought, the more outlandish his ideas became. His sudden fear was that Sam might be on the mission with Jamie and Tim. Perhaps Tim had not had time to mention it? Jamie and Tim would not know that Sam had tried to kill him. Sam could be out there in the desert with them and he would make sure that Christian was never rescued alive. In fact, Sam could have put the whole thing together to finish the job.

Christian fingered the razor-sharp tip of the knife. He felt better knowing he had a weapon. It created more options. He slipped it carefully into the top of his trousers and covered it with his shirt. The light increased in his cell, as did the activity outside.

With a hollow feeling in his stomach, he felt sure things were coming to a head, one way or another.

29

Tim hurried along the river bed for 400 metres. Then, to his right, he saw Jamie squatting in amongst some large stones with his hand slightly raised. Glancing around, Tim made his way over and tucked himself in the rocks beside Jamie.

'So, what on earth did you see? Did you actually see him?' whispered Jamie.

'Well, yes, yes, I did I—' replied Tim, in a tone of bewilderment.

'Like how?' interrupted Jamie.

'Well, I saw a window with bars on it and tapped on it with my knife. I just had a feeling he might be there – all the other windows were just open gaps or had shutters,' continued Tim.

'Or it could have been the fucking guard room,' snapped Jamie.

'Yes, but a second later Christi appeared and I saw

his face. I told him we were here to get him out and at that moment a fucking truck appeared around the corner and I had to scarper.'

'Well, that puts a very different angle on things,' Jamie whispered, exhaling audibly.

'Are you saying you didn't think we'd ever actually find him?' asked Tim.

'No, not exactly, but I didn't think it would be quite like this. The question is how the fuck we let Dev know he's here when we are on a bloody climbing holiday in Europe?' said Jamie.

'We don't necessarily have to, do we?' replied Tim. 'The fact is that we're here. Their guys are definitely not expecting company; otherwise I couldn't have wandered in there like a fucking tourist and poked around. We could just hold on, watch the place and bust him out tonight. Then we get back home, and, lo and behold, Christian has escaped. He's hardly going to dump us in it when we were the ones who risked life and limb . . .'

'And career . . .' slipped in Jamie.

'. . . to get him out of the soup,' finished Tim.

'The fact is these guys are a bunch of rag-head recruits doing summer camp – "Learn to fire an AK" – before heading back home to grow up and stop being so dumb, aren't they?' hissed Tim, with an excited ring to his voice.

'Well, yes and no.' Jamie sounded unconvinced. 'The plan was to get down here and find him. We weren't going to get all macho and whizz on in, armed with out-of-date war souvenirs in fancy fucking dress. There must be at least eighty of these dudes knocking around in there. We could get him out OK but it's the home run that would worry me. We'd have about four hours' head start max and then every working pick-up south of the Sahara is out looking for us.'

'Listen, we need to see what they are all up to before we decide what to do. For all we know, they may all fuck off somewhere for training today, in which case in we go. We need to get an idea of what they're all doing.'

'OK, let's agree to lie up and watch for the time being, get a feel for things,' answered Jamie.

They climbed out of the river bed and made their way carefully to the trench. Jamie lay down and Tim covered him with a groundsheet so that he was nearly invisible except for a small opening at the front for observation.

Tim crawled back onto the top of the ridge and hid himself just over the skyline in a position where he could cover Jamie's rear. Although they were less than 50 metres apart and could talk over their radios, both men kept quiet, allowing the implications of the situation to settle in their minds. By 06.00, the sun was visible to the east.

Jamie scanned the area with his binoculars. He counted the men and the vehicles. He was surprised to notice a small herd of goats being driven out of the village by a young man. More surprising was that he was the only person not carrying an automatic weapon or wearing an ops vest.

As the sun rose, the insects started. Small jumping flea-like creatures hopped about in the sand in front of Jamie. Very quickly, they seemed to have worked out that he was unable to move and took full advantage. They stuck to his face and crawled up his sleeves. With tiny movements, Jamie wiped his face and squeezed his lower arms to squash them. After twenty minutes it was pointless and he accepted a full invasion.

'There's fucking sand lice everywhere round here,' he heard Tim say over the radio.

'Tell me about it,' Jamie replied, pleased to hear he was not the only one being harassed.

'What's going on in town, then?' continued Tim.

'Well, not much, mate. But I've counted thirty-four people so far and that's not including the herd of goats that just went by.'

'OK,' said Tim.

'I can see the tail of the heli really well now but can't see any ID markings. There've also been three vehicles coming in and one going out. This is one busy little place, that's for sure,' replied Jamie.

By 07.45, Jamie felt the heat of the sun through the groundsheet over him and wondered how he was going to survive in the midday heat. He was watching people wandering around when he suddenly spotted a clean-shaven white face. A second later, another European-looking man emerged from the building by the communications tower. They walked over to the wooden platform and entered into some kind of debate.

As Jamie adjusted the focus of his binoculars, one of them produced a coil of steel cable. He clambered onto the platform and looped one end of the cable over the beam. As he climbed down, a pick-up truck pulled up by the platform. The second European was now kneeling in front of the pick-up attaching the end of the cable to a winch mounted on the front of the vehicle.

'Shit,' he spoke into the radio, as a chilling sensation passed throughout his body. 'Tim, there's something going on here and I don't think it's looking very nice,' he continued

'What . . . like what?' answered Tim immediately.

'That wooden platform thing, it's a fucking gallows or maybe worse. They're rigging up a wire round the beam and they have a winch. You need to see this.'

Twenty seconds later Jamie heard movement behind him as Tim slithered over the skyline of the ridge. Tim lay on the ground next to him with his binoculars trained on the village 400 metres away. Neither man spoke. They just watched as one end of the cable was linked up to the winch. The other end dangled menacingly over the beam.

One of the Europeans produced an electric drill and

busied himself screwing something to the floor of the platform below the beam.

'This is getting medieval,' whispered Tim, almost to himself.

'We need to get moving, this is serious, they are going to fucking tear him to pieces with that thing. It's a fucking rack,' Jamie croaked. He turned to Tim, fear all over his face.

'Right, right, you stay here, I'll phone Hereford right now,' Tim replied, turning and sliding off on his stomach.

Just as he was slipping down the far side of the ridge, he heard Jamie's voice on the radio.

'Now they've got out a video camera on a tripod. They're going to film it.'

Tim whipped open his grab-sack and snatched out his sat phone. He pressed the 'On' button as he flipped the aerial round. The display appeared agonisingly slowly. Once it confirmed he was connected to a satellite, he started dialling the guard room at Stirling Lines, knowing the phone was always answered. Once a sugary-sounding female American voice had told him he had $100 credit left, he heard the faint ring tone.

'Hereford 899123,' answered a bored-sounding voice.

'This is Symonds, Trooper Symonds. I need to speak to Colonel Deverall immediately.'

'Let me just check for you,' replied the voice, 'although I don't think he's in yet.'

A bolt of rage erupted in Tim's mind.

'This is a life and death situation, I need him right fucking now or anyone senior in D Squadron, like Day, Cornwallis, anyone,' he snapped, suddenly wishing he had not sworn, in case the man on the other end of the phone decided to hang up.

'I can re-route your call to his mobile if you like?' said the voice.

'Yes, thank you, thank you,' answered Tim, trying to keep calm.

30

There was a second ring tone, this time from a mobile. Tim's heart was in his mouth as he prayed Deverall would answer.

'Deverall speaking,' sounded a slightly irritated but familiar voice. I am driving at the moment; let me find somewhere to pull over.'

'Sir, it's Trooper Symonds,' gulped Tim.

'Yes, tell me what's going on,' Deverall said in a business-like tone. 'Enjoying France, are we?'

'Er, well, no, not really,' stammered Tim. 'I'm not actually in France, sir.'

'Go on,' replied Deverall.

'I am in Mauritania with Corporal Baxter, sir,' continued Tim.

'And how's the climbing there?' answered Deverall.

'Sir, it's a disaster. We have found Christian at one of the camps you showed us on that map and it looks like they are about to rip him apart on a primitive rack and film it. The plan was to find him and get him out. We . . . we thought there was a chance he might not be dead and then you told us about the high-profile hostage and we thought it could be him so we came down to see.'

'OK, OK. I see exactly. Which camp are you at?' snapped Deverall.

Tim garbled out the coordinates and Deverall repeated them back to him.

'You are to call me back in precisely ten minutes. I will get things moving this end.'

Derevall's car roared out of the gateway where he had pulled over on a country road. It was 07.56 and he reckoned he could be in the barracks by 8.05. He flicked through his contacts on his phone and dialled.

'It's Deverall, we have a hostage situation. Mauritania, Africa. It's one of our own men. Get everyone, and the PM; we'll need the RAF, too. Priority Desert Red, full fucking alert.'

'Yes, sir, wilco,' replied Major Cornwallis.

In less than two minutes, telephones were ringing all over Stirling Lines and Hereford. Breakfasts were abandoned, cigarettes stubbed out and men were running in all directions. Those living in the barracks were first to make it to the store house where each man had his desert warfare kit neatly laid out in preparation for rapid reaction. Lines of pre-packed desert-camouflaged bergens were arranged in a row, with similar jungle, arctic and NBC packs behind them.

By the time those living locally burst into the stores, three Lynx troop-carrying helicopters had their rotors turning on the parade ground. Of the forty members of D Squadron, only eighteen were present, the minimum acceptable staffing levels for immediate deployment.

They were shouting to each other, desperately asking if anyone knew what was going on. Blank faces all round made everyone think it was just a training exercise.

'If it was a frigging training exercise, it would be three o'fucking clock in the morning, yer twat,' yelled the Beast at the man next to him, while swinging his 80 lb bergen onto his shoulder as if it were made of polystyrene.

'This one is for real,' shouted someone else. 'Otherwise the MOD plod on the gates would have stopped us and wanted to see ID cards.'

As the members of D Squadron piled out of the stores with their bergens on their arms, the sump of Deverall's car thumped loudly into the sleeping policeman between the main gates and the car park. Knowing looks were exchanged by those in earshot as he darted into his office building and up the stairs to the Operations Room. He pushed open the heavy set of double doors, strode inside and made for the large meeting room on his left. A dozen people already present looked up nervously as he shouted to the Communications Officer to get Brize Norton on the phone, then the Prime Minister.

'The priority is to get them into an aircraft and on their way down there. We will then have time to work out the plan. Every second counts,' he shouted.

At that moment, his mobile phone rang.

'Deverall,' he barked.

'Sir, it's Symonds with full sitrep.' Tim sounded nervous and formal.

'Go ahead,' Deverall replied curtly.

'I confirm Corporal Baxter and I are here, sir, and we have visual and verbal contact with Captain McKie. I repeat Captain McKie. He is not dead as believed. He is being held in a cell at the village at 540 397.'

'Go on,' said Deverall.

'We believe there is a strong possibility he may be executed in the very near future and request immediate back-up,' continued Tim.

'How long to do think we have?' snapped Deverall.

'Impossible to say, sir, but it could be any time. They have built some kind of scaffold and it looks like they are going to rack him first. They have a winch and some cable,' Tim said, panic in his voice.

'What? What do you mean, "rack him"?' replied Deverall.

'It looks like they have built a giant rack to torture him with, sir.'

The colour in Deverall's face drained away. He paused.

'Sir?' said Tim, wondering if Deverall was still there.

'I'm here,' said Deverall quietly. 'Right, I need you and Baxter to watch and let me know exactly what happens. You need to let me know if they get close to starting anything nasty. This is now official, and so are you. A team is on the way but it could take six hours. You need to hold on. I want you to call me in thirty minutes with as much info on the place, numbers, weapons, you know, vehicles, etc., as possible.'

'Yes, sir, thank you, sir,' answered Tim.

Even in the time Deverall had been talking to Tim, more staff had flooded into the Operations Room. Desks filled and screens were alive with images and data. Anxious-looking people communicated in short concise language, all trying to bring up as much information on Mauritania as possible. The political liaison desk talked to the French and Moroccans about troops flying through their airspace, the transport and logistics group frantically analysed satellite imagery of the area and looked for aircraft landing sites while a lone meteorologist assessed the likely winds and ground temperatures.

Deverall stood up and stepped back in the Operations Room, now a buzzing hive of activity. Cornwallis appeared through the double doors and approached him.

'Sir, we have eighteen D en route to Brize. I have been onto them personally and have the G4 waiting on standby. We'll have them out of our airspace within half an hour. Could be ready to insert at around one p.m. our time,' he said.

'OK, OK, this is bloody strange stuff,' Deverall replied, quietly enough so only Cornwallis could hear.

'Sir, it's very strange.' Cornwallis looked uncomfortable. 'My understanding was that McKie was confirmed dead. It's great news but we are now piling in eighteen-plus guys into a nest of vipers in broad daylight, sir. We have not planned this and there is only so much I can brief Major Day over the aircraft radio. We really are going in blind.'

'Well, yes and no. We do have eyes on the place with Baxter and Symonds. This is a fuck-up from start to finish.' Deverall sighed.

'Sir, you knew they were going?' replied Cornwallis, looking perplexed.

Deverall strode towards the meeting room, gesturing to Cornwallis to follow. He closed the door and checked the phone was not on intercom.

'The fact is I have thought from the day we got back from Barras that something was wrong. Surely you could feel it too?' he said earnestly.

Cornwallis nodded. 'Well, yes, sir, we certainly never got the full picture, did we?'

'The fact is that something happened in that village and someone knows the truth. Carter, Symonds and

Baxter all knocked out verbatim reports, then we hear from GCHQ about the chatter and the high-profile hostage but no one's missing anyone. You have to agree it's all very fishy, or what? So, I sowed a seed and let the three musketeers have a little information just to see what they would do. Within twenty-four hours, Baxter and Symonds are asking for leave. What a surprise, they took the bait.'

'OK, this is starting to make sense.' Cornwallis nodded, the beginnings of a smile on his face.

'I reckoned,' continued Deverall, lowering his voice conspiratorially, 'that we couldn't send anyone down there officially because we aren't missing anyone officially, and that I could get Baxter and Symonds to do the job on the basis that they'd know what did or didn't happen to McKie.'

'I like it, sir, and in their own time, too,' interjected Cornwallis.

'Exactly,' said Deverall, with a wag of his finger. 'But what I didn't bargain for was a phone call saying they are about to chop McKie's head off at any moment. I reckoned they would get back and somehow let me know if they found anything without putting themselves in the frame.'

'Well, at least they are there, otherwise we wouldn't have a clue, would we?' replied Cornwallis.

'True, but the one card we still have to play is our friends the Yanks. When there is the possibility of a rotten apple in the barrel, I thought it might be best to outsource. There's always a US frigate in that part of the world and I did warn Admiral Farraday we might need some Seals and a couple of helis at short notice. Problem is, I was not expecting a village load of thugs, daylight and the threat of our boy being tortured.'

'Tortured?' The smile left Cornwallis's face.

'I don't know exactly, but Symonds said they have built some kind of scaffold and may use it . . .' Deverall's voice tailed off. 'We need more information from Symonds and Baxter. I don't want anyone panicking just yet. First we need to brief the Americans and find out exactly what they've got in the area. Farraday said there's always a frigate round there that carries a couple of Black Hawks and a Navy Seal team. The problem is going to be distance and numbers. It's a long way for the helicopters and it's not really fair to expect six or eight Seals to take on upwards of eighty terrorists on home bloody ground, however good they are,' Deverall said gravely.

There was a knock on the door and a balding head appeared.

Major Bury glanced inside and spoke. 'Sir, D are nearly at Brize Norton. We've got a packet of information waiting there for them. It's good sat images of the village, surroundings, etc., so they'll have something to read on the flight. Also, USS *Pindar* is on alert and scrambling everything she's got. We still don't quite know what she has got, but should do soon. Farraday sends his best wishes too, sir.'

'Thanks, Nick. And thank God for the bloody Americans,' replied Deverall, giving him an encouraging nod.

Once the door closed Cornwallis spoke again.

'So, what are we going to do if these guys start on McKie before we get anyone down there?'

'Fuck only knows.' Deverall shook his head and inhaled sharply. 'In theory, we already have men on the ground. But I can't send in two guys, otherwise we really will end up in the shit.'

As Deverall and Cornwallis made their way back into the Operations Room, the eighteen members of D Squadron were piling out of the back of the Lynxes and running across the tarmac at Brize Norton.

'That aircraft, there, the G4,' yelled a man in a green boiler suit, pointing at a small white jet with its engines already roaring.

They covered the 80 yards at a full sprint and bundled themselves up the steps and into the stripped-out interior of the aircraft. There were basic plastic seats down each side and where the central aisle would have been on a normal aeroplane, was a row of parachute packs. Before the men had even sat down, the door was shutting and Major Day had his head in the cockpit telling the pilots to get going.

Ignoring every flight procedure ever written, the aircraft pulled forward abruptly, sending a couple of guys in the back falling over the parachutes, cut straight across an area of grass and took off the wrong way down the main runway. Once airborne, and when the whoops of excitement had settled down, the G4 banked steeply and set off, at maximum cruising speed, for Africa.

Jamie twitched with nerves when Tim wriggled back into position next to him.

'So what did he say?' he asked aggressively. 'Are we in the shit? He must be fucking furious. He'd probably just bomb the whole bloody place with napalm if Christi wasn't here.'

'Well, actually he sounded OK,' replied Tim breathlessly.

'Did he? What, you mean, not too fucked off?'

'He said we have to hold on and report back every detail we can see, and that a team is already on the way, but might take six hours—' continued Tim.

'And what . . . ?' interrupted Jamie, folding back a piece of the groundsheet so he could see Tim's face.

'We have to phone back in half an hour with more info – you know, numbers, the usual shit. And, it's now official and so are we, which helps, doesn't it?'

'It's not going to make much difference if this lot see us, is it?' Jamie replied, sounding panicked.

'Man, we just have to stay put, keep low and report in, just like we normally do. This is now a normal operation,' said Tim.

'There's nothing normal about this bloody .375. Where's the grenade launcher, my M16 and the other half of the patrol? This is all Sam bloody Carter's fault. Without him, none of this would be happening,' Jamie hissed, sounding scared and angry.

'Just go with it. We need to keep calm and watch the place, like usual,' said Tim. He sounded confident.

Half an hour later, Tim still lay next to Jamie. He switched on the sat phone and dialled Deverall's number. Cornwallis answered.

'Tim, good, now how is everything? I need to know exactly what you can see and what your precise position is,' he said.

Tim spent the next five minutes describing their position on the ridge, the numbers of men in the village, the helicopter and the layout and depth of the dry river bed. Cornwallis ended the call, telling him to ring back with any other relevant facts as they occurred.

Cornwallis repeated the details to an intelligence officer who immediately started adjusting the aerial-view sketch of the village and surrounding area which he was drawing on a large map table.

Deverall was back in the meeting room, pacing around nervously, telephone in one hand, coffee in the other.

31

By the time Farq slid his breakfast under the bars into his cell, Christian was in a near frenzy of anticipation. Something different was going on and he could feel the tension. Farq looked ultra nervous, the machine tools were going full blast outside and Jamie and Tim were lurking in the sand dunes nearby. Something had to happen.

Once he had forced himself to eat his stew and drink as much water as he could, he lit his penultimate cigarette. He pushed the lighter into the top of his cycling shorts for safe keeping.

As the Gulfstream 4 reached the French coast, a French Eurofighter Typhoon appeared and circled the aircraft once, before locking in just behind as an escort. Inside, the soldiers scrabbled around, going through their kit and checking their weapons. They were similarly armed as on the operation in Sierra Leone, except in lighter-coloured desert combat clothing with matching body armour.

Major Day appeared from the cockpit and raised his hand for quiet.

'Listen up,' he said. 'I've got a load more information through, including some basic images of the village. As you know, there is nothing ordinary about this job, but this is really going to surprise the living fuck out of you.'

With blank faces all round, he paused to savour the moment, then carried on.

'Well, even you lot may have guessed we are off to rescue a hostage.' He paused again, looking round.

'But you're not fucking going to believe this,' said Day, shaking his head and taking a deep breath.

'Come on, sir, who is it, Maggie Thatcher?' shouted someone from the back of the cabin.

Day waved his finger in a mock show of authority. Still shaking his head and breathing heavily, he spoke again.

'It's Christian McKie. Our lad, Christian. He's not dead and it's definitely him.'

A split second of silence was taken over by an almighty roar as the realisation swept around the room.

'Yup, it's Christian and what's more, the reason we know it's him is because Baxter and Symonds are already down there and have seen him.'

The stunned expressions changed to those of total bewilderment. Men exchanged glances and shook their heads.

'No, it's not my idea of a sick joke,' continued Day, 'it's true and we are off to get him, well, all of them, out of there. But, there is more to it than that.'

After a second of silence, a huge roar of elation erupted from everyone in the aircraft. The pilots turned around in their seats with huge grins on their faces as the men of D Squadron whooped and hollered, punching the air and hugging each other.

Major Day was pleased to have a moment to compose himself before raising his hand and shouting for calm.

'But, listen up, lads, there is more to this,' he said, but still no one was listening. They were all shouting questions and comments to each other.

'Only a bloody Scott like McKie could get shot up somewhere like that and make it out,' yelled the Beast.

'He's not Scottish, he lives in Hampshire, you Glaswegian tit,' replied Day to a roar of approval.

The Beast's retort was drowned out by more questions and the slapping sounds of high fives.

Day tried again to speak and, finally, was successful.

'Listen, guys, this is not going to be as easy as it sounds.'

The noise in the cabin resumed to a level where he could be heard. Day explained the full situation, the fact that Christian could be brutally executed any second and that Jamie and Tim were there unofficially, with all the wrong kit.

Just as soon as it arrived, the carnival atmosphere abated. Day walked down the middle of aircraft distributing a sheet of paper to each man showing a rough map of the village. The lines of houses were shown along with key points such as Christian's cell and Jamie and Tim's position.

With one hand pressing against the roof of the cabin to steady himself, Day started to run through the battle plan.

'We have practised this sort of thing a thousand times, but there is no such thing as routine or planning once these things are on for real. In about four and a half hours, we will be at twenty-two thousand feet over the village and out the rear door – HALO [high altitude, low opening] descent in four-man clusters for 1.5 minutes in free fall, and pulling the chutes at eight hundred feet like normal.

'We will group up on the north side of the ridge,' he said, stabbing a finger at the map, 'where we should be out of sight of the village. We will be behind Baxter and Symonds and able to move over the ridge onto the target. The fact is they will only know we are coming when we pull the chutes, but we will be out of sight once we hit the ground.'

Day paused and looked around at the faces of his men.

'I will allocate you into units in a minute but I want

to cover the high-level battle plan first,' he continued. 'I want the specialist sniper team of three to get to the top of the ridge asap along with the two Minimis. I want the snipers taking out anyone they can see and the two Minimis putting down so much automatic fire that they shit themselves. I will then lead the rest round via the river bed to the middle of the village. We punch through some of the alleys between the houses and then move to left and right in two groups, clearing as we go.'

He glanced around to see nodding faces and carried on.

'These guys are not expecting us but from what I hear they are all armed, some will be pro or semi-pro and there will be a splattering of loonies who will be unpredictable. There are also two Europeans in there that we need alive if possible. These two appear to be in charge and they are looking to give Christian the chop and may film it for some reason we would like to get to the bottom of. I don't want this to cloud your judgement, but they have built some kind of rack with a winch and may be planning on torturing Christi first.'

Cursing broke out as eyes narrowed and hands tightened around weapons.

'I knew you wouldn't like that,' said Day, still standing in the middle of the cabin. 'Right, I'm now going to allocate you into groups and specific roles. Just one more thing: there are a couple of Black Hawks with about ten US Rangers or Seals on board heading for the area. If things get going before we get there, they may be sent in as they are a lot closer than us. The only thing is they have to refuel somewhere on the way, which won't be easy. Also, there will only be ten of them max, which, good lads as they are, could be a bit rough against eighty plus. But anyway, we'll have more info later.'

As Day meandered his way through the piles of kit, back along the cabin towards the cockpit, two UH-60 Black Hawk helicopters crossed the Mauritanian coastline flying fast and low. In each helicopter were two pilots, a gunner and a ground assault team of five. Captain Dwight Rodriguez of the US Navy Seals was in command of both groups. A small, dark-haired man of Hispanic origin, he was briefing his men simultaneously in both helicopters over the radio.

'We have an ETA of two point five hours' fly time, excluding a fuel stop at a destination still to be ascertained,' he said, looking at a map.

The men in his helicopter nodded, looking down at the hand-drawn maps of the village they had each been handed as they piled aboard. Rodriguez continued to talk over the radio while the Seals carried on checking their weapons and adjusting their kit. Under an hour ago, most had been either asleep or playing volleyball in beach shorts on the deck of USS *Pindar*.

'This is not, I repeat not, going to be anything like what we normally do,' Rodriguez continued. 'The Admiral says this guy is going to get it from the terrorists, but we are looking pretty outnumbered and have orders only to go on in if things look OK.'

'Sir, how many terrorists are there?' replied one of the Seals, raising a hand to speak.

'We reckon there could be as many as eighty, armed and dangerous,' said Rodriguez. 'But we may find a couple of birds in the sky is enough to send most of them running; who knows till we get there? But we need fuel first. We're not going to get there just to run out of gas.'

32

Christian heard more vehicles arriving. Several four-wheel drives parked immediately outside his window and he could see the faces of the men inside. They seemed like local Arabs in long coloured shirts and baggy trousers. The common denominator was that they all looked excited and carried guns. As the latest arrivals disappeared from his view, he heard voices and then footsteps in the courtyard outside.

To stop his hands shaking, he gripped the bars of the cell. The metal door clanged open and Mo appeared with Farq and the two South Africans. Christian immediately detected a change in atmosphere from the last time he had seen them.

Conrad Lennep and Martin Roote stepped into the building with very different expressions on their faces.

'Handcuff him, now,' Lennep said to Farq, in his clipped South African accent.

'What the hell's going on?' shouted Christian.

'You, shut up if you know what's good for you,' Lennep barked at Christian.

Christian turned to Mo.

'What, what? When am I being released?' gasped Christian.

'I said, shut up,' yelled Lennep. Before Christian had a chance to think, he found himself staring down the barrel of Roote's machine pistol.

Christian descended into a spin of confusion and panic. He had not been convinced by these two men in the first place and yet it had been easiest and most comforting to him to believe what they said. He thought of going for the commando knife, but could not see the point with a gun pointing straight at him. He felt hands grab his arms and push him hard against the rear wall of the cell.

With his hands secured in metal cuffs behind his back, Christian's vision blurred with fear. Lennep held the chain between the cuffs with one hand and gripped Christian around the neck with the other, to frog-march him out of the cell and into the bright sunlight of the courtyard. Christian was in a state of overload. A tiny piece of him thought that maybe Lennep and Roote were for real and simply employing heavy-handed tactics to make sure they had full control of the situation. He knew hostages could mess things up for their liberators and had to be controlled, but this was going too far. His next thought was of Jamie and Tim. Where were they and what on earth were they doing now? Surely they would be nearby and doing something to help?

Farq pulled open the outer door of the courtyard and Lennep thrust Christian through with such force that he lost his footing and bashed his bad shoulder into the wall. The shock of the pain snapped him out of his stunned state of panic. He looked around and saw a sea of local militia men, all staring and pointing, some laughing or jeering.

He clung to the thought that Lennep and Roote might be manhandling him roughly to please the crowd. The thought was soon dispelled as the crowd parted to form a corridor, leading to a wooden platform that he had not seen before but now realised he had heard being built. Still not sure what was going on, he felt Lennep yank the handcuffs sharply upwards, making him lean forward to the point he was bent double. His next feeling was his chest crashing into the side of the wooden platform and someone swinging his legs up.

Lennep stepped up onto the platform and hauled Christian towards the centre, under the beam. Christian found himself in a kneeling position, looking around wildly at a sea of faces only a few metres from him – some chanting, others clapping their hands.

Lennep and Roote stood either side and raised their hands for calm. Once the jeering and shouting had died down, Mo joined them and spoke in Arabic. He pointed at Christian and talked quietly at first. The crowd listened. Mo walked around the platform, wagging his finger aggressively as he spoke. He then turned to Christian and spoke in English.

'You have come to our country,' he said, in a bitter but controlled way, 'to kill, steal and rape. But things are different now and you will answer any question and you will explain to me and everyone here who you are, how you operate and everything we wish to know about your Special Forces. We will show the world that you are not so special and, when we have finished with you, you will beg me for death.'

He turned back to the crowd and carried on his rhetoric with increasing volume and gesticulation. Christian was so shocked and scared that he could only think of one thing: be the grey man. Don't be tough, don't be hard, look scared and make Mo feel big and important. He looked at the wooden planks in front of him and tried to keep his balance. Sweat ran down his face into his eyes and dripped from his chin. His shook visibly and he felt he was likely to be sick. In the background, he heard either Lennep or Roote telling him to keep still. Above him was a thick wooden beam and a metal coil. He needed no imagination to know they were there for his benefit.

Where the hell were Jamie and Tim? He looked up and over the crowd. Little did he know that the cross-hairs in the sights of Armalite's .375 buffalo rifle were squared up in the middle of Lennep's face.

Jamie's finger rested gently on the trigger as Tim whispered, 'A head shot's too good for that wanker.'

'Yeah, I'll blow his guts out instead,' Jamie replied, slightly lowering his aim.

'Don't forget that's a very heavy bullet, it's going to drop a bit over four hundred yards,' said Tim, staring through his binoculars.

'You call Cornwallis and tell him what's going on. Tell him we can see Christian and they need to get a bloody move on. And the Yanks, too,' replied Jamie.

While Tim updated Cornwallis on the sat phone, Jamie scanned the scene before him through the rifle sight. He could count at least a hundred armed men and thirty vehicles in total. Christian was still in the kneeling position and the two Europeans held him in place. As he watched, the Arab addressing the crowd was handed a video camera, which he placed on the tripod.

'The Squadron are still over Southern France, won't be here for at least four hours and the Yanks are two hours away. So that leaves us,' said Tim.

'OK, OK, but tell me what benefit is there to filming all of this,' Jamie whispered as Tim slipped back into position beside him.

'Hard to say, but they are probably going to need evidence of what they are doing. Whoever is paying for all this is going to want something to prove they've had an SAS man and that it's all genuine,' replied Tim.

'It's bloody outrageous, one way or another, this whole thing has been about money. We wouldn't have been here without those fucking diamonds, and now this. These fuckers are going to sell the film to the highest bidder and then claim they can kidnap anyone they want,' continued Jamie, sounding furious.

'Well, as they say, mate, who pays the piper . . .' replied Tim.

Mo looked into the viewfinder on the video camera and signalled he was about to start filming. Lennep and Roote rolled down their shirtsleeves, pulled shemaghs around their faces and put on sunglasses, as did some of the crowd.

Mo moved into view of the camera and started to speak, first in Arabic and then in English. He spoke slowly and deliberately to make sure his words were not muffled by the shemagh covering his face. He pointed to Christian who was still kneeling, staring at the floor once again.

'Tell us your name and confirm you serve with the British SAS,' he said, 'and you will raise your head and address your words to the camera.'

After a short pause, Christian looked up.

'McKie, Welsh Guards, 231609, sir,' he replied.

Hardly had he uttered the last digit of his ID number when the butt of Lennep's pistol crashed into the side of his head, sending him spinning onto the floorboards. With stars dancing before his eyes, he was grabbed by Roote and pulled back into position. Blood oozed from his temple and right eyebrow. The crowd roared with approval.

Jamie and Tim exchanged agonised glances.

Tim spoke. 'If they start on him too badly, we are going in, aren't we?'

'They nearly knocked him out just then. We have hours of this to go until the others get here. He just needs to sit tight and say the right thing for as long as he can. Every second is crucial,' replied Jamie.

'Yes, but it may come to it,' Tim continued.

'Of course, I know it. I'm not going to lie here with a ringside view of Christi being thrashed by these motherfuckers. But he is a tough bastard and we need to hold off until—'

'Until when?' interjected Tim.

'Until . . . until it looks like it's getting properly nasty. It might take ages for them to build up, you know,' replied Jamie.

'I know, but if it gets too rough, you are going to need to open up on the place and I will sneak in round the side and get him out.'

'Fabulous, truly inspired. How the hell do you come up with plans like that, Mr Bloody Desert Fox? So much for the "Let's pop down there for a quick recce shit",' said Jamie sarcastically, with a nervous grin.

33

Mo stood immediately in front of Christian with a pistol in his hand.

'Since you arrived here, I have made sure you have had everything you needed. You have been fed, had water and cigarettes, and had medical treatment. You will cooperate with me now or else I will have no alternative but to allow these two gentlemen to do their job with you. I don't want any of the name, rank, serial number shit. I need facts about you, the SAS and their connections with both MI6 and the CIA. I want to know about covert operations in Columbia, the Middle East, every theatre of operation. We will discuss training, weapons, intelligence and interrogation techniques. I want names, places, addresses, moles, safe houses. There won't be a secret left. The mystique of the SAS will be broken once and for all.'

With the blow to his head, combined with the noise

of the shouting crowd, Christian had trouble hearing what Mo was saying. He turned to look at Mo and made to say something but felt so dizzy and confused that no words came out.

'I think it may be time for you to see a little of what our friends here have in store for you,' Mo said, waving his hand towards Lennep.

Christian swayed on his knees and looked into the crowd. He saw a blur of faces, some of whom he partially recognised from the training on the ranges. He half expected to see Jamie and Tim among them. Then he heard a bizarre, high-pitched squealing. He looked around and saw to his amazement a large pig being dragged onto the platform by four men.

'What the hell are they doing now?' whispered Tim to Jamie.

'God only knows, but . . . this is getting sicker by the second,' Jamie replied, squinting into his rifle sight.

As they both looked on, ropes were tied around each of the pig's legs as it thrashed and kicked, letting out the most hideous squealing noises. With a struggle, the four men managed to link up the two ends of the ropes to the ring on the floor and the other two ends to the steel cable. Roote signalled to someone and the winch on the front of the pick-up started to turn slowly. Within a few seconds the pig was suspended spread-eagled in the air, diarrhoea pouring from its back end.

With Roote now holding a pistol to the back of Christian's head, Lennep raised his hands for quiet. The crowd ceased shouting and yelling. Christian detected a change in mood and could see that some among them looked as shocked and confused as he felt.

Lennep spoke. 'Listen here, McKie, the anatomy of a pig is very similar to that of a human. They are intelligent animals and strong, too. You are now going to see what will happen to you. The more information you give us, the quicker this will be for you. That's the deal.'

With that, he pointed to the winch. There was an electrical whirring as the motor turned. The metal coil became tense and started to stretch the pig. It writhed and bellowed. Christian looked on in horror as the pig tried to twist and turn. He could see some men in the crowd had their hands over their mouths while others hollered in delight. Some taunted Christian, pointing at the pig and then at him.

Lennep signalled to the man on the winch to ease the pressure and then he turned to Christian.

'I can assure you I have done this before and can make it last anything up to two days. That's my personal best. It's amazing what a man will say when every tendon and ligament in his body is at breaking point. There is nothing in your training that can prepare you for this.'

He moved towards Christian and carried on.

'You think interrogation involves being without sleep, hungry and being in a stress position for a few hours, don't you? You know, a couple of your own guys from Intelligence in Chinese uniforms trying to freak you out.'

Lennep laughed and turned to Roote. 'We do things a little differently in our part of the world, don't we, mate?'

Roote laughed too and said, 'That's right. And working on an SAS man could be good. It'll make some great footage having you denounce everything you have ever stood for and believed in. And what's more, no one is ever going to know quite what we did to you, why you talked. You'll just look like we roughed you up a bit and you told us the lot. Nothing heroic about that.'

Christian stared at the ground and wished he had used the knife when he'd had the chance. He started to reckon that Jamie and Tim had most likely left the area and gone off to summon help. He saw Sam's face once again and wished he had just put the bullet straight in his head and been spared all this. To all intents and purposes, he had been a dead man from the moment Sam shot him. The double tap to the head would have been much simpler for everyone involved.

Christian looked up and tried to make eye contact with Mo who was standing at the side of the platform. Mo avoided his eyes but Christian detected a feeling of shame. As Lennep stretched the pig for a second time, Christian looked around for Farq, who was nowhere to be seen.

This time the pig writhed and thrashed even more wildly. It let out a blood-chilling whine as the ropes strained. Christian saw the pick-up truck slide an inch or two in the dust due to the strain. Lennep shouted to some of the crowd to get in the back to weigh it down. Black veins appeared all over the pig's body as the tension increased. Its eyes bulged and blood poured from its mouth, ears and nose.

Christian shook his head and yelled at Lennep, 'I think you have made your point, but you'll find that the pig doesn't know much about the covert operations of the CIA.'

Lennep turned to Christian and smiled menacingly. 'So you can talk,' he bellowed over the desperate squeals

Christian knew Lennep had won this point but was hoping for another bang on the head to get him to the point where he might be unconscious and have proceedings delayed. It did not work. Lennep signalled to the man on the winch to increase the power. The squeals became even more horrendous, to the point where Christian could see that some of the crowd had drifted away.

The pig was now about half as much longer than its natural shape. Its formerly low-hanging belly was now a similar width to its head. The feeling of horror was quite unbearable and increased by clearly audible popping and snapping noises coming from the pig's body. To make things worse, Lennep stood by with a matter-of-fact look on his face, as if he were carrying out a daily chore.

After a few more minutes, Lennep started to wander around the platform like an entertainer. He invited a man from the crowd to step up and feel the tension in the pig's body. A young man in tatty combat trousers and an ancient US Army issue flak jacket willingly accepted the offer. Clearly enjoying the attention, he looked on with a twisted fascination as Lennep offered him a knife. Then Lennep pointed to a part of the pig's back leg and instructed his new apprentice to stick in the knife.

The pig flinched as the tiny tear in the skin tore open and became a huge gash due to the tension. Lennep turned to Christian.

'We have not even started yet, you know. And this is in fast forward, just to show you what's in store for you,' he said, with a sarcastically pleasant tone. 'This pig will suffer about five per cent of what's coming your way. I have worked out the secret to this. It's making sure the pig doesn't have a heart attack.'

Christian had no idea what to say or do. He could feel Roote standing right beside him but there was no point trying to make a break for it as no one was going to shoot him and ruin all the fun. He just tried to switch off his mind and pray this was just some elaborate mind game. But the more he concentrated, the more alive his senses became. He could feel the heat of the African morning, the sounds of the pig and the crowd were deafening, his knees hurt from kneeling, as did his shoulder from being bent behind his back. Time had slowed, forcing him to experience his surroundings in an enhanced way.

Through the barrage of noise and trauma, Christian identified what sounded like approaching vehicles. He glanced up and saw Mo looking up and over the heads of the crowd. A glimmer of hope flickered in his mind. New arrivals could somehow help or cause some delay or distraction. He turned to look as the engines got louder. Lennep looked up too.

The crowd were also aware of approaching vehicles but seemed more interested in the convulsing pig. Christian's tiny moment of hope was short lived as he caught a glimpse of more local militia turning up, no doubt to enjoy the spectacle. Mo waved enthusiastically to a huge fat black man in military uniform standing in the turret of an armoured US Humvee. Next in the convoy were two armoured personnel carriers with faded UN paintwork still visible down the sides. These vehicles were followed by more dusty pick-ups and Land Cruisers. Christian stared at the ground again. The Humvee pulled up next to the wooden platform, allowing the man in the turret a bird's-eye view.

'Who the hell's that?' said Jamie, turning to Tim.

'Looks like Rommel meets Idi Amin,' replied Tim.

'More Boss Hogg meets Idi Amin,' retorted Jamie. 'That looks like a .50-cal on top of the Humvee and those APCs are fully bloody armoured. These guys look like the local army, not a bunch of trainee terrorists.'

'Shit, this is getting worse and worse,' hissed Tim. 'I'd better let Deverall know.'

'Tell him there are now about a hundred fighting personnel, they have armour and a fully mobile .50-cal. He's not going to like it.'

Tim flipped round the aerial on the sat phone and dialled. Cornwallis answered instantly. Tim relayed the details, unaware he was on loudspeaker to the whole of the Operations Room. When he mentioned the pig, there were gasps of shock from the Intelligence staff.

'Just hold on; just hold on as long as you possibly can. Our team are well into Morocco and should be with you sooner than we thought, around two hours,' said Cornwallis.

'What about the Seals, sir? I thought they were going to be here a bit sooner,' Tim answered nervously.

'Well, as I said, they need aviation fuel and that's not easy to come by. We reckon D may be with you first. It just depends,' replied Cornwallis.

'Yes, sir, I understand, sir.'

Back on the platform, Christian was trying to get a feeling of who the new arrivals were. He was careful not to make any eye contact with the fat guy poking out of the turret of the Humvee, but guessed he had to be a local bigwig. Mo talked to him in a familiar way. Neither man seemed bothered that their relaxed banter was conducted over the agonised squeals of the pig. Christian's mind was on the point of overload when to his astonishment a scruffy young man appeared with a tray and passed up a small glass of tea to Mo's new arrival.

The man looked pleased and gestured to Lennep to continue. The brief interval was over and Lennep set to work once more.

'We have two hours to go,' said Tim to Jamie.

'That's too long,' Jamie replied, turning his head slightly to look at Tim. 'They are not going to stretch that pig any further. When it dies, they are going to start on Christian. The pig is going to last twenty minutes max. Let's face it, the guys aren't going to get here in time, are they?'

Tim paused before replying. He took a deep breath and said in a resigned way, 'This is pretty much suicide.' He wiped the sweat from his eyes and continued: 'Mate, you know neither of us can lie up here and watch them rack Christi. We put him there and it's our fault, every bit of it. No point blaming Sam now.'

There was another pause before Jamie replied.

'Well, I think it was Wellington who said he would rather die in glory than live in shame.'

'Listen,' replied Tim, 'I'm going to get my arse down into the river bed and get round to the back of the houses. No one is going to see me as they watch the bloody circus. If it looks like they are going to start on Christian, I want you to start taking out key targets from up here. I'll give them a full magazine and a couple of grenades, then slip into the mayhem and get Christi into a vehicle. You keep putting the rounds down and then leg it while you can. Radios on now.'

Before Jamie had time to reply, Tim was crawling back over the top of the ridge with his grab-sack. He disappeared from view briefly and then Jamie saw him making his way along the dry river bed towards the houses.

Jamie pumped with adrenalin. He felt alone and guilty that Tim had taken on the more dangerous role. He knew he was probably the better sniper and that Tim would stand out less than a man of six-foot-six with a fake suntan, but still he felt bad. He could feel his hands shaking and his heart beating, both of which would hinder his aim.

34

Lennep continued to make small strategic incisions in the writhing pig. The winch whirred, the overhead beam creaked and the crowd roared. Christian found it hard to breathe as the pig stretched still further. Its head twitched and its tiny eyes bulged. The flow of blood from its mouth, nose and ears dripped onto the wooden boards and formed a crimson pool. To the delight of the crowd, blood started to drip from its anus, too. More popping and tearing noises came from inside the animal.

'Now, this is the best bit,' yelled Lennep, starting to look enthusiastic about his work. He placed the knife between the pig's hind legs and cut a straight line up to the base of its ribcage. He paused theatrically before cutting another shorter incision across the pig's belly. He only just had time to jump back to avoid the guts and stomach as they exploded out of the pig's body. The pig squealed its most harrowing note yet.

Christian felt panic and could taste the smell of fresh guts. The pig was far from dead and still thrashing wildly.

'We could play with this pig for another hour,' Lennep said, waving his hands for quiet. 'But I don't want to delay things too long. As I said, this is just a warm-up.'

Still talking to the crowd, Lennep produced a small can of lighter fuel from his pocket. The pig's guts hung from its body and some parts lay in a gory pile on the floorboards.

'These guts and stomach are still all alive and fully functioning. You could push then back inside, sew up the pig and it would survive – crazy really, but true,' he said.

Lennep sprayed the pig's intestines with lighter fuel, produced a lighter and set fire to them. The flames were hard to see in the bright sunlight but the reaction was extreme. The pig let out the most horrific noise Christian had ever heard, while its body shook violently. The guts sizzled in their own fat and gave off the smell of cooking sausages.

Lennep eyed Christian and said, 'About five per cent of what we can do with you. And don't forget no one will know why you talked. They will just know that you did.'

With that, Lennep drew his pistol and shot the pig through the head.

Jamie pulled the mouthpiece of his radio to his mouth. 'Fucking hell, they have shot the pig and . . . and . . . get a move on,' he gasped.

Tim replied in a breathless gasp, 'I guessed that was what the shot was. Nearly there.'

Jamie saw Tim emerge from a narrow piece of river bed about 100 yards to the rear of the houses. He stood up and walked purposefully across an open area of ground to the rear of the closest house.

As Tim disappeared from Jamie's view between two buildings, Lennep pushed his pistol into the holster on his belt and began cutting down the ghoulish remains of the pig with his knife. The guts smouldered and continued to cook in their own fat.

Knowing his time was coming, Christian felt light-headed with fear. He was sure the cuffs would have to come off if they were going to rack him like the pig. This would be his moment. He would go for the knife and hope to get shot in the scuffle that would ensue. With this thought in mind, something caught his eye. Tim was standing there in the crowd on the opposite side of the platform. He leant casually against the side of the Humvee and stared intently at Christian to get his attention. As Christian focused on him, he pulled his shemagh briefly away from this face and mouthed the word 'grenade' several times. Then he winked. With that, he pulled up his shemagh and discreetly pulled his mouthpiece down to a speaking position.

Christian jolted with surprise. This was the ultimate close-quarters recce. His next thought was Jamie. If Tim was standing there, where was Jamie? Christian looked around in the crowd, knowing that Jamie would be at least a head taller than anyone else. Then he clicked. Jamie could not be seen as he would stand out far too obviously. He would be in the background as the fire support team.

The elongated body of the pig crashed onto the floorboards, its head lolling lifelessly. Lennep turned to Roote and nodded. With the help of two of Mo's guards, Roote hauled Christian to his feet. With his hands still secured in the cuffs, they tied a length of rope to each of Christian's wrists. A guard holding each rope, Roote unlocked the cuffs. Christian's arms were immediately pulled out sideways and gripped by the guards.

The crowd roared their approval as the guards started to pull Christian forward. Instinctively, he pulled back, and several things seemed to happen at once. A grenade landed with a thud in the middle of the wooden platform, the side lever upright in the detonation position. Tim bellowed the word 'GRENAAAADE', Jamie squeezed the trigger of the .375 and Christian's world crashed into blurred slow motion.

Before anyone even heard the shot, a large-calibre bullet capable of felling a charging buffalo hit Roote in the side of the head just above the ear, the impact lifting him off his feet. His body landed in the front row of the crowd, his head, minus eyeballs and brains, dropped more or less where he had been standing on the platform.

All eyes fixed on the grenade still spinning on the centre of the platform. Then total bedlam broke out as everyone turned and dived for cover. Having removed the primer, Tim knew the grenade would not explode and confidently stood his ground. As his adversaries hit the deck, he opened up on the screaming and writhing men with a full magazine of the AK. He tore a 60-degree arc of fire before flicking off the empty magazine and replacing it with a full one that he had tucked under his arm.

Jamie had intended to get Lennep with his next shot, but by the time he had snapped the chamber shut and repositioned the rifle, his target was out of sight. He moved the rifle a fraction and fired again at the one remaining guard still hanging onto one of the ropes attached to Christian. The man folded instantly, leaving Christian free.

Christian whipped the commando knife out of his trousers and leapt from the platform into the heap of men still scrabbling around on the ground. One man still standing grabbed the rope attached to Christian. The .375 boomed again and Christian continued on

279

his way through the mêlée, desperately making his way to the pick-up truck with the winch. Just as he approached the vehicle, a large bearded man in Arab headdress slammed shut the driver's door and turned the keys in the ignition. As the engine started, a small hole appeared in the windscreen, followed by the boom of the .375. The driver slumped forwards. Christian tore open the door, pushed the man across towards the passenger seat and leapt in, still trailing the ropes from his wrists.

Tim had fired off the second magazine in short coordinated bursts. Men lay all over the place, dead or screaming from their wounds. Less than ten seconds had passed since Tim had lobbed the unprimed grenade in the air, but already he could feel the edge of the surprise beginning to fade. Some men had reached the safety of buildings and adopted defensive positions behind walls and vehicles. The more experienced had their guns ready, looking for targets. Mo and Lennep crouched by the one of the APCs, their pistols drawn.

Christian slammed the pick-up into reverse and pressed his foot to the floor. The vehicle lurched backwards, pulling the remains of the pig up and over the beam. Christian could not see Tim but knew roughly where he would be. He crunched the vehicle into first and roared forwards and around the side of the platform. Tim still fired as he moved backwards away from the Humvee, making his way to the alley between the houses. Christian swung around towards him and hit the brakes. Tim saw his chance and made a lunge towards the open back of the pick-up. As his raised his leg to jump, Lennep appeared around the side of the APC with his gun raised. Christian did not hear the shots but saw Tim hit in the head and chest. His body crashed to the ground, lifeless. With bullets slamming into the vehicle all around him, Christian pushed his foot against the accelerator and slipped down as low as he could in his seat. The pick-up revved to the red line and careered along the row of houses.

Jamie pressed his eye against the sight and fired. He had to keep the mayhem going as long as possible The bullet missed Lennep. Knowing he only had two more bullets for the .375, he took one more shot without looking to see if he had hit anything. He then saw a man in a green army uniform appear on top of the Humvee and lower the barrel of the .50-cal. Jamie fired and missed. Taking this as an omen to get going, he reached for his grab-sack and leapt to his feet, flinging off the groundsheet and camouflaging debris. Rounds from the .50-cal tore up the ground 20 feet in front of him as he bounded up the rise and over the crest of the ridge.

Christian raised his head just enough to see where he was going through the shattered, blood-spattered windscreen and slipped the groaning engine into third. He saw the last house in the row flit past and then sat up to start driving properly. The unmade sandy road bent round to the right and cut through some sand dunes. He glanced in the rear-view mirror and caught a glimpse of several vehicles already giving chase. As he rounded the first corner, an idea flashed through his mind. He pushed down on the brakes and brought the vehicle to a halt. He reached over and pulled the Heckler & Koch MG4 machine gun from under the body of its former owner. Stepping out of the pick-up, he slid back the action and checked it was loaded and ready to fire. He then propped himself against the side of the pick-up, just in time for the first of the pursuing vehicles to appear around the bend.

Clearly not expecting to be ambushed under a quarter of a mile into a chase, the men in the lead vehicle were totally unprepared for a hail of bullets. The windscreen shattered and the vehicle swerved off the track into soft sand. Before the first vehicle had come to a rest, Christian fired at the second as it appeared around the bend. At a range of less than 100 yards, the effect of the automatic fire on the soft-skinned vehicle was devastating. The second vehicle swerved and then rolled as the driver lost control. Christian fired the last two or three rounds from the magazine as a third vehicle appeared. The driver slammed on the breaks and roared backwards in reverse gear out of sight. Christian slipped into the cab, put the pick-up into gear and accelerated away, still towing the head and front legs of the pig. His next thought was how he could help Jamie but he could be anywhere by now and there were no agreed twelve- or twenty-four-hour RV points. Surely he would have a decent evacuation strategy in place?

Jamie ran headlong for the river bed. Although he had no more ammo for the .375, he did not want to abandon it, so he looped it over his shoulder. He heard firing coming from the village. He guessed that the terrorists would not know there was only one man sniping on the ridge and would be pretty reluctant to reveal themselves. He slipped down the bank of the dry river bed and ran as fast as he could along the rocky bottom.

After a couple of hundred yards, he could no longer hear firing. This would mean they were now aware there was no longer any sniper threat from the ridge and would be giving chase. Still running, Jamie pulled a grenade out of the grab-sack. He ripped off his shemagh and used it to wrap the grenade. He then pulled the pin out of the grenade and placed the bundle on the ground in an obvious place, the side lever secured by the cloth.

Powered by adrenalin and fear, Jamie sprinted on at full pace, hoping that a less experienced recruit would see the shemagh and pick it up. He glanced behind him but could see no signs of pursuit. He fumbled in the grab-sack for the sat phone. Slowing up slightly and trying to catch his breath, he pressed the redial button. He put the phone to his ear and after the infuriating message about his remaining credits, he heard Cornwallis.

'Yes, any change?'

'It's Baxter, yes. Contact, contact. One man down, need urgent assistance. Retreating to the south along river bed system,' gasped Jamie.

Jamie did not hear Cornwallis's reply. He heard the noise of an engine and shouting voices. He turned around and looked back: a Land Cruiser was bouncing along the bank, 200 yards away. Jamie ducked down and carried on running, knowing he just needed to keep ahead of them until the rest of the Squadron arrived.

He ran at full pace, trying to avoid patches of soft sandy ground. Every second was crucial. He reckoned, worst-case scenario, he had about an hour and half to hold on. Without warning, he heard the crackle of machine-gun fire and saw dust kick up 10 metres to his left. Looking for a place with cover, he heard a deep boom echo along the river bed. The second grenade-trick of the day seemed to have worked.

Jamie threw himself to the ground behind a couple of small rocks. He unlooped Armalite's .375, resigned that he was going to have to dump it. He rested the machine pistol on the rock and took out his two remaining grenades. He would make a small stand here and then move on. The Land Cruiser appeared again. Jamie could see it full of men, some of whom were leaning out of the windows with their weapons at the ready. He opened fire, wishing he had an M16. Because of the distance, he was not sure if he had done any damage but the vehicle disappeared from view.

He was about to move when he heard shouts. He glanced left and saw several men running along, following his tracks. Jamie repositioned the machine pistol and fired a short burst at the lead man who fell. The other two immediately hit the deck and returned fire in his general direction. Desperate not to get pinned down, Jamie popped up from his position and fired again, before turning and running. He could hear shots from behind and could now see figures appearing along both sides of the river bank.

He knew he had to keep moving – there was no way he could sustain any kind of siege or stand-off with one small automatic pistol and two grenades. With bullets kicking up all around him, Jamie stopped running and turned. He raised the pistol, took aim and fired at the men running on foot between the bushes along the river banks. The minute he fired, they all dived for cover. More vehicles appeared, driving along the river bank, and several overtook him. He could see that it was only a matter of minutes before he would be cut off. He also knew that the moment he left the twisting course of the dry river bed he would become an easy target. This was now the last chance for a change of strategy. Rather than run headlong into the force that were trying to cut him off, he would turn back and ambush those chasing him, try to punch through and somehow hope to cause confusion.

Jamie seized a grenade from his pocket and pulled the pin. He turned and ran back down the gully of the river bed the way he had come. He rounded the first bend and almost collided with the first of his pursuers. Not expecting a wild man of six-foot-six coming their way firing a machine gun, the reaction was total panic. Jamie sprayed the area with fire, and tossed the grenade in the air. Two men fell, and several others hit the ground to avoid the grenade, which went off with a muffled thud in the soft sand it had landed on.

Jamie tore on. He had to maintain momentum and the element of surprise. He approached the next bend in the river bed. He extracted his last grenade and slowed enough to lob it high and far into the next section of the river bed. He rounded a bend just in time to see the grenade explode 50 yards ahead of him in a pile of rocks. The boom echoed, but the blast was largely contained. Three men had taken cover but were instantly back on their feet. Jamie fired the machine pistol from the hip, still running at full pace. One man sank to his knees but the other two opened fire at relatively close range.

His next sensation was cartwheeling through the air as bullets tore into both his legs and stomach. He

twisted as he hit the ground, roaring with rage.
Fumbling to find the pistol that had fallen from his
hands, he felt the sudden impact of two men jumping
on top of him. Unaware of quite how serious his
injuries were, he swiped a punch into the face of the
man now sitting across his chest trying to pin him
down.

Jamie's resistance ended with a blow to the side
of his head from an AK. He saw a flash of white and
his mind went blank.

35

Aboard the Gulfstream 4, the soldiers of D Squadron had been told there had been a contact on the ground. Worried faces stared at Major Day, who imparted the news from the end of the cabin.

'That's all the information we have. Cornwallis just said that Baxter had reported a contact and someone may be down. This does change things. But, we are still due to drop in less than an hour. Unless I hear to the contrary, this mission is on. Having said that, things are fluid and we no longer have eyes reporting from the ground.'

Day answered a series of questions as men tried to extract every possible ounce of detail from him. The prospect of Jamie and Tim going in against around a hundred armed terrorists prompted a mixed reaction, ranging from 'Greedy fucking buggers' to agonised expressions of deep concern.

'The only other bit of info I have,' continued Day, 'is that the Yanks have not even filled up with gas yet. They are fannying around, about an hour's fly time away, trying to secure some gas at a military airfield in the middle of God knows where. Anyway, we can forget them for the time being. It's just us, folks.'

Jamie opened his eyes a few seconds later. His vision was blurred and he stared directly up at the sun. He could see blue sky and splashes of green that were the bushes that followed the line of the river bed. He could not hear anything but was suddenly aware of a thumping pain coming from his lower body. He was conscious of movement and of hands holding onto him. The pain seared up through his body like nothing he had ever experienced. He tried to scream but did not have the power in his lungs. His head lolled back and he gasped for breath. He saw the faces of some of the men carrying him. They were silhouetted against the bright blue sky

Suddenly it was as if the sound had been switched back on. It came as a shock. He could hear shouts, yells and engines. With the sound came increased pain. His senses started to function. He was being carried along the bottom of the river bed where only a few minutes before he had been running. He was now a crumpled, broken wreck. He had no idea quite where he was hit, because the pain was not specific to one place. He longed to be put down on the ground.

Having been manhandled up the river bank, Jamie became aware of more and more people gathering round. The shouting seemed to be getting louder and he felt hands slapping his face and fists hitting his head. Out of the corner of his eye, he caught a glimpse of houses to his right.

At that moment, he realised what was happening. With the shock of being shot and the bang on the head, he had not been thinking straight. But now, he felt he knew for sure what was happening. He was being carried back into the village to take over where Christian had left off. Absolute panic erupted in his mind. His wounds were no longer of any importance. It was all about what was going to happen next.

With these dismal thoughts, he was dumped down on his back on the wooden platform. All around him men shouted and screamed with delight. He could see the devastation caused and understood why these men were on the edge. There were dead bodies all over the ground around the platform where Tim had cut a huge swathe through the crowd. There were dark pools of blood and some men wandered around looking dazed, in blood-soaked clothing.

Jamie struggled to think, such was the pain and fear, but he knew he had a tiny chance of survival if he could hold on until the Squadron arrived. The one card he held was that he knew they were coming and his captors did not. They would be in no hurry to finish him off. This would mean that going along with them would buy time. He had to do anything – say anything – as long he could delay things. Every fraction of a second would be a lifetime if they got him on the rack.

'Well, it looks like the party's only just beginning,' croaked Lennep, looking down on him.

'You might think you are in a bad way, but you're still well able to star in my little film,' he continued. 'We are going to patch you up, stop the bleeding and then get to work. Judging by what I have seen of you, you must be SAS too. Just for information, your mate's dead, shot him myself, and McKie won't get far in a shot-up pick-up with the whole country looking for him. And just in case you have any more jokers out there in the desert that fancy some amateur heroics, I am placing a load of troops round this place.'

Jamie heard the words but said nothing. He had to play as grey as possible. Lennep gestured to someone and Jamie felt his combat trousers being torn off. He raised his head slightly to see what was going on and was horrified by what he saw. His entire torso from his chest down was soaked in deep crimson. His shirt was yanked up and off over his head. He could see a bullet entry wound just above his left hip. He was aware of bandages being applied but could not see who by. He didn't care. The longer they took the better, and if they stemmed the flow of blood, he was better off.

Ten minutes later, Lennep reappeared in Jamie's view. Mo stood next to him, looking shocked and angry.

'They have done a good job on you,' said Lennep. 'But, we don't want you checking out too soon. But if you do, it is nothing to worry about; I have all the kit necessary to give you a blood transfusion to keep things going. McKie may have taken my winch but we are pretty dammed innovative down here in Africa, we have to be.'

'Just use another vehicle, any will do,' interjected Mo, jerking his thumb over his shoulder.

'Tie a rope to the front bumper.' Lennep continued to look down at Jamie. 'You don't just turn up here, shoot up my men and expect to run away, do you? You've ruined my business and I'm going to see to it that you pay.'

Jamie felt his body start to shake. The initial shock was wearing off and the protective adrenalin was fading. He nodded and tried to look at Mo in an appeasing way. He reckoned it was now twenty minutes since he was hit and that he had about an hour to go before anyone turned up. Then, when it seemed impossible that things could get any worse, they did.

It occurred to Jamie that the rescue mission might well be called off due to his phone call to Cornwallis.

It would be obvious to anyone that two men stood no chance against a hundred, and Deverall would have to assume that he and Tim were dead. Why would he then send in a team and risk more casualties? This thought nearly killed him. While he had a plan, he had hope. He was still operating and playing the game – kind of. This new thought changed everything. The attack would surely now be called off. His only hope was Christian, a wounded man on the run, whose life he had ruined.

Impossible. His eyes glazed over and closed. This was it.

Jamie saw Mo re-erecting the video camera on the tripod when Lennep, with the help of two men, dropped Tim's dead body down beside Jamie. Lennep rolled Tim's head, already crawling with flies, over to face Jamie and then spoke. 'Yes, I suppose all's fair in love and war. You got my mate right through the head and if you look, you'll see that I whacked this guy through the head too. Is he a mate or just a colleague? I guess if there are really only two of you here, you guys must have been pretty close?'

Jamie looked up at the sky and switched off any focus. Lennep tapped him on the side of his head with his pistol and continued, 'Actually, there is a difference. I didn't really like the guy you killed. What's more, I was going to have to cut him in the money I'm earning out of this. So, if you put it that way, you've kind of done me a favour, haven't you? Much appreciated.'

Lennep laughed and stood up. He busied himself looping two ropes up and over the wooden beam and to the front bumper of a Land Cruiser.

'I would have liked to use that yank Humvee, nice and heavy, but I rather like knowing it's up there blocking the entrance to this place. Don't want McKie, or anyone else you had with you, dropping in and spoiling things,' Lennep said, with a smug tone.

Jamie could see things progressing too fast and made the decision to speak. Struggling to get the words out, he mumbled, 'So, so what do you need me to do? I'll go along with it.'

'I don't doubt that for a second,' Lennep replied, grinning at Mo. 'Unfortunately for you, these guys need to see some revenge.' He gestured to the group of scowling and shell-shocked men standing around the platform. 'Things have moved on from just making a video of an SAS man revealing everything there is to know about British Special Forces. This is also about giving something back to the guys you've just been killing.'

Mo nodded and started to address the group standing around. He needed to reassert authority, demonstrate he was in control and dealing with the situation. He barked instructions to Farq, who moved nervously forward holding several lengths of rope. The men around him moved out of the way and Farq glanced over his shoulder, as if he were expecting a sniper's bullet in the back of the head.

Mo pointed and clicked his fingers. Ropes were tied to Jamie's wrists and legs.

Jamie shouted out, 'Listen to me, we can offer better terms than anything you are being paid. I am a British serviceman and my lot will pay you. I know we do. I can sort things out, just let me.'

Lennep attached the ropes around Jamie's wrists to the ropes over the beam and those around his ankles to the ring in the middle of the platform.

He put his face a centimetre from Jamie's and shouted, 'Yes, this is all about money, you're right, but these guys want to hear you scream first. We have all the time in the world for you to talk. And you are going to tell me everything you have ever fucking known. There won't be a single secret left about any tiny aspect of British Special Forces, MI bloody 5, Northern Ireland, government sanction of torture – you name it. You are going to blow the whole gig wide open and the world is going to see it. People I know are prepared to pay a load of money to be the ones to put that on air. It will make their cause the most publicised in history.'

Despite the agony of his wounds, Jamie's mind was functioning sufficiently to know there were two aspects to what was happening. One was Lennep's video of breaking an SAS man and getting a load of secret information; the second was showing the frenzied mob that they were in charge and going to make this guy suffer for the deaths of their comrades.

Jamie remembered his training. He knew if it got to the point of torture that it was essential to make the torturer think he was winning and causing the desired amount of pain. With this in mind, he heard the rev of an engine and felt himself pulled up and into the air. His arms were pulled up over his head and he was suspended at forty-five degrees to the ground.

As the ropes tightened the crowd roared. Several more vehicles entered the village and men jumped out, eager to see the spectacle. It was not the tension on his body that caused Jamie to scream out in pain, it was simply being pulled out of the foetal position he had adopted to protect his wounded stomach.

Lennep waved his arm towards the driver of the Land Cruiser again. The engine revved and Jamie found himself taking the full pressure of the reversing vehicle. He felt the oxygen leave his body and unbelievable pain tear through him. He was unable to offer any resistance as tensing his muscles made things worse.

He did not want to give anyone the satisfaction of making him scream but he had to give the baying rabble something. He saw shouting faces contorted with rage and heard yells of delight. Lennep stood back with a satisfied grin.

Again the engine revved and the pain increased.

Jamie bucked and writhed, his brain blank to anything except the agony. Lennep lowered his hand and the driver took his foot off the accelerator. The ropes slackened and Jamie felt a brief moment of respite.

Lennep walked up close to Jamie and shouted, 'It's amazing to think we could do this for about two days, without stopping. Obviously, I need to get some fluids into you, but it's quite a thought, isn't it? I bet you'll be regretting coming in here and fucking with us. I don't know how much you could see of our friend the pig, but I bet you shit yourself in the next couple of stretches. You'll probably hear a few interesting pops and twangs as your first ligaments snap.'

Jamie was too scared even to think about what Lennep had said. His eyes were filled with sweat, dust and tears. He blinked and looked to the horizon. He could not believe this was happening. He was meant to be doing a recce, nothing more. He had not come down to Africa looking for a fight. He was simply trying to find a friend and to put right a wrong. This outcome was inconceivable. How could his good deed have backfired so massively? He had thought the worst-case scenario would be being chucked out of the army, but this?

Lennep raised his arm again. The ropes tightened and Jamie's moment of relief was over. This time the pain was worse. He was unable to think, he just had to endure. He roared, he writhed and gnashed his teeth. The crowd now meant nothing. He was no longer in control of any single facet of his mind, or life. He was alone with the pain. It was just him and the time when the pain would stop.

After thirty seconds, Lennep signalled again to the driver. The ropes slacked and Jamie felt the agony subside. Lennep was talking, but Jamie could not make out the words. He looked up into the sky where he saw the thin white trail of a jet. He followed the white line along and could make out an aircraft, out of which a string of tiny black dots appeared.

Jamie narrowed his eyes and looked again, before allowing himself to believe.

The tiny dots formed four larger shapes as the soldiers of D Squadron linked into clusters by grabbing onto each other's wrists. Jamie knew the procedure. They were falling at 120 mph. They would stick in the groups of four until about 3,000 feet, then release and free fall the next 2,200 on their own. At 800 feet, their parachutes would open with a crack and a few seconds later they would be on the ground.

No one appeared to have noticed either the aircraft or the free-falling parachutists. Jamie was the one tilting back facing the sky and the crowd were all looking at him. Despite the wrenching pain, he felt a wave of triumph flood his mind. He could take another wrench of the ropes, knowing that by the time Lennep eased the pressure D Squadron would be on the ground.

Lennep's arm signalled and the ropes tightened.

Jamie screamed and roared once again, this time with purpose. He wanted to distract anyone from looking around for as long as possible. He bellowed and thrashed about, his mind swimming in unthinkable pain. After an eternity, the pressure eased once more. Gasping for breath, he blinked the sweat and tears out of his eyes and looked up. The sky above the ridge was full of opening parachutes. Some were already dropping out of sight behind the ridge.

And then Jamie heard shouts and saw the crowd around the stage disperse and run in all directions.

36

Mo and Lennep shouted instructions and some of the men fired their AKs into the air above the ridge. Jamie found himself alone on the platform, except for the buzzing flies and Tim's body. He had been abandoned so he just hung there, watching as Mo mobilised his troops.

Behind the ridge, the eighteen-man group hit the ground and flicked off their parachute harnesses. Day shouted instructions through the personal role radios as the sniper team ran for the ridge and the assault team made for the river bed.

Jamie looked on and saw the Humvee pull back, parallel to the end of the row of houses. Already the .50-cal machine gun was firing with its deep, large-calibre roar, which was so distinctive from the clatter of smaller hand-held machine guns. The top of the ridge had disappeared in a cloud of dust caused by bullets, sprayed in wide sweeping movements.

Lennep ran for his helicopter. Jamie felt rage replace pain as he saw the rotors begin to turn. He knew helicopters took a while to get going and prayed someone would put a bullet in Lennep before he managed to take off.

The three-man sniper team, accompanied by the two soldiers carrying Minimis, ran at full sprint up the back of the ridge. As they approached the top, they dropped down and proceeded over the crest, crawling at speed on their fronts looking for cover. The assault team slipped into the dry river bed and ran along the soft sand towards the village.

Mo's men were spread out in a semicircle at the edge of the village. Most were positioned in houses and were poking out from windows and doorways or behind walls. Dust swirled from the downdraught of Lennep's rotors, billowing in all directions. With his eyes only a crack open, Jamie saw the skids of the helicopter move and then leave the ground. Lennep skilfully manoeuvred the helicopter into the air and towards the platform. At about 15 metres from the platform he turned it sideways to Jamie and slid back the window. His arm appeared holding a pistol. He took aim and fired a full magazine at close range. Jamie's head fell back and his body hung loose in the ropes. Lennep pulled the throttle, sending the helicopter up and over the row of houses and away to the west.

Seconds later, the first shots rang out from the snipers on top of the ridge. The opening volley was followed by the rough grunt of the two Minimis opening up on pre-designated areas of the village with automatic fire. The first casualty was the gunner on top of the Humvee. He slumped forwards, then slipped down inside the turret. Several more of Mo's men crumpled whilst others either took cover or fired their weapons in the general direction of the ridge.

Mo sheltered behind a wall, yelling at his senior men to put down suppressing fire. He knew full well that regular troops could not perform HALO para-chute drops and that very few military units would operate in such minute numbers. It could only mean one thing.

He glanced up and over the wall but could not see anything, due to the swirling dust kicking up from the relentless Minimi fire. He called to those around him to spread out, preserve ammunition and watch out for a flanking manoeuvre.

By the time Mo's orders had filtered around the village, Day and his team reached the point where the river bed ran closest to the village. He raised his hand and shouted, 'Smoke grenades, now!'

Anticipating his order, his soldiers obeyed imme-diately. Each man hurled first a smoke grenade, and then a fragmentation grenade, high into the air. The grenades bounced down all over the dusty area between the river and the dirty white houses. The smoke grenades had only just started to spew thick white smoke when there was a deafening explosion as a dozen grenades exploded within a second of each other.

Day was first out of the river bed. He ran headlong into the wall of smoke, firing his M16. Leaving Trooper James Powell to hold the river bed and to snipe from a different angle, the rest followed him in groups of twos and threes. Just as he reached the back of a house, halfway along the row, he heard one of the sniper team talking over the personal role radio.

'Baxter is down, Baxter is down. Confirm visual contact. Strung up in the centre. Can see him swinging there.'

Roars of rage erupted from the twelve men in the assault group as they pressed themselves against the buildings, waiting for the last group to catch them up. Day's eyes bulged with fury, his face glowing crimson.

He clenched the end of his microphone stick in his fist to prevent his words being broadcast and possibly heard back in the UK over one of the radios. 'No fucking mercy now,' he bellowed, over the deafening tirade of gunfire. The men around him had already been psyched up to the point of frenzy before the news of Jamie's brutal death but now boiled in a state of unbridled primal rage.

Releasing his hand from the microphone, Day's voice resumed its normal sound and pitch, 'Go, go, go,' he shouted, tossing a grenade down an alley between two houses.

As the boom sounded, the two groups of six set off between the houses, their weapons pressed into their shoulders. They burst out into the central area by the platform where two soldiers took up defensive positions covering any threat from the houses on the other side of the row. The remaining members of the assault teams kicked in the doors of the closest buildings and lobbed in grenades. With dust and debris flying out all over the place, they stormed inside, firing.

Mo was aware that the assault was coming from the side. He also knew that with the accuracy of the sniping from the ridge, his men were now too scared to reveal themselves. The result would be annihilation unless he could get his men outside to fight. He had around a hundred men, either cowering behind walls or firing off random bursts at the snipers tucked in on the top of the ridge nearly 400 metres away. He shouted to the men around him, 'Use the smoke before it clears, get in the river bed and round behind the ridge. I want the ridge cleared. Do it now.'

A few seconds later, twenty of Mo's men were running through the smoky haze towards the river bed. Trooper Powell lay on the bank staring into the clearing smoke, desperately looking for targets. Alerted by one of the snipers, he looked to his left and saw the first figure appearing through the smoke. Hesitating to make sure he was certain it was not one of his own, he swung his M16 around. At a distance of less than 50 yards he pulled the trigger and the outline fell.

As the man had hit the ground, a dozen more appeared out of the smoke. Powell swung his weapon in an arc of automatic fire, dropping more of the running men. By the time he had fired again, his magazine was empty and more figures appeared, firing their guns towards him. He ripped his Sig Saur pistol from his leg holster and kept firing, until the last man fell 5 metres from his position. Powell replaced the magazine on his M16 and carried on sniping from the flank.

By the time the smoke had cleared enough for Mo to see his sortie party had been cut down, the assault team clearing his side of the village were only a few houses away. His men were in a state of panic and being shot to pieces each time they showed themselves. Some had made it to their vehicles but, once inside, made easy targets for the Minimis.

By now, every member of the assault group had seen Jamie's limp and blood-soaked body hanging below the beam on the central platform. The Beast, ribbed by his mates as being a softy for smacking the bottom of a young West Side Boy who had stabbed him in the leg with a hunting knife, had changed. The gentle giant had transformed into a wild killing machine. The red mist was down as he tore through buildings killing with bullets, his bayonet and the butt of his rifle. His friends closed in around him, recognising the signs of a man on the edge.

Mo's men were bunched up in two remaining buildings on the end of the row. The Minimi gunners were running low on ammunition and had cut back their rate of fire. The result was more heads popping up, putting greater pressure on the assault teams who were desperately trying to maintain momentum. Day's group had reached the far end of the village and were about to cross over to neutralise fire coming from the other side. They had one man down with shrapnel in his chest and another treating him.

'Heading across the way; need covering fire now,' he called into the radio set.

The Minimis came back to life, pouring fire into the central strip. Before the dust settled, Day bolted across the open space, followed by three men. They kicked in the door of the building next to the communications tower and found two terrified men kneeling on the floor with their hands in the air. Without the manpower to deal with prisoners, Day shot them both at close range before turning and heading to the next building.

More of Mo's trainees burst out of doors, some pushing their hands in the air to surrender, whilst others ran among them still shooting. In the last building, Mo urged his men to keep going as the straw roof caught fire. With no options left, the dozen or so men were forced to run for it. With Mo in the lead, they charged out of the flimsy wooden door, out into the bright sunlight, their weapons firing, in a desperate dash for their vehicles.

Alerted by the smoke, the Mimini gunners expected a mass exodus and had their sights trained on the exit. Within a couple of seconds, all lay either dead or wounded, having been cut down by the last rounds from the Minimis with the support of the snipers. The Beast and his team appeared a moment later and finished off any left alive in the writhing heap of bodies with a blast of automatic fire. Mo lay among them, holding his pistol in one hand, his car keys in the other.

Having cleared their side of the village, the Beast and his team poured with sweat and shook with nerves and adrenalin. They were also running low on ammunition and grenades. They reported their progress to Day who was still battling his way through the buildings along the other side of the village.

By the time the Beast and his group had made it across the open space between the rows of houses to assist Day, the resistance had pretty much collapsed. The remainder of Mo's men had either been shot or the lucky ones had made a run for it into the desert. Day emerged from the last building in the row, still barking instructions into his microphone.

'I want this place searched from top to bottom, but

before anyone does anything, I want Baxter off that fucking thing, like right now, and find McKie and Symonds. They're coming home,' he yelled, pointing to the wooden platform.

While some of the assault group took up positions on the outer perimeter of the village, the others ripped through the houses and buildings, looking for anything that contained information on the people that had lived and worked there. Day was extracting the hard drive from the computer in the communications building when one of the snipers entered.

'Just been clearing the river bed and came across this,' he said, handing Day Armalite's .375. Day looked at it and smiled sadly. 'Leave it with me. I'll look after that,' he muttered.

37

Sixty kilometres to the west, Lennep cruised at 7,000 feet. He had recovered from the shock of the morning and was smarting at the financial implications of a wasted trip to Mauritania. Still, he was chuffed to have brushed with the SAS and come out on top. He looked at the map and reckoned he would clear Mauritanian airspace in ten minutes' fly time when he heard a strange humming noise. He glanced at the gauges, which looked normal, and then up and over his shoulder towards the engine. What he had in fact heard was the sound of a pair of Black Hawk helicopters flying 50 metres behind him.

Lennep smirked as he looked over his shoulder, waiting for the Black Hawk to force him to land. Sure, there would be legal grief to deal with but he had contacts, and in Africa he could buy his way out of more or less anything. McKie would not get far and there were not exactly a whole load of reliable witnesses for the prosecution. Nothing he couldn't handle.

Captain Dwight Rodriguez pressed his piece into his ear and spoke: 'This is Pindar Black Hawk Super G1, we have close visual. Awaiting confirmation, Hereford. We hear this is one nasty son of a bitch, over.'

Deverall pushed back in his chair and kicked shut the door of the meeting room. He looked at Cornwallis, put his hand over the telephone handset and spoke.

'They've found one of them escaping in a heli. It's sure to be one of the torturers. Our friends are flying along right behind him now. Need our say-so. Do we make him land or drill him?'

'No brainer,' replied Cornwallis, shaking his head.

'Yes, Super G1, this guy is as nasty as they come and we don't want any issues with his government. Take him out.'

'We have a couple of options, sir. We can give him a rocket or shoot up his rotors and let him fall. Up to you, Hereford,' Rodriguez answered, in a matter-of-fact way.

Deverall relayed the choices to Cornwallis, a hint of malice in his voice.

'Goodness me, the agony of choice,' mused Cornwallis, inhaling sharply.

'Let him fall over,' replied Deverall.

'Roger that, Hereford,' replied Rodriguez, signalling to the gunner to slide back the rear door.

As Lennep glanced over his should a second time, the gunner in the lead Black Hawk made ready the massive belt-fed Howitzer. Aiming at the gearbox positioned just below the rotor blades, he pulled the trigger. Lennep's helicopter jerked sideways as oil and bits of gearbox casing filled the air. It spun around, flipped upside down and dropped like stone. Twelve seconds later, there was a small red flash in the desert below.

By 02.30, D Squadron had recovered as much intelligence material as possible and dragged ninety-six dead bodies into a heap. They drained fuel from the assortment of abandoned vehicles and collected anything flammable, including enemy weapons, ammunition and all but two of their own parachutes. They then set fire to the mound of bodies, creating a huge, stinking funeral pyre.

Having given the outlying areas one more sweep for signs of Christian, the final task was to torch the communications building and the remains of the shot-out Humvee. They wrapped Jamie and Tim's bodies separately in the remaining parachutes. With two men holding each end and two supporting the middle of each bundle, they set off on a northerly bearing towards the extraction site 10 kilometres away, to meet two lightweight PC12 RAF aircraft capable of landing and taking off on soft sand.

'Well, I guess that's the easy bit done,' Deverall said to Cornwallis, still sitting at the head of the table in the meeting room. 'Now we have to explain why we have been into Mauritania, shot the shit out of some village and don't have a hostage to show for it. Just two more funerals and another guy full of shrapnel.'

Cornwallis paused before replying, 'Well, we know McKie probably isn't dead, that's something. We are going to have to tell his folks. At least someone's going to be pleased.'

'Yup, that's something, I suppose,' replied Deverall, in a despondent tone.

Sam had just disappeared into a small wood to discreetly check the answerphone messages on his mobile. He glanced about and then pulled his phone out of a small waterproof bag that he had stashed in his webbing.

The survival training course in Scotland had been going well. He was leading a good bunch of guys who looked up to him and gave him the sort of respect he liked. He had leaked snippets of information about his role in Sierra Leone and had the men of the Coldstream Guards on tenterhooks for more details of a real close-quarters fire-fight.

He had not played his messages for two days and deleted several mundane ones.

The last message, however, almost stopped his heart. John, a friend in A Squadron, had heard that D had lucked out again and were off to West Africa to bust out a hostage, apparently a British serviceman. John was desperate for more details and was wondering if Sam was going. Sam replayed the message. It had been left at 10.21. Sam glanced at his watch. It was nearly 16.00. By now, Christian could well be halfway back to the UK and would have already told everyone the truth.

As he was just about to call Stirling Lines, a group of young Guardsmen ambled through the under-growth towards him, dressed in filthy bin bags and agricultural fertiliser sacks.

'No fucking mushrooms round here, lads,' Sam grunted, slipping his mobile into a pocket. The soldiers nodded and continued their woodland forage. As soon as they were out of earshot, Sam dialled the office at Stirling Lines. After an agonisingly pointless chat with the RSM, he ended the phone call. All he had learnt was that something had taken place in Africa and the lads were due back sometime that night.

It was going to be a long wait and he needed a drink

38

Christian was utterly exhausted; he had spent the entire day driving south. Having made his getaway from the village, he had almost immediately dumped the body of the Arab. But not before he had stripped him of some very useful accessories, including a battered sat phone, just over $400 and three full packets of Benson & Hedges. He had reloaded the Heckler & Koch MG4 and had it lying across the passenger seat. He had also done his best to tidy up the pick-up; pushing out the remains of the shattered windscreen and scrapping out some disgusting pools of congealing blood, mixed with chunks of skull and blobs of brain. He reckoned that from 20 yards off, the pick-up would look fairly normal by local standards.

He had imagined that the sensation of liberty would be utterly euphoric. He had gone from almost being ripped to pieces by a psycho to cruising along in a vehicle with cash in his pocket, a phone and gun at his side. But Christian felt appallingly low. He had not really been able to digest the full horror of what had happened to him. At the time, it had all just seemed surreal. Now it dawned on him how close he had been to death. He had teetered on the edge of an abyss.

He lit another cigarette and thought of the pig, pulled apart and its guts burnt. He shuddered. Then there was Tim. His mate was dead and it was very likely Jamie would be too. He looked at himself in the mirror on the back of the sun visor. He saw a scabby, frightened old man staring back at him with sunken dead eyes.

He had two choices. The simplest thing was to find the first official-looking building and announce himself as a British soldier. There would be a few phone calls, a night in some British consulate and then the next available plane to Heathrow. This was all well and good, but it would be breaking a promise he had made to himself. He had sworn he would have revenge, a desire that had only increased as things had got worse and worse.

Sam's actions had not just resulted in Andy's death in Gheri Bana and his own captivity, but in Tim being shot and probably Jamie too. The soft option of going home was easy but it would be just his word against Sam's. Most people would believe him, but it would not stand up in any court, military or otherwise.

With the light gradually fading, Christian's spirits improved. There would be no soft options. He had a plan, it was a good one, and he would stick to it.

The eighteen members of D Squadron, along with their two fallen comrades, touched down at a military airbase near Marseille to refuel. It was 23.30 and the mood was bad. It could have all gone so well if only Jamie and Tim had stayed put and not gone in. Everyone agreed that their bravery was second to none, but there was still confusion as to what they were doing there in the first place.

Day sat on a pile of camouflage netting with his back against the fuselage. His eyes were shut but he was not asleep. He had had enough of answering questions about the mission and found this was the only way of getting any peace.

Three hours later, the slow-flying PC12s reached Brize Norton. Everyone was knackered and pissed off not to have helicopters waiting to take them back to Hereford.

By the time they drove through the gates at Stirling Lines, news had reached not just the rest of the Squadron, but the whole regiment. Sam finally got a call. Apart from the hip-shaped half-litre bottle of vodka in his hand, he was alone in his room in the Sergeants' Mess at the Cameron Barracks near Inverness. His hand shook as he answered his phone and put it to his ear. It was the RSM who had promised to ring him with any news. The call was brief but music to his ears.

'The long and short of it is that Symonds and Baxter were off on a wild-goose chase to find McKie and now I'm afraid that they're all dead,' said the RSM gravely.

'Not all three?' said Sam. 'They didn't find Christi's body so he could have made it? There must be a chance, surely?'

'Well, if Symonds and Baxter were killed, we've got to assume McKie was too. Let's face it, he was an unarmed hostage. They'd have drilled him the minute Symonds and Baxter went on in. That's if he was even there in the first place. No one really even knows that for sure,' the RSM continued.

The call finished with condolences from both men, before Sam hung up. Having pressed 'End' on his phone, he promptly marched over to the washbasin in the corner of his room and watched himself silently yell 'Yeahhhhhhhhhhhhhhhh' into the mirror. He then spun round and picked up his phone to make double sure it was not still connected. Confident he was totally alone and the RMS was not still on the line, he performed a drunken victory dance of karate kicks, whoops and air punches.

The next morning, Deverall summoned the seventeen fit members of D Squadron to a debrief in the smaller of the two lecture rooms at Stirling Lines. He stood at the lectern, a sombre look on his face, his demeanour reflected by all present.

He stood still for a moment, taking in the men before him. They looked exhausted; some even still had desert cream around their ears.

'The fact is you have been on two of the most unusual SAS-led missions since the Second World War. You have trained for the unexpected and the unusual and you have certainly had all that. Barras was the first time, since we kicked-off the invasion of Sicily in July nineteen forty-four, that this regiment has operated at Squadron strength. Two weeks later, with some of you still rattling with shrapnel, you were dropped into the frying pan again, this time to rescue one of our own.

'This is not normal soldiering, but,' said Deverall, with a mournful laugh, 'this isn't a normal regiment. You have exceeded all expectations, mine included, and probably even your own. We lost people yesterday, good people, yes, but you played your part and we sent a clear message to the terrorist organisations of the world. Mess with us at your peril. That's an important message and will save lives in the future. Well done, all of you. I will now hand over to Major Cornwallis who will go through the mission with you in detail.'

Sam had spent the day demonstrating how to use snares to catch small prey such as rabbits and hares.

The soldiers on the survival course were now even dirtier and hungrier than they had been the day before, when Sam had shown them how to identify edible mushrooms. He apologised that he had not been out with them overnight and promised them they would have something to eat that day. He tried to suppress any signs of total and utter elation and appeared relaxed and pleasant. He had four days left leading the course, which suited him perfectly. It meant he could avoid any unusual questions in Hereford.

He then had two weeks' leave to look forward to and could finally enjoy being the hero of Operation Barras without any nagging worries.

39

After three and a half days on the road, Christian had passed through Mali and guessed he was in Sierra Leone or was at least getting close. There had been no formal border points so it was hard to tell. His first stop had been in a small town where he had bought diesel, food and a map with the US dollars he had taken off the body of the dead Arab. His main problem was that none of the settlements he passed had any signs or place names. His only form of navigation was setting the odometer to zero as he passed each place and recording how far it was to the next one, then cross referencing with the map. It was basic but worked.

Despite the constant ache from his shoulder, he found driving a preferable option to parking up for a rest. The moment he killed the engine, he started to analyse the situation and gloom filled his thoughts along with gnawing paranoia of recapture. He found himself glancing in turn at the wing mirrors and the rear-view mirror. On the move, he only had to focus on one field of vision. Also, if he had to abandon the pick-up, every mile covered would be one less on his feet. It could only be a matter of time till someone pulled him over.

Smoking was tricky on the move without a windscreen. Over about 30 km an hour, tiny sparks of burning tobacco flew back in his face and his precious few remaining cigarettes burnt at twice the rate. He felt pathetic holding each one down by his knees out of the airflow and bending forwards to take a drag.

The temptation to call his parents on the sat phone nagged him constantly. He had dialled their number and allowed his finger to rest on the call button. He longed to tell them he was alive but worried that such a call would jeopardise everything. He knew they would persuade him to come home and that they would be right. Being dead and buried gave him an advantage and the world's greatest alibi, both of which he was going to need.

Lost in reverie, he hadn't noticed that the road had suddenly changed from bumpy mud to tarmac. A memory flicked in his mind. He remembered a feeling of relief when he was in the back of Cambodia's pick-up on the day of the battle. He had been bouncing along dirt tracks jolting his wounded shoulder around and then, suddenly, he had been on smooth road.

Wondering whether it could possibly be the same place, he rounded a slight bend and saw three armed men standing in the middle of road, with large oil drums acting as a roadblock.

Approaching at speed, and without changing his course, he continued to drive towards the men who were now less than 300 yards away. Holding the steering wheel in his knees, he reached for the MG4 and slipped it across his lap. At 100 yards, he could see tyre marks where vehicles had driven slightly off-road and around the drums. A tiny piece of him thought there was a chance he might be waved on and could slip round the block without having to stop. Dismissing the thought, Christian glanced down and pushed the safety catch round and forwards to the fire position. As he looked up, one of the men walked slowly down the road towards him with his hand in the air. The other two were close behind, all three had machine guns in their hands and the unmistakable WSB gangster gait, tatty shorts and reversed baseball caps.

Christian usually tried to avoid unnecessary blood-shed, but after everything he had been through recently there was no way he would take more risks. He lifted his hand in a friendly wave, hoping to put the three young WSBs at ease. Then, still holding the steering wheel in his knees, he raised the MG4 and opened fire from a range of 40 yards. The closest WSB had not moved a muscle when he was hit by a hail of bullets. The other two grappled their guns from their sides, but they were cut down too. Christian guessed from the reaction that the three WSBs had not noticed the missing windscreen that had allowed him to shoot directly at them and were taken by complete surprise.

Looking around for anyone else lurking nearby, Christian swerved around the oil drums. He moved up through the gears and was soon travelling at 80 km an hour, taking full advantage of the decent road surface. He was sure it would not take long for there to be some reaction to the burst of automatic gunfire and he wanted to clear the area as fast as possible. Every 30 kilometres he could travel by car would save a day's walking, if it came to it. With the occasional nasty little slap in the face from a fly, he cruised through increasingly green and jungle-like country. Then, just as suddenly as it had started, the tarmac came to an end. Christian dropped back down to forty and continued bouncing south.

Passing through depressed-looking villages, Christian became increasingly worried as to how he would ever find the remote and, hopefully, abandoned Gheri Bana. The Rokel Creek was clearly marked on the map. In theory, all he had to do was find it, follow it downstream and he would be there.

In the next village he came to, Christian broke with Special Forces convention.

He leant out of the window and shouted to a young

man in a dirty Aston Villa football shirt. 'Excuse me, I'm lost. Can you help me, please? Villa are the best,' he added, with a big, cheesy smile.

The young man nodded. Christian got out of the cab and managed a few more words about football before getting to the point.

'Gheri Bana?' he said slowly.

The man repeated the words and then nodded. He walked around to the front of the pick-up and, to Christian's delight, started drawing a basic map with his finger in the dust on the bonnet.

The young man's exaggerated snipping gestures with his fingers helped Christian establish that the wiggly line down the left was where crocodiles lived and therefore must be the Rokel Creek. Christian nodded enthusiastically and offered his new friend a cigarette. Various roads were then added, accompanied by monkey noises and scratching, suggesting they ran through jungle.

After five minutes of Christian trying to extract as much detail as he could, a small crowd had formed around the pick-up. People pushed their fingers into the bullet holes and muttered aggressively. It was time to go. Christian pulled open the door and got inside, and not a moment too soon. The atmosphere had deteriorated and people were making the obvious connection between bullet holes and Gheri Bana.

The clock on the dashboard showed 14.30, which gave him enough time to make the scene of Operation

Barras before nightfall, assuming the young man's directions were correct.

He did not encounter another roadblock, but the body of a man, hanging from a large burnt tree, sent shivers down Christian's spine. As he drove past, he slowed to see strange voodoo-style feathers in a garland around the decaying figure's neck. Both the lower arms were missing. Even driving past he could catch the acrid smell of rotting flesh. Deverall's words, about not underestimating the WSBs, reverberated in his ears.

40

Forty minutes and three cigarettes later, Christian rounded a bend in the jungle road and saw the murky brown waters of the Rokel Creek. This was the river that had brought him into hell and would hopefully be his ticket out. According to the map on the bonnet, he just had to turn left and follow the track down the side of the river and it would bring him right into the village. He was certain the place would have been abandoned after the slaughter and destruction, but he had no intention of driving straight on in. He drove off the track, heading for an area of thick jungle. He got out with the MG4 in his hand and made his way back to the track, taking care to tread in the most obvious tyre tracks in the soft jungle earth.

Keeping the track just in sight, he followed its course from 10 metres into the jungle. After twenty minutes he felt his nerves build in his stomach. He was taking a massive risk and was desperate to succeed.

As he trudged on through the thick jungle, wiping insects from his face, a strangely positive and re-assuring thought came to him. He had noticed that he was once again doing something that he had been trained to do. He was engaged in a piece of textbook SAS soldiering. He was making a tactical approach to an objective through thick tropical jungle. He was handrailing off the only obvious landmark and using it to guide him into position. The fact that he was knackered, filthy and with all the wrong kit – well, that all felt fine, too.

Frequently stopping to listen, he pushed on through the foliage, still keeping a careful eye on the track. After a few more minutes, he saw a lighter area of jungle in front of him and guessed he was approaching either a clearing or, more likely, the village.

He listened carefully again. He sniffed the air, hoping to pick up any scent of wood smoke or cigarettes. There was no sound other than the usual jungle chatter of birds and the odd call of a monkey. He could smell nothing other than his own body, and the damp aroma of jungle. He inched forwards, the MG4 raised.

Christian saw that he was now only a couple of metres from open ground. He parted the leaves in front of his face and suddenly knew where he was. He had spent several days observing the place and probably understood the layout better than the inhabitants themselves. He was on the edge of the village, close to the hostage house. He could see the extent of the damage. Every square foot of wall that still stood was riddled with bullet holes. Roofs had caved in, there were craters everywhere and endless casings glinted in the grass.

He was confident that he was alone. No one, however desperate, would want to live amongst this. He drew level with the shattered shell of a building next to the hostage house. He poked his head inside the doorway. The walls were charred a dirty black and the remains of a burnt mattress lay against the back wall.

He knew exactly where he was going, but turned around to look at the wooden veranda at the front of the hostage house. He paused. This was the scene of the crime, the place where his world had been taken from him.

He stepped onto the veranda and looked down at the dark stains. The last time he had stepped on these pieces of wood, he was heading for Cambodia's pick-up. He looked at the doorway and hesitated. His eyes narrowed and he felt a need to raise the MG4. He had no particular requirement to enter but something drew him forwards. He stepped inside slowly and looked to his right, to the room where the Rangers had been held. He moved forwards, to the end of the hallway, and looked through the remains of the door to the right. He saw the rubble that had covered him where the wall had collapsed. Dirty brown streaks stained the three remaining walls. The bodies had gone, but the smell of death remained.

He was repulsed and desperate to leave, but stood there to confront the evil he sensed. It screamed at him to go, but he stood there. He saw Sam's bloodshot eyes and the desperate look on Foday's face as he pleaded for release. He saw the old man who had looked down on him when he was pinned under the rubble. He saw the hairs on his chin and tasted the alcohol on his breath.

When he could bear it no more, he walked quickly back down the hallway and out across the veranda. He had to get on with the matter in hand. He made his way up the row of houses towards the site of the OP. He was surprised how few leftovers there were of the battle and guessed the village would have been fully looted by the remains of the WSBs, or by local people.

He pushed his way into the jungle and had no problem finding the site. The destruction caused by the Claymore mines was still obvious. He squatted down and picked up a few empty bullet casings. He could see some from the M16s and many more from the Minimi. He had wondered how he would feel if he ever made it back to the OP. He had imagined himself feeling angry and emotional but instead he felt strangely disconnected from the place. It was utterly different now, just a partially collapsed hole in the ground and not the place where he had stood and fought for his life. He looked around and saw the ragged remains of a blood-stained T-shirt.

He made his way over to the tree and hauled himself up. This had been his vantage point and a place of sanctuary. He found the branch where he had sat and once again looked out across Gheri Bana.

He saw the hostage house and remembered the Rangers sitting outside, smoking joints. He cast his eyes around and tried to concentrate. He had to remember something that, at the time, had been highly unremarkable and that had only subsequently become important.

He had seen Foday disappear quietly on his own into the jungle and squat down. At the time, he had thought nothing of it but although it was only a hunch, in the long hours in captivity, Christian had had time to think and it did make sense.

Shutting his eyes, Christian replayed one more time that piece of memory. He opened his eyes and found himself looking at the bit of jungle at the far side of the village. He locked onto certain trees and used them to get his bearings. He slithered down and set off across the village at a fast walk; there was probably only an hour of daylight left. He crossed the football pitch, noticing large scorch marks in the grass from the massive exhaust pipes of the Chinooks.

Christian looked straight ahead, aiming for the trees he had identified. As he drew closer his hunch began to feel increasingly far-fetched. He could be safely back in England by now instead of being on some wild-goose chase.

Christian stood at the base of the large tree that he was certain marked the place where Foday had been. Going on the fact that he had only been out of sight for a matter of a few seconds, Christian reckoned any hiding place would have to be within about 10 metres, but there was nothing immediately obvious that might mark a point.

He thought back to his brief spell in Northern Ireland when he had been trained to find underground weapon stores out in the countryside. He had been told to look for a place that had nothing to identify it at all; the more featureless the better.

Christian marked out a square by poking four sticks in the ground. He would follow the search procedure and take a systematic approach. He rested the MG4 against a tree and pulled off the end of the stock to access the cleaning equipment stored inside. He screwed together the cleaning rods to produce an eighteen inch steel probe. Then he knelt down and began a detailed search of the jungle floor. He ran his fingers through the upper layer of dead and rotting leaves, into the soft and crumbling earth below. Every six inches he would push the probe into the soil as deep as it would go.

Working as fast as he could, he reckoned it would take an hour to cover the square. After twenty minutes, he started to tire. His shoulder was not responding well to him being on all fours and he was tormented by the swarms of freshly disturbed insects that buzzed around his head. Suddenly his fingers detected something that felt like a tree root, although of different texture. Christian froze and then slowly withdrew his hand; worried it might be a booby trap.

He carefully brushed some topsoil away and examined the area in front of him. He could see a piece of rusty wire poking out of the ground with a small loop on the end. A surge of excitement flowed through him. He took a deep breath and looked about him, suddenly concerned he was being watched, but there was nothing, not even an animal in sight.

With shaking hands, he removed one of his bootlaces and tied the end through the wire loop. He then stood up slowly and pulled a creeper off a nearby tree. He attached the other end of the bootlace to the creeper and positioned himself behind a tree. He gave the creeper a yank and immediately covered his ears. Nothing happened. Just as he was about to pop out from around the tree, he remembered the words of the bomb-disposal course leader. Christian put his hands back over his ears and waited. Twenty seconds later, there was an ear-splitting boom and debris rained down through the trees.

'Clever little weasel,' Christian muttered to himself, as he emerged from behind the tree to see white smoke drifting around a foot-deep crater in the jungle floor.

He approached cautiously, knowing that there could well be more than one booby trap, and squatted down to look into the crater. Seeing a shattered paving stone, he began to use the probe, prodding the ground around the stone, feeling for hard objects. Then, realising that he was probably in more danger from WSBs turning up to investigate the cause of the explosion than from a possible second booby trap, he leant forward and pulled up the pieces of paving stone to reveal a square-shaped biscuit tin.

Still shaking with nervous excitement, Christian dug around the tin and slipped his hands underneath it. Feeling no wires or anything hard, he pulled it out of the ground. Very gently, he prised the lid a couple of millimetres open and squinted inside. Confident there were no more nasty surprises in store, he pulled off the lid.

The first thing Christian saw inside was a brand-new silver 9 mm Remington pistol. The rest of the tin was packed out with a number of dirty, white cloth bundles with numbers marked on them in black marker pen. He picked one up and immediately knew what it contained from its weight and feel. Glancing about like a school kid raiding the tuck shop, he unwrapped the bundle to confirm his expectation. Sure enough, the bundle the size of a bar of soap contained fifteen large uncut diamonds of similar sizes.

Mixed emotions pounded through Christian's mind. These simple, rough-looking objects had caused unspeakable suffering. They were the reason so many had died. They funded wars, terrorism, dictators and psychos like the WSBs and were aptly named 'blood diamonds'.

Christian knew that he, too, had been influenced by them. He had travelled through three countries risking life and limb, indeed killing on his way, just on a hunch that he might find them. He held one between his finger and thumb and examined it in the fading light. As the diamond glinted in the setting sunlight, he made himself a promise.

He checked over the Remington and tucked it into his belt, feeling better with a reserve weapon. He noticed that one bundle looked larger than the rest. He unwrapped it carefully, to reveal a clear plastic freezer bag containing shiny white crystals and powder. The final surprise, in the bottom of the tin, was two passports, one American, the other French.

Christian secreted the contents of Foday's emergency stash into his pockets. He kicked some earth into the crater in a quick effort to cover his tracks. With the rush of excitement subsiding, he became acutely aware of his vulnerability. He had just shot three WSBs, asked for directions to the scene of a recent massacre and let off a hand grenade to confirm his exact whereabouts.

The familiar ache of fear took hold once again. He checked the MG4 and began walking back towards the pick-up. Taking some comfort in the rapidly fading light, he pulled out the sat phone from inside his shirt. He had thought out his plan so carefully but still felt the need to pause before dialling. This was the tipping point when he would reveal his hand. Once he had been updated on his remaining credit, he dialled a number he knew well.

He was still surprised at how quickly he heard a ring tone. It felt extraordinary that he was about to connect with the world he had left behind, a world to whom he was a dead man, quietly pushing up daffodils in a military cemetery.

'Hello,' sounded the familiar voice of Oliver Daily, the RAF Flight Commander who had secured Christian a seat in the cockpit on the flight down to Freetown.

'Oliver, Oliver, are you on your own?' Christian said, trying to sound as normal as he could, but acutely aware of sounding high-pitched and stressed.

'Hold on a sec, just moving outside, bit noisy in here. Who is it?' Oliver shouted over the obvious background noises of a busy pub.

'It's Christian, it's me . . . you probably think I'm dead but I'm not . . . it's really me,' Christian gasped, pushing his way through the jungle vegetation.

There was a pause before Oliver spoke again. 'Christian . . . ? What? Hang on . . . Christi, man, are you fucking serious?' he replied incredulously.

'Yes, it's me, and you need to listen. Sam Carter shot me and left me for dead. I am in the bloody jungle and there are fucking West Side psychos all over the shop. And you need to get me out of here.'

'What do you mean, I need to get you out of there?' answered Oliver.

'Listen, I'm on a nicked sat phone and I have to be quick. Sam shot me, I ended up in a terrorist camp and Tim is dead, trying to bust me out. Apparently, Jamie was there too. I need to get back to the UK without anyone knowing. Otherwise Sam will get away with it,' blurted Christian.

'Shitting hell, mate, this is unreal. You obviously don't know that half of D have just got back from covert ops in North Africa, a mate of mine picked them up in the desert somewhere in Mauritania,' replied Oliver.

'Listen, I have about two minutes left on this phone. When are you flying the next Herc out of Lungi, you know the airbase where you dropped us off?'

'It's not my rota but the next one goes in tonight, flying out about two a.m., into Lungi for around midday local time and out tomorrow night. We are picking up the last of the Para kit and some Int. guys. The flight's coming out about this time tomorrow and it's the last one for a month or so.' Oliver had a hint of panic in his voice.

'You need to swap things round and get on that flight somehow. Do it. I thought you were the bloody boss anyway? Forget your career for once, and don't worry. If you get booted out of the RAF, I'll buy you your own frigging airline,' Christian snapped, trying not to shout.

'OK, OK, I can do it, I can do it. I can wing it . . .' Oliver hissed, sounding both stressed and excited at the same time.

'Good man,' replied Christian. 'Now listen again, you need to bring a small kit bag with the following things in it. A flight suit like the one you wear, a razor, washing kit – you know, I need to clean up if I'm to walk onto that plane with you. I look like shit, stink to hell. Get me a baseball cap, and shades too. And I will need a bergen, sixty-litre plus sort of thing. You'll need to stash it near the perimeter. I'll call you tomorrow evening, keep your phone on and charged up. No room for fuck-ups. And one last thing: put some credit on this phone, that is, if you can see the number on your screen.'

'Yeah, I can see it, long sat number, right?' Oliver sounded more under control.

'You're a fucking star. Now, if I never make it out of here you need to tell Deverall that I caught Sam Carter beating the shit out of the West Side boss trying to find his diamonds. He then shot me. But only if I don't make it, OK?'

'Yes, Christi, got it,' replied Oliver, his tone serious.

'Good man, over and out.'

41

Christian pressed the 'End' button and listened to the sugary American lady tell him he had sixteen dollars of credit left. He dropped the phone back down inside his shirt and continued to push his way back through the jungle towards the pick-up, whilst trying to visualise the maps of Sierra Leone he had studied three weeks ago.

He remembered Sam saying that if the shit hit the fan they could walk out in two days, no problem. That was all very well, on the basis they were super-fit and well-fed SAS men. Sam's statement did not factor in losing at least two stone of body weight and being shot before setting off.

His calculations were interrupted. He froze. He had a heard a voice. It could not be far away due to the thickness of the vegetation. As he stood there, rooted to the spot, he heard another voice. It was not a shout, just someone talking in a loud voice. Christian guessed it was a maximum of 50 yards away and out to the right, probably on the track.

With the MG4 in his shoulder, he inched forwards, wishing he had done things by the book. If he had done things properly he would have boxed round the roadblock and found a way of disarming the booby trap. Now every operational WSB in the country would have been mobilised.

He crept away from the voices, counting a hundred paces before turning right through ninety degrees and proceeding in the direction of the pick-up. The problem was that he now had about twenty-four hours to cover 50 ks, through what was very hostile country.

By the time Christian found the pick-up, the light had faded to the point where he could hardly see it. Realising there was absolutely no way he could risk starting the engine, he squatted down in the bushes nearby to think. Suddenly, he heard a vehicle approaching and people shouting. Shaking with nerves, Christian retreated further into the jungle and sat down at the base of a tall tree to listen. The vehicle was driving along the track and had what sounded like at least four people shouting to each other in excited, aggressive tones.

He cursed himself for being so gung-ho. He knew he could have made it into Sierra Leone covertly if he had taken the time and been bothered to walk. The prospect of blowing his plan, having got so far, infuriated him. In theory, his timing could have been perfect. He could easily have made it to Freetown in a day, to catch the flight out. But now he faced the prospect of either ending up dead or being stuck in Africa with no real passport and enough drugs and diamonds to put him in prison for the rest of his life.

Sitting in the darkness, he assessed his options. The worst choice was getting in the pick-up and just taking his chances. The tracks would be crawling with heavily armed and mobile WSBs. He gave this a ten per cent likelihood of success. The next possibility was to force march it, but he knew from experience that 50 ks through thick jungle at night, with hardly any food or water, was almost as unrealistic.

Then he had a flash of inspiration. The river. He came in up it and by God he could leave down it. He had seen how fast it flowed. It had to be the answer. Christian lost no time in standing up and creeping back to the pick-up. Once he found it, he listened carefully for signs of life before pulling the tool kit out from under the front seat.

Within twenty minutes, he had removed the four wheels and, including the spare, pulled off the tyres. Next he fumbled in the darkness with a spanner to remove the driver's seat. Having piled up his collection of reclaimed buoyancy aids, he set about stripping out the wiring that ran from the battery, down the length of the vehicle, to the rear lights.

It took him two trips to carry the tyres and seat

down to the edge of the Rokel Creek, about 500 yards away. He was sweating heavily and was deeply paranoid about making any noise that might give him away.

Finally positioned by the water's edge with his pile of scrap, he needed to figure out how best to make some kind of raft. He had not seen any crocodiles on his way up the Rokel Creek but knew they would be around. He racked his brain as to whether or not they hunted at night and concluded he would rather be eaten by a croc than barbecued by the WSBs.

He laid out four tyres in a square shape and tied them together with strips of the reclaimed wire. He secured the fifth tyre in the centre with the car seat on top. With a feeling of relief building inside him that his craft was nearly ready, Christian fumbled around in the darkness trying to find a suitable branch to use as a punt. Just as he was about to break down a young tree, he caught the smell of cigarette smoke. He froze, his hands still wrapped about the trunk of the tree. He heard a cough and saw the orange glow of a cigarette end about 10 yards away, moving towards him.

The orange glow then paused, lifted several feet and glowed more strongly for a second as the invisible smoker dragged on the cigarette. Christian felt agonisingly vulnerable. He had laid down the MG4 at his feet in order to use both hands to snap the sapling. He could move for the gun but it might well give his position away. A jumpy young WSB would probably open up with a full magazine. Christian remained stock still and waited.

The seconds passed – obviously the smoker was in no particular hurry. Christian remained motionless, wishing this guy would just move on. After another minute of hideous tension, he saw the outline of the man move. He heard him pushing through the vegetation, heading towards the river.

Christian's desire to climb on his raft and get going could never have been stronger but still he waited. The worry was that the WSB would stumble across the raft. Taking slow steps with the MG4 in his shoulder, Christian crept back towards the water. He had only gone about 5 metres when he saw the silhouette of the man standing by the river in exactly the same place as the raft.

The temptation to put a bullet in his back and just push off into the river was overwhelming but Christian decided to do the proper thing. He crouched and waited.

The next half-hour crawled by. Christian began to think the man had been positioned on the bank to watch the river. The man muttered under his breath and mumbled the odd lyric from what sounded vaguely like rap songs. He was chain-smoking and seemed fidgety. Behind him, Christian heard the noise of vehicles and voices approaching.

Every minute he stood there was one less minute

he had to get to Lungi airport. The temptation to take the man out grew greater and greater. Christian decided to let the man have one more cigarette and if he had not moved on, it would have to be his last.

He reached slowly into his pocket and pulled out one of the remaining pieces of wire he had removed from the truck. He wrapped one end several times round his hand and then used his teeth to peel back the plastic coating to reveal the single strand of wire within. He wound the other end around his other hand with about 60 centimetres between his clenched fists.

He had practised the savage art of silent sentry removal ad nauseam whilst on 'Continuation', in the days after Selection, but had never imagined himself doing it for real. Knowing that letting the man finish his cigarette was really only procrastination, Christian crept forwards, the slight crunch of his movements drowned by the noise of the flowing water.

The secret was not to hesitate. In training, he remembered sneaking up behind a sentry to find at the last possible moment it was a woman. He had paused, whereupon the woman had turned around and shot him with a blank. He advanced in a crouching position to within a couple of metres of the man before making his move.

With his forearms crossed in front of his face, he sprang forward and pulled the loop of wire around the man's neck. In one smooth movement, Christian stood up and twisted round until he was back to back with his victim. With his hands clasped together just over his right shoulder, he flicked his torso forwards and down. There was a tiny gasp from the man as his body flipped over backwards, his hands grabbing at the wire that had already severed his windpipe and jugular vein.

Christian hauled on the wire with all his might. He felt the man writhe against his back in his last moments of life. Despite the searing pain from this shoulder, he increased the pressure and pulled his hands from left to right in a sawing motion. He had more or less pulled the WSB over his shoulder and now lay on his lifeless body. He felt the warmth of blood down his neck, back and shoulders, yet still he pulled and sawed.

After ten seconds in the deathly embrace, Christian was sure the man was dead and there was no chance of any last-moment cries, or a twitching finger pulling a trigger. Slowly he released the pressure and let go of the wire. This was killing on a new level. Sure, he had shot people at close range in Gheri Bana – he had seen the whites of their wide and fearful eyes –

but he had never engaged with them like this. This was different. Blood was in his eyes, face, hair and ears; he could taste it, feel its texture. He had chosen this man's moment of death and heard his last gasp. He had felt him buck and writhe, shared his last agonised seconds of life. Again, it all boiled down to Sam and a nasty load of diamonds.

Christian felt light-headed from adrenalin and shock. He stood up and took a breath. He gave himself a moment to get a grip, then bent down and ran his hands over the dead man's body. He pulled the gun off the man's shoulder and a packet of cigarettes from his pocket. He grabbed a leg and slid the man's body off the bank, into the water.

Without dwelling further on the horror, he pulled the sat phone from the inside of his shirt and gripped the aerial in his mouth. He hauled his makeshift raft into the water. Immediately, it was waist deep and Christian felt his feet gripped by thick mud. He pulled the raft around, pushing it out and away from the bank. With the water halfway up his chest, he pulled himself up and onto the raft. It instantly submerged. He splashed about trying to get his balance without letting go of the sat phone. After a couple of seconds, he managed to get his legs through the front two tyres and his backside onto the seat in the centre. He steadied himself and found he was sitting waist deep in water with the majority of his craft under the water-line. His final adjustment was to slip the sat phone into the top pocket of his shirt and to shorten the sling on the MG4 so it hung high across his chest.

His objective was to get out into the middle of the river where the flow would be fastest. He hoped this would also be the place that would have fewest crocs. He kicked his legs and used his hands to paddle. He knew the river was about 100 yards wide but could not see how far across he was. He felt he was moving fairly fast and guessed he just had to keep upright and, eventually, he would reach the sea.

Christian heard the noise of engines and the occasional shout coming from the jungle to his left. He caught a glimpse of headlights and guessed a full-scale search was on for him. Despite the darkness, he tilted forward, keeping as much of his chest under water as possible without soaking the phone. They would surely find the stripped pick-up and work out what he was doing.

After an hour or so, Christian realised he had not heard or seen any signs of activity in the jungle for a while. His new focus was the swirling and gurgling of the Rokel Creek. Not knowing if crocodiles hunted at night, his hand instinctively grabbed at the stock of the MG4 with each splashing sound.

As the sun rose around 05.00, he shook with exhaustion and cold. He had spent the most arduous night of his life trying to stay afloat, crashing into sand bars and disentangling himself from mangroves. Fine alluvial mud had found its way into every pore in his body, and his hands, knees and shins were grazed and cut all over. Christian looked around as the sun climbed in the sky. He had been going for at least eight hours. He guessed he had been moving for about three-quarters of the time, which equated to a satisfactory twenty or so miles if the river flowed at four miles an hour. Being able to see the jungle on either side made him feel better in some respects, but more vulnerable in others. The darkness of the night helped him stay hidden, but the approaching daylight would turn the tables. He would make an easy target, bobbing along at walking pace at a range of less than 100 yards. Even the most inept, drug crazed zombie would be able to pick him off.

In theory, Christian should have got off the raft, destroyed all evidence of it, holed up somewhere for the day and then walked into Freetown under cover of darkness. But if he did that, he would miss Oliver's flight out. It was either staying on the raft or walking in daylight. The factor that tipped the balance was that he did not have the energy to walk 20 or 30 miles in 35 degrees of heat, having been battered all night by the Rokel Creek. He would stick on the river for as long as he could.

42

Oliver dropped the ailerons on the wings of the C-130 by ten degrees to lower the nose of the aircraft and get a better view of the crumbling runway at Lungi. He had managed to rejig the flight rota with comparative ease, due to his seniority and some rubbish about missing his wedding anniversary. He had two main worries. Firstly, how he was going to get Christian into the aircraft. There would not be the usual amount of hanging around this end. It was a quick in-and-out and there would not be hours when the aircraft would be unattended. Secondly, it was almost guaranteed that Christian would not be there on time, if at all. He had therefore taken the precaution of reporting a minor malfunction with the electrics on the flight deck that could be elaborated into a full-blown fault if necessary.

*   *   *

With the sun came swarms of flies and bugs in all colours, shapes and sizes. Every inch of Christian soon crawled with life and as he lay there, half-submerged, flicking creatures off his face, he noticed that the left bank of the river had become cultivated farmland. This meant he was probably out of the day-to-day jurisdiction of the WSBs. He knew they occasionally dipped into the government-run areas, but not too often. This was a good sign.

Whilst he felt buoyed up that he might be out of the clutches of the WSBs, his next worry was being caught by whatever government forces were present in the southern part of the country. He surely had a life sentence's worth of cocaine in his pocket, not to mention the diamonds and guns. He knew he could blag it – say he had every intention of handing them in to the authorities – but it would still look deeply suspicious.

The next thing to catch his eye was a small settlement on the river bank. There was a makeshift pontoon and a collection of grass-topped houses by the water's edge. He could not see anyone but had a feeling it was only a matter of time. Whilst he was making good progress on the water, having not hit a sand bank or mangrove for several hours, he knew it was time to ditch the raft while the going was still good. On terra firma, he would at least always have the option of being able to run or hide.

He paddled slowly towards the bank until his feet

touched the soft muddy sludge of the river bed. He pulled his feet awkwardly out of the front two tyres and slipped into waist-deep water. Brushing the flies off his face with his hand, he waded forwards then crawled up the slippery mud bank on all fours. At the top he flopped onto his stomach and lay in the dusty grass, breathing heavily.

Hungry and muddy, he set off down the river bank along a well-used track. He passed two young men and had to control his natural reaction, which was to fire off half a magazine of suppressing fire and run. Instead, he smiled and walked on past.

By midday, Christian reckoned he had covered at least 10 kilometres and was half expecting to see signs to Freetown. He had seen lots more people and wandered through several basic-looking settlements on the river. He had stripped down the MG4 and had it in component parts in an old fertiliser bag he had picked up.

He rounded a bend of the river and finally saw what he had longed for. On the horizon, he could make out the distant sight of Freetown. It did not look like much but it was a major, major milestone on his journey.

He reached inside his shirt and pulled out the sat phone. He pressed redial and paused while the connection was made. The call went straight through to Oliver's message service. With a pang of irritation, Christian left a brief message telling Oliver he was on time for their drink and was looking forward to seeing him later on.

Unnerved by the lack of certainty, he marched on. He just had to get hold of Oliver and get on that Hercules.

43

Feeling ever more conspicuous the closer he got to Freetown, Christian decided he needed to hole up somewhere safe and get hold of Oliver. There was no point marching into Freetown, risking an encounter with the local police or UN Forces, unless he knew Oliver was there.

He wandered into an area of tall grass and bushes right by the river and sat down. He decided he would wait an hour before calling Oliver again. Within twenty minutes his finger hovered over the call button. He pressed it and to his delight heard a ring tone.

'Hello,' snapped a voice.

'Oliver, it's me. Where are you?' hissed Christian.

'We are here and it's all fine so far,' Oliver replied.

'Good, that's great. When are you due to take off?' continued Christian.

'I've already caused a delay and there's no way

we'll fly before twenty-two hundred hours. So you need to get your arse in here. I have the bag and will stash it once it's dark. It'll be in the wrecked control tower on the south side of the airfield and that area isn't patrolled, I've checked. Call me when you're ready and I'll bring you in the gates with me.'

'Roger that, roger that, over and out,' Christian replied, grinning for the first time in weeks.

The afternoon wore on very slowly. Due to the proximity of the water, Christian was dogged by endless mosquitoes and he constantly heard voices of people walking along the path. His extreme experiences in captivity had given him the feeling that everyone was out to get him and he had to remind himself that the voices he heard were not those of search parties. He did not dare sleep in case he slept too long, so he sat in the long grass cleaning his weapons and counting and recounting the diamonds.

Once the light had finally started to fade, Christian set off down the river, heading towards the slight glow of orange light which hung over Freetown. Within half an hour, he saw telephone poles, which meant he had to be getting near. People wandered around and some sat on the doorsteps of their simple houses, watching the world go past.

His walk-in plan was simple. The river would lead to the sea and the sea would lead him to the port that was only a ten-minute drive from the airport. The first part was easy and he soon found himself wandering past ancient containers and rusting cranes. With a sea breeze in his face, he followed the line of the coast through the port area out into open country. After an hour, pushing through waist-high vegetation, he reached into his shirt and pulled out the sat phone. He squatted down low and covered the illuminated screen with his hand as he dialled.

Oliver took no time to answer. 'Christi, Christi, where are you?' he snapped.

'Lost in the sticks . . . Must be somewhere near the bloody airport, but it's a total black-out round here,' Christian said, looking around.

'Hold on, I've got an idea. They're still checking the electrics so I'll get in the Herc and test the landing lights and I'll put on the landing beacon. You'll see it for miles.'

'Nice one, brilliant,' replied Christian.

'And when you see the plane, the old control tower is about six hundred metres behind, right by the sea. But watch out, there is security out there after all. Then call me and I'll get you in because there's a fence around our bit,' Oliver went on.

'Roger that, over and out,' answered Christian, ending the call.

Two minutes later, a bright white flash caught Christian's eye in the distance. It winked every three seconds. Christian pushed on through the vegetation until he walked into a barbed-wire fence. He pulled back 20 yards and followed its line along.

The sound of voices stopped him in his tracks. He froze and slowly lowered to a crouching position. He listened again and distinctly heard two men talking in front of him. He waited, trying to get a better feeling of where they were. He edged carefully away and boxed around them.

Picking up the line of the fence once more, he continued around the perimeter fence to the point where he could hear waves breaking. He swung around to the right and pushed on, keeping an eye on the beacon, which still winked away in the darkness.

The disused control tower was not hard to find. It stood 30 feet high and the remaining shards of glass in the smashed upper windows reflected in the white light of the beacon. He approached carefully, guessing it was the sort of place a lazy nightwatchman might settle down in for a kip. He stepped onto concrete and listened, before putting his head very slowly though the empty doorframe. The smell of urine immediately reminded him of his awful arrival in Mo's cell. He listened again before stepping inside. Gingerly, he felt his way around the walls at the base of the abandoned tower until he came to a set of concrete steps. Just as he was beginning to give up, his hand brushed against something soft. He bent down and felt the familiar texture of Gortex. He scooped his arm through one shoulder strap of the backpack and made his way out.

Around the back of the control tower, he sat down against the wall. He pulled open the pack and felt around inside for food. Within three minutes, he had devoured the contents of a twenty-four-hour ration pack and glugged a litre of mineral water.

Then, with the aid of a small torch, he began to concentrate on the remaining contents of the pack. To his satisfaction, it seemed that Oliver had delivered exactly what he'd asked for and more. Along with the RAF flight suit, sponge bag and baseball cap, there were clean boxer shorts, socks and a T-shirt. There was also a clipboard with various documents relating to a C-130 Hercules and an envelope with the words 'Open Me' on it. Inside was a hand-drawn map showing the whole airport and, most importantly, the various points where security guards were located. He winced when he realised he must have walked straight past at least two static sentries.

Christian splashed some water onto his face and squirted a ball of shaving foam into his hand. He daubed the foam all over his face and proceeded to attack three weeks of beard as best he could in the dark. Then, finding it impossible to get the cheap plastic comb through his matted hair, he pulled on the clean gear. He neatly folded the clothes he had been wearing and slipped them into the pack, along with the diamonds and guns.

Shielding the light of the torch with his hand, Christian orientated Oliver's map and set off, following the perimeter of the outer fence. He made two detours around points that were marked with sentries and soon came to a track. The smell of wood smoke confirmed that he had to be by the houses that were drawn on the western side of the runways. He picked up the track and followed it for 500 metres before finding himself behind some large industrial units. Looking around, he saw lights coming from the airport to his right and knew he had to be close to the gates.

Trembling with excitement, Christian pulled out the sat phone and dialled. Oliver answered immediately.

'I am right outside, just been down the track on the south west side of the main runway,' hissed Christian.

'Good, er, very good,' replied Oliver, his formal tone suggesting that he was in company. 'OK, OK, that should be fine. I just need to check a few details.'

'You what?' said Christian, sounding confused.

Then he heard a much quieter voice. 'Can't talk, get round to the main gates – marked on the map – and wait there. See you in exactly ten minutes. Be there, OK?'

'Sure, sure, roger that,' answered Christian quickly.

Christian heard activity coming from the far side of the warehouses as he passed by, hugging the perimeter fence again. He was making for a point marked on the map as VCP1/RV. He guessed this was the main gate he had driven through in the back of the battered old van at the start of the operation. He crept forward slowly, ever grateful for the total absence of electric light. In any normal country it would have been impossible to wander round a large built-up area at night without being seen.

Suddenly the beacon on the Hercules stopped. Christian took this as a sign that Oliver had to be making his way to the Vehicle Check Point 1. He saw light coming from several buildings in front of him and could make out the distant whirring noise of a generator. He inched forward.

He saw the outline of a single-storey building with three illuminated windows. He edged forwards and squatted down, knowing it had not been a full ten minutes since he had spoken to Oliver. The last thing on earth he wanted was to make any polite chit-chat to a bored sentry from the Irish Rangers, while waiting for Oliver to pitch up. A minute later, he decided to move. He pushed slowly through the grass to the point where he could see a barrier blocking a tarmac road leading out of the airport.

A figure appeared by the barrier. The man raised his arms in a relaxed way and the barrier lifted. Christian guessed this was his cue. He stood up and walked forward quickly, the pack slung over his shoulder, the clipboard under his right arm.

He stepped into the area of light near the barrier. He saw a soldier in desert kit with an SA80 standing by the open door to the guardhouse. He walked towards Oliver, who raised a hand and called out, 'I assume everything was OK and they gave you the fuses?'

Christian needed a moment to think, but replied, 'No problem at all. They are a bit bigger than ours but will work fine.'

Oliver glanced up at Christian with a nervous grin before turning to nod at the sentry who was already standing half back inside the guardhouse. Christian walked under the red barrier with a Stop sign bolted to it, staring intently at the papers on his clipboard. Oliver locked onto him and they walked, two abreast, towards the dark shape of a hangar.

Oliver turned his face slightly towards Christian and spoke through clenched teeth.

'You have no idea the shit that's been going down since Barras. Didn't want to say anything on the phone but D Squadron's been in pieces. It's—'

'Well, I can assure you a fair bit of shit has gone down my end, quite a lot down my throat,' interjected Christian. 'Now, what the fuck happened to Jamie and Tim? I saw Tim go down in a hail of bullets but what about Jamie? Did they get him, too?' His tone was desperate.

'Listen, I'll tell you everything when we get you on the Herc. But, yes, they got Jamie and badly. But shut up for a second, we need to get you on the plane. Just keep looking at the clipboard and don't look up. Most people are off duty right now but there are still a few loadies pratting about.'

Oliver steered Christian round the outskirts of a Portakabin and down the side of the main hangar towards the open rear tailgate of the C-130 Hercules. A forklift appeared out of the shadow cast by the wing and a man in a luminous yellow waistcoat nodded in a friendly way.

Oliver marched Christian up the ramp, pointing with his hand as if drawing his attention to some aspect of the loading gear. Christian's mind was elsewhere. He had imagined that the moment he stepped into an aircraft bound for England, he would be walking into a world of light and sense but the news that Jamie had been killed 'and badly' reignited in him horrible thoughts of Lennep, the rack and the squealing pig.

'Please don't tell me they killed him without shooting him,' murmured Christian in a trance-like state.

'Hold on, just let's get you between these containers and I'll tell you everything I know,' Oliver replied firmly.

Christian did not reply. He felt hands on his shoulders directing him between two wooden crates. He was aware of the familiar smell of aviation gas and army kit, but not much else. He saw the rack and Lennep's sweating face. He heard the baying mob and the tearing of sinews.

Oliver pushed Christian into a seating position behind the crates and sat down next to him.

'Listen, mate,' he whispered, 'I can't imagine what's happened to you or what on earth you're up to, but I can tell you what I've heard my end.'

Christian nodded and took a deep breath.

'Well, everyone thought you were dead,' Oliver went on. 'Sam Carter said he saw you go down in the hostage house. No one else saw it, but obviously his word was good enough. The whole operation was deemed a success overall but everyone knows something went wrong and that the perimeter was not held properly, because people were chasing round after diamonds. It's not official but it's what people are saying.

'So there's this horrendous atmosphere at Stirling Lines and Deverall is doing his nut. Then I get approached by Jamie and Tim, needing a covert drop into Mauritania. They reckoned you weren't dead and wanted to recce some training camps in the desert, just in case. Armalite was in on it too and supplied the weapons, etc. I didn't like the idea of it but the thought of you getting your head cut off was quite motivating.'

'Thanks, mate,' Christian muttered.

Oliver paused for a moment before carrying on.

'So, we insert Jamie and Tim and the next thing we know is there's a full alert and the whole bloody regiment's scrambled, Desert Theatre. About eighteen guys from D drop out of the G4 over Mauritania and flatten a hundred terrorists and some village, but find

Tim and Jamie both dead. Apparently, they'd seen you there. The tragedy is that they went in to get you out only about forty minutes before D got there. It was their call and they went for it. I guess they felt they couldn't hold on. Does that make sense?'

'Yes, it does. It makes total sense,' Christian replied under his breath.

'Then, of course, you weren't there after all. Sounded like you had run for it,' Oliver continued.

'Yup, I took a vehicle and bolted. I had no idea at all the Squadron was on the way, thought it was just Jamie and Tim being nutters. So, did they torture Jamie for long?' Christian whispered.

'Well, no one really knows for sure. But he was shot in the end. From what I heard, everyone went well and truly berserk when they saw what had happened. No survivors. The Yanks shot down some bloke in a heli, too.'

'Did they? Too good for that bastard. He was the torturer. He was the one that would have racked me and then did Jamie. They were going to film it, too – unreal really, and all caused by Sam Carter and his bank balance. Unreal,' groaned Christian.

'So what actually happened in the hostage house with Carter?' said Oliver.

'He was after Foday's diamonds. Everyone knew the West Side Boys control the diamonds in Sierra Leone and Sam obviously reckoned he could find them in the middle of the fire-fight. Tim and Jamie were in on it, too. They left their part of the line unmanned to fuck off and find Foday, leaving Andy to get overrun and machete'ed. And then I walked in on them in the middle of it,' said Christian.

'*What?*' Oliver said in disbelief.

'They were in the hostage house where no one could see them. They had Foday and it looked like they had shot him once and were beating the crap out of him so he would reveal where his diamonds were. If only they had asked me, I could have probably worked it out for them. It would have saved a whole load of grief.'

'So you knew where the diamonds were?' Oliver sounded more confused.

'Yup, well, I didn't know I did at the time, but it turns out I did,' replied Christian.

'Now this is getting weird. So you did know where they were but you didn't?' Oliver exclaimed.

'I worked it out sitting on my arse in a prison cell. Had plenty of time to think things through, you know. When I was in the OP, I saw Foday messing about in the jungle. At the time I reckoned he was taking a shit and thought nothing of it. But then I clicked that there was a good chance he wasn't shitting but checking his stash. That's why I'm here now. I trekked down from Mauritania and back to the village to see. It would have bugged me for ever not to have known. Nearly blew my head off getting round his crafty little booby trap. Anyway, I now have all one hundred and sixty stones and a few other bits and bobs, to boot,' said Christian, turning to look at Oliver in the darkness.

Oliver did not reply for a moment. He stared at Christian before opening his mouth to speak.

'And you said Tim and Jamie were nutters?' he said incredulously.

'Desperate times call for desperate deeds, or whatever,' answered Christian.

'So what do we do now?' asked Oliver.

'Well, the other thing I had time to think about was how to deal with Sam. His disgusting greed led to Andy getting chopped up, Tim being shot in the head, Jamie ripped to pieces medieval style, an entire village being wiped out and four more West Side Boys getting drilled. Oh, and not to mention me being shot and a pig being racked, gutted and partially barbecued,' hissed Christian.

'A pig? A pig being barbecued?' said Oliver, sounding confused again. 'I thought Muslims didn't eat pork?'

'It wasn't quite like that,' Christian snapped. 'They made me watch a pig being racked, gutted and burnt so I could see what they were going to do to me. Nice guys.'

'Fucking hell. No wonder you want to get Carter. But why not just tell Dev? There will be a court martial and he'll do twenty years for attempted murder and whatever else,' said Oliver.

'I can assure you I did think of that. It would have

saved me an eight-hundred-mile road trip, nearly getting blown up by a grenade, having to decapitate some bloke with a cheese wire and white-water rafting the whole way down the Rokel Creek on a car tyre.'

'Starting to sound a bit like my gap year,' Oliver interjected, putting his hand over his mouth to prevent a nervous laugh.

Christian looked at him angrily in the darkness before suppressing a laugh too.

'It's not fucking funny, you know,' said Christian, shaking his head and grinning.

'Sorry, mate, it's not funny, it's just the way you put it. It's all so utterly mad, completely mad. I just can't get my head around it. But what's the plan, then?' said Oliver.

'Well, it's simple really. OK, actually it's not, but it is clever. So bloody clever that our mate Sam is going to wish he was getting a court martial and a twenty-year stint inside. That would be a picnic compared to what I've got planned,' answered Christian.

'What? Are you going to rack him, gut him like the pig and then barbecue him?' replied Oliver.

'No, I am not,' said Christian. 'That's simple, boring copycat stuff. I said my plan was clever. Let's just get back home and I'll talk you through it.'

'OK.' Oliver looked at his watch. 'You need to stay here and don't move. There will be people up the front – screened off – but you never know, someone could come back to stretch their legs. We take off in about four hours. Flight time is about nine hours. There's water and scoff in this bag, a bottle to piss in and a bag if you really need to shit. Just don't make any noise, for goodness' sake. When we land, wait for me. I'll walk you off and hand you over to Armalite. He's going to get you back to his place where you can stay till you know what you're doing. It's arranged. OK?' said Oliver, standing up.

'OK, roger that. And thanks, I'm really grateful. If you get caught, remember I promised that I'd buy you your own airline.'

'Shut up and get some sleep,' answered Oliver, disappearing between the crates.

44

Christian stretched himself out on the hard aluminium floor of the Hercules. He was uncomfortable but pleased there were no mozzies buzzing around and that it was dry. He thought of his parents. He had deliberately kept them out of his mind to stop himself calling them. He hated the fact that one call could end all their suffering, but it would put them in an impossible position. He knew his mother would tell his aunt, her only sister. She would tell her husband, who had a famously big gob and a drink problem. It would get out and in no time the whole country would know he wasn't dead. And, for the time being, being dead made his plan a whole lot easier.

Mulling over these thoughts, he drifted off to sleep. The next thing he was aware of was a sliding feeling. He opened his eyes and found himself being pushed against a crate as the Hercules gathered speed down the runway. Christian braced himself, loving that he was finally leaving Africa. He had dreamt of going home and now it was actually happening. The noise and shaking of transport aircraft normally irritated him, but this time it felt fantastic. As the C-130 levelled off, he stretched out once again and shut his eyes.

The next time he woke, his face pushed into the rough wood of a packing case, he knew the aircraft was landing. He sat up, feeling light-headed and desperately thirsty. He fumbled around for the water bottle and took a long drink. Next, in an awkward kneeling position, he managed to urinate a dark stream of piss into the empty bottle Oliver had provided.

Just as the C-130 was finishing its taxi, a pang shot through Christian. This was the moment when he officially became a smuggler of drugs, diamonds and guns. He knew he was not going to have to walk through the customs section of the airbase like normal returning service personnel would, but it still felt bad. He had the ultimate cover story but still he would be lying.

He heard the ramp hit the tarmac and the winch-motor stop with a clunk. This was it. Any moment now the loadies could start moving boxes. He stood up and made ready. He did not know the exact time but he could see daylight flooding into the plane. He was sure he would stand out horrendously in compar-ison to the fresh, clean-shaven people around the aircraft. He had only had a basic wash; he was still encrusted in weeks of grime, sweat, blood and mud. He could smell himself and had seen how bad he looked in the rear-view mirror of the pick-up.

Footsteps approached up the ramp. More voices. Christian had to move. He slipped through the gap between the wooden boxes and turned away from the rear ramp. He walked along the centre of the Hercules, staring intently down at his clipboard.

Where the fuck are you, Oliver? he mouthed silently, through gritted teeth.

He reached the end of the cargo hold and looked through the window into the seating area. There was no one there. As he opened the door, Oliver appeared from the cabin adjacent with a nervous look on his face.

'I need those checks done now, if that's OK,' Oliver called back over this shoulder, gesturing to Christian to stand still. Then, turning to him and pulling the metal door to the flight deck shut, he whispered, 'Armalite's just sent a text. He's stuck in traffic and he'll be here in a few minutes.'

'Bloody typical. Nothing changes round here, does it?' replied Christian, looking out through one of the small round windows.

'Don't worry, everyone else is off and my co-pilot will be busy for ages in there,' Oliver said, sounding more relaxed. 'How about a coffee?' He gestured to a large green canteen.

'A coffee?' answered Christian incredulously. 'Do you realise I'm packing about fifty million pounds' worth of diamonds, enough coke to kill the whole of the RAF, a stolen machine gun, a— '

'OK, OK, I'll call him now.' Oliver pressed his phone to his head.

'Don't bother, I can see him,' Christian said, staring out of the window. 'He's just down there.'

'Good, we just need to . . . er, you follow me. Out the side door and down the steps we go.'

Christian followed Oliver out of the side door just behind the passenger seating area and down some metal steps. Around the aircraft, numerous ground staff were already busying themselves and a stream of green forklifts unloaded boxes. Christian glanced over the top of his clipboard to see that no one was taking any interest in him whatsoever. He saw Armalite standing by the door of a muddy, long wheel-base Land Rover, a roll-up cigarette in the corner of his mouth.

'Hop in the back, lad,' he said calmly, a slight grin appearing beneath his moustache.

Christian nodded to Oliver, opened the back door of the Land Rover and got in. Armalite started the engine and drove slowly away towards the row of hangars with his hazard lights flashing.

'All right then, Christi?' he said, without turning round.

'Well, kind of, I guess,' Christian replied, pushing the backpack under some camouflage netting.

'When I say so, I want you to slip down onto the floor and pull the netting over you. Just stay put until I say so, OK?' said Armalite, in a matter-of-fact way.

Christian slid onto the floor and pulled the netting over his head without saying a word. He felt the Land Rover slow up, bounce over a couple of sleeping policemen and then start to gather speed.

'OK, lad, all clear. Right, climb over and get up here in the front and tell me what the fuck's being going on.' Armalite sounded friendly but firm.

'Sure,' replied Christian, easing himself over the seats, 'but not until you roll me a fag.'

'Didn't think you smoked,' said Armalite, shooting Christian a sideways glance.

'Well, I do now,' answered Christian.

'That bad, eh?' Armalite passed Christian a tatty-looking bag of tobacco and a packet of rolling papers.

He eyed Christian's schoolboy attempt to roll himself a cigarette. Then, pulling over into a lay-by, he leant over and plucked the torpedo-shaped mess out of Christian's fingers.

'For fuck's sake. Rolling a decent fag obviously wasn't part of the course at Sandhurst, was it?' he said, grinning in a condescending, NCO kind of way.

'OK, you do it, then. Even the WSBs have proper smokes. Don't know why you can't,' replied Christian.

Once Christian had the rollie in his mouth, he began telling Armalite the tale, starting with the fire-fight. Armalite gasped with anger when he heard that the line had not been properly manned and then roared with rage when he heard the exact details of Andy's death. His face went red and he smashed his good hand against the window.

'Fucking stupid goddam bastard,' he yelled, as they rounded a roundabout on the quiet Gloucestershire A road.

'You've heard nothing yet,' said Christian. 'But pull into that petrol station; I have got to eat something before I go on.'

Two minutes later, Armalite emerged from the petrol station shop, his arms laden with sandwiches, bags of crisps, bars of chocolate and two large coffees.

'Right, there you go, Christi. Start on that. By the way, the plan is to go back to my place. You can stay there until you decide what to do.'

'Nice one, I'm really grateful. But the thing is, what are we going to do about Sam? I do have a plan but I'm going need your help. May need Oliver, too,' said Christian, chewing on a sandwich.

'You can count on anything you need from me. Anything, anything at all. Just name it. I'm right there, Christi. We need to get this fucker – never liked him much anyway – and get him hard, the cunt!'

Christian suddenly cried out in pain as he took a swig of coffee.

'Shit, that's hot,' he spluttered. 'My gums are totally shot, ulcers galore, bloody agony.'

Forty minutes later, Armalite told Christian to get

back in the back of the Land Rover as they approached the outskirts of Hereford. With a half-eaten chocolate bar still in his hand, Christian hid himself under the camouflage netting once again. It was not long before he heard the engine turn off and the squeak of a hand-brake. A couple of seconds later the back door opened.

'Out you get, it's that one there,' said Armalite, jerking his thumb towards a neat-looking red-brick house at the end of a long terrace. Christian slithered out the back and made his way quickly across the pavement and up the steps into Armalite's house.

Christian smiled to himself as he looked around. It was exactly as he had imagined – the typical home of an unmarried Special Forces soldier. Every square inch of the sitting-room walls was covered in neatly hung pictures depicting military scenes. There were early-looking Land Rovers traversing sand dunes, parachutists dropping into jungles, endless regimental photos and framed certificates of the army courses Armalite had completed. The mantelpiece over the small gas fire was crammed with models of military aircraft, vehicles and men carrying huge bergens. Even the cushions on the sofa bore the SAS insignia.

'Come on, lad, let's get us some brews and sit in the garden. It's a beautiful evening and I need some air.'

'Sure thing,' Christian replied, deliberating with himself as to whether he could maybe ask Armalite if he could have a shower first and sort himself out.

Christian followed Armalite through the kitchen and out through the back door. It was immediately clear why Armalite had suggested sitting out of doors. Christian stood and gazed at the most immaculate vegetable garden he had ever seen. It stretched back, 30 yards of perfectly maintained raised beds, to a group of apple trees growing at the far end, which provided perfect shade for some wooden chairs and a table.

Armalite walked down the central path with a four-pack in his good hand and plonked himself in one of the chairs.

'It's just gone six now,' he said. 'Should be nice and sunny here for at least another hour, mate. This is where I like to sit when I need a bit of peace and quiet.'

Christian sat down opposite Armalite and pulled the ring pull off his beer. The two men drank a can each before resuming any kind of conversation.

'That fucking Sam Carter,' said Armalite. 'I've always thought he had a dodgy look to him. I was a bit surprised when he passed Selection in the first place. I said standards were slipping but, of course, I was told I was out of touch and a purist. Could have told you that he was trouble.'

'Well, personalities aside, his actions have resulted in some good guys going down. Jamie and Tim got sucked in by him and his bullshit. Look at what they did to try to save my arse. From what you are saying, they went in against a hundred armed guys. That's fifty to one,' replied Christian.

'And you know what, all they had was my buffalo rifle, a dodgy blinged-up AK souvenir from Iraq, a couple of tiny machine pistols and a few antique grenades. Appalling,' answered Armalite, shaking his head.

The two men finished off the beer in the remainder of the warm evening sunlight, then retreated inside. Christian walked upstairs and found the bathroom, where he stripped off and stepped into the shower. The sight of his emaciated face in the mirror came as no surprise but seeing every bone in his body protruding from tight grey-looking skin worried him. His shoulder was still an angry purple and black with bruising but the entrance wound seemed to have healed well.

He winced as the hot water cascaded over him. Every nick, scratch and graze stung like hell. There did not seem to be an inch of his body that had not been affected by something. His scalp was full of raw patches from scratching, his hands and arms were all grazed from the bashing he had taken on the Rokel Creek, his feet were swollen and rancid. The rest of him was covered in a vast array of insect bites, some just red and angry, others bleeding, oozing and infected. The shampoo and soap felt like sulphuric acid.

He had imagined a shower would make him feel

better. The reality was that he had broken the now well-established equilibrium between his body and filth in which he had co-existed for some time. He wandered downstairs in a towel and asked Armalite to roll him a cigarette. He sat on the sofa drinking more beer and listened to Armalite tell him why, if he had had his way, Sam Carter should have failed Selection in the first place.

By 22.00, Christian was yawning uncontrollably. He had told Armalite his plan in broad brushstrokes, and was pleased that he had not thought it was too far-fetched. It would have made life a lot easier if Armalite had pulled the plan to pieces. That would have meant he could have given up and dealt with Sam along more conventional lines. Armalite had not only offered to help, he had also made a couple of suggestions that improved things and reduced the risk.

He awoke the next morning to find a note on the kitchen table from Armalite saying he would be back about lunchtime. Christian wandered down to the end of the garden in a too small T-shirt and tracksuit bottoms that he had found neatly folded on the floor outside his room. The mid-morning sun was strong, bright and warm. He sat quietly munching on apples, enjoying the calming background noises of birds singing in the trees and children playing a couple of gardens along.

Access to unlimited food, tobacco and coffee felt like the ultimate treat. By the time he heard a key turning in the front door and heard Armalite shout, 'Honey, I'm home,' he felt bloated from too much toast and jittery from far too much coffee.

He looked up as Armalite walked into the kitchen with a purposeful expression.

'Morning, darling. Sleep well?' said Armalite, lowering a sports bag carefully onto the table.

'Good, thanks. Got everything?' chuckled Christian.

Armalite unzipped the bag, pulled on some leather gloves and placed the contents on the table.

'A Siggy, two spare mags, grenade, new pay-as-you-go phone, four pounds of Semtex and a couple of detonators,' he said.

45

Christian was pleased to get a visit from Oliver that evening. They sat with Armalite in the chairs at the end of the garden and drank more beer. Christian went over the plan in a quiet voice, wondering if the less gung-ho Oliver would buy in to the same extent that Armalite had. When he had finished, Oliver paused, before replying that at no time in his life had he ever felt more strongly that a man needed to be brought down. He told Christian that he had loved playing his part in things so far, had never felt such a sense of purpose. He was one hundred per cent behind Christian and would not stand by and watch Sam lie his way out of justice.

Christian summoned Oliver and Armalite inside. He unwrapped the little white bundles and laid the diamonds in neat lines on the kitchen table.

'If it weren't for these little fuckers, there's a load

of people who would still be around today. We all know who. Quite frankly, it's a miracle I'm here. I don't deserve to be, but the cookie crumbled my way about six times. I shouldn't have made it. I fucked up at every stage but I'm here. You know what?' he said, looking at them before continuing: 'It feels shit in some respects. But, I'll put things straight. If either of you want to take anything off this table, please feel free. Pay off your mortgages; buy a fucking Ferrari, for all I care. I'll only need a few to fund the plan, the rest of the evil little sods can be disposed of,' said Christian.

There was pause. Armalite looked at Christian and then at Oliver. With a smile on his face he spoke: 'Don't be such a self-righteous twerp, Christi Let's not go crazy like a bunch of lotto winners, but I can assure you the lads that died would think we were the biggest load of pricks on earth if we decide to dump this lot in the sea.'

'Yeah, quite right,' added Oliver. 'You take what you need to fund the plan and let's divi up the rest, give a few to charity. I'd love a fucking Ferrari.'

'Me too . . . Actually, a Bentley or a big Merc might be more me,' said Armalite, nodding.

'OK, guys. You both take a couple of bundles each. No idea what they're worth but it must be quite a bit. I need to get up to London and shift some for cash. I've been on the internet and found some places that offer cash for jewellery; they might be the sort of places that like a hooky uncut diamond.'

The rest of evening was spent discussing the fine details of how best to nail Sam and how to spend a load of money without friends getting suspicious. More beer was consumed, and Christian and Armalite were caught eavesdropping at the door as Oliver slipped out to call his wife to say he was too pissed to drive home. Christian and Armalite wailed with laughter, attempting to imitate Oliver's grovelling conversation.

By midnight, the three men were standing outside smoking rollies. Armalite had taken his top off and, with ever-increasing bravado, narrated an endless stream of war stories to an increasingly wide-eyed Oliver who leant against the kitchen wall, nodding respectfully at all the right moments. When Oliver began asking Armalite about his tattoos, Christian knew he had had enough and slipped off to bed.

He woke as the front door slammed shut. He rolled over in bed and checked the time. It was 06.30 and he guessed the slamming front door had to be Oliver rushing off, no doubt in trouble with his missus, and probably late for work. After five minutes trying to get back to sleep, he gave up, got up and made his way downstairs to join Armalite in the kitchen.

'Right, today is going to be a day of action,' Christian declared, scratching an insect bite.

'Yup, as I said, I'm here if you need me and for fuck's sake don't let anyone see you. Any shit, you just let me know. And before I forget, here's the cash you wanted,' answered Armalite, swigging some coffee from a mug with a winged dagger on the side.

'You know how grateful I am. This is a big deal for all us and I do appreciate—'

'Shut up, sort out Carter and don't get seen. I'll find out exactly what he's doing and let you know his movements. Right, I'm off. See you in a few days,' replied Armalite, heading towards the door.

Christian just nodded.

An hour later, he was heading for the station in the back of a taxi. He pulled his baseball cap down over his face and slouched in the seat to keep low. Glancing nervously out of the window, Christian enjoyed seeing day-to-day life in Hereford trundling on as usual. His world might have been smashed to pieces but it was reassuring to see that everyone else seemed to be getting on OK.

At the ticket counter, Christian asked for an open-ended return ticket to London. Then he bought a newspaper to hide behind and made a beeline for the far end of the platform. Arriving at Paddington three hours later, he hailed a cab and headed straight to Oxford Street to buy some clothes that looked more normal than his borrowed, too small, military PE kit.

His next destination was an address in Hatton Garden. He had a list of possible places that he had found on the internet that he thought might buy diamonds. They fell into two categories: there were those that dealt in gold bullion and other precious metals and those that offered to value and purchase jewellery.

Feeling nervous, Christian entered what looked like a pawnbroker just off the Whitechapel Road. Its sign declared, 'All Gold and Jewellery Bought'. He pushed open the door and stepped inside. He looked around at the shabby display and immediately walked out, knowing he was wasting his time.

The next two places he visited turned him down, saying they were not interested in uncut stones. The fourth address turned out to be an office based over a bookie's shop. Christian climbed the stairs, feeling sure he was still wasting time. He opened a door and approached an elderly Asian man behind a wooden desk. After a sentence or two of idle banter, Christian skirted around to the question of who would buy uncut diamonds.

The man paused before telling Christian that there was no market for uncut diamonds in London. Christian turned and descended the stairs, thinking the diamonds were cursed. So far, everything connected to them had been bad. In an ironic way, it made sense that after all the trouble they had caused, they might now be impossible to sell.

He stepped out into the bustling East End street wondering what to do. He felt removed from the busy, purposeful people passing him. He had just lit a cigarette when he heard a polite voice behind him say,

'Excuse me, but I couldn't help hearing your conversation just now.'

He turned around and looked at a middle-aged Asian man in a dark blue suit.

'What conversation was that?' Christian answered cautiously.

'You mentioned you have diamonds to sell?' replied the Asian man.

Christian avoided a direct answer.

'What are you saying?' he said.

'Come with me. I know someone who might be able to help you. Do you have any samples with you?' the Asian man answered.

Christian's instinct was to deny all knowledge of any diamonds and walk away. He looked at the man and tried to read him. He seemed respectable, just, but Christian knew that everything he was doing was dodgy, and the people involved had to be that way too.

'I have one small sample on me, just the one, but access to more, OK?' he said.

The man smiled and gestured to Christian to follow him. Christian kept a couple of yards behind as they made their way back in the direction he had come from. The man took out a mobile phone and made a call. Christian could hear the words, but could not even make out what language was being spoken. Instinctively, he reached around and touched the Sig Saur tucked in the back of his jeans.

They rounded a corner, walked another 50 yards and into a pub. Christian was relieved he had not been directed into an alleyway or a disused warehouse, but knew he was still playing with fire. The man guided him to an empty table and proceeded to look around, his confident smile now a nervous grin.

Five awkward minutes passed during which neither man spoke. Christian hated the situation but sat quietly watching the door of the pub, making sure he kept a neutral expression on his face. Then, to his surprise, two casually dressed men who had been standing at the bar all along turned around and approached the table. They did not look like Lennep and Roote, but Christian was nonetheless reminded of them and felt his hackles rise.

One looked about forty and wore a smart new black leather jacket and a fitted grey shirt. The other was younger-looking with spiky blond hair and a pock-marked face. Christian remained expressionless as he looked at them. Then the older man spoke, in an east London accent.

'I understand you may have some stones for sale?'

Christian nodded and thought before he spoke.

'Yes, that's right,' he said quietly.

'OK, well, I'm going to need to see a sample before we can do anything,' the man replied.

Christian reached into his pocket and produced one of the large uncut diamonds. He leant forward, put it on the table, getting the reaction he wanted. All three men stared at the stone and then glanced around nervously.

'So, eh, right,' said the older man, picking up the diamond and looking at it. 'How many of these have you got, then?'

'Two hundred,' Christian replied, dead pan.

There was a pause and the three men looked at each other, then at Christian. The Asian man looked delighted.

'Two hundred, you say?' replied the older man, looking stunned.

'Yes,' replied Christian.

'I assume you know how much these could be worth if they are any good?' he continued.

'Yes,' answered Christian, still dead pan.

'These are coming out of Africa. Ex-soldier doing security on a diamond mine, right?' the man said quietly.

'Yes,' said Christian, nodding slightly.

'OK. I'll tell you what I can do.' He looked intently at Christian. 'Now, I don't know you from Adam, so I'm going to keep this stone and check it out. If it's rubbish, you've lost nothing and if it's good, we want more. The deal is ten thousand pounds cash per stone. If it's the real thing, I will be outside here tomorrow at ten a.m. Don't be late, bring fifty and we'll look at them. Got that? Any bad ones and you don't get paid.'

'Yes,' replied Christian, standing up.

'Right, I'm Danny. And one more thing: no funny stuff, right?'

Christian nodded and made his way to the door. He kept seeing Lennep and Roote and felt nauseous. He hated what he was doing and wanted to get out. He turned and walked away down the street, lighting a cigarette. His mind raced, trying to analyse whether he was being a fool or whether he had stumbled on the right people.

It took several minutes for his thoughts to settle. He saw an underground station, went inside and bought a ticket. He stood on the crowded platform and waited for the next train. The doors opened and he stepped inside. He glanced about casually, then, just as the doors started to close, he stepped back out onto the now empty platform.

Confident that no one was following him, he left the tube station and hailed a taxi.

'The Taunton Hotel on Park Lane, please.'

46

On the journey across London, Christian reminded himself how he had made up his mind back in Sierra Leone that he would stop taking risks and do things properly. The problem he had was that there were no standard army operating procedures or protocols for becoming a gangster. And that's what he felt like. He was peddling a load of nicked blood diamonds to a bunch of hoods in a grotty pub in east London. It was a far cry from swearing allegiance to Queen and Country on the parade ground at Sandhurst. He drummed his fingers on the seat and looked out of the window. He passed Buckingham Palace and saw guardsmen in their red jackets and bearskin hats standing to attention. A world apart from where he was now. Had he been corrupted by the diamonds like Sam?

He was pleased to arrive at the hotel. It meant he could stop thinking about things and get on with what he had to do. He checked in, using Armalite's credit card, and went upstairs to an expensive junior suite. He stashed the diamonds on top of the cupboard and opened the minibar. He devoured two bars of chocolate and then a packet of shortbread.

Christian moved over to the window and looked out across Park Lane towards Hyde Park. He liked the view of the trees with the late-afternoon sun getting low in the sky behind them.

He sat on a small sofa and pulled out the pay-as-you-go mobile. He dialled Armalite's number.

'Hello,' said the voice, not recognising the number.

'It's me,' said Christian quietly.

'Oh, OK. How are you getting on, lad?' Armalite sounded interested.

'Well, looks like I've found a load of hooky guys to buy some stuff,' answered Christian.

'Nice one. You'll have to give me more details when I see you,' said Armalite cryptically.

'Sure, no problem. Now I'm going to need my bag in a day or two. Will that be possible?' Christian continued.

'Yup, I could bring it up this weekend if that's OK.'

'Fine, that's totally fine,' said Christian.

'And the other point, I've had a look into things and can confirm our friend is up north right now, but will be in your part of the world soon. Will have more details when I see you, OK?' said Armalite, knowing Christian would understand.

'Yes, good, thanks. Got a busy day tomorrow but I'll let you know how things go.'

'Keep yer head down then, lad,' replied Armalite, a note of worry creeping into his voice.

'Roger that,' said Christian, pressing the 'End' button.

Christian lay on the bed and turned on the television. He flicked through the room service menu and ordered steak and chips and three beers. He knew what he was going to do in the morning and did not want to spend the whole evening worrying about it. He ate his dinner, drank his beer and fell asleep by 20.00.

The alarm call woke him at 06.00. Before he had got out of bed, he could feel adrenalin pumping around his body. He washed and dressed quickly and then ordered breakfast. He counted out fifty diamonds and slipped them into a soft felt bag that had contained his complimentary hotel slippers. Next, he stripped the Sig Saur down to component parts on the desk.

Due to his high state of tension, he jumped when he heard a knock at the door. He knew it was his breakfast arriving but still felt paranoid. He laid a towel over the desk and opened the door to his room.

It was still only 07.00 by the time Christian had eaten his breakfast and checked the Sig Saur again. He tried watching the news to pass the time but felt too twitchy to sit down. He picked up his kit and left the room.

Getting a taxi on Park Lane was easy. In the quiet early-morning traffic, it took him only twenty minutes to get to the East End. He got out a few hundred yards from the pub and walked down the street, which was already showing signs of life. People were on their way to work, some shops were open and the traffic was starting to build. Christian walked past the pub, glancing through the windows. He walked around to the back, looking for doors and generally familiarising himself with the area. Next, he toured round the neighbouring streets to recce the wider area.

Satisfied he had a good feel for the place, Christian sat in a coffee shop and watched the minutes pass by on the clock on the wall. He had to proceed on the basis that these guys were going to try to do him over, or simply not turn up at all. He felt nervous. At 09.50, he left the coffee shop and approached the front door of the pub. He glanced through the windows and saw a man mopping the floor of the empty bar area. Turning around, he noticed a blue Mercedes had pulled over 50 yards up the street. He looked at his watch. It was 10.00.

Christian concentrated on keeping calm, when he heard a voice.

'Glad to see you made it on time,' said Danny.

Christian turned to him and nodded.

'Got the goodies, I take it?' Danny continued.

He produced his phone and pressed a button. Ten seconds later a silver people-carrier appeared and pulled up right by them.

'We have a specialist on board who needs to have a look at the stones for obvious reasons. You can either get in with us or wait here,' he said.

Christian looked into Danny's face, trying to read him.

'You saw a stone yesterday, now I need to see the money,' he replied gruffly.

Danny did not answer but walked up to the window of the people-carrier and said something to the driver who looked like the younger, fair-haired man from the pub.

'Look on the seat,' he said, with a perceptively condescending tone.

Christian took a couple of steps forward and peered through the window. The fair-haired man had a brief-case open across his lap containing wads of cash.

'OK?' said Danny.

'Sure, you guys are for real,' Christian said with a nod.

Danny slid back the side door and gestured to Christian to get in. The six seats in the back were arranged in two rows facing each other. As he got in, he saw a big, tough-looking man sitting on the far side. He had short grey hair, a big red face and wore a long, grey overcoat. Opposite him was a smaller man with receding hair, in a blue-striped suit, an anxious look about him.

Christian sat down facing forwards, next to the big guy. Danny pulled the door shut and the vehicle moved off. They rounded a corner and Danny leant forward and spoke to Christian. 'So are you carrying?'

'Yes,' answered Christian, slowly opening his jacket to reveal the Sig Saur tucked into the top of his jeans.

Danny leant forward and slowly pulled it out. He slid out the magazine, popped out the rounds and slipped them in his pocket. He smiled and passed the gun back to Christian.

Then he said in a polite voice: 'Kneel down on the floor, please. We need to check the rest of you.'

Christian slipped off the seat and kneeled down, while the tough guy and Danny ran their hands all over him. Christian felt Danny's hands pause and then squeeze the two lumps in the inside pockets of his jacket.

'The diamonds,' said Christian.

Danny nodded, glanced at the tough guy and then sat back in his seat with a satisfied expression on his face. He picked up his phone and dialled.

'Clean, sir. He's clean, sir,' he said.

A few seconds later, the vehicle stopped and Danny slid back the door. A small, immaculately dressed black man in a tailored suit got out of a Mercedes which looked like the one parked near the pub. He stepped up into the people-carrier and, with an exhausted-sounding huff, sat down next to Danny.

'Come on then, Danny boy, aren't you going to shut the door?' he said.

His voice amazed Christian. It sounded bizarrely upper class to the point of being theatrical. The vehicle moved off again. Christian said nothing. He was looking at the black man's city-style chequered shirt and matching tie.

They drove for another minute before entering a multi-storey car park. Christian felt his body press against the tough guy as they went up the spiral ramp to the top floor, which was almost empty of cars.

The fair-haired driver parked the vehicle in the middle of the wide-open space and kept the engine running. Christian sat there, silently trying to work out the black guy sitting in front of him who was obviously the boss.

Danny then spoke. 'Right, let's have a look at them.'

Christian pulled out two felt bags each about the size of an orange. He put one in his lap and passed the other to the nervous-looking man in the blue suit, who was holding out his hand. The man pulled the drawstring and tipped some of the contents onto a white tray. He shone a torch onto them from the side and bent forward to inspect them with an eye scope.

It suddenly occurred to Christian that Foday was the sort of slippery shit that might have had a stash of fake diamonds. With the thought still in his head, the gemmologist sat up and raised his eyebrows. Christian felt panic welling inside him.

'Where did you get these?'

Before Christian had time to reply, the black man interrupted.

'So are they any good?' he squeaked, irritably.

'Eh, yes, Derek,' replied the specialist. 'They are really very good indeed. They must have been sorted already as they are the same size and quality.'

The man called Derek smiled and turned his attention to Christian. He looked him up and down and narrowed his eyes.

'So, young man, you seem to be onto something here, don't you? Now, it may come as a surprise to you but my family own most of Africa and we like to control what comes in and out. So, I think it's time you told us just where these little babies came from?'

Christian was still utterly baffled by Derek's extraordinarily posh accent. It sounded contrived and affected, yet he was immaculately well dressed and his men seemed somehow in awe of him.

'Well, to be honest, I don't know exactly where they come from. A mate of mine, ex-army, is working in Zaire and came across them. I don't know how or where from, but he's in the security industry. He asked me to shift them for him. It's really as simple as that,' replied Christian, sounding as sincere as he could.

'I see,' said Derek, turning around and reaching for the briefcase on the front passenger seat. 'And we are all meant to believe that, are we?'

Christian stayed silent. As far as he was concerned not an honest word had been said by anyone and he could not see any point in making up anything else.

'Well, I am certainly not a military man myself, but it would seem to me, soldier boy, that you are in a bit of a fix. Now, I am used to dealing with legitimate businessmen who play by the rules, so I'm not quite sure how to deal with you. As I see it, you're here with us, got some nice little diamonds and an empty gun. That's definitely not a good situation for you, is it?' he said silkily.

Christian felt anger building inside him.

'Well, there are plenty more where these came from. I could set up a regular supply for you,' he said, staring at Derek intently.

'Well, in my experience, you normally only get to rip off a mining company once,' Derek replied, in a much more aggressive tone. 'Now, I'm not a nasty man, but Mr Jones sitting next to you is,' he continued, back in his pompous sing-song voice.

The hard-looking man next to Christian smiled and produced a pistol from the pocket of his overcoat.

'Let me show you these ones. They're even better,' gasped Christian.

'Oh, very good,' answered Derek. 'Go on, let's see then.'

Christian untied the drawstring on the second bag and reached inside. Derek's eyes bulged and he let out an excited camp-sounding sigh. Christian gripped something hard. As he withdrew his hand, he slipped his thumb through the safety pin on the grenade inside the bag and pulled it out.

'What the fuck is that?' Derek shrieked, slipping into a south London accent. Mr Jones sat up violently and Danny's hand automatically reached for the door handle. The gemmologist pressed himself into his seat, as if trying to put distance between himself and the grenade.

'It's two things, actually,' Christian shouted, jerking his thumb backwards to release the pin. 'Firstly, it's a Type 61 hand grenade, Russian, but very reliable I can assure you, and, secondly, it's my way of ensuring you amateur, low-life arseholes don't fuck with me.'

Derek gulped and Danny slowly slid back the side door of the people-carrier a few inches, saying, 'Relax, we're all here to do business.'

Knowing the shock would not last for too long, Christian made himself shake as if he were losing control. Then he started to stutter, 'We, we, we can all die, I don't fucking care, makes no fucking goddam difference to me.' He waved the grenade in the air. All four men recoiled in terror. The fair-haired driver flung open the driver's door of the vehicle, jumped out and bolted.

Suddenly, Mr Jones made a grab for Christian's arm. As his hand gripped Christian's wrist, Christian released the grenade. The handle sprang up and the grenade fell to the floor, bounced and disappeared under the seats.

Instantly, Danny ripped open the door and dived out, followed by Derek, Mr Jones and the specialist. Derek lost his footing as he landed and fell to the ground. Mr Jones's boot crashed down on Derek's shoulder, smashing him into the concrete. The specialist leapt sideways to avoid Mr Jones. All four ran madly away from the vehicle, looking for cover behind concrete pillars.

Christian sprang out a moment behind them, took one small step and leapt in the driver's seat. He rammed the vehicle into 'Drive' and pushed his foot flat to the floor. The engine screamed and the people-carrier careered forwards, the door simultaneously slamming shut. He drove straight towards the exit and momentarily hit the brakes to make the turn onto the ramp. As he started the turn, shots rang out.

With the tyres tearing against the concrete kerb, Christian struggled to keep the vehicle from tipping over. The front faring slammed into the ground at the bottom of the ramp and Christian looked for the next set of exit signs. He roared around the middle floor of the multi-storey car park and down the next ramp to the bottom floor. He saw a yellow barrier by a row of ticket machines. He pushed his foot to the floor again and smashed straight through it. He swung the vehicle around to the right and joined the traffic in the street, oblivious to gawping members of the public, shouting and pointing.

Still in getaway mode, he took the first turning he saw and roared down a residential side street. After 300 yards, he pulled over, and immediately turned round in his seat to check the briefcase and diamonds were still on board. With a deep sigh of relief, Christian lit a cigarette and drove off again, this time at a normal speed.

Conscious that some passer-by would have called the police, he was keen to dump the people-carrier. He drove around the back of a rundown tower block and got out, leaving the keys in the ignition and the engine running. He grabbed the briefcase, the unprimed grenade and the bag of diamonds and set off on foot, confident that the nearly new people-carrier would be nicked within a matter of minutes.

Glancing at his watch, he was amazed to see it was only 10.14. He was sweating, slightly out of breath and his hands were shaking. He needed to calm down and think through what had happened. As far as he was concerned, he had ripped off a bunch of gangsters who certainly were not going to report anything to the police. He had intended to do a genuine deal with them and had only taken them on once it had become clear they were going to play dirty. Sure, there were a couple of bullet holes in a multi-storey car park and a broken barrier, but there was no way of linking things to him. It was Derek's car that would be seen on the CCTV, if there was any.

Keeping the sun behind him, Christian walked west. By the time he saw parts of London that he recognised, he was feeling a lot better.

47

It was getting on for lunchtime when Christian strolled across the lobby of the Taunton Hotel. He extended the length of his stay with the receptionist and took the lift to his room. He called room service and picked up the mobile to call Armalite. Despite speaking in riddles, he relayed the morning's activities, as Armalite crowed with delight.

'The fucking grenade trick always works, particularly on civvies!' he yelled, dropping his guard for a moment.

'You should have seen them,' Christian answered, giving up the covert talk. 'They nearly shat themselves. I've never seen anyone move so fast in my entire life. The security bloke actually stamped on his boss as they all piled out.'

'Priceless,' replied Armalite. 'I can't believe I

missed it. Fuck, what a shame. I'd make such a good gangster.'

'I bet you would,' said Christian, suddenly sounding a bit more serious. 'But back to business, can you make it up here with that bag tomorrow?'

'Yup, tomorrow is fine. Got a bit more detail on you-know-who and his movements. Will fill you in when I see you.'

'Roger that. See you here any time tomorrow.'

With his lunch on a tray in front of him, Christian flicked on the computer on the desk and let it warm up. He used the mouse to access the internet. He surfed around for a few minutes before reaching for his mobile.

'Oh, hi there,' he said, trying not to sound too nervous and awkward.

'I'm on your website at the moment and was wondering if you have any girls available?'

'Yes, we have lots of ladies available this afternoon and this evening,' said a friendly-sounding female voice. 'Is there anything in particular you are looking for?'

Christian gulped before answering.

'Well, yes, there is actually. I want a girl who is into motorbikes and stuff, you know.'

There was a slight pause before the female voice replied.

'You mean you like girls in leather?'

'Yes, that sort of thing, but I really need a girl who can ride a motorbike.'

'Sure, sure, I understand,' said the voice in a tone that suggested Christian's request was totally normal. 'We have Helena, who is a beautiful biker girl. She is five foot seven with long blond hair and blue eyes. She has good conversational English and a bubbly and lively personality. Very popular; four hundred pounds per hour.'

'OK, she sounds nice. Can you send her over to my hotel, please?' said Christian, clicking on a thumbnail photo of a stunning-looking blonde.

He spent the next hour pacing around the room feeling awkward. He cleaned his teeth and looked in the mirror. He definitely felt a lot better and had put on some weight, but still looked a wreck compared with his normal self. His skin was grey and there were bags under his sunken eyes. He tried to watch some television to pass the time when suddenly the buzzer went.

He took a deep breath and opened the door. The very attractive blond who he had seen on the computer screen an hour earlier stood before him. She smiled and said, in a husky central-European accent, 'So, can I come in?'

Christian realised he was blocking the door and stepped back to let her in. She walked into the room and looked around.

'Nice place you stay,' she said, still smiling.

'Oh, er, not too bad really, I suppose. I am only here for a day or two,' Christian replied, trying to sound relaxed.

'I am Helena. What is your name?'

'I'm Dave,' said Christian, half-raising his arm as if about to shake hands.

Helena looked at Christian and smiled again. 'So, let's take care of business first and then we can enjoy ourselves, yes?'

'Yes, of course.' Christian passed her the money that he had put on the desk ready for her.

Helena counted it and then turned to look at Christian.

'Your first time like this?' she said.

'Well, not exactly, but this needs to be slightly different. I have an unusual request, but I am happy to pay you big money if you are prepared to do it.'

48

Sam was pleased to have finished the course in Scotland. He felt out on a limb and wanted to get back to his house in London to relax and catch up with a few people who would be able to tell him more about the operation in Mauritania. He still felt elated that the only people who could have given evidence against him were actually dead, and not just presumed dead.

He had his kit packed up and had been round to the Sergeants' Mess to say a few goodbyes. He got a lift to the station and was soon on a high-speed train heading for London. He would be there just in time to meet some mates for a big Friday-night pub crawl and then had a full week off before he needed to be back in Hereford.

Sam's train pulled into King's Cross at 18.50. He swung his kit bag onto his shoulder and barged his way aggressively through the crowded station towards the tube, thinking that the bustling commuters would probably get out of his way a bit quicker if they had any idea of what he was capable of.

Forty minutes later, he unlocked the front door of his house in Romford and was clearing a pile of post out of the way with his foot, when he heard a foreign female voice behind him.

'Excuse me; can you help me, please?'

The irritated look on his face melted into a smile as he set eyes on Helena. She wore fitted black motor-cycle leathers and a tight T-shirt.

'Yeah, of course,' he said, as if he had all the time in the world.

'I just do a delivery near here and now I must go to somewhere else. I don't know where to go. I have only been in London for one week,' she said, widening her eyes and looking directly at Sam.

'So, er, where are you looking for, then?' Sam asked, trying not to stare at Helena's breasts.

Without answering, Helena pushed a parcel into Sam's hands. He flipped it over and looked at the address.

'This is in the West End, quite a way from here, I'm afraid,' he said, pulling a sympathetic look.

Helena's expression changed from confident girl-about-town to lost child. She did not say anything and did not take the parcel back from Sam's outstretched hands. She muttered something in Czech, with her hands on her hips. Then she looked back at Sam and spoke.

'I have only been doing this courier thing for one week and London is big place. Please, you tell me the way to West End?'

'Well,' said Sam, 'it's not that easy from here but— '

'Maybe you draw me a map, please, please,' interrupted Helena, swapping her look back to sexy girl-about-town.

'Well, I suppose I could, yeah, no problem,' answered Sam, gesturing to her to come inside. He put the parcel down on the coffee table in the sitting room, picked up a piece of paper and started drawing.

Helena hovered by his side, pointing at the map and asking for more detail.

'So I am looking for number twenty-three South Street,' she said. 'Where is that, then?'

Sam scribbled away and marked the middle of South Street with a cross. Helena kept smiling and allowed her gloved hand to brush against his as he pointed at the piece of paper.

'There you go. That's the best I can do. So tell me, how are you finding London life?' Sam said, trying to sound relaxed and not as if he were attempting to engage her in conversation.

'Is OK, but I have only been here for a week. I live with my sister; her boyfriend get me the job as a courier because I can ride a bike. I don't know anyone here and—'

'Well, if you ever need anyone to show you around . . .' interrupted Sam.

Helena paused, allowing Sam to continue.

'I'm off work this week and could always show you around a bit, er, that's if you have time?'

Sam hoped the language barrier would have softened his clumsy tone.

Helena beamed at him and said, 'That would be so nice. You call me tomorrow.'

Sam jotted down Helena's number, part of him thinking that he should probably get her out of the door before he said anything stupid, another part weighing up if he should invite her out with his mates that very evening. The prospect of being 'reluctantly forced' to reveal what a hero he had been in Sierra Leone by his ultra-impressed-looking mates in front of this Czech beauty was heavenly. He was just clearing his throat to speak when Helena made the decision for him.

'Thank you so much. I had better go and deliver before I get fired,' she purred.

'Yes, of course,' said Sam, picking up the parcel and passing it to Helena. He opened the front door for her, hoping that the slight sheen of sweat he felt on his face was not too visible.

'Call me,' she said, with a slight sideways glance and a little wave of her hand.

Sam closed the door quietly, stepped over the pile of post and flopped on the sofa feeling turned on by the smell of perfume that he could still just detect in the air. He folded the piece of paper with her number written on it and placed it carefully under the clock on the mantelpiece.

The next morning, Christian was woken by a call from Armalite.

'Morning, lad; got good news and bad.'

'You've woken me up,' groaned Christian. 'Go on.' He rolled over to look at the bedside clock. 'Let's start with the bad then.'

'Well, the bad news is I'm downstairs already and coming up right now for breakfast. The good news is everything is sorted with your mate Oliver, but it hasn't been easy skiving off Battle Camp.'

'Battle Camp, what a nightmare,' replied Christian.

'Yup, the same old crap. We've got the usual load of TA lads scattered all over the Beacons. I'm doing the weapons course all bloody week, but I don't need to be back until late this afternoon.'

'OK, I'd better call room service and get a couple of full English breakfasts.'

'I want two eggs and flipped, OK?' continued Armalite, talking to himself as Christian had already hung up.

Christian hauled himself out of bed and into a white fluffy dressing gown. A moment later, his cosy private world was invaded by a loud knock on the door, followed by Armalite storming in, demanding more details on exactly how he had dealt with the diamond dealers.

Once they had finished breakfast and Armalite had stopped wandering around the suite saying how unnecessarily posh everything was, they got back to the matter in hand.

'So what time is the Czech bird coming round, then?' asked Armalite.

'Well, I said ten a.m., and bearing in mind how much we are paying her, I doubt she's going to be late,' replied Christian.

'And is she really fit, then?' continued Armalite, a pained expression on his face.

'Well, you do get super-model fit for four hundred pounds an hour it would seem,' said Christian, with a grin.

'Maybe we should get her to do a little show for us when she gets here. We've bags of cash, haven't we?'

'Honestly, she's a crucial part of the team. We can't expect her to get her kit off and start dancing round here while we eat our bloody breakfast. For fuck's sake!' replied Christian, laughing. 'You can have her number after all this is done if it makes you feel better.'

'OK, lad, just thinking about morale, that's all.' Armalite was grinning from ear to ear. 'Don't worry, I wasn't serious.'

'Bollocks, of course you were!'

'Listen, I've had another chat with my MI5 mate,' said Armalite, sounding businesslike once again.

'The ex-Hereford one?' interjected Christian.

'Yup, that's the one, known him for twenty years. He's agreed to help but doesn't know anything. All you have to do is get your Czech bird to lure Carter out of his house at an agreed time. The access specialist needs about forty seconds max – sometimes they can do it in ten.

'He will walk up to the door, open it and walk away. It's best you don't even see him. You just turn up one minute after the agreed time and the front door will be unlocked. You do your stuff inside, come out and pull the door shut behind you. They'll be watching and will then lock it properly, once you've gone. Does that make sense?'

'Sounds absolutely fine to me,' replied Christian.

There was a knock at the door. Armalite's eyes widened and Christian adjusted his towelling robe, making sure it was properly done up. He opened the door and in strode Helena, carrying the parcel. She looked around suspiciously and then spoke.

'So, I have done my job. Now you pay me the other half, yes?'

'Yes, of course. No problem,' answered Christian, passing her a wad of notes. 'Now there is something else we'd like your help with.'

Helena glanced up from counting the notes. 'OK. Same deal like this?' she said.

'Same deal, but even easier,' answered Christian, smiling.

'You are very strange men,' continued Helena, now focusing her attention on Armalite, who was looking on quietly from the sofa.

Christian suddenly became aware of just how peculiar Armalite did in fact look. His handlebar moustache, slightly grown-out crew-cut and missing fingers looked the norm at Stirling Lines, but pretty odd on Civvy Street.

'Sorry, this is my friend Andy; should have introduced you, sorry,' said Christian.

'Hi,' croaked Armalite, nodding stiffly.

Christian spent the next twenty minutes chatting to Helena about what he wanted her to do. The atmosphere relaxed and Armalite joined in the conversation. Christian produced another £5,000 in cash as an upfront payment and sent Helena on her way with an excited smile on her face.

'You really are a smooth-talking creep, Christi,' grunted Armalite, as the door closed. 'Sitting there in your dressing gown, like Steed out of *The Avengers*, honestly!'

'*The Avengers*?' replied Christian. 'People of my age have never heard of *The Avengers*, and Helena definitely won't have done. You're thinking of James

Bond, surely?' continued Christian, dodging a flying piece of toast.

Buoyed up from his surprise encounter with the mystery Czech blonde, Sam had been on a big night out with his mates. There were seven of them in total and they had cruised around various pubs and bars in Romford. Sam had strategically revealed more and more about his role in the fire-fight, revelling in the attention and respect. Despite consuming eight pints of lager, he had not had to put his hand in his pocket once.

He had been thinking about calling Helena from the moment he woke up. He had resisted calling too early, but felt that anything after eleven would be fine. Not too keen, he thought, but showing he was too mature to play silly games.

Her accent sounded ultra-sexy as she answered the call. Again, he felt the language barrier was going his way and helped to cover any awkwardness on his part.

'So we could meet anywhere that's good for you,' suggested Sam, in a helpful tone.

'But I don't know anywhere in London,' answered Helena. 'Oh, I know somewhere you know. How about we meet on South Street, where you showed me yesterday. I know where that is.'

'Yeah, that would be perfect. I could be there in an

hour or so. Maybe we could have some lunch and I'll tell you all about London?'

'Good, I will see you there,' Helena replied.

Christian and Armalite were still grazing on the remnants of breakfast, when Christian's mobile phone rang. He instantly recognised Helena's accent.

'I have an appointment with your man in one hour. I will keep him with me for two hours. OK?'

'That's very good. Thank you,' Christian replied, making an exaggerated thumbs-up sign at Armalite. 'Have the meeting just like I said, call me and then you can come and collect your money.'

'Good. I see you later then,' she replied.

Armalite whipped out his mobile phone and dialled, muttering, 'Bloody hell, mate, your bird doesn't half operate fast. I just hope my man can move as fast as her.'

'Tell him to drop everything. It's Saturday, for fuck's sake. No one else is paying him twenty thousand for forty seconds' work, are they?' snapped Christian in reply.

Fifteen minutes later, Christian was in a taxi heading east, across London. He was prepared but still rattled by the speed at which his plan was unfolding. He told the driver to drop him three streets away and then walked slowly around to get an idea of the area. It was a pleasant enough neighbourhood; far too pleasant for Sam, he thought.

At 12.00, Christian positioned himself at the end of Sam's road. He knew that any moment an MI5 access specialist would appear from somewhere. He also knew that any compromise would result in whoever it was aborting. Christian walked slowly round the corner and then around the block. He looked at his watch. It was approaching 12.05. He held on for one more minute before walking back into Sam's road. He looked up and down and seeing no one, strolled casually down to number 42. The front door was very slightly ajar. Christian pushed it open and stepped into Sam's world.

The inside was not at all what he had expected. The sitting room was freshly painted in off white, with two large sloppy-style sofas on either side of a glass coffee table. The floor was modern stripped pine. There were the compulsory army photos scattered about, but nothing like Armalite's wall-to-wall coverage. He climbed the newly carpeted stairs, noticing his own face in a D Squadron photo halfway up. He put his bag down on the landing and set to work.

Sweating slightly from tension, Christian was relieved to pull the front door shut a few minutes later. He walked off down the street as fast as possible, knowing that within a minute or so the door would be locked. He had now passed the point of no return.

Back at the hotel, he tried to relax and watch television but found his thoughts drifting back to Sam. An uncomfortable feeling of doubt kept creeping back. He knew Sam was to blame for everything that had happened but, on balance, Christian decided that Sam's fate was almost worse than anything the West Side Boys, or even Lennep, could lay on. Was it really fair? It had certainly felt so, back in Mauritania, but lying on a bed in a five-star hotel suite made things feel different.

Helena's arrival interrupted his negative thoughts. He fished out another £5,000 in cash from Derek's briefcase and gave it to her. She took the cash and said, 'So then, do you have any more jobs for me?'

'No, but you could help me with one of these bottles of champagne. I may need a bit of Dutch courage later,' Christian replied, flipping open the door of the minibar.

Helena smiled and sat down on the sofa with her legs tucked up under her. Christian prised the cork out of the champagne and sat on the chair opposite. Their conversation lasted the best part of an hour before Christian said he had to go. He closed the door behind her, respectful of the fact that she had asked nothing about the extraordinary things he had asked her to do.

Christian moved over to the window and looked out. The sun was setting over the horizon on the far side of Hyde Park. He sat quietly on the sofa and watched the light fade. It was 7.45 p.m. when he decided it was time to go. He tucked the Sig Saur into the back of his jeans, picked up his bag and left the room.

Emerging onto the pavement outside the hotel, he lit a cigarette to calm his nerves. He had planned his route and timings. He knew that in less than twenty minutes he would be back and that the final piece of the jigsaw would be in place.

He walked fast, passing relaxed and happy-looking people heading out for the evening in the West End. A group of young girls, their names written on the backs of their matching pink minidresses, screamed past him in a parallel universe. Christian paused in a shop doorway just long enough to light a second cigarette from the dying embers of his first. He set off again at a fast pace, pulling his baseball cap lower over his face.

As he turned into South Street he tucked his chin into the scarf loosely tied around his neck.

49

Armalite had made it back down to Hereford by mid-afternoon. He changed into combat gear and reported for duty at the Sennybridge Training Centre, on the edge of the Brecon Beacons. With his mind anywhere but on the job, he stood in the flood-lit parade ground and took a group of exhausted and filthy TA recruits through a weapons drill on the M16 assault rifle. He could tell no one was really listening, having been up all night on a forced march across the Black Mountains.

'Right then, lads, you have finished with me for the time being, but you will be seeing me later on in the week. It's time for some scoff over there,' he said, pointing at a building the far side of the parade ground.

Once the recruits had picked up their kit and shuffled off in the direction of the canteen, Armalite whipped out his mobile and dialled.

'All OK, lad? How did it go?' he blurted the moment he heard Christian's voice.

'Well, fine, I think. I've only just got back to the hotel now. Need to pick up my stuff and head on down, as soon as. Should be in before ten; I'll get a cab from the station,' replied Christian, lying on the bed.

'Fucking marvellous . . . Well done, lad! The key's under the mat like I told you. Make yourself at home and I'll try to see you before you go, if I can get any more time off this bloody course.'

'How's it going, anyway?' said Christian, trying to sound interested.

'Well, it's the usual thing. Across the Squadrons, there are probably a couple of hundred TA lads prattling around the hills. The fact is, we know about one per cent will pass, so what's the bloody point at lobbing so much resource at it?' Armalite grumbled.

'Tell me about it,' replied Christian, over the sound of a knock at the door. 'Hold on a second, need to get the door, don't want my dinner getting cold.'

Christian put the mobile down on the bedside table and made his way across the room to the door. He turned the handle but, before he had even begun to pull it open, the door burst open with such force that it hit him in the face. He found himself slammed backwards into the hallway wall behind him, as four men burst in. Before a coherent thought had passed through his mind, the first two men through the door had piled on top of him. The third had run through into the main section of the suite, and the fourth had covered the door.

'Shut the fuck up,' hissed a high, aggressive north London accent from behind a balaclava.

Christian had been taken entirely by surprise but knew from his training that he needed to cooperate for the time being. He felt handcuffs snapping shut and pain searing forth from his right shoulder, as his arm was yanked back. A hood went over his head. He felt his body physically leave the floor and being dropped somewhere in the seating area of the room. He was pulled into a kneeling position and he felt a hard object pressed against the back of his head.

'Right, you piece of shit, we want your name first,' said a different voice, sounding calmer than the first.

Christian did not answer. He paused for thought. He needed to know who these guys were and would have to test them.

'Angelus Phelps, New York Police Department,' blurted Christian.

There was a pause that lasted several seconds before the voice replied. 'Who?'

Christian thought for a second and concluded that whoever it was did not know exactly who he was. 'I said my name is Angelus Phelps. I am a US citizen, seconded to the London Metropolitan Police, sir,' Christian gasped.

There was another pause. Christian's brain churned

but he was at least buying thinking time and getting some idea of what his captors did or didn't know about him. His next sensation was the hood being pulled sharply off his head.

A man sat on one of the chairs in front of him wearing a smart dark suit, his face obscured by the balaclava. He had a mobile phone in his hand and looked at the screen.

'Would you be the same Angelus Phelps that nicked a load of cash and tried to blow up a load of people with a grenade?' the man said, sounding more in control.

Christian guessed the man was probably reading a description of him on this phone.

'Yes, that would be me,' Christian replied, looking at the floor immediately in front of him.

'Well then, Mr Yankee policeman, whoever the fuck you are . . . You have two choices. Either you tell us where you have put the five hundred grand and those diamonds or we torture you for the next week and then you'll tell us where the fuck it all is. And one small detail. We torture in twenty-four-hour incre-ments, so that means we will only allow you to offer information every twenty-four hours. Does that make sense? Our sources tell us you have paid for this very comfortable-looking suite for a few more days. Ideal really, we won't have to clear up the mess.'

Christian thanked God Armalite had taken most of the stash back down to Hereford.

'OK, you win. I have hidden the money with the diamonds. Fuck it, you can have the whole lot. I thought this was a shit idea from the start,' he muttered.

'So, where the fuck are they then?' snapped the man.

'It's all down in Wales, where I come from. It's stashed; I mean, it's buried. I am so sorry for all this. I hope I didn't mess up your VW too badly?' stammered Christian.

'Shut up! Right, you even smaller piece of shit, it looks like we are all heading off to Wales, then. That's once we've taken this place to pieces. You'll lead the way and defuse any nasty little booby traps. I've heard you like grenades. And if, for any reason, we don't find exactly what we are looking for immediately we arrive, you are on for your first twenty-four-hour instalment. That's enough time to pull out each of your teeth, eyes and fingernails. Then, depending on time, we might have time to break a couple of joints – knees, ankles, elbows, etc. – and start twisting them around. That sort of thing, you know? It doesn't kill you, but twenty-four hours will feel like a year. Are you starting to understand me?' The man spoke in a pseudo-friendly tone.

Christian nodded. After more questions, the hood went back on. He heard the frenzied sound of tearing fabrics and draws crashing onto the floor. A satisfied grunt indicated they had found the remains of the cash.

He was pulled back onto his feet and pushed towards the door. With the handcuffs securely fastened behind his back, he was bundled out of the door and down the corridor to some stairs. One man held his cuffed wrists, another dragged him by the shoulder and the two others led the way. They descended five sets of stairs.

A moment later, Christian felt his knees hitting something sharp and metallic and his body fell forwards onto a hard surface. There was the sound of slamming doors and an engine. He was in the back of a van. He felt the vehicle move off and up a steep, twisting gradient, which had to be the ramp of an underground car park. There was the jerk of a gear change and the sensation of gaining speed. All the time, he felt the pressure of a knee in the small of his back.

Taking deep breaths, Christian tried to gather his thoughts when he heard the scream of a siren. Then he heard another and another. Over the din, he heard his captors speaking.

'What the fuck is going on in this fucking city?' snapped someone.

'No fucking idea,' said a more distant voice from the front of the van.

The vitriolic chatter continued over the sound of the radio as Christian lay still, taking in the information and building a picture.

After twenty minutes of stop-start traffic, Christian

was conscious that they were moving at a more constant pace, which he guessed meant they were either on the dual carriageway leading out of London or maybe even on the M4. He tried to picture where they might be and reckoned it was probably somewhere near Heathrow.

The surge of adrenalin had faded, leaving Christian able to think straight and analyse. He had written Derek out of the picture entirely. His plan had been going perfectly except he had not even considered the remotest chance of the East End diamond mob re-entering the frame. Sam's grinning face flashed before him. The whole perfectly conceived and brilliantly executed plan was now most likely ruined.

The chit-chat settled down and it seemed the woes of the London traffic were behind them. Then the nine o'clock news broke. Christian listened hard, hoping the cavemen would not switch it off.

'This is the Nine O'Clock News from the BBC . . .' sounded the familiar voice of a BBC newsreader. 'A bomb has been detonated in Central London, bringing chaos to the capital. The device is thought to have been placed outside the Egyptian Embassy but has only partially detonated. A spokesperson from the Metropolitan Police has confirmed there are no reports of casualties at this time.'

'That'll be what caused the fucking traffic,' snarled one of the men in the front of the van. A second later the news was flicked off and music started up, but

Christian had heard all he needed. He rested his face on the rough plywood floor and tried to deal with the rising feeling of panic within him. There were several options. He either had to break free or offer to buy them off and somehow deliver, or he would be tortured to death and dumped down a disused mine shaft in the Welsh valleys. At least his broken body would rot in Wales, not Romford or Sierra Leone.

Option three was unacceptable. Option two was going to be very tricky as he no longer had the diamonds or the cash in his possession. This left Option one. The problem was that his captors were taking no chances. He assumed Mr Jones was one of them and no doubt paranoid about messing up again, hence the thugs, handcuffs and hood.

After a couple of hours' driving, the van slowed up and the driver's window wound down. Christian heard the driver grunt the word 'Cheers', which he knew had to be the toll section over the Severn Bridge. The van accelerated away.

'Right, sit up in the back there and start giving some directions,' shouted someone in the front.

Christian felt the pressure on his lower back release and a hand on his shoulder pulled him up roughly. The hood was ripped off his head.

'Where are we?' he said.

'We've crossed the fucking bridge and are in Wales, still on the M4. You said you stashed it out in the sticks in the middle of nowhere. Now, where are we going?' replied the driver, slightly turning to look over his shoulder.

'We need to come off the M4 and take the A4042 towards Abergavenny and then keep heading north. Just one thing, though, there is no way I am going to be able to find it in the dark. We are going to have to hold on till the morning,' said Christian, in a scared-sounding voice.

There was an explosion of anger from the four men in the van. Christian was thrown back on his face while each of the men shouted at him. With a pistol pressed against his cheek, Christian stammered, 'There's nothing I can do. It's not my fault. I hid them somewhere in daylight and that's that. Shoot me, but it won't make any bloody difference.'

Despite having the hood forced back over his head, Christian knew when the van came off the motorway. He felt the incline of a slip road and the right-hand turn off the roundabout at the top of the motorway. He did not know for sure, but was pretty much convinced the man in the front passenger seat was Mr Jones. He lay on his front listening to the men arguing about how to spend the night. Each scenario involved kicking the shit out of him first.

As they wound along the A4042, towards Abergavenny, Christian thought of happier times when he had driven along this stretch of road. He knew it well. It seemed ironic that he had made it halfway across Africa, negotiated the Rokel Creek on a load of car spares, crossed swords with the WSBs, dodged mercenaries and professional terrorists, to end up being beaten to death by a bunch of second-rate yobs in his own back yard. It would not be a soldier's death. It would be humiliating, drawn-out, and a painful load of shit.

At least the WSBs had known who and what he was. Mo and his men had been fearful of him and treated him like a dangerous animal. He was now at the mercy of some arguing wide-boys for whom life was cheap. He had worked out a plan but he knew it wasn't a very good one. It did have one advantage, though. If it went wrong, which it probably would, he would end up with a bullet in his back as opposed to having his teeth pulled out first.

50

The night crept past. Christian remained handcuffed, with the hood over his head. Nasty second-rate thugs they were, but they were not taking any chances. He had no idea where they were parked but it was a couple of hours' drive from the motorway. With the exception of being allowed to take one piss, Christian had stayed in the van. The four men took turns to guard him and judging by the smell of alcohol, had found somewhere to buy some booze.

Christian was not aware of having fallen asleep, but having the hood ripped off his head came as a startling shock. He looked around, blinking. The van was full of light and he could see the faces of his captors for the first time. Immediately, he recognised Mr Jones. He looked tired, grey and angry. The older man from the pub was there, too. The other two were hard-looking ex-military types that

Christian guessed would have been chucked out of the army.

Mr Jones put his face close to Christian's. Before he opened his mouth to speak, Christian smelt a nasty mixture of coffee, alcohol and cigarettes.

'You have pissed me off twice so far and I suggest you don't do it again. You need to take us to the stuff right now or we start work on you. There's no one round here to hear you scream.'

Christian could feel the anger and tension radiating from him.

'Just get me to the car park, two miles south of Llanspyddid, and we'll be there in no time. It's on the right with a big sign, you can't miss it,' Christian replied, holding the other man's stare.

Twenty minutes later, Christian felt the van slow, turn to the right and then bounce slightly. This was the car park where he had unloaded a thousand times.

'Get the fuck out and start walking,' Mr Jones shouted. 'And if we pass anyone, you make sure they don't spot the cuffs and don't you say a word or even look at them, right?'

'Right. Follow me,' Christian replied quietly.

He led the way across the main road and through a small gate that led into a rough gorse-scattered field, from which rose a large mountain range. He set the pace deliberately too fast, waiting for the first complaint. Within a minute he was told to slow down.

With Christian at the front, the group followed a

well-trodden path for a couple of kilometres then veered off across country. The sight of dawn breaking over the hills buoyed Christian. This was his country and he knew exactly where he was going. He knew the bearing they were following and, within a minute or so, when they would reach each way point.

They had covered less than 5 kilometres, at a slow walking pace, when Mr Jones needed a break. Christian turned round to see his face flushed with colour and sweat pouring from his brow.

Lazy cunt, flashed through Christian's mind, but for the time being he needed to keep his cool.

They followed a sheep-track uphill. Christian heard satisfying amounts of wheezing behind him and pushed the pace a fraction. With seconds Mr Jones was yelling again.

'We're nearly there,' Christian called over his shoulder. They followed the contour around the bottom of a hill and found themselves looking into a very long, slightly rising valley with steep sides. Without a word, Christian pressed on, following the line of the small stream flowing down the middle of the valley.

By the time they reached the halfway point, the sun had risen sufficiently to fill the valley with warm autumn light. Christian looked around at the green and gold colours and took a deep breath. He always felt strong in the hills, but he was going to need a hell of a lot of luck.

Ignoring the puffing and cursing behind him, he walked on at a steady pace. Then, to his surprise, he saw a figure sitting on a stone several hundred yards ahead. Christian was sure he had not seen anyone in the valley and assumed it was the poor light.

Immediately, Mr Jones called out, obviously seeing the figure too.

'You two get ahead,' he gasped, 'and you,' pointing at Christian, 'keep your hands out of sight, head down and keep walking.'

Christian had no intention of trying to involve an innocent walker in his nasty gangster world. Enough lives had been ruined.

As they got closer, Christian glanced up and saw a small figure in a blue anorak sitting on a large stone studying a map. At 10 yards, the figure lowered the map and a smiling face with stubble and a grown-out moustache appeared.

Lightning passed through Christian.

'Excuse me,' said the man, in a strong Welsh accent 'I reckon I'm lost and would be ever so grateful for your assistance.'

'Can't help,' grunted the closest of Mr Jones' men, not even slowing the pace.

Armalite stood up and blocked the path. 'Well, that's not so very friendly is it, then?' he continued.

'Get the fuck out of the way,' hissed Mr Jones, looking at Armalite's missing fingers.

'Yeah, get out of the way, you filthy fucking leper,'

growled the lead man, reaching out to push Armalite out of the way.

'Thalidomide, more like,' interjected one of the other men.

Christian saw colour appear in Armalite's cheeks despite the beard growth. He prayed his old friend would keep his cool.

Armalite stepped back nimbly and deflected the push. Having recovered from the initial shock of seeing his comrade, Christian suddenly had a bad feeling. He had bragged to Armalite about what a bunch of amateur idiots these guys had been and how he had outwitted them with the good old grenade trick. He had made it sound like some sketch from a 'B' movie and that Armalite had missed out on all the fun. It dawned on him that Armalite would not be prepared for the nasty, more hardcore professionals that had been drafted in this time round. They were probably ex-military and, so far, had not cut any corners.

Armalite flicked the map to one side to reveal a small pistol that he had concealed between the folds. With his legs in a widened stance, he raised the pistol and pointed it at Mr Jones, who he seemed to have identified as being in charge.

'Right, who's calling me a fucking leper now?' he yelled, losing the Welsh accent.

Within half a second there were four pistols pointing straight back at him. Armalite's eyes glanced uneasily from one large-calibre weapon to the next.

'Put that fucking pop gun down now, you little toss pot,' yelled Mr Jones. 'I guess you're the jerk that's been nicking diamonds on the job in Africa. Right? You small-time, petty thief.'

Christian shook his head in disbelief. How could Armalite have lost his cool so quickly? Armalite was lowering his weapon with a desperate expression of defeat all over his reddened face.

'Not so big and tough now, are we?' taunted one of the other men, pointing his weapon in Armalite's face.

Armalite dropped his gun on the ground. Christian met his gaze and watched Armalite raise his hands in the air. Thoughts of Tim being shot in the head flashed through his mind. Then a momentary image of the twisting pig filled his view. Sam's face. It seemed that everyone connected in any way to these diamonds would end up dead. They were cursed.

As Christian looked on in stunned disbelief, Armalite's raised right hand moved slowly from fingers outstretched into a clenched fist. Christian detected a tiny twitch in the corner of his mouth.

With no warning, the bracken around them swirled and came to life as twenty-four heavily armed infantry soldiers in full combat kit sprang up in a full circle.

The tremor in the corner of Armalite's mouth gave way to a huge, impossible-to-hide sneer of victorious delight. Christian glanced around at the soldiers, all carrying M16s with fully camouflaged faces and helmets covered in bracken.

'British Army. Drop your weapons, now!' roared Armalite.

Mr Jones and his men looked at Armalite in bewilderment. Then they looked at each other and at Christian. Mr Jones was the first to drop his gun and raise his hands, followed immediately by the other three.

Armalite took a step forward and spoke, just loudly enough that only Mr Jones, his men and Christian could hear. 'Who's the toss pot now?'

Then, turning to a soldier behind him, Armalite shouted, 'Corporal Anderson, pick up these weapons and flexi-cuffs on.'

'Yes, sir,' barked Anderson, sprinting forwards with three other soldiers. A few seconds later, Mr Jones and his men were kneeling, staring at the ground, their hands flexi-cuffed behind their backs.

'Find the keys and get the hostage released,' Armalite snapped next.

Anderson yelled at the group to reveal who had the keys to Christian's handcuffs. Mr Jones raised his head and stuttered, 'Er, in, in . . . in my coat pocket.'

Once Christian was released, Armalite handed him one of the captured pistols.

'Cover these tosspots while I dismiss the unit,' he said, grinning from ear to ear. He turned to Anderson and spoke: 'Very good, form the men up over there.'

The soldiers formed a small semicircle around Anderson and either squatted down or dropped to one knee. Armalite moved forward to address them.

'Good work, A Squadron. That was a basic counter-terrorism operation. In reality things could have been very different and it's usually the sort of thing the police, MOD Plod or M16 would do. Could be useful, though. The important element has to be surprise and speed. You need them cuffed and down before anyone gets any big ideas. Are there any questions?'

Armalite paused and looked around before continuing.

'Your next RV point today is 209654 and I will give you a slight clue. The obvious route won't necessarily be the fastest, so don't just look at your map, read the map, understand the features, feel the topography. That's all, now move.'

As the soldiers leapt to their feet and moved off up the valley, Armalite walked back to where Christian stood, still beaming. He stood in the front of the four kneeling men and spoke. 'Right, you gobby bunch of cretins, you have no idea who you fucked with today. You will remain here for precisely thirty minutes and then you will return to your vehicle and drive directly to London. You will be followed. You will forget everything you have ever known about this. One word, one drunken whisper, and you will be killed. You have no idea who you have crossed. If you weren't so fucking low down the food chain, you would now

433

be in the food chain. There is a sniper on that hill so don't move a muscle or he will shoot. Thirty minutes from now.'

With that, he picked up the remaining pistols from the ground, nodded to Christian and set off down the valley. As Christian caught him up, he turned his head and appeared to be suppressing laughter. Christian shook his head and grinned back at him.

At a safe distance, Armalite put his hand over his mouth and laughed. Christian looked back up the valley to see the four men still kneeling. He was about to speak when Armalite beat him to it. 'Told you I'd make a great gangster, didn't I?' he gasped.

'You fucking legend, I cannot believe you worked it out. Fucking genius, that was first class,' Christian said, still shaking his head.

'Well, I could hear everything. We were in mid-conversation and you put your mobile down when you went to answer the door. I could hear the whole bloody thing. Nearly shat myself. I was sure that any second it would be noticed and switched off. I assumed you meant to get in the reference to VW?' replied Armalite, with a mixture of excitement and worry in his voice.

'I knew the mobile was still on but I had no idea if you could hear anything. I was so surprised, it took me a moment to twig you might still be on the line. I needed to think of somewhere I could bring them where you would intercept and I thought of here, good old VW valley.'

'That's what I thought you meant. I couldn't see any other reason on earth why you would be apologising for smashing up their car. It worked perfectly because we've been doing drills with the TA all weekend round here. I took over the A Squadron lads about two a.m. I force-marched them over and got them set up from about five. I guessed you would be here at first light.'

'But surely someone is going to mention it to someone senior, who knows there wasn't meant to be a mock terrorist handover on the schedule for Battle Camp,' Christian said, looking concerned

'When was the last time you can remember a bunch of Twenty-one TA guys talking to someone senior in Twenty-two? We've laid on a week of messing about for them, from log races to fast roping, weapons, foreign weapons, demolition, climbing, the whole bloody lot. That was the most boring thing they've done. No chance, mate,' answered Armalite confidently. 'Piece of piss. Now, we need to get you out of here before anyone recognises you. Everything is ready with Oliver, but we need to get you to Brize, like right now.'

'I owe you big time,' replied Christian.

'Lad, you already sorted me big time with them diamonds. It's me that owes you. And anyway, it's time I had some of the fun.'

'I don't think this whole thing has been that much fun, to be honest. Just need to finish off now. There is still every chance this whole escapade could go to rat shit,' Christian said, frowning.

'Whatever,' answered Armalite. 'Anyway, at least it's a nice day for it!'

After a short pause in the conversation, Armalite stopped in his tracks. He turned to Christian with an inquisitive look on his face. 'So what were you going to do?'

'I was hoping you weren't going to ask,' replied Christian. 'Well, I had about three options. I thought there was a tiny chance you might have picked up on the VW bit, or more likely, I was hoping to run into a TA unit somewhere in the hills before they got pissed off walking around the place. Last option was heading up the dam and leaping off into the lake. Probably would have drowned or been shot, but I thought that was better than be tortured to death by that lot.'

'Yeah, well, I guess that makes sense. Anyway, we got the wankers, didn't we?' replied Armalite, in triumphant mode.

51

Deverall was at a dinner party with some family friends when he was informed of the failed terrorist bombing in London. Part of him was secretly delighted to make his excuses and leave the table. He went to his car and spoke to the Operations Room in Hereford, who were automatically alerted by the police to any terrorist incident.

He heard from the Duty Officer that the Met believed that only the detonator of a large bomb had gone off outside the Egyptian Embassy. It was believed to have been an extremist Islamic group, but no one quite knew who as yet. He made an appearance in the Ops Room and was relieved to be stood down to Amber Alert by MI5, who had assumed control. He decided to sleep on the camp bed in his office and woke early to attend a briefing in the Ops Room.

He swirled his coffee and pondered as the meeting

room filled. The thing that surprised him most was that only the detonator of the bomb had gone off. Anyone who could get their hands on a pile of good quality Semtex would know how to make it explode. It was easy. Also, why plant a bomb to go off on Saturday night, when the embassy was closed and no one would be about? There was more to it. He would sit through the briefing and then head out for a walk to clear his head.

By the time they approached the barrier at Brize Norton, Christian could tell that Armalite was getting twitchy. The drama of the ambush had worn off and the practicalities of disappearing for a couple of hours in the middle of an exercise were more real. They had listened to the news on Radio 4 and got as much information as was available on the bombing in London the night before.

'It's quite amazing what a load of bollocks the news is when you know what really happened,' commented Christian from beneath the tarpaulin in the back of the Land Rover.

'I know,' snapped Armalite. 'Now shut up; we're going in any second. This has to be one seriously fast turn-around, otherwise I'm in the shit.'

A minute later, Christian heard the clunk of the back door opening.

Armalite's voice sounded confident and reassuring as Christian emerged from under the tarpaulin and walked towards the back of the Hercules, wearing the RAF flight suit he had worn before. He walked up the ramp and disappeared once again between the wooden containers. He sat down in the same dark void and checked through the bergen that was waiting for him. Everything was there.

Sam woke early for a Sunday morning. Having had a big Friday night, he'd felt a bit off colour on Saturday, but had at least managed to be on form for lunch with Helena. Sure, she had kept him waiting for a few minutes, but that was what sexy girls did. They had lunch together in a nice French restaurant and afterwards, he had walked her round the West End.

He had an early night, wanting to get back on track for Sunday and hopefully for another encounter with her. He reckoned he only needed to see her once more before he could make a move. Ideally, he needed to select a few of his most presentable mates and do something in a group where she would pick up on just how respected he was.

Musing over this next step, Sam made himself breakfast. He wondered what sort of breakfast Helena would expect him to have. He poured himself a bowl of cereal, with chopped-up banana on top and then poured milk over it. He knew yogurt would look better but he didn't have any. He took his first mouthful as the doorbell rang.

He put down his spoon, got up from the breakfast

table and sauntered to the front door. It was probably her. Wiping the corners of his mouth with his thumb and forefinger, he pulled the latch down.

With the velocity of an avalanche, a wall of CO19 armed policemen burst through the door. Within four seconds, there were fourteen firearm officers in black boiler suits and helmets in the house, shouting 'Armed police, clear; armed police, clear, clear' to each other as they stormed from room to room.

Sam was hit in the chest by something or someone. He hit the ground knowing there was no point resisting. He was grabbed and dragged outside. The next time his feet touched something solid was in the back of a police van. He shook his head in astonishment and opened his mouth to speak.

'Shut up,' yelled a highly aggressive-looking man in casual clothes, sitting between two armed policemen opposite. Sam tried to move his arms and only then noticed he was handcuffed. There was a scream of sirens and the van moved off. Sam could tell by the speed they were going that there had to be outriders. He was pressed against the white metal caging which protected the rear door of the van as they careered through the quiet London streets.

Sam's mind was in overdrive. Was this the most utterly mad counter-terrorism exercise ever? Maybe he had been selected for MI5 or MI6 and this was some bizarre test or initiation ceremony? It could be some big mistake, a mistaken identity? That was most likely. Whatever it was, he had done nothing wrong and had nothing to worry about. He would be released in a few hours with an apology, once they realised who he was. In fact, once they identified him as a respected SAS officer, someone else would be in deep shit. It could be fun.

He decided he needed to play the part properly. It would get back to people. This was a chance to confirm his status as a tough nut who couldn't be pushed around by anyone, even the police.

Arriving at Paddington Green police station fifteen minutes later, it occurred to him that there might be reporters and cameramen. Just in case, he adopted a hard, expressionless scowl as he was bundled out of the van. He could imagine his mates taking the piss if they thought he looked scared or ruffled.

He was pushed through a side entrance and into a lift, which dropped several floors. He was shoved out and along a bright, white-tiled corridor to a small meeting room with a table and chairs and a mirrored window. He looked around. The white tiles from the corridor were still on the floor but the walls were a bumpy grey cardboard, which he guessed had to be something to do with sound proofing. In front of him sat the casually dressed man from the van. He was wearing a navy blue shirt with an almost matching suit jacket. His hair was short and black. Sam thought he had a military look. He hoped so.

Next to him sat another man, older, portly, with

short grey hair and glasses. He looked pensive. A police officer stood by the door with his hands behind his back.

'My name is Chief Inspector Danes and this is Mr Ingram from the Metropolitan Counter-Terrorism Unit. Now this is all being recorded but will be off the record until a solicitor gets here for you. For the benefit of the tape, it's nine twenty a.m. It's myself, Mr Ingram and Police Constable Davies present,' said Danes.

'Now you are probably thinking we don't know who you are but, unless we are very much mistaken, I think we do. Are you Sam Carter, currently serving with Twenty-second SAS?'

Sam found himself speaking in a softer than usual voice with his head tilted slightly to one side.

'Yes, sir, that's correct, sir,' he said, with an exaggerated nod.

Danes continued. 'Well, would you like to tell us what you are doing here with us?'

'I'm sorry, sir, I have absolutely no idea why I am here,' Sam replied, in a tone that sounded more like his normal voice.

'What do you know about the bombing that took place last night in Central London?' continued Danes.

'Well, I heard about it on the news, sir. I think everyone would have done. Nobody hurt, some device that failed to go off is what the BBC said,' answered Sam, looking baffled.

'OK, so are you saying you know nothing about it?' said Danes.

'Yes, sir, that's what I am saying,' replied Sam.

'Are you sure?' said Danes.

'Yes, I'm sure,' Sam replied, unable to hide a hint of aggression.

'That's not what I think, Mr Carter,' said Danes. 'Now, I have a tricky situation on my hands. We have had a bomb go off outside the Egyptian Embassy. It's world news and it doesn't look too good, the fact we let it happen. Sure, it may not have gone off properly but as far as the world out there is concerned, we let a bomb go off in Central London.'

'So what's it got to do with me?' said Sam gruffly

'Well, what hasn't it got to do with you, Mr Carter?' answered Danes, shaking his head. 'What hasn't it got to do with you?'

There was a knock on the door and a uniformed policeman walked into the room. He nodded to Danes and put a file down on the table in front of him.

Danes' eyes flashed as he opened the folder, but his face remained expressionless. He was not going to reveal anything about what he was reading. He slid the file over to Ingram, who also flicked through the contents.

Finally, Danes looked up and spoke.

'I don't know whether you remember or not, but all Special Forces soldiers have a sample of their DNA taken during a medical, along with fingerprints, etc.

I think it's so you can be identified even if there isn't much left of you.'

'So?' grunted Sam, with a slight shrug. He felt pretty sure now that Danes was not ex-military.

'Well, sorry, I'm jumping around— ' replied Danes. Before he had time to carry on Sam interrupted.

'If you think I had something to do with the bombing last night, hurry up and give me some evidence. This is a waste of my time,' he blurted, wishing he had put less emphasis on the word 'my'.

'Very well. It may not be us you really need to explain yourself to, but I am happy to present the evidence we have. A bomb exploded last night at the Egyptian Embassy on South Street.'

'Yes, tell me something I don't know,' snapped Sam.

Danes paused and glanced at Ingram. He continued.

'The Semtex device was contained in a sports bag, packed with a mixture of nails and ball-bearings. You know the sort of stuff, to cause maximum damage. Now, because only the detonator went off, we have the bag, which would normally have been vaporised. In that bag we found various things that bring us to you.'

Sam's narrowed eyes widened with surprise.

'Yes, Mr Carter. We found your DNA – you know, skin, hair, etc. – in the bag. We also found a hand-drawn map of the area, marking the site of the embassy in what, according to your MOD records, looks like your handwriting. We have CCTV footage of you hovering in the street outside where the explosion took place.'

In Sam's mind was a growing realisation that something was very, very wrong. He nodded as if asking Danes to continue.

'So all this led us to you. And according to this report,' said Danes, pointing at the folder on the desk, 'certain other materials have been found at your house, including a machine gun that our firearms people say has been fired, nearly a kilo of cocaine, another gun, two fake passports and a pen that looks like the one that was used to draw the map. And, Mr Carter, a very, very large sum in cash . . . £191,214, to be precise. And before you tell us the whole lot was planted by your mates as a big, very funny practical joke, Mr Carter, your bloody prints are all over the box the money is in,' growled Danes aggressively.

Sam's mouth opened and shut. The possibility that this was some form of misunderstanding was no longer an option. He thought of Helena. He had drawn a map for her, he had been on South Street, he had hovered about. Yes, all true, but his DNA, in a bag containing a bomb? That was crazy, and the weapons, passports, cash? This was simply impossible. Narrow-eyed again, he paused before he spoke. He knew what was going on. This evidence was being made up to trick him into saying something, to make him confess to something he had not done.

'Listen,' said Sam, leaning across the table towards

Danes, 'I was in the West End yesterday. I met a girl. Is that still OK in this country? She told me to wait for her on South Street. I had no idea the Egyptian Embassy was even there. Why should I? I waited for her, she was late. End of story.'

Danes looked at Ingram.

Sam regained some control and carried on.

'I've got no idea about any guns in my house. I am a respected army officer and I have no idea how they got there, if they were there,' he stammered. 'They were planted there by someone, that's if they were there at all. And I'm not saying they were.'

Ingram looked at Sam and spoke for the first time.

'Mr Carter . . . Sam . . . Tell me about the money. A man on £39,000 a year with £191,241 in cash hidden in the loft, it seems unlikely to me. Why would someone plant a sum like that in your attic? Sure, a couple of guns and some drugs, possibly, but a big box of cash, I don't think so. Wouldn't it be easier to tell us where you got it? The box has your prints on it, so you must have put it there.'

Sam felt his body shake. He realised that Helena had to be part of some drugs ring and he had been set up. He had no idea why he had been picked, but she must have been using him.

'I won't say anything else until I have a solicitor present. It's my right,' he snapped, looking around behind him as if he expected to be ambushed from the rear.

'That's fine, Mr Carter. Anyway, this isn't really anything to do with us,' replied Danes.

'What?' shouted Sam.

'Well, to be quite accurate, you have not committed a crime in our jurisdiction. Sure, you have a couple of guns and some coke. Big deal, we get that every day of the week. Could be six years, out in three, that kind of thing. Not interested, really. What you have done, though, is commit an act of terrorism on Egyptian soil, because an embassy is sovereignty. Now I know it's a minimum of twenty-five years' hard labour down there for that or, if you're lucky, death by hanging.'

Ingram nodded slowly and gathered up his papers. Sam's mouth hung open, his eyes bulged, sweat dripped down the inside of his shirt.

'Yes,' said Danes, 'we are not really interested in you at all. Mind you, we wanted to know internally what you have been up to, but as far as we are concerned you committed the more serious crime in Egyptian legal jurisdiction and not on our patch. So, Mr Carter, that's it from us. We will be handing you over to the Egyptian authorities, who have already applied for extradition and will probably have it by now because they requested it from a judge at the Old Bailey an hour ago.'

Sam's eyes cast around the mean little room. He was about to speak when suddenly he lunged forward, pushing the table towards Danes and Ingram. He turned and sprang at the policeman by the door. He grabbed him by the front of his shirt and pulled him out of the way of the door, hitting him on the side of the face at the same time. Sam ripped open the door and bolted down the white corridor, heading for the lift. He had only got a few yards when alarms sounded.

Two policemen appeared at the far end of the corridor. Without hesitation, they ran at Sam who was able to deflect the first one with his shoulder, but was knocked to the ground by the second. As they struggled, the policeman appeared from the interview room and piled on top, followed by Danes.

Sam kicked, writhed and bellowed. Cuffs were snapped on his hands and his thrashing body was dragged towards a cell. The door shut with a clang behind him.

52

Christian's afternoon was very dull. He had been told the flight was going to leave any minute, but for some reason, as was always the case with the RAF, things had been delayed. He had nodded off with his head resting on his pack when he found himself waking up with a start as the Hercules finally began to move. A couple of minutes later, he was in the air on the last leg of the plan.

Sam was also on an aircraft. It was small private jet taxiing along a runway at Biggin Hill. The only reason he knew he was on an aircraft was because of the slight smell of aviation fuel. None of his other senses worked, due to the black hood over his head secured with masking tape to keep the ear defenders on. His body was encased in a mental hospital-style strait-jacket and his hands were tied in small black mittens to prevent any sensation of touch. He was in a highly uncomfortable position, lying on his front with his feet tied up tightly in a hogtie position. Worst of all was the nappy the Egyptian secret service agents had pulled him into.

Pressing his head hard into the carpeted floor, Sam was able to push the ear defender covering his right ear back, just enough to make out the odd snippet of conversation over the drone of the engines. He soon lost track of time but realised the nappy was not just a form of humiliation. He held on as long as he could, but eventually gave way and felt the warmth of his own urine spreading around his crotch and up his stomach.

No longer having to concentrate on needing a piss, Sam analysed the situation again. He established the bombing could not be pinned on him. He could not work out what Helena possibly had to gain by implicating him. He understood why she might have played some part in providing a safe place to hide guns and drugs. That was easy. She was probably part of a Russian drug ring and had been told to stash some gear somewhere safe.

The point that baffled him most was the cash. It was a lot of money to leave in someone else's attic. It had to be drugs money put there for safekeeping. For a moment he wished he had found it himself. He could have dumped the guns and drugs and kept it.

Then something vague passed through his mind. It was part speculation, part memory. His brain was suddenly in overdrive. He took a desperate breath and tried to think.

Then it clicked and his vision went white with anger, his stomach churned and he felt himself pissing into the nappy with frustration. His back arched upwards and he flipped on the floor, between two rows of seats in the back of the jet, like a fish out of water. He bellowed in torment, until a foot trod his head back down onto the floor of the aircraft where he lay, a sobbing, twitching wreck.

He knew what it all meant. It could only be one thing. Sure, he knew he had been set up, yes, everything had been planted, but now he knew who was behind it. The amount of money was £191,241. Those were the coordinates of the 24-hour RV in Sierra Leone. The place they would meet if things went wrong in the jungle.

That was the figure Christian had joked about in the back of the van on the way to the port in Freetown. That was the figure the whole patrol had committed to memory because it could not be marked on a map, in case the map fell into enemy hands. This could only mean one thing. Christian had made it out, somehow, and this was his revenge. Even worse, that would mean it was watertight. The whole thing would be thought through perfectly. He knew Christian well enough to know that. The more he thought about it, the more sense it made. Danes' words echoed round his head: 'Twenty-five years' hard labour or, if you're lucky, death by hanging.'

Oliver took an order for coffee from his colleagues and left the flight deck, his glove casually positioned over the light that glowed to show the rear door opening. He strode casually down the back of the aircraft, checking the cargo netting was all in place. Once he passed the rear cargo section, he darted forwards and slipped between the wooden containers to find Christian ready and waiting.

'Nice one, Oli. I can't tell you how grateful I am,' Christian whispered.

'You'll be back in England before me,' replied Oliver, an excited grin on his face. 'Now, go, we're over the drop zone now.'

Christian positioned himself and made ready. Oliver slid the door back and in a second Christian was out into the darkness.

Before he had opened his parachute, he saw the lights of Samara in the Moroccan desert. He reached for the metal D on his chest and released his chute. There was the familiar crack above his head, then silence.

Christian used the altitude to his advantage, knowing how much walking he could save himself. After ten minutes of descent, he knew he was within

5 kilometres of the edge of the town and should land there.

His feet touched down on soft sand. He pulled in the parachute and looked around in the moonlight for somewhere to hide it, along with his flight suit. He flicked on his hand-held GPS and set off across the sand. It felt strange being back in the kit he had worn in Sierra Leone. His shirt was stiff with blood and dirt, his trouser pockets full of silt from the Rokel Creek.

With the GPS showing 3 kilometres to destination, Christian climbed a ridge of sand and sat down, looking out over the town before him. He slowly lit a cigarette and watched the sun gently appear in the sky to the east. Very soon, he would be alive again and part of the real world. This was the last moment of his parallel life, a life he hadn't asked for or wanted, but one to which he had become accustomed. Being dead had been liberating and made extraordinary things possible, but now it was time to return.

He stubbed out the cigarette and stood up, leaving the rest of the packet lying on the sand. With the aid of the early-morning light and the GPS, he had no problem finding the British High Commission in the centre of the town. He pressed a buzzer on the wall outside and waited.

After a few moments an English voice crackled through the speaker, 'Yes, what do you want?'

'I'm a British soldier. Please open up, I need help,' said Christian, earnestly.

'OK, someone will let you in,' the voice replied.

The large wooden gates swung open and Christian stepped into a smart-looking courtyard. A moment later, he found himself speaking to a middle-aged Englishman in a T-shirt and linen trousers, who had clearly only just woken up.

'Now, what is going on?' he said sternly.

'I am a British soldier,' Christian replied with a tone of authority. 'I have been held hostage by terrorists for weeks and just escaped. I need to speak to my commanding officer immediately.'

The man's tone changed.

'Come this way, you can use the telephone in my office,' he said, looking alarmed.

Christian sat down in a leather office chair and dialled the guard room at Stirling Lines knowing that, with the time difference, it was still only 07.00 in the UK.

'I need to speak to Colonel Deverall immediately,' he said.

'Who's calling?' came the reply.

'Just put me through if he's there. It's important,' snapped Christian.

Cornwallis moved across the busy Operations Room, heading towards the meeting room. He looked exhausted, having been up half the night trying to deal with the political storm that had ensued from a serving SAS man being charged with a terrorist atrocity.

Deverall sat at the head of the table drinking coffee. He looked depressed, careworn and grey. Deverall nodded to Cornwallis to pick up the phone.

'Yes, yes, Cornwallis speaking,' he said, in an irritable way.

'Sir, it's Captain McKie, may I speak to Colonel Deverall, please? This is not a joke. I am alive and have escaped and I have made it to the High Commission in Morocco,' Christian said.

Cornwallis paused. He looked at Deverall and then back at the phone.

'Who is it, then?' Deverall mumbled, looking at some papers on the table in front of him.

'It's McKie,' said Cornwallis quietly. 'Says he has escaped and made it to our High Commission somewhere in Morocco.'

There was another pause.

Deverall's tired-looking eyes twinkled and traces of a smile broke across his face. 'Identify him,' he said.

'OK, if it's you, McKie, tell me what sort of dog your commanding office has,' said Cornwallis, in a challenging tone.

'A Springer spaniel; a black, incontinent one,' replied Christian, without hesitation.

'It's definitely him, sir,' Cornwallis said, shaking his head and passing Deverall the receiver.

Deverall took it, and spoke: 'Christian, I am lost for words, it's quite incredible. This . . . this . . . is quite remarkable. Are you OK?' he blurted, unable to contain his delight.

'Yes, sir,' said Christian calmly. 'You know, train hard, fight easy, and all that.'

'Well, well, very impressive, Christian. Pure genius, really, I'd say,' replied Deverall, winking at Cornwallis.